THE BOURNE ESCAPE

ROBERT LUDLUM'S™

BRIAN FREEMAN is the bestselling author of the Jonathan Stride and Frost Easton series. His novel *Spilled Blood* won the award for Best Hardcover Novel in the International Thriller Writers Awards, and his debut novel, *Immoral,* won the Macavity Award and was a finalist for the Dagger, Edgar, Anthony, and Barry awards for Best First Novel. He lives in Florida with his wife, Marcia.

Follow Brian on @BFreemanbooks
www.bfreemanbooks.com

ROBERT LUDLUM was the author of twenty-seven novels, each one an international bestseller. There are more than 225 million of his books in print, and they have been translated into thirty-two languages. He is the author of *The Scarlatti Inheritance, The Chancellor Manuscript,* and the Jason Bourne series – *The Bourne Identity, The Bourne Supremacy* and *The Bourne Ultimatum* – among others. Mr Ludlum passed away in 2001.

THE BOURNE SERIES

Robert Ludlum's The Bourne Vendetta (by Brian Freeman)
Robert Ludlum's The Bourne Shadow (by Brian Freeman)
Robert Ludlum's The Bourne Defiance (by Brian Freeman)
Robert Ludlum's The Bourne Sacrifice (by Brian Freeman)
Robert Ludlum's The Bourne Treachery (by Brian Freeman)
Robert Ludlum's The Bourne Evolution (by Brian Freeman)
Robert Ludlum's The Bourne Nemesis (by Eric Van Lustbader)
Robert Ludlum's The Bourne Initiative (by Eric Van Lustbader)
Robert Ludlum's The Bourne Enigma (by Eric Van Lustbader)
Robert Ludlum's The Bourne Ascendancy (by Eric Van Lustbader)
Robert Ludlum's The Bourne Retribution (by Eric Van Lustbader)
Robert Ludlum's The Bourne Imperative (by Eric Van Lustbader)
Robert Ludlum's The Bourne Dominion (by Eric Van Lustbader)
Robert Ludlum's The Bourne Objective (by Eric Van Lustbader)
Robert Ludlum's The Bourne Deception (by Eric Van Lustbader)
Robert Ludlum's The Bourne Sanction (by Eric Van Lustbader)
Robert Ludlum's The Bourne Betrayal (by Eric Van Lustbader)
Robert Ludlum's The Bourne Legacy (by Eric Van Lustbader)
The Bourne Ultimatum
The Bourne Supremacy
The Bourne Identity

THE COVERT-ONE SERIES

Robert Ludlum's The Patriot Attack (by Kyle Mills)
Robert Ludlum's The Geneva Strategy (by Jamie Freveletti)
Robert Ludlum's The Utopia Experiment (by Kyle Mills)
Robert Ludlum's The Janus Reprisal (by Jamie Freveletti)
Robert Ludlum's The Ares Decision (by Kyle Mills)
Robert Ludlum's The Arctic Event (by James H. Cobb)
Robert Ludlum's The Moscow Vector (with Patrick Larkin)
Robert Ludlum's The Lazarus Vendetta (with Patrick Larkin)
Robert Ludlum's The Altman Code (with Gayle Lynds)
Robert Ludlum's The Paris Option (with Gayle Lynds)
Robert Ludlum's The Cassandra Compact (with Philip Shelby)
Robert Ludlum's The Hades Factor (with Gayle Lynds)

THE

ROBERT LUDLUM'S ™

BOURNE ESCAPE

A JASON BOURNE NOVEL BY BRIAN FREEMAN

HEAD of ZEUS

An Aries Book

First published in the US in 2025 by G.P. Putnam's Sons,
an imprint of Penguin Random House LLC

First published in the UK in 2025 by Head of Zeus Ltd,
part of Bloomsbury Publishing Plc

9 7 5 3 1 2 4 6 8

A catalogue record for this book is available from the British Library.

ISBN (HB): 9781035919994 ; ISBN (XTPB): 9781035920013
ISBN (ePub): 9781035919987 ; ISBN (ePDF): 9781035919970

Printed and bound in Great Britain by
CPI Group (UK) Ltd, Croydon, CRO 4YY

MIX
Paper | Supporting
responsible forestry
FSC
www.fsc.org
FSC® C013604

Bloomsbury Publishing Plc
50 Bedford Square, London, WC1B 3DP, UK
Bloomsbury Publishing Ireland Limited,
29 Earlsfort Terrace, Dublin 2, D02 AY28, Ireland

HEAD OF ZEUS LTD
5–8 Hardwick Street
London, EC1R 4RG

To find out more about our authors and books
visit www.headofzeus.com
For product safety related questions contact productsafety@bloomsbury.com

THE
BOURNE
ESCAPE

ROBERT LUDLUM'S™

The Past

THE BULLET FROM THE TARGET RIFLE BURNED LIKE A RAZOR BLADE across David Webb's neck and landed in the heavy rubber trap to which he was bound. Where he felt the sting, a single trickle of blood dripped down his skin.

Each of the earlier bullets had come close without actually striking him. The first had landed two inches to the left of his shoulder. The second, an inch away from his right ear. The third, half an inch below his groin, in the valley between his muscled legs. The fourth, immediately above his head, had parted his swept-back muddy-brown hair and singed his scalp with its heat.

Now he'd been hit.

Was that deliberate—a way to maximize his fear? Or had the shooter made an error?

It didn't matter. David felt his muscles begin to tighten, but he restrained his body's instinct to flinch at the impact. His mind stayed calm, his limbs motionless. Sweat bathed his skin, but he ignored the dampness. He measured out each breath and focused on slowing down his heartbeat, which stampeded in his chest. Inside his mind, danger didn't exist. This was nothing but a circus, where a knife thrower showed off his skills to impress the audience.

In this case, the audience was one man in a Savile Row suit, standing on a third-floor balcony above the manicured garden of his Marnes-la-Coquette estate.

The target where David was bound had been positioned at the rear of the garden, near a stone wall that separated the mansion from the green lawns of the *parc sportif.* He was posed like da Vinci's Vitruvian Man, arms outstretched, legs spread-eagle, his wrists and ankles secured with Velcro straps. The old woman who'd tied him—*Je m'appelle Madame Aubert*—had taken his Glock and shoulder holster. Then she'd waited with outstretched arms for him to undress. Her eyes, still hungry despite her age, followed his movements with erotic interest until he'd given her all his clothes and was completely naked in front of her.

When you are exposed, you are vulnerable.

When you are exposed, you cannot hide.

Those were the rules of the Monk.

David kept his head perfectly still as he anticipated the next bullet. The slightest twitch meant the difference between life and death as the marksman took aim. Even so, David's eyes moved constantly, memorizing every detail of the garden. The circular pond in the middle of the narrow rectangular lawn, with a single fountain bubbling out of green water and lily pads on its surface. The conical trimmed bushes—eight on either side of the grass—

casting arrowhead shadows in the morning sun. The statue of Zeus atop a marble pedestal, bearded, a wreath around his curly hair, a gold-painted lightning bolt clenched in his upraised fist. No one but the king of the gods for the owner of this estate.

Later, assuming the Olympic medalist fifty yards away didn't make a mistake and kill him, David would need to describe the setting with perfect recall. He didn't know which details he'd be asked about.

That was part of the test.

"This exercise is about maintaining your ability to function in the face of lethal threats," his mentor had told him. *"You will be afraid, but you cannot let fear rattle you or make you panic. It's essential that your mind continue to operate. Think, observe, strategize, remember. Is that clear? You can't pause an operation simply because you're under attack. The intent of this lesson isn't to harm you, David, but even the most competent shooter can miss on a given shot. If he does, you may be injured, or you may die. That's the risk you accept by doing this. It's my belief that training should replicate as much as possible the actual conditions an agent will experience in the field."*

His mentor.

David Abbott.

The man after whom he'd been named. David Abbott, the son of an auto-industry billionaire, whose wealth had given Abbott the financial freedom to devote his brilliant, bold, and calculating mind to the clandestine intelligence services. To his allies, he was the Monk, a black-ops pioneer always two steps ahead of everyone else, anticipating new global threats from the smallest of clues. To his enemies, he was a pirate, reckless and ambitious, not caring how many lives he put at risk with his schemes.

David Abbott. The man with whom he'd lived for almost a decade after his parents were killed. The two of them had shared a brownstone on East 71st Street in New York for most of that time. Then, six months ago, without warning, Abbott had moved them out of his Manhattan home base. The building was being renovated from top to bottom for a special project, he said, but someday David would see it again. Since then, the two of them had traveled around the world to Abbott's various homes. Iceland. Norway. Turkey. Vietnam. Singapore. Hawaii.

And now Paris.

In each location, Abbott had arranged a new lesson, increasing in difficulty.

"Until now, I've emphasized your physical and mental fitness, David. Your strength and dexterity, your stamina, your language skills, your knowledge of history and politics. But it's time for your more specialized training to begin. When we return to the brownstone in New York, you need to be ready."

Ready for what?

Abbott hadn't told him. But now he knew.

David stared across the garden at the marksman holding the benchrest .22-caliber Anschütz rifle. He couldn't see the man's face; it was hidden by a mask, and the man's body was protected by a plexiglass shield that allowed only a small square egress for the barrel of the rifle. David heard the action of the bolt, but he didn't know when the next bullet would come. The time between shots had varied from eleven seconds up to six minutes, in order to keep him off balance, in order to increase his anxiety.

"I've run this same exercise with fourteen men and women," Abbott had

told him. *"One, and only one, succeeded completely. Two made it through the range test, but failed to pass the cognitive recall. Two survived the challenge itself, but passed out as soon as they were released. One soiled himself. Seven panicked and ripped off the Velcro straps, after differing numbers of bullets, from the first to the ninth. One turned his head at the wrong moment and unfortunately was killed."*

The rifle once again spat flame.

David felt his skin burn, this time on the inner flesh of his left thigh. Another hit.

He barely had time to process the pain before another bullet landed below his right ear. Then, barely five seconds later, another clipped skin from the tip of a middle finger, and then the last one in the sudden barrage burrowed into the rubber target immediately adjacent to his hip. Shocked by the ferocity of the assault, his muscles and bones developed a mind of their own, desperate to fly, to leap out of the line of fire into the grass. His brain struggled to control his body, hold his arms and legs back from lurching free of the Velcro bonds, keep his mouth from screaming. He concentrated all of his thoughts on the empty eyes of Zeus, and he turned himself into stone, like the statue.

A long pause followed. The garden became completely still, except for the hum of bees. A gentle breeze blew away the smoke. Five minutes passed. Then ten. Was this the end? Was the test over?

But the shooter remained behind the rifle, a new bullet ready.

David's stare drifted to the estate, which rose immediately behind the garden. It was two hundred years old, built of classic French limestone, its chambered windows high and narrow. Abbott was no longer alone on the third-floor balcony, behind the intricately carved iron railing. A woman stood beside him, far enough away that her exact features were difficult to distinguish. She looked to be a few years older than David, perhaps thirty. She held her body with a grace that was reserved but extremely attractive, half fire, half ice. Her wavy blond hair cascaded below her shoulders. She wore a black dress that barely made it to her knees, and her legs seemed to go on forever before ending at stiletto heels. Even at that distance, he could see the deep red flash of her lips, like a rose at peak bloom.

She didn't hide the fact that she was staring at him, but he saw no smile to go along with her cool gaze, only scientific observation.

Then a new motion in the garden distracted him. Between the conical bushes, he saw Madame Aubert returning toward him across the grass, his clothes neatly folded in her hands, his gun and holster on top of the clothes. She wore a sensible dress over sensible shoes, and her silver hair was short and neatly coiffed. Her mouth was a thin line, almost a smirk. She stopped ten feet in front of him, arms extended to offer him his clothes.

Her body stood between him and the shooter now.

The rifle suddenly cracked one more time.

Jesus!

Madame Aubert shuddered, a tremor rippling through her body, her gray eyes widening with surprise. Her expression turned empty, her jaw going slack. His clothes spilled out of her arms, and her body slumped sideways to the ground.

David heard the snap of the bolt. Another bullet was coming. With Madame Aubert no longer in the way, the barrel was again pointed at his chest.

Using simultaneous pressure in both arms, David ripped his

wrists out of the Velcro bonds and threw his body forward, just as the next shot thudded into the rubber target where the middle of his neck had been two seconds earlier. He felt his ankles disengage as he fell, and his body crashed down six feet into the soft grass. As he hit, he somersaulted, and his hand smoothly scooped up his Glock from where it lay next to the old woman's body. Then he rolled again, his mental clock warning him of the next bullet.

The rifle spat another shell that kicked up turf and mud inches from his face.

He kept rolling, but he aimed and fired as he did. Shoot, roll, shoot, roll—four shots in a tight group thudding into the plexiglass fifty yards away. But the shield held. He fired once more, and this time he placed a bullet into the two-inch gap around the barrel of the rifle. The shot struck the marksman in the meat of his shoulder, and the voice of the masked man erupted with a loud French obscenity. Blood sprayed. The shooter jerked backward and tumbled off the platform where the gun was mounted.

A voice shouted from the balcony over David's head. Abbott's voice. *"Arrête!"*

Stop!

David did, but he was slow to understand what was going on. He got to his feet, keeping his Glock trained on the nest where the marksman was hidden. But out of the corner of his eye, he saw Madame Aubert getting slowly to her feet, too.

She wasn't dead. Her grim smile told him she hadn't even been shot.

It was a fake. A ruse. This was all part of the test.

David lowered his gun and ran to check on the man he'd nearly killed.

"IMPRESSIVE," THE WOMAN SAID.

Abbott smiled. "Indeed. You have competition, my dear. You're no longer the only person to pass the entire test. Although even you didn't make the shot through the shield. I really didn't think anyone could pull that off, which is the only reason I didn't have my man wear a vest. Unfortunate. I hope he's not dead. The French will pitch a fit if they lose him, with the Summer Games coming up next year."

"He looks fine," the woman commented, noting David Webb helping the shooter to his feet and tending to the man's wound. "But I wouldn't count on another medal. My guess is, his nerves will be permanently scarred after this."

"C'est la vie."

Abbott gripped the iron railing with strong hands. He was tall, and even in his late fifties, he was muscled and lean, maintaining the form that had marked his own Olympic swimming career decades earlier. His hair was silver-gray and wavy, and he wore a neatly trimmed salt-and-pepper beard. He had intense blue eyes and a sunburnt face etched with parallel wrinkles on his high forehead.

"So what do you think of David Webb?" he asked. "I wanted you to see him in action."

"He's just as you advertised. Physical skills, poise, mental agility. You can always see intelligence in the eyes."

"He noticed you," Abbott said. "He notices everything."

"Yes, he did."

"You noticed him, too, darling. Don't think I wasn't aware of that. I've never seen you react like that to a man. I hope this won't be a problem, Marlen."

She brushed her blond hair nonchalantly from her eyes. Abbott only called her Marlen when he wanted to talk about personal things. Which wasn't often. Their private bond was something they avoided showing in public. It was safer for her, safer for him. Abbott had built his career by having no weaknesses his enemies could exploit. But Marlen was a weakness for him and always would be.

So most of the time, the Monk used the other identity he'd given her.

Shadow.

"I find him attractive," she admitted, "but that's all it is. You know me. Mind over matter."

"Good."

"So when do I get to meet him? You've studiously kept us apart all these years. It made me wonder why, but now I gather you've been worried we would fall into bed. Does he even know I exist?"

"No, he doesn't, and for now, we'll keep it that way. But the two of you will meet soon enough. In the field. You're the only one I trust to vet his psychological readiness, and that won't work if he knows who you really are. Or if he learns about our . . . relationship."

"Except now he's seen me," Shadow pointed out.

"If he asks, you're the daughter of a colleague in Germany who came looking for a job."

"Oh, the tangled webs we weave. But you know best." She kept watching the young man in the garden, and she surprised herself by realizing it was hard to look away from his face and body. "I've begun reviewing his file. That will take me some time. Your level of detail is impressive, as always, so there's a lot to go through. Does he know you've kept him under constant surveillance since he started living with you?"

"Of course not."

Shadow frowned. "Well, best to make sure he never finds out. Given the loss of his parents, I imagine trust issues will be a problem for him. Anyway, I need to go. I've got to catch a flight to New York to check on the conversion of the brownstone."

"You'll find everything ready," Abbott replied. "That's why I've been pushing so hard on David's training these past six months. And why I need you to do your usual thorough analysis of his strengths and weaknesses. I want David Webb on board with us as soon as Treadstone is officially born."

PART ONE

1

AS JASON BOURNE AWOKE IN THE MIDDLE OF THE NIGHT, HE FELT THE violent sway of the Mediterranean water tossing the boat around like a floating toy. The belowdecks cabin was pitch-black, leaving him blind. When he reached across to the other side of the bed, he realized that it was empty. Johanna was gone.

He pushed his fingers underneath her pillow, but he didn't find the Ruger that she usually kept there. She'd taken her gun with her.

Where was she?

He swung his legs out of bed and stood up, balancing himself gracefully as the floor made a seesaw motion under his feet. His own Glock was invisible on the table by the bed, but he knew exactly where it was, and he took the cool grip into his hand. When he listened for noises on board, he heard only the furious slap of the sea. The engine was idle, the Fairline Squadron 65 anchored a few miles off the French coast. He crossed the cabin and felt along the wall for the gap that marked the narrow stairwell. Finding it, he grabbed the railing with one hand and ran up the steps.

On the main deck, Bourne slipped through glass doors onto the windswept stern of the *Stormy Weather.* Tonight the boat was aptly named. Dark clouds erased the stars, the high waves churned, and staccato flashes of lightning lit up the horizon. It would be pouring down rain soon from the warm summer sky. He checked the water for the signal lights of other boats, but for now, they had this corner of the Mediterranean to themselves. They were one tiny speck on a vast empty sea.

Below him, the Zodiac was still lashed to the deck. Johanna hadn't slipped away.

Bourne made his way along the port side of the cruiser. The boat lurched under the impact of a high wave, nearly throwing him overboard. Bent over, his body slammed into the railing, and he saw black water raging against the hull. He steadied himself, tightened his grip on the Glock, and staggered forward. Where the prow came to a point, he saw her.

Johanna.

Lightning lit up her naked body. In the wind, her long blond hair seemed to defy gravity as it made a tornado around her head. She was tall and scrawny-thin, her shoulder blades visible, her spine rippling through the valley of her back. She stood with her legs slightly apart, her bare feet gripping the deck and rolling smoothly with the wild motions of the boat. She stared northward at the unseen French mainland, as if searching for something. Or waiting for something to happen.

He shouted her name, but the wind deadened his voice. She didn't react. Bourne approached her and called again, and this time her head turned sharply at the noise. The next flash of lightning illuminated her pretty face, buried under the nest of her hair. Her sapphire blue eyes had a cold intensity, and shadows played across her high, angled cheekbones. Her expression was full of solemn foreboding, the way it had been for weeks.

Seeing him, she bent her pale lips into a smile. When she turned around, the sight of her body aroused hunger in him the way it always did. But he also noted the gun clutched securely in her right hand, barrel aimed at the water.

Bourne came closer. "What's wrong?"

Johanna didn't answer immediately. She leaned into him, her breasts against his chest, her soft mouth kissing him. Their passion for each other rose as their bodies pressed together in the night air. Then she broke away, and the odd darkness returned to her face. They stood inches apart from each other, bodies moving up and down as the sea tried to wrest the boat from its anchor and yank it free.

"I don't know," she replied in a voice he could barely hear. "I woke up and couldn't sleep. I have a bad feeling."

He studied the dark water in every direction, looking for threats. He saw nothing, and his instincts set off no alarms. At least for the moment, they were alone, and they were safe. "No one's coming for us."

"Aren't they? We can only hide for so long, Jason. Sooner or later, they're going to find us. Whoever they are."

Bourne said nothing, but he knew she was right.

Four months earlier, in February, killers had confronted Johanna and tried to abduct her during a port stop in Positano. They'd been looking for *him*. Since then, the two of them had lain low, keeping to the water, only stopping on land every few weeks to resupply the boat. But life on the run was a losing game. Eventually, a spy would spot them. Word would get passed.

We've found them!

Men would come to take them down on the water. But *who were they?*

Was it the Russians? Jason knew he was still in Putin's crosshairs for killing the assassin known as Lennon. The Russian leader was patient and determined, and sooner or later, he'd find Bourne and exact his revenge. But in the meantime, there were plenty of other enemies from his past who might be on the hunt for Cain.

That included Shadow. She was the head of Treadstone, and she'd warned him—*ordered* him—to stay away from Johanna, without giving him a reason. He hadn't listened; he hadn't obeyed. If Shadow knew they were together, she wouldn't hesitate to send agents to kill them both.

So yes, they were living on borrowed time.

But none of that mattered. Jason savored every moment he could get with this woman. She was beautiful, skilled, unstable, and treacherous, but he loved her. He'd walked away from Treadstone to be with her. They'd cut ties with the rest of the world in order to live in a kind of isolated paradise on the sea. It was a bubble where nothing else mattered—but bubbles were also fragile and fleeting.

It was as if she could read his mind.

"I don't want this to end," Johanna murmured. "I never want to let go of this time."

"Neither do I."

"These months with you, they've been the best of my life."

"Mine, too."

"But it will be over soon. I feel it, Jason. Something wicked this way comes."

"Don't think about that."

"I can't think about anything else."

He kissed her again, trying to ease her mind. She slid an arm around his waist, her face settling into his chest. But her heartbeat thumped against him, crazy fast. He felt something intense and extreme emanating from her, a strange desperation.

Extreme desire. Extreme fear.

"I need to ask you something," she said without looking up at his face.

"Of course."

"What do you remember about David Abbott?"

Bourne pushed Johanna away in surprise. He took her chin in his left hand and lifted it up, staring deeply into her blue eyes, looking for answers. "Abbott? Why are you asking about him?"

"He started Treadstone. He recruited Shadow. He recruited *you*. It all started with him."

"I know, but David Abbott's been dead for years. You never mentioned him before. Why ask about him now?"

Johanna hesitated. A wrinkle slithered across her forehead like a snake. He tried to read her face, but she was good at keeping secrets. Too good. She was also good at lying. He didn't know whether to believe anything she told him.

"A month ago, I took the Zodiac into port near Dubrovnik," she said. "Remember? I was late. You were worried. The thing is, in the Old Town, I spotted someone I knew. A Croatian agent. He was obviously surveilling the area, looking for someone. I wondered—I wondered if he was hunting for us. It didn't feel like a coincidence that they'd station someone near the water who knew *me*."

"*Jesus!* Why didn't you tell me?"

"I—I wanted to, Jason. But I knew as soon as I did, it would be the beginning of the end. From that moment forward, we'd never be free."

"So what happened?" Bourne asked.

"I followed him after his replacement showed up. He went to a bar, he got drunk. After dark, when he left, I took him down in an alley. I needed to know what he was doing there. I needed to know if we were in danger."

"And?"

"I interrogated him, then I killed him."

Bourne saw no regret or guilt in her eyes. She'd made the only decision she could. Once the Croatian saw her, once he *recognized* her, he had to die. "What did you learn?"

"He wasn't there looking for you, but he confirmed what we already knew—that there's a dragnet out for Cain. A bounty on your head. Mercenaries all over Europe are on the hunt for you, Jason."

"Is it Putin?"

"He didn't know."

Johanna stopped, her face still dark. There was something more.

"What else did he say?" Bourne asked, his eyes narrowing. "Why was this man in Dubrovnik?"

"Surveillance, just like I thought—but we weren't the target. He was searching for someone else."

"Who?"

"David Abbott. He was looking for *David Abbott.*"

Bourne stumbled backward, pressing a fist against his skull. Lightning flashed again, thunder boomed, but this was in his head, not on the sea. Pain jabbed like the thrust of a knife behind his eyes. He tried to remember Abbott, but he couldn't, because nothing was there. David Abbott, like every other part of his past, was nothing but a ghost without substance, lost in a mist that never cleared.

"That's impossible," he said. "That makes no sense."

"The agent told me Abbott had been seen in Dubrovnik. The ID was definitive."

"Abbott is *dead*!" Bourne insisted.

"Is he, Jason?"

"Of course he is."

Johanna grabbed his hand tightly. "How do you know? Because Treadstone told you so? Do you think Shadow's not capable of keeping the truth from you if it serves her interests? She's done it over and over, Jason. You can't trust her. For that matter, you can't trust David Abbott, either. Treadstone is evil. It has no soul. That's why we're *out*. That's why it's just you and me now. We don't owe anything to anyone."

Bourne shook his head.

David Abbott. *Alive?*

That couldn't be true. He'd read the letters and emails between them, going back for years. He'd seen the photographs of the two of them together. He'd been to Abbott's grave in Calvary Cemetery in New York.

But what did he really know about the man who'd been his surrogate father?

Only what he'd been told. Only the story that Treadstone— that *Shadow*—had crafted for him. And time and time again, what he'd been told about his past was a lie. His whole life had been nothing but layers of deception.

Johanna repeated the question she'd asked at the beginning. "What do you remember about him? What do you know about David Abbott?"

"Almost nothing," he admitted. "After I lost my memory, Abbott didn't exist for me at all anymore. He was just a few disconnected flashes. A face. A voice. Fragments of memories. But you're right, he was the mastermind of Treadstone. He planned everything, like a puppet master pulling the strings. He sent me on the mission where I got shot, where I lost who I was. The whole scheme was his idea. And when he found out I was still alive, he was the one who gave the order to have me killed."

Jason stared at the hidden coast of France to the north. The few memories he did have always came back like fire, hot and intense.

"It happened right here," he went on, anger creeping into his voice. "We're practically in the same place, the same waters. Somewhere out there in the darkness is the French village where the fishermen took me. That's where they found the doctor who saved me. My life began on a small island in the Mediterranean called Ile de Port Noir."

He looked down into Johanna's blue eyes, and he tried to make sense of things that made no sense at all. "David Abbott can't be alive."

"He is, Jason."

Bourne wondered if that could be true.

The impossible is always possible.

That was one of the Monk's rules. One of Treadstone's rules.

He felt a sharp stinging across his body, needles all over his skin. The rain came, a soaking downpour blown sideways with the howling wind. The *Stormy Weather* jerked and twisted, a dog anxious to break its leash and run.

Johanna's words echoed in Bourne's mind. *David Abbott is alive.*

Then he thought: *What does that mean?*

But he had no answer for that question. They'd run out of time. His gaze drifted to the water, and his hand tightened around the wet metal of the Glock. Johanna was right. Something wicked was headed their way. From the French coast, lights blinked in and out of the night, arriving like monsters out of the sea. They weren't alone anymore.

Other boats were out there now. Closing in.

———

HIS EYES OPENED.

He stared up at stars winking in the clear night sky. Had there been a storm? He had a vague memory of pelting rain. But if so, the storm had passed, and now the water around him was as still and calm as black glass.

Water.

Where am I?

The man turned his head, feeling a jolt of pain travel into the muscles of his neck. He saw a wide-open sea, far from land, illuminated by tongues of flame licking at debris that floated in the water. Wood. Metal. Fiberglass. The field of wreckage drifted around him, feeding smoke into the air in clouds that choked the sky. It filled his nose, and he gagged with a raspy cough shuddering through his chest.

Moving made the pain worse. His whole body was nothing but pain. Every muscle screamed. He touched his face, wincing at the barest pressure, and his fingers came away with blood. Then his chest, his legs. More blood. Blood everywhere.

Beneath him, heat warmed his skin. *Burned* his skin. He examined his surroundings and realized that he lay on his back on a scorched fragment of wood, barely as long as he was, so narrow that his hands and feet dangled in the water. The wood smoldered, hot and black with char. It would break apart soon; it wouldn't hold him much longer.

How did I get here?

The man blinked, trying to remember. But nothing came. Darkness closed around his mind, an emptiness as wide as the sea where he floated.

What happened to me?

He had no idea.

Below the surface of the water, something brushed his foot. A creature, large, curious, bumped past him. Was it a tiger shark? They were relatively rare in the warmer waters of the Mediterranean, but any shark would smell blood at great distances and be drawn to the scent. He drew his limbs out of the water and squeezed his hands and feet onto the fragile sanctuary.

He knew some things. Strange.

He knew about sharks. He knew about the Mediterranean; he knew this *was* the Mediterranean. He knew—he could easily call up the details in his mind—the coastlines and countries bordering the sea. He also knew he was going to die soon if he wasn't rescued. He would die of blood loss, or he would drown when the burning wood cast him into the sea. Or the sharks would eat him. He knew all of that.

But it was night, and he was alone.

No one was coming to save him.

The man's eyes drifted shut again. He couldn't keep them open anymore. Sleep—or unconsciousness—won the battle over salvation.

One last question tormented him before the world turned black.

Who am I?

2

HIS EYES OPENED.

He blinked at the dazzling sunshine.

Half a dozen men loomed over him. Rough hands grabbed him under his shoulder blades, dragging his almost-lifeless body into a rubber Zodiac. He had no strength to move, to help them, or to resist. Who were they?

Guttural voices shouted in French, and hooked poles stabbed the water.

"Allez! Allez! Pas de déjeuner aujourd'hui, connards!"

Somehow the man knew they were driving away the sharks, telling them they would have no meal today.

"Est-il mort?"

"Non, non, regarde ses yeux!"

No, he was not dead. Somehow he had survived the night. He had a vague recollection, not much more than a dream, of the burnt plank disintegrating beneath him, pitching him into the water. He remembered intercepting a larger piece of debris before the sharks got to him and rolling his exhausted body onto it. As the wind blew, he drifted, leaving fire and smoke behind. His mind went blank.

And yet he had one more memory from the night and the explosion. He saw a body face up in the water, dressed in black, eyes wide open. Dead. A man with a bullet hole in the middle of his throat.

He knew—*how did he know?*—that he'd shot that man. Himself. He was a killer. He'd aimed for the neck to sever the man's spinal cord, pulled the trigger on his Glock, and the stranger had fallen back into the sea like a pirate.

Why would he need to kill someone?

Who was he?

The Zodiac motor whined. The boat rose high in the water, each jolt making him shiver with pain. The men scooped buckets from the sea and poured them over his body, washing away the blood, but making his cuts and bruises sting from the salt. Then they tipped cold water—no, not water, beer—between his cracked lips, and he tried to drink. His eyes opened and closed. The men shouted questions at him in French, and he understood their Marseilles accents, but he couldn't drag words from his chest. Besides, it didn't matter what they asked because he had no answers to give them.

The boat slapped across the water at high speed. He smelled the heavy stink of dead fish in the air, mixed with body odor, cigarette smoke, and raw onions. He heard laughter and listened to dirty jokes and insults hurled among the men. Every couple of minutes, one of them kicked him hard to make sure he was still alive. When he grunted in pain, they ignored him again.

He slept.

He slept a long time, unaware of what was happening, troubled by nightmares. In his dreams, he saw a woman's face, someone he knew, someone he *loved*. He heard her scream; he saw her rising into the air in the midst of fire and going into the sea. If he thought hard enough, if he held her face in his mind, he thought he could remember her name and what she meant to him. But his unconscious brain was a sieve, and when he awoke, her face melted away like falling sand.

The sun had been replaced by darkness again. Night had returned. He felt the up and down of the waves and knew he was on a larger boat. A sliver of the moon glowed through a porthole. He was in a dirty, cramped space, surrounded by heavy nets and rusted metal walls. Water dripped from the ceiling. Damp crates filled the floor; he lay on two of them pushed together. A couple of burlap sacks had been thrown over his body to keep him warm. His wrists were tied together with rope, and so were his ankles. The fishermen, skilled with knots, had taken care to secure their prisoner. But they couldn't strip the room of sharp objects, and somehow his instincts told him exactly what to do.

He rolled, letting himself fall three feet down to the floor itself. His body landed hard with a bolt of agony from head to toe. He shrugged off the pain, then slithered toward a large wooden reel, three feet in diameter, with edges that were jagged and splintered. Ten minutes later, as the rope frayed where he sawed it against the reel, his wrists came loose. Thirty seconds after that, he'd untied his ankles. He was free. But when he tried to get up, his knees buckled, and he fell sideways onto his back. Whatever had happened to him had drained him of his strength.

"Où vas-tu, mon ami?"

The prisoner glanced up from the floor when he heard the voice.

He saw a man in the doorway to the storage room. Something in the way the man carried himself made it clear that he was the captain of the vessel. He was at least six foot two, with tree-trunk arms and legs that had been honed by hard labor and a beer belly drooping over his belt. His face had been colored to a deep mahogany by years in the sun, and greasy brown hair crept from under a beret and hung below his ears. He was probably forty, but maybe as old as fifty. He wore old jeans that were a tapestry of rips and stains, plus a plaid shirt with the sleeves rolled up and heavy unlaced boots.

In his left hand was an open bottle of Bordeaux.

In his right hand was a Beretta 92FS.

The man raised both of his hands high in the air.

"The lady or the tiger, eh?" he continued, now in thickly accented English. "What's your choice, *connard*? We can drink wine together, or I can shoot you in the head and dump you in the sea. Makes no difference to me. My men brought you back, but it's less trouble if we leave you to the sharks."

The prisoner pushed himself up so that he could stretch out his legs across the nets and lean his back against one of the wooden crates. "Wine."

"Smart man."

The captain slid down to the floor next to him, exhaling with a sigh and a belch. He offered him the bottle, and the prisoner tilted it to his lips and drank. He realized his hands were shaking, and some of the wine spilled.

"I assume you prefer English, eh?" the man asked, taking back the bottle and draining a third of the wine with a long swig. He shoved his gun in a jeans pocket. "You're American, yes? That's what it says on your passport. Generally, I hate Americans, but you—you're interesting. Very, very interesting. See, most Americans don't turn up in the middle of the sea with a passport and fifty thousand euros in cash strapped in a plastic pouch to their leg. Yes, *mon ami*, you make me very curious."

"Your crew saved my life?"

The man nodded. "Lucky for you, my brother was on the Zodiac, too. Otherwise, I imagine they would have grabbed your money and dumped you overboard. You were pretty close to dead anyway, they said. But Jacques thought I'd want to see you for myself. My brother, he knows opportunities."

"You want the money for yourself? Take it."

"Oh, I will, you can be sure of that. But where there's fifty thousand, Jacques thinks there must be more. I think so, too. Either you can pay me to rescue you, or—and this is where my brother is very good at smelling possibilities—there are other people who will pay even more to put you in their hands."

The prisoner found it interesting that turning him over to Interpol wasn't one of the captain's options. That was something he could work with. Whatever he did to this man, whatever deal he worked out, there would be no repercussions.

A dishonest man is easier to play than an honest man.

He knew that was true, because lessons like that had been taught to him, drilled into his head, a thousand rules for staying alive. But where did they come from?

"Why would you think someone wants me?" he asked.

The captain drank more wine. "We saw an explosion on the horizon last night. A fireball through the storm. A boat blew up, which is a rarity even in our rough little community. So naturally, we headed that way to investigate. That's where we found you almost dead. What happened to you, *mon ami?*"

"I have no idea. I don't remember."

The other man studied his face, as if trying to determine whether his prisoner was lying. "You don't know why you were out there?"

"I don't."

"Who blew up the boat? Was it you?"

"I don't know."

"Are you playing a game with me, *connard?* That's something I don't recommend. I've spent thirty years dealing with drunk crew, cheating owners, and crooked competitors, and I've learned to use a tough hand. People who get in my way get squashed like fucking mosquitoes."

"I'm not lying. I don't remember anything."

The captain dug cigarettes from his pocket and offered one to the prisoner, who shook his head. "All right, we'll assume you're telling me the truth," he went on, lighting the thin European cigarette and blowing smoke into the air. "My name is Henri, by the way. Henri Joub. What's your name?"

The prisoner grimaced and squeezed his eyes shut. He searched for something, anything, that his mind could grab. His past. His identity. But nothing came. "I don't know that, either. I have no idea who I am."

"A mystery man, eh? Actually, I already know who you are. I have your passport, remember? I've done searches on you, and I've come up empty. It's like you don't exist. That's quite an art these days. Could be because your ID is fake, could be because you're a man with secrets. Or both. Jacques and I, we're betting anyone with that much to hide is a valuable commodity."

The man on the floor took hold of Joub's shoulder. Some of his strength was coming back; he gripped the shoulder hard enough to make the man's face flinch. "What does my passport say? Who am I?"

A little nervousness crept into the captain's eyes.

"Your name is Jason Bourne."

———

JASON BOURNE.

He let go of the captain's shoulder and closed his eyes. The name rolled around in his brain, and he realized: *Yes. That's who I am.* He knew nothing of his past, of who he was, of why he'd been on that boat, of how it had exploded. But he could picture his face now, as if he were staring at a mirror. Blue-gray eyes, as hard as rough jewels. A square line to his jaw, his skin pale, his mouth devoid of any expression. Expressions gave away too much. Swept-back hair, cut short, so dark brown it was almost black, except when he needed to dye it blond to become someone else.

Why would he need to do that?

What kind of life did he lead?

But that could wait. He had a name. *I am Jason Bourne.*

And yet he was not. Somehow he knew that even his name was a lie. He was Jason Bourne, but he was not Jason Bourne. There was another identity in his past, an identity he'd left behind long ago.

He tried to remember, but a spike of pain in his head took his breath away.

Henri Joub eyed him with a curious smile. "That means something to you, eh? Do you know who you are now, Monsieur Bourne?"

"The name is right," Bourne replied, "but that's all. I don't remember anything else."

Joub shrugged. "No matter. Someone will know who you are. Someone will pay to get you back. Or they'll pay for your corpse."

"Why do you think that? I could be just a man who had a boating accident."

"You're not. Oh, no, most definitely not. You see, Bourne, we found something more than debris at the scene."

"What?"

"Bodies," Joub told him. "At least five bodies. Five men, dressed in black, the kind of men who you know have skills, eh? Assassins. They'd all been shot. Every one of them, a kill shot to the throat. Precise."

Bourne's fists tightened, and his eyes closed. A flash burned through his mind like lightning. A firefight. Bullets flying, bullets aimed to kill, men with rifles dying. Then it all ended in a millisecond as an explosion ripped the boat apart.

"Ah, this does not come as a surprise, does it?" Joub commented, watching him closely. "See, I think you killed those men, Bourne. You strike me as a survivor, someone with skills yourself. A hunter."

Bourne frowned, because he was sure Joub was right. He *was* a hunter. But why was he being *hunted*?

"Did you find a woman's body?" Bourne asked.

Joub's eyebrows arched. "A woman? No. Just men. Who is this woman?"

"I don't know."

But to Bourne, the question felt important, almost more important than the questions about his own life. He'd been on a boat, men had come, men had been killed, the boat had exploded. But there had been a woman. He'd lost her.

Outside the storage room, boots clanged on a metal floor.

Someone was coming.

His instincts came to life, and Bourne tensed, ready to fight. His eyes found the nearest weapon, a rusted screwdriver on the floor. He gauged the distance to the doorway, the number of steps it would take to get there, the best way to roll, grab the screwdriver, and charge. Go for the eyes. Plunge the tool into the man's brain.

Those calculations went through his mind in less than a second. Joub watched him curiously, then put a restraining hand on Bourne's thigh. "It will be one of my crew. I would really rather you not kill them. Too much paperwork."

A man, barely more than a boy, appeared in the doorway. He was no taller than five foot two, his skin ghostly white and dotted with acne. Nineteen or twenty years old at most. His rust-colored hair was buzzed almost to his scalp, and he had staring brown eyes with large whites and nostrils as wide-open as caves. The kid danced nervously on his feet.

"Capitaine?"

"*Que veux-tu*, Boris?" Joub replied impatiently. "*Je suis occupé.*"

"*Oui, Capitaine. Une nouvelle tempête arrive.*"

Bourne understood him. A new storm had descended on the boat. That was obvious. The metal of the hull groaned as the waves climbed higher, and lightning illuminated the darkness of the porthole. Another sensation came and went in his brain. There had been a storm before the explosion, too. His skin felt the pinpricks of heavy rain; his body swayed with the surge of the sea. In the lightning, a face came and went, but he couldn't see it clearly.

A woman's face.

Joub waved at the crewman with disgust. "Am I blind?" he snapped in French. "Deaf? Go away, Boris."

Boris.

A Russian? No, he was from Belarus. Bourne already knew that. He'd identified the source of the teenager's accented French and analyzed his Slavic features. But Russia or Belarus, Putin or Lukashenko, the politics were the same. When a soldier in Minsk eats beet soup, a spy in Moscow farts.

Why did he know those things?

Boris turned to leave, but as he did, the boy's gaze lingered on Bourne, and their eyes met. It lasted only a second, and then the squirrelly foreign crewman disappeared. But Bourne knew—in that moment, he knew—that Boris had appeared with a needless weather report solely for the purpose of seeing him. The teenager had wanted a close-up look at his face, to describe him, to identify him.

Why?

When Boris was gone, Joub exhaled a large sigh and put down the empty wine bottle. He pushed himself wearily to his feet, then withdrew the Beretta from his baggy jeans. The captain waved the gun at Bourne on the floor.

"Up, *mon ami*. I need to be on the bridge. We'll be approaching Marseilles soon, and Jacques will run us on the rocks, the fool. When we get there, we will begin asking questions about you. Never fear, someone will have the answers. Someone will tell me what you're worth."

"I can't stand up," Bourne replied. Which was a lie. He could feel his strength and his adrenaline surging like a wave. But he shoved himself up, then fell back down with an exaggerated groan of pain. "I can't even feel my legs."

"You can stand, or my men will hog-tie and carry you. Your choice."

Bourne bared his teeth, as if the slightest motion brought pain. It did, but he ignored it. Pain was irrelevant; pain could be managed; pain would go away. He rolled awkwardly, getting on his hands and knees at Joub's feet. His elbows bent under his weight. He breathed loudly and let his head fall forward as he gasped an obscenity. "I can't do it."

"Up," Joub repeated. "Move!"

With another grunt, Bourne straightened his arms, twisting the kinks out of his neck. Then, fast as a cat, his left hand shot out, grabbed hold of the captain's right ankle, and yanked it into the air. Off balance, the captain flew, and so did his Beretta. Joub landed with a booming thud on his back, his skull cracking against the metal floor. Bourne was immediately on top of him, knee crushing the man's chest. He already had Joub's pistol in his hand with the barrel squeezed into the captain's windpipe.

Bourne's whole body screamed at the exertion, but he didn't care.

"We aren't going to Marseilles, *Capitaine*," he told Joub. "Don't worry, I'll pay you for your troubles. Five thousand for you, five thousand for your brother. And you stay alive, rather than me shooting you both in the throat. *D'accord?*"

Joub's face screwed up with rage. He inhaled as if to spit, then thought better of it as he saw Bourne's finger curl around the trigger of the Beretta. "Who the fuck *are* you?"

"That's what I need to find out," Bourne said.

"Where do you want to go?"

Bourne didn't hesitate. He already knew. He could picture the place in his head. He knew the bars and hiding places; he knew where the streets went; he could see the high cliffs over the sea. And there was someone who could help him there. Someone who'd helped him before. A doctor.

How did he know that?

"We must be near an island off the French coast," Bourne said. "A little village. Ile de Port Noir. Take me there."

3

PORT NOIR.

It was a town that time had forgotten, still part of Old France, before the tourists invaded. Once upon a time, the city fathers had entertained dreams that the village would become another Mediterranean playground, snatching money from places like Ibiza and Capri. The A-listers of Hollywood and Wall Street might not come here, but minor starlets would adorn the beaches and lesser financial gods—millionaires, not billionaires—would renovate the hillside estates. It never happened. Port Noir crept along decade by decade much the way it always had, a few thousand people fishing by day and drinking by night, inhabiting weathered homes of white stucco along cobblestone streets.

Bourne knew he didn't have much time. He'd kept Henri Joub's fishing boat a few miles offshore, then used a Zodiac to make his way to the harbor on the southern coast of the island. But Joub wasn't a man to be trusted. No doubt he had friends who would spread the word in Port Noir. By nightfall, the entire village would know about the mystery man, and Bourne would have a price on his head.

He'd exchanged clothes with one of Joub's crew, but they didn't fit well. He stood out on the Old Town streets, and he didn't want to be noticed. Using some of his cash, he bought new clothes and shoes, nothing fancy, nothing to brand him as a rich American. He stuffed most of the clothes into a backpack and then wore a striped shirt with a Henley collar, khakis, and boat shoes as he returned to the street.

He found a café and began asking questions.

Le docteur? Where is he? Where can I find him?

But the waitress at the café told him he'd made a mistake. There are no doctors on the island, monsieur! If you are sick, you go to the mainland! Why would rich men like doctors live in this place?

Bourne didn't believe she was lying. Somehow, among his skills, he knew how to read body language and look for tells in people's faces. It made him wonder if his instincts had been wrong. Perhaps there was no doctor on Port Noir who had helped him in the past. Perhaps he was on the wrong island hunting for the wrong man. Or the doctor had died or left the island years earlier.

He didn't know. He didn't *remember*!

If Bourne was alone, then he couldn't stay here much longer. Men would be coming for him. Somewhere on the waterfront, he needed to find another boat, another captain, who could ferry him to Toulon or Marseilles. He wanted to be back on the water by midnight. That meant getting more money. The windfall strapped in a pouch to his leg—*where did it come from?*—wouldn't cover the bribes necessary to get people to break the rules. He would need to find more cash in the village.

Fortunately, he also had the skills to identify wealth, to smell corruption, to pick locks, to interrogate contacts, to speak multiple languages, to find weaknesses that could be exploited. How and why he had learned those skills, he didn't know. But Jason Bourne was just what Joub had called him.

A survivor.

By the time daylight turned to nightfall, he had increased his cash supply to nearly one hundred and fifty thousand euros. Most of it came from the wall safe of a Spanish expat who used his spice exports business as a cover for smuggling cocaine around the Mediterranean. Faced with the barrel of the Beretta in Bourne's hand, the Spaniard had given up the combination of his safe and all of the money inside. Bourne had also found a Pro-Tech TR-3 switchblade, which made a useful addition to his armory, given that Henri Joub's Beretta only had three bullets left in its magazine.

The Spaniard also gave him the name of a man with a boat for hire who didn't ask a lot of questions. It was time for Bourne to get out of Port Noir.

Most of the local dockworkers drank up their paychecks at a bar two blocks from the water cheekily called Tant Pis. It lived up to its name as too damn bad. By ten o'clock, when Bourne arrived, four men had already gotten themselves kicked out to the street, where they lay in a soup of vomit and urine. He went inside and found that he had to squeeze through a crush of people to get to the bar. Mean eyes followed him; he was a stranger, and strangers always drew attention. Best to get in, find the man who could ferry him off the island, and get out before the drunks came looking for a fight.

He ordered a shot of absinthe, then found an empty wall near the toilet. No one wanted to stand there and smell what wafted out when the door opened and closed. From this vantage, he surveyed the bar. Most of the occupants were men, most of them drunk and getting drunker. However, he realized that some were only pretending to be drunk, watching for opportunities among the careless men who'd had too much. They were spies on the hunt for whatever they could grab. A stolen wallet or passport. Car keys. Or just gossip about a boat's secret cargo that might prove lucrative.

Bourne took note of who they were. Spies were always useful.

There was one woman among them. She sat by herself, shooting down the men who approached her. Two whiskey glasses, one empty, one full, sat on the cocktail table in front of her. She was Black, attractive, with a few deep purple streaks swirling through her shoulder-length hair. She wore a burgundy leather vest over black Lycra, plus blue jeans and calf-high boots. Her eyes passed over Bourne without seeming to notice him, and then she picked up her second shot of whiskey and drained it with a single swallow. But her casualness was an act. Her fiery eyes had identified Bourne as a threat.

He did the same with her. His mind registered her, classified her—the man with no memory could call up details on every face he'd seen since he awakened on Joub's boat—and then he moved on. She was a spy, but also a distraction.

Never allow distractions to get in the way of the mission.

Why did he know those rules?

He had one job in the bar. Find a man with a boat. He knew

the man's name was Raren, rhymes with Karen. But he didn't need an unusual name to find him. The Spaniard had said that Raren had flaming-red hair, and only one man in the bar met that description. He sat by himself, drinking coffee rather than the hard stuff. He was in his fifties, and he had the look of a by-the-book sailor, someone who put ship and crew first. That was also the kind of man who didn't go back on a deal.

Bourne shoved through the crowd, still feeling eyes that watched him everywhere in the bar. He sat down in the empty chair across from Raren and took the man's measure. The boat captain was small but wiry, with the kind of hidden strength a wrestler would have. Raren carried weapons, too. Bourne noted the barrel of a Ruger jutting from inside the man's jean jacket, and the way his cargo pants bulged at his calf suggested a backup gun. Despite his age, he was not someone to mess with. However, he also had a six-inch, freshly stitched cut on the left side of his neck, which would limit his mobility if someone came at him from that direction.

Jesus! Why did his brain think that way?

"You know who I am?" Bourne asked.

Raren sipped his coffee. When he spoke, his accent was American. "Manuel said someone wanted to get to Marseilles."

"Did Manuel also say to kill me once I was on board?"

A smile broke across the man's freckled face. "In fact, he offered me all the cash you're carrying—he said it was a lot—to do just that. But that's not my line of work. I'm a courier, that's all."

"How much?"

"Twenty thousand."

"That's steep," Bourne said.

"The transport is only a thousand. The rest is for keeping my mouth shut and asking no questions."

"Fair enough. When do we leave?"

"When do you want to leave?" Raren asked.

"Midnight."

"Then we leave at midnight." The man checked his watch. "Ninety minutes from now. The boat is docked on the south side of the harbor. If you're not there on time, the deal's off. But I wouldn't stay here until then. Find a place to lay low. You've already been spotted, and they'll be planning to take you out. I suspect you can handle yourself in a fight, but these boys won't go down easy."

"Thanks for the advice," Bourne said.

"See you at midnight."

Bourne was about to get up, but he glanced at Raren and played his instincts again. He gestured at the cut on the man's neck. "How'd you get that?"

"One of my men was careless with a hook. He doesn't work for me anymore."

"It looks recent."

"Yesterday."

Bourne frowned. "Who stitched it up for you?"

"Why do you care?"

"Because I'm looking for a doctor, but I heard there wasn't one on the island."

Raren winced as he touched his neck. "He doesn't advertise. Man's half dead from drink, but if you catch him on a good day, he won't kill you."

"That's quite the recommendation."

"You live on Port Noir, you take your chances."

"What's his name?"

"Washburn."

The pain behind Bourne's eyes stabbed him instantly as a memory flooded back.

Washburn!

Yes, that was the man; he *knew* that man. Washburn, gaunt and frail, with hands that shook and sallow skin that hung on him like a bad suit. Washburn, a drunk who'd run away from London in disgrace after killing two patients on the operating table. *I could have gotten away with one. Not two.*

Washburn, who'd gone dry for thirty-six hours and then operated on a man who'd been shot in the Mediterranean and been dragged at the brink of death to the doctor's doorstep. A man who awoke with no memory.

My God! It had happened before!

He'd lost himself, he'd lost who he was, in this same place. And right here, with help from Geoffrey Washburn—yes, *Geoffrey*, that was his name—he'd taken the first steps on the road to discovering who he was.

He needed help again. He needed answers.

"You all right?" Raren asked.

"I'm fine," Bourne replied. "This doctor, Washburn. Where can I find him?"

———

THE STREETS OF PORT NOIR WERE MOSTLY DESERTED IN THE LATE EVE-
ning. Bourne headed away from the bar along a stone walkway that

led beside the water. In the harbor, sailboats bumped their rubber fenders together as the wind blew off the sea. Across the street, in the doorway of one of the seaside storefronts painted in fading pastel colors, he spotted a prostitute on her knees servicing a customer. They paid him no attention.

He was looking for rusted steps beyond the port that climbed in switchbacks to the top of the island's steep hill. Up there, according to Raren, he'd find a white cliffside cottage that belonged to the English doctor named Geoffrey Washburn. But Bourne soon realized he had company. His boots clapped sharply on the cobblestones, and behind him, at least fifty feet back, he heard what sounded like echoes of his footsteps. But this was no echo. He'd been followed from the bar.

His ears zeroed in on the sound. Three men moving fast, getting closer. Three against one. He didn't have time to wonder who they were, whether they were simple thieves or something else.

Raren had said: *These boys won't go down easy.*

Bourne had Joub's Beretta and the TR-3 knife. That was all. He gauged the openness of the harbor and concluded he didn't have the advantage here. If he wanted to turn things around, he needed a confined space and the element of surprise. Casually, hands shoved in his pockets, he turned away from the water and crossed the street to walk beside the row of shops. The men followed, matching his movements. Where the street ended, he turned into a narrow alley that dead-ended at a ten-foot brick wall. Water-stained walls of four-story buildings rose on either side, their windows dark. Bourne only had a few seconds to ready himself. He removed the nylon leather belt from his jeans and let it dangle in his right hand, the heavy brass buckle swinging like a club. With his other hand, he gripped the Beretta, but he was conscious of his lack of ammunition. Three bullets, three men.

He waited around the corner of the alley. The footsteps came closer, slowing as the men anticipated a trap. He smelled the first man, only inches away, and listened to his loud breathing. Bourne timed his assault, gauging the man's location. He knew what to expect. The first man would run or roll toward the other side of the alley to draw his attention; the second would spin around the corner, firing; the third would wait a beat, then spin around as backup. In a few seconds, they would take Bourne down in a crossfire.

If they wanted him dead.

Who are they? Why are they trying to kill me?

Bourne lashed out with the belt. Like an attacking cobra, it whipped around the corner of the building, and the buckle hit home, slapping the first man's face and yielding a howl of pain. Bourne charged out of the alley, throwing himself at the man, who tumbled like a bowling pin into the men behind him. The second man lost his balance; the third nimbly stepped out of the way. As the first man fell to the street, Bourne landed a fierce kick between his legs with the toe of his boot, and the man grabbed at his groin with a scream. The second man recovered his balance and stabbed at Bourne with a long dagger. Bourne didn't have time to aim the Beretta. Quickly, he bent his arms, blocking the blow, but taking a cut to his forearm. He spun backward—*how did he know to do that?*—then punched out with his leg as the man charged again. His boot drove into the man's stomach. The man let out a wheezing gasp, but kept coming. Bourne had no choice; he dropped the Beretta, then grabbed the man's knife arm with two hands just as the point of the blade penetrated his chest. He bent the arm sharply back, dislocating the elbow. The knife dropped; the man screamed.

The third man had a Ruger. Bourne threw himself sideways as the man fired, and he landed hard against the building wall. The bullet missed, breaking a store window and spraying glass. The second man, now with a broken arm, lurched toward Bourne again, stumbling into the line of fire and taking a bullet in the middle of his back. It didn't stop him. The man's good arm shot out, and his strong fingers curled like a vise around Bourne's throat, choking him. Bourne pounded the man with his fists, but his iron grip refused to yield. Struggling, close to blacking out, Bourne grasped for the TR-3 in his back pocket. He flicked it open, then plunged it into the man's stomach and dragged it upward, cutting through organs, fat, and muscle. A river of blood poured out. The man's fingers finally loosened, and Bourne freed himself with a heavy shove.

Another bullet. The third man had fired again.

Bourne spotted the Beretta on the ground. He dove, snatched up the gun, and fired as he swung his arm around. Somehow he had perfect aim. A red hole dotted the third man's forehead, and he pitched forward. Bourne swung the gun again, this time toward the second man, who lay on his back, dark red blood pulsing from his abdomen. He wasn't worth the bullet; he'd be dead in minutes.

The last man, still writhing from the blow to his groin, saw the writing on the wall and tried to run. Bourne took him down on the first step. He spun the man around and saw a gash where his belt buckle had torn open the man's face. But he *recognized* him. He knew that face. This was Boris, the Belarusian teenager from Joub's boat. Bourne dragged the kid into the darkness of the alley, then pushed him against the wall and shoved the hot barrel of the Beretta under his chin.

"Why did you come after me? Who do you think I am?"

"We all know who you are," Boris spat back. "Every Russian in Europe knows your face. Putin wants you dead. He'll pay for your body, dead or alive. You killed his assassin, and Putin never forgets. That's what you do. You kill people. You're going to kill me, too, so just fucking get it over with. Pull the trigger, Cain."

Another lightning bolt stabbed through Bourne's brain.

Cain!

Despite himself, he stumbled backward, releasing the teenager. His eyes squeezed shut, trying to drive out the blinding pain. Vaguely, he was aware of Boris running, escaping, but he didn't try to stop the boy this time. He was too consumed with his past, with the reality of who he was. He couldn't hold back images rocketing through his head, memories of strangers, all dead, their bodies at his feet.

Yes. That was what he did. He killed people. And he was good at it.

He stumbled out of the alley, leaving behind the bodies and the guns in a wave of self-loathing, trying to get as far away from this awful scene as he could. Two men dead on the street. Dead at his hands. It had been so easy. So natural. They were the latest bodies in a long list of victims.

Behind Jason Bourne was another identity.

I am Cain.

4

ON TOP OF THE CLIFF LOOMING OVER THE VILLAGE OF PORT NOIR, Bourne knocked on the door of an old white cottage. He knew—*he knew*—that he had been here before, however long ago that was. Time had been cruel to the house in between. Storms had torn shingles off the roof and chipped away the paint. The flowers in the garden and in the pots by the door were all dead, taken over by weeds. A single iron chair sat in the long grass near the drop-off to the sea, its metal frame corroded by rust. No one had sat in the chair for years.

Bourne heard footsteps dragging from inside after he knocked. When the door opened, he realized that time had been cruel to Geoffrey Washburn, too. One look at his sunken eyes and gray skin told the truth. The doctor was dying.

He was also a stranger. Bourne knew Washburn, but he *didn't* know him at all. He didn't recognize his features, didn't remember his face. When he reached for memories, none came back. But the doctor's eyes widened at the sight of him, and he immediately stepped forward and pulled Jason into a fragile embrace.

"Dear God, it's you," he murmured, his raspy voice unmistakably British. "After all this time? What a treat for me before the end. I'm so pleased to see you again, old friend, but why are you here, Jason?"

Bourne held the doctor at arm's length, still searching for something familiar about the man and finding nothing. Washburn was very tall, two or three inches taller than Bourne, but his frame stooped as if he were carrying a heavy weight. Every breath carried a deadly rattle, and the smell of alcohol oozed from his pores. But there was genuine warmth in his expression. They were friends; they'd shared something important. How could this man simply vanish from his mind?

"So it's true," Bourne said. "My name is Jason. You and I, we know each other."

Washburn blinked, not understanding. Then the loose skin of his forehead furrowed into wrinkles. "Oh my God, I'm so sorry. Your memory? It's gone again?"

"Yes."

"Do you remember anything at all?"

"Almost nothing. I get flashbacks of people and places, but they don't mean anything to me."

"Including me? Including our relationship?"

"Yes. I don't know what to say. I don't know you at all."

Washburn didn't look offended. "That's understandable, old man. I'm hardly memorable. But obviously, you *do* know me on some level. Your instincts carried you here to me. This is where your life started once before, so it's no surprise that you would come back to find it again. Tell me, do you know what happened to you? Where were you when this latest cloud settled over you?"

"I was on a boat."

"As you were before," Washburn said. "That's important, too. The parallelism probably makes it worse. Do you remember what happened?"

"There was an explosion. Or so I'm told."

"You don't remember it?"

"I remember a body in the water," Bourne said. He hesitated before going on. "It was a man I killed. I shot him. That's what I am, isn't it? I'm a killer."

Washburn let out a wheezing sigh and draped an arm around Bourne's shoulders. "You are many things, Jason. A killer is certainly one of them, but that's only the beginning of the story. Let's go inside, shall we? I definitely need a drink."

———

THEY SAT ON EITHER SIDE OF A BOTTLE OF GLENMORANGIE AT A TABLE near the fireplace. It wasn't a cold night, but Washburn needed the heat to warm his scrawny frame. They took turns drinking shots.

"You'd been shot in the head," the doctor told him, seemingly pleased to reminisce even about a dark episode in their lives. "Some fishermen found you floating in the Med, and they brought you to me. It was a delicate operation, particularly for a surgeon not exactly in his prime. I don't know whether it was a surgical mistake by me that harmed your memory, or whether it was the bullet that did that. Perhaps a bit of both. But you came through it. We spent weeks together after that. Your physical recovery was long, and by the time you left, your emotional recovery was just beginning. I gather it's still going on. You weren't just trying to find your memories, Jason. You were trying to understand the kind of man you are."

Bourne stared at the fire. "That seems pretty obvious, doesn't it? Given my skills. Given what I do."

"Don't be so sure."

Bourne looked around at the heavy Victorian-style furnishings of the doctor's cottage. "I spent weeks with you here? You'd think I'd remember something about it. Why did you do so much for a stranger? Not just saving my life, but letting me recover in your home, too."

A sly grin crossed Washburn's face. "Oh, trust me, I'm not altruistic, Jason. I had a motive for myself, too. When I was examining your body, I found a microdot implanted in your hip with the numbers for a Swiss bank account. I saved your life, I helped you, because I thought you might ultimately help me. Which you did. You wired funds to me from Zurich. You were extremely generous. That's what has kept me alive since then, even if I haven't exactly made the most of my time."

Washburn downed another shot of Glenmorangie.

"Did I ever tell you what I'd found out about myself?" Bourne asked.

"Some. But only some. You called me a couple of months later to see how I was. That's when you told me your identity—Jason Bourne. Although I gather that was a cover story more than the truth about who you were."

Bourne nodded. "It feels that way to me, too."

"You were more interested in finding out how *I* was. Checking on me and my health, making sure the money had reached me. Which should tell you something about the man you are, Jason. Other than that, you were pretty secretive about the life you'd uncovered. Honestly, I gathered it was one of those 'I could tell you, but then I'd have to kill you' sorts of things. In your case, I suspected that was literally true."

"Did I say *anything* else?" Bourne asked.

"Very little. As I say, I think that was for my own safety. But yes, there were two things you mentioned that might be important to you now."

"What were they?"

"First of all, Paris," Washburn replied. "You were in Paris when you reached out to me. I gathered you'd made your home base there. It seemed to have meaning for you. You transferred your money from Zurich to the Valois Bank in Paris, and you told me if I were ever running low on resources, I could contact a banker there who would replenish my accounts. His name was Antoine d'Amacourt. Does that mean anything to you?"

D'Amacourt.

Bourne had an image in his mind of a scared, oily French banker. A man who could be pressured, a man who could be bought. Was it real, or was he inventing someone out of his head?

"Maybe," he said. "There's something about d'Amacourt that triggers memories. He was a small fish, a means to an end. But why would I remember someone like that if I don't remember you? You were far more important to me."

"The brain works in its own way, Jason," Washburn explained with a shrug.

"You said there were two things. What was the other?"

The doctor frowned. "Are you sure you want to go down this road?"

"What do you mean?"

"I mean, is a tabula rasa really all that bad? You get a chance to start over with a blank slate. It doesn't matter who you were. Paint your own canvas."

"Except people are trying to kill me," Bourne replied. "Just like they were years ago. Nothing's changed."

"All right, then I have something to show you." Washburn pushed himself out of the wooden chair by the fire, which required significant labor. He went to a bookshelf on the other wall, where he maintained a small collection of hardcover books, most of them on medical topics. He seemed to know exactly which volume he wanted—a history of the plague in Europe—and he took the thick book down from the shelf. Rather than bring it with him, he opened it and drew out a folded, yellowed piece of newspaper from inside the back cover.

He brought the paper to the table and laid it out in front of Bourne. It was an old article from the *New York Times* about a NATO security conference in Bonn, Germany, in 1979. The accompanying photograph showed then–secretary of state Cyrus Vance along with his German counterpart, Hans-Dietrich Genscher, and a handful of U.S. State Department aides behind them.

"Does anyone in this photograph look familiar?" Washburn asked.

"From 1979? I wasn't even born then."

"Look anyway, Jason."

Bourne studied the photograph. He focused first on the two principals, then went face to face among the aides behind them. At first, none of the men—they were all men—looked familiar to him. But he found himself going back to the face of a young aide, probably in his mid-twenties. The man was tall and obviously charismatic, with a confident hand placed on Vance's shoulder. Only an aide with a healthy-sized ego would dare to do that. He had a crown of blond hair, a strikingly handsome face, and a fit physique.

He was a swimmer.

Why did that idea pop into Bourne's head?

Jason checked the caption, but the young man wasn't identified.

"Him," he said, pointing. "I don't know who he is, but I'm sure I knew him. Or at least I did when he was much older."

Washburn smiled. "Good. Very good. You're right. That suggests to me that your memories are still there, Jason. Blocked, but there. And when the memories exist, then there's reason to believe they will come back to you."

"Who is he?" Bourne asked.

"Well, I'm afraid you would know that better than me. You mentioned him when you called. You were upset. You'd just found out that this man was dead, and you told me that he was the closest thing you had to a father. He'd been your mentor for years. But you didn't give me any information about who he was or how he'd shaped your life. Nonetheless, I was curious. I used the name you gave me to do research. When I was back in London visiting my sister, I spent a day at the Senate House Library to see what I could find out about him. He proved to be every bit as much of a mystery man as you, my friend. I found oblique references to him in articles about intelligence strategy and black operations, but nothing to give me any personal background about him. The only photograph was this one, and as you see, he's not even identified. But this article was cross-referenced in the library indices under his name."

Bourne picked up the brittle piece of newspaper and studied the face again. "What was his name?"

"David Abbott."

———

BY MIDNIGHT, THE GLENMORANGIE WAS GONE, AND THE FIRE WAS DYING down. Bourne sent a text to the boat captain, Raren. *An extra ten thousand to reschedule our journey.* The captain's agreement to the new deal came within seconds. Whenever he chose to go to Marseilles, he had transport.

Bourne got up and paced on the worn carpet in Washburn's small cottage. He had more clues about his past, he had new direction, but the biggest mysteries remained outside his grasp. Forcing himself to remember brought nothing but pain.

"So you think my memories are intact?" he asked. "You think I can get them back?"

Washburn fiddled with the empty shot glass on the table, his lips puckered together in thought. "Those are two very different questions, Jason. Are the answers somewhere in your brain? Very likely. Can you recover them? I'm not sure. It's like I told you years ago. There are no rules when it comes to amnesia."

"What can I do?"

"Allow yourself to free-associate. That's the best advice I can give you. See what comes. See where your brain takes you. When you can, when the situation allows it, step outside yourself and observe."

Bourne shook his head in frustration. "But there's no rhyme or reason to it! I hear the name of a French banker, and I can picture what he looks like. But you, who were so much more important to me, you're a stranger. Some kid on the street tells me my identity is Cain, and I see images of bodies—people I *killed*! I know I did. But I don't remember who they were, or why they had to die, or who gave me the assignment. Hell, I'm the one who killed Lennon, and I can't even remember his face."

Washburn stared at him. "Lennon?"

"Putin's private assassin."

"You didn't mention him before," the doctor pointed out.

"I'm sure I did."

"No, Jason. You didn't. Did the teenager from Belarus tell you his name?"

"I guess he did . . ." Bourne began. Then he revisited his conversation with Boris, and he realized he was wrong. "No. He didn't. He talked about Putin, but he didn't give me Lennon's name. And yet I know I'm right about that. He was an assassin who called himself Lennon, and he and I—we had a lot of history."

"History?"

"He was with me in the agency. He was a mole."

"What agency?"

The name fluttered on the tip of Bourne's tongue, but then it slipped away. "I don't know, but it had something to do with David Abbott."

Washburn nodded happily. "You see, old friend? Things are

already coming back to you. There may be no rhyme or reason to how it comes, but they are all pieces in the puzzle."

Bourne sat down at the table again. "What I really want to know is what happened two nights ago."

"You may remember more about that than you realize. You just have to let it come back."

"How do I do that?"

"Don't think. Don't try. Let your senses do the work. You were on a boat."

"Yes."

"It exploded."

"Yes."

"How?"

"A bomb," Bourne said, not even knowing where the answer had come from. "They attached it to the hull."

"They?"

"An assault team."

"How many men?"

"Four boats, twelve men. There was a firefight."

"You lost."

"Yes and no. We were outnumbered. We didn't have a chance. But we killed eight of them. I was beginning to think we might get away alive. Except I didn't see an operative maneuver a boat behind us from the other direction to plant the charge. That was it, that was the end. Next thing I knew, I was getting rescued by Henri Joub's crew."

The doctor stayed silent for a long time. He stared hard at Jason's blue-gray eyes. "We?"

Jason cocked his head, not understanding. "What do you mean?"

"You said we. *We* were outnumbered. *We* didn't have a chance."

Bourne's voice dropped to a whisper as his own words echoed in his mind. "*Jesus!* You're right. I wasn't alone. Someone was with me on that boat."

"Who?"

Jason shook his head. "That's the problem. I don't know."

5

BOURNE SPREAD A BLANKET ACROSS THE SOFA IN WASHBURN'S LIVING room. The doctor went off to his bedroom after the two men shared a warm embrace. Jason felt a surge of regret, knowing that this man was counting down the last days of his life. They'd been close. Bourne could feel that, even if he didn't remember it. When he left in the morning, he would be leaving behind the only friend he had in the world.

His eyes closed as he lay on the sofa in the darkness. Exhaustion overtook him, and almost immediately dreams crept into his brain as he slept. The dreams started out peaceful. He was with a woman; they were in bed. She faced away from him, but she had long, straight blond hair down to the middle of her back, like a field of gold. He traced her shoulder with his fingertips, then followed the line of her body to her hips and legs. A rumble of pleasure came from her throat as he caressed her. He eased in close, molding himself against her, ready to make love. She arched her back, and he opened his mouth to whisper her name, but he didn't remember what it was. He knew her, he *loved* her, and yet he didn't know her at all. She was this perfect nude mystery, a calm in the midst of a storm. All he could do was hold her in his arms, their bodies rocking as the boat swayed—

The boat.

Yes, they were on a boat.

But they were no longer in bed. The dream changed like a quick cut to a new scene in a movie. His body twitched, feeling scorched heat, hearing the crackling fireworks of gunshots in his ears. It was just the two of them on the deck of the boat, two of them holding off an army. They were surrounded. He aimed and fired, aimed and fired, and so did she, a professional, an expert. But her back was to him. He still couldn't see her face.

Who are you?

The attackers drew in closer, their boats tightening in a circle around them. He aimed and fired; she aimed and fired. Another body fell; there he was, dead in the water, dressed all in black. Bourne counted eight down, five kills for him, three for her. He could see fear in their faces now. They hadn't expected such a fierce counterattack. He stared at the mystery girl at the prow of the boat, and she finally glanced back at him with a cocky grin, sure that they were winning. That was the moment when fire and sound erupted. The sky lit up; night became day. She flew. An explosion launched her into the air, and all he heard was her scream as she disappeared.

Her scream to him.

"Jason!"

Then she was gone. He was alone, drifting on debris, and there was nothing but smoke on the water.

Bourne's eyes shot open.

He was awake now, but choking smoke followed him from his dream. He found himself gasping, his eyes tearing. He rolled off the sofa to the ground for a breath of air that didn't contain poison. Thunder roared in his ears, the devil-growl of a monster snapping its teeth and licking at the walls.

The cottage was on fire.

Tongues of flame taunted him from every direction. Flakes of ash and ember landed on his clothes. A window shattered, spraying the room with hot glass. He shouted Washburn's name, but got no response. Through a black cloud, he snaked along the floor toward the doctor's bedroom and pushed inside. The heat and sting made it impossible to open his eyes, and he had to feel his way forward, his skin burning. His hands bumped against a body, motionless, sprawled across the old wood floor.

Washburn had made it out of bed, then collapsed.

Bourne draped the doctor's torso over his shoulders and hiked him off the floor. He took a breath, but inhaled nothing but venomous fumes. Staggering, he carried Washburn toward the seaside window, which was framed in rippling streaks of fire. With his elbow, he punched out the glass, then cleared away the shards and maneuvered the doctor's body through the hole and eased him to the ground. Bourne followed, climbing outside. He took Washburn under the shoulders and dragged him away, close to the cliff's edge, where sweet sea air blew off the water. He could still feel the heat. Behind them, the fire spread, consuming the walls, hissing through holes in the roof.

Washburn still didn't move.

"Geoffrey!"

He shook the doctor by the shoulders and got no response. The man's pulse stuttered, his breathing ragged, his face streaked with black soot. When he tapped his friend's cheek, Washburn's eyes finally fluttered open, and he hacked out a cough, clearing smoke from his lungs. After a moment's confusion, he managed to focus on Bourne, and the doctor gripped his wrist with surprising strength.

"Jason, go! Get out of here!"

"You need help."

"There's no help on the island, and I'm done anyway. Go! This was meant for you! They're after you!"

As if to punctuate the warning, gunshots laced the cliffside. Through the clouds of smoke, Bourne saw two black silhouettes moving toward him from the south side of the cottage. He got up and ran, drawing them away, the bright flames illuminating his body. Bullets chased him toward a dense stand of trees. When he reached the cover of the woods, he dove forward, then stayed low and changed direction. He crawled through the dirt and brush, watching from the shadows as two men with body armor and HK416 rifles closed on his original location. Now he wished he'd taken the Ruger from the body in the alley the previous evening, rather than leaving it behind. Next to these weapons, the Beretta—with only two bullets—was a flyswatter.

There was a time to fight and a time to run. But if he ran, Washburn was dead.

Even if you stay, I'm dead!

That was what the doctor would tell him.

Bourne aimed the Beretta at the first of the men, but at that distance, in the flickering light of the fire, he had almost no shot, and the man's body armor offered little vulnerability. He shoved the gun back in his belt and dropped to the ground. Silently, he made his way inch by inch through the brush, letting the two men get ahead of him. They were pros; they spread out and moved carefully, their rifles ready, their fingers on the triggers. But the deafening whoosh of the fire gave him cover. They couldn't hear him.

He drew the TR-3 blade into his hand. He timed his movements with the men in the woods, slowly closing the gap. The nearest man seemed to have a sixth sense for danger. With each step now, he turned, aiming his rifle backward at the woods. Bourne had to stop and hope the night gave him cover, even when the man seemed to be looking right at him. He closed to within ten feet. Then five.

If the man looked back, looked down, he would see him now. Bourne was exposed. He watched the man's shoulders, waiting for him to circle around and guard his six. He bent his left knee, foot pushed against the ground like a sprinter, and envisioned the swing of the knife in his hand. He felt rather than saw the movement of the other killer, twenty feet away, close enough to unleash a punishing rain of fire from the 416 as soon as he spotted Bourne's location. But there was nothing he could do about that.

Wait for it, wait for it!

Bourne was practically at the first man's heels, looking up at him. He saw the first twitch of muscle, the man's shoulders beginning to turn. The killer swiveled, exposing the side of his face and the jutting artery in his neck. The man sensed Bourne immediately, heard and felt the rush of air behind him, began to whip the barrel toward the threat. But Bourne already had the TR-3 buried to its hilt in the man's carotid artery. In the same instant, he yanked the man to the ground as blood sprayed over him like a fire hose.

The man's finger twitched as he died. The rifle fired like a warning flare.

Instantly, the other killer charged toward the noise. Bourne heard heavy boots pounding directly at him in the woods. He stripped the rifle from the dying man, then fell onto his back and fired up, spraying the trees around him in a semicircle. None of the bullets hit home, but he forced the second killer to take cover. Bourne scrambled away, changing locations, staying low. So did his enemy. His target. They were both on the ground now, both crawling, circling, trying to find the other.

Where are you?

The sickening thunder of the fire continued to drown out nearly every other sound. Bourne's eyes moved constantly. The burning core that had once been Geoffrey Washburn's cottage was as bright as the sun, and smoke spread in a black fog through the woods. Wind tossed the trees around, making every shadow look alive. Bourne kept the rifle poised as he backed away. Nearby, the air felt cooler and fresher. He was near the fringe of the woods, close enough to hear the crash of waves on rocks.

The two of them found each other at the same instant. Their bodies practically collided, so close that neither one of them had room to turn and fire. Bourne dropped his rifle; he needed both hands. In body armor, the killer was practically an invincible robot. Bourne grabbed the man's arms, hammering the rifle against a tree trunk until the other man let go of his weapon. A gloved fist hit Bourne's cheekbone and snapped his head back. A metal-plated knee kicked the air from his chest. Bourne gasped, then used his whole upper body as a battering ram to throw them both forward. The two men spilled from the trees onto a narrow stretch of tall grass, barely three feet wide, where the land ended and sagged off the cliff.

They hit the ground. Bourne saw dark open eyes below him. He aimed a fist at one eye, and then with another downward pound, he broke the man's nose. The killer roared in pain, then hoisted Bourne sideways with a thrust of his chest. Jason skidded and felt half his body go over the edge, slipping down with avalanches of dirt and rock. He dug his fingers into soft ground and scrambled back. The killer was half on his feet, right hand stripping a Ruger from a holster on his leg. Bourne jumped as the barrel came up. He pushed the man's hand wide, a bullet firing off the cliff and disappearing into the sea. Then his shoulder landed hard and low, throwing the man off balance.

The killer stumbled back one step.

Then two.

But there was no second step behind him. Just air. The man pawed at nothingness. He swung his arm and fired again as he fell, but he was already tumbling backward, and the angle sent the next bullet harmlessly over Bourne's head. The killer disappeared, sucked away in a cartwheel toward the rocks. Bourne watched the man's body land in the sea a hundred feet down, pushed and pulled by the waves.

He sank to his knees, breathing hard and gathering his strength. When he could walk again, he found the body of the other killer and retrieved his small arms. Two Rugers. Backup magazines. Another knife. He left the rifle behind; he needed weapons he could conceal. When he was done, he limped out of the woods toward the silhouette of Geoffrey Washburn stretched out in the grass.

The doctor hadn't moved from where Bourne had left him.

The fire in the house was almost out. There was nothing left to consume, the cottage gone, the walls collapsed inward. Smoke lingered in the air, but the sea wind had already begun to dissipate it into the sky.

Washburn's eyes were closed. His face had a serene look, his old body now relaxed and unmoving. There was no breath, no movement in his chest. Bourne knelt next to him and put a hand on the man's face and found the skin still warm, but that was from the heat of the fire, not from the pulse of blood. He checked for a heartbeat, but he already knew the truth. The doctor was dead. The man who'd saved his life was gone.

He'd found a friend and lost a friend in the same night.

Bourne didn't have time to mourn. All he could do was leave Washburn behind for the police. He had to find the captain named Raren; he had to get on a boat and get out of Port Noir before daybreak.

The next secrets of his missing life were waiting for him, and he knew where he had to go to find them.

Paris.

6

THE WOMAN WITH THE CODE NAME SHADOW CROSSED TO THE TOP-
floor window in the Washington, DC, brownstone located in the
northwest part of the city. She assessed her nighttime security on
both ends of the quiet residential street. One Treadstone agent
staked out the nearest intersection from inside a black Escalade.
Another was parked two doors down from her front door in a Mercedes sedan. A third walked her German shepherd across the
street, dressed like a DC suburban government worker who'd finally gotten home after a late day at the office. Two more agents
staffed the first floor of the brownstone.

Their reports indicated no threats, but Shadow evaluated the
street for herself, watching for anything the agents might have
missed. Every security net had vulnerability. Years earlier, in the
first Treadstone headquarters on East 71st Street in New York,
the deadly threat had come from within the organization. A double
agent had gained access to the inner sanctum and proceeded to kill
nearly the entire Treadstone leadership.

Initially, Shadow had believed the agent who perpetrated the bloody massacre was Cain. She'd been wrong, but she didn't regret the error. Shadow regretted nothing. She never looked backward. All the evidence of the break-in had pointed to Cain, and she had no way of knowing that it had been planted specifically to implicate him. In fact, David Webb—in his identity as Jason Bourne—had *acted* guilty because he'd lost his memory. Of himself, of Treadstone, of her, of David Abbott. But even if she'd known about his amnesia, Shadow would have suspected Bourne as the killer.

A man with a broken psyche was capable of anything.

Cain. David Webb. Jason Bourne.

One man. Multiple identities.

Of course, she'd lived under many identities herself. For years in the field, she'd used the legend of Monika Roth. That was what she'd called herself when she first met David Webb as a teacher at a private school in Switzerland. For months, they'd been sexually and romantically involved while she pursued her real agenda, which was to analyze his psychological readiness for Treadstone. She'd never admitted to him—she'd never admitted to herself—that some of the feelings she had for him were real.

Now, as the head of Treadstone, a role for which she'd been groomed by David Abbott since the very beginning of the agency, she was known only as Shadow. There were days when she didn't even remember that her birth name was Marlen. The life she'd known as a child in Germany might as well have belonged to someone else.

Shadow retreated from the window to her desk. A piano concerto by Brahms played softly from hidden speakers. The office with its antique walnut furniture and gold-and-black wallpaper was lit only by a single Tiffany lamp. She liked it dark. Darkness was her friend. She sat down behind her desk, but she left her laptop closed. Her personal gun—a Tanfoglio Domina 9mm—lay within reach. She still prided herself on being the best sharpshooter among her team of agents. Except for Cain. He still managed to beat her. Shadow didn't mind; it only made her focus harder in order to best him.

In reality, it aroused her to find a man who was better at anything than she was.

Shadow fondled the Domina with her nails. She was tense. The call she'd been expecting all evening was late. She hated not knowing what was going on; she hated being without information. Her obsession was knowing *everything*. But she'd spent the last month navigating the most dangerous crossroads in her life, and she'd been mostly blind. No intel. No contact. No way to get answers.

Finally—*finally!*—her phone rang. Shadow snatched it into her fingers. "You're late. Next time you're late, you better be dead."

"Well, I'm alive," the agent known as Vandal replied.

"And?"

"I found Cain."

Shadow squeezed her eyes shut. A little sigh of relief breathed from her chest. Some of the tension of the past month evaporated. "Where are you?"

"France. An island off the coast called Port Noir."

"*Port Noir!*" Shadow hissed. "What the hell is Cain doing there?"

"That's not clear to me. I found him largely by accident. You were right that he was with Johanna, but the reason I couldn't find them is that they've been living on a boat. That's why every contact report came up dry. By the time I got there, they were already gone. Out to sea."

"So how did you find them this time?"

Vandal hesitated. "I got word of an explosion in the Med. A boat blew up. I played a hunch that Cain might be involved, and I was right. I got a chopper over the site. It was a disaster. Debris everywhere and multiple bodies in the water. We pulled one up. Looked like a mercenary. No ID."

"But Cain survived?" Shadow asked.

"Yeah. I'm not sure anyone can kill that son of a bitch. I monitored local radio traffic, and I got word of a commercial vessel pulling a man out of the water. Description matched Bourne."

Shadow picked up the Domina in her hand. The coolness of the barrel comforted her. "What about Johanna?"

A long pause went by on the phone.

"She didn't make it. The man they rescued was alone."

"More good news," Shadow replied coldly.

"I thought you'd feel that way."

"The more important question is, who was behind the explosion? Who do we think is targeting Cain?"

"I don't know. As I say, the one body we retrieved had no identifying information. But the obvious players would be the Russians. We know Putin put out a bounty on Bourne after he killed Lennon. Using mercenaries would keep his hands clean."

"So how did you find Bourne?" Shadow asked.

"I remembered rumors around Treadstone about Cain spending time in Port Noir after he got shot and lost his memory. The location of the explosion wasn't far from the island. I thought if Cain had contacts there, he might go to Port Noir to resupply. I was right. I was in a locals bar this evening, and he showed up."

"That's good work, Vandal."

Another long pause.

"Thanks, but the news isn't all good."

"Oh?"

"When Cain left the bar, three men followed him. Cain dispatched them and disappeared before I could get to the scene. Two of the men were dead. I put a squeeze on the third man and got him to talk. He was a Belarusian teenager—so definitely a Russian connection. But I think this was a crime of opportunity, not a targeted hit. This kid wasn't involved in the attack on the boat. He spotted Cain on the fishing boat that picked him up, and he realized that their mystery man matched the description of Bourne going around on the Russian chat rooms on Telegram. So he saw an opportunity to make some money if he and his buddies could take him down."

"And Cain?" Shadow asked.

"I lost him."

Shadow aimed the Domina at the wall of the brownstone, but resisted the urge to fire in frustration. "There's a doctor on the island. Geoffrey Washburn. He's the one who helped Cain after he lost his memory the first time. Odds are, he's the one Bourne would go to. Find Washburn, and you'll find Cain."

"Unfortunately, someone already figured that out," Vandal reported. "They burned down Washburn's cottage. Cain got away. I found out he did a deal with a boat captain on the island. The captain's gone now, and so is his boat. Bourne escaped."

Shadow shook her head. "So Cain's on the run again?"

"Yes. He's in the wind."

"Goddamn it, Vandal."

"I know. I'm sorry. He's been one step ahead of me for weeks. But listen, there's one weird thing. I don't know if it means anything, but I didn't like it. When I was in the bar and Bourne came in, he ordered a drink and sussed out the place the way an agent would. He *saw* me. Our eyes met. I wasn't in disguise, and he looked right at me, but he didn't acknowledge me at all."

"That's his training," Shadow pointed out. "And yours. Take note of your ally, make contact later when it's safe."

"I know. Exactly. That's what I was planning to do. That's why I followed Bourne out of the bar. I assumed *he* would be looking to make contact with *me*. But he didn't. He's on the run, he sees another Treadstone agent—and he doesn't check in? That makes no sense. The thing is, when our eyes met, he definitely saw me, but . . ."

"But what?"

"I'm not sure he recognized me," Vandal said.

"What do you mean? You said you weren't in disguise."

"That's right. He had to know it was me, but I'm not sure he did."

Shadow eased back in her chair in the dim light of the office. "Shit. I was afraid of something like this."

"What are you talking about? Afraid of what?"

"I told him last winter that we didn't have a full understanding of the impact of his memory loss. I warned him it might come back under stress."

"Jesus. You think he lost his memory again?"

"Port Noir. Geoffrey Washburn. That's where it all started for Bourne. If he was lost in a vacuum again, I think that's where his mind would take him."

"So what do you want me to do?" Vandal asked.

Shadow's mind traveled backward.

She remembered an afternoon in a garden outside Paris, watching a handsome young man stare down a sharpshooter who was there to test his nerves. More than anything, she remembered that moment when their eyes met, when he stared at her and she stared back at him. She could picture him in her memory as vividly as if it had happened yesterday, and she could still feel the heat of arousal in that stare.

You noticed him, too, darling. I've never seen you react like that to a man. I hope it won't be a problem, Marlen.

Shadow got up from the desk and went to the closet in her office. Her go bag was there, ready for instant travel. With one call to the airport, she would have the Treadstone jet waiting to take her across the Atlantic.

"Are you there?" Vandal asked when the silence lingered on the phone. "What are your orders? What should I do?"

"Don't do anything," Shadow told her.

"I don't understand. A month ago, you said finding Cain was our number one priority."

"It still is," Shadow replied. "But for now, stand down. If I need you, I'll reach out, but this is a situation I need to deal with myself.

I'll find Bourne. If he really has lost his memory, I know where he's going."

———

VANDAL HUNG UP THE PHONE.

Under the starlight, she tramped through the aftermath of the fire at the top of the cliff. Embers of the fallen walls glowed orange where the cottage had stood. The burnt, smoky smell lingered in the air, stinging her nostrils. She'd found the body of Geoffrey Washburn stretched out in the grass, gray ash fluttering down over his clothes. Next she found one of the killers in the nearby woods, awash in his own blood. She noted that his small arms had been taken. Bourne had resupplied himself.

The other killer bobbed in the water at the base of the cliff. The boat, the fire, and more than a dozen hired killers, and still Bourne had managed to slip through the net. Vandal shook her head. Chasing Cain was like chasing a magician.

She stared at the phone. Part of her wanted to toss it off the cliff into the sea and then run. Find a place where no one would ever find her. But there was no such place anywhere in the world. Sooner or later, they would track her down and drag her back. They'd dump her in prison for the rest of her life, and she knew—she'd been *promised*—that it would be the toughest time she'd ever done.

Her fingers punched the buttons. She knew the digits by heart. Holly Schultz of the CIA answered on the first ring.

"Vandal."

"Cain's still alive," Vandal told her, not sugarcoating it. She could feel the chill from Holly halfway around the world.

"In other words, you failed again," she snapped. "First the boat. Johanna died, but Cain got away. Now he got past you a second time. Either you're incompetent, or you're deliberately sabotaging the assignments I've given you. Which is it?"

Vandal swallowed down her fury. "You know Cain. You know he's good."

"I do, but you're good, too. And you're *motivated*. Do I need to remind you of that?"

"No."

"Then do your job."

Vandal hesitated, searching for a way out, any way out. "Look, we may not need to do this. Things have changed."

"What do you mean?"

"I talked to Shadow. I described Bourne's behavior after the explosion. She thinks his memory is gone. Again. If he can't remember anything, then he's no threat."

Silence followed. Vandal could almost hear the gears clicking in the woman's mind.

The reputation of Holly Schultz inspired fear throughout the intelligence community. Holly had started out on the CIA's Russian analysis team, but as she climbed the ranks in the agency, she'd carved out a role for herself in managing the blackest of black ops. Domestic ops, the ones that supposedly didn't exist. Manipulating elections. Peddling disinformation. And—according to the rumors—facilitating assassinations.

Vandal had only met Holly once, but the meeting had validated what everyone said about her. Holly found a person's weakness and pushed hard until she owned them. Vandal had been serving a twenty-year sentence in California for murdering her husband—at a time in her life when she was addicted to cocaine—until Nash Rollins of Treadstone pulled her out and gave her a new identity. Thanks to Nash, Vandal was free, but Sylene Jasper—the woman she really was—was still wanted as a prison escapee in Los Angeles.

So Holly had given her a chance that was no choice at all.

Serve two masters, betray her Treadstone bosses, or return to the hardest of jail cells.

"Bourne's memory has a way of coming back at inconvenient moments," Holly replied finally. "Even if it doesn't, he's not the kind of man to let things go. If Cain finds out what's really going on here, it will be a disaster. You need to take him out. He's too much of a risk to all of us."

Vandal's eyes closed as she stood on the clifftop with the sea wind cooling her face from the heat of the fire. The breeze parted the strands of her black-and-purple hair. She thought again about tossing her phone onto the rocks below her. Or maybe she could take a shortcut and throw herself to the rocks. She went so far as to put one foot over the edge, into air, and imagined what it would feel like as her body fell.

Then she took a step back.

"All right," she told Holly. "I'll make sure it happens. I'll kill Cain myself."

7

BOURNE SAT ON MOSSY STEPS BELOW THE SOOT-STAINED COLUMNS OF L'église de la Madeleine in Paris. The church offered a vantage across the plaza toward the six-story limestone building that housed the Valois Bank. There was no sign on its tall oak doors designating the location. Private banks such as the Valois didn't need to advertise their services to the public. If you knew, you knew—and somehow Bourne knew. His brain had directed him here to the Place de la Madeleine without even needing to look up an address.

He remembered what Washburn had told him about the beginnings of his prior life. He'd transferred money from the Gemeinschaft Bank in Zurich to the Valois Bank in Paris. His contact there was a banker named Antoine d'Amacourt.

Soon d'Amacourt would get a visit from one of his best customers.

Bourne didn't hurry to go inside the bank. He knew—damn it, *how* did he know?—that he needed to analyze a situation before rushing into it. Watch for security. Watch for traps. Evaluate ways in, ways out, emergency getaways, places to hide. Make a plan for every contingency. Know what to do when things go wrong, because things will always go wrong.

Those were the rules.

But where did the rules come from?

Bourne ate *frites* from a paper cone. From behind his sunglasses, his eyes moved constantly. He watched the people come and go, dodging tour buses and motorbikes. It was a warm June morning under blue skies, and the wind blew a dank smell from the Seine a few blocks away. He let an entire hour pass on the steps of the church. The other reason not to hurry was to follow Washburn's advice about free-associating. *See where your brain takes you. When you can, when the situation allows it, step outside yourself and observe.*

His instincts told him that he was home. He felt comfortable here. The city noise felt like an old friend. He knew every twist and turn of the streets, every alley, every stop on the Métro map. He'd arrived from Marseilles the previous day on an early-morning train with nothing but a leather satchel over his shoulder. He'd wandered the city for hours, anticipating what was around each corner and describing landmarks in his head before he saw them. There was no doubt.

Jason Bourne lived in Paris.

Finally, he decided that the area outside the bank was safe. No one was watching. He got up and crossed the plaza toward the northwest corner, where the Valois Bank was located. He pushed through the outer doors the way he suspected he'd done hundreds of times in the past. Inside, an armed security guard waited at a desk outside the building elevators. Bourne tensed, wondering whether he'd be searched and his guns would be discovered. He had visions in his head of another bank—Zurich, yes, it was Zurich!—where his visit had dissolved into gunfire.

But seeing him, the guard's impassive face broadened into a smile of recognition.

"Monsieur Bourne! Welcome back. You've been away several months. Shall I alert Monsieur d'Amacourt that you are here?"

Bourne returned the smile. "Please."

Not even a minute later, a twentysomething French woman, small and trim with brown hair tied in a tight bun and dressed in a severe gray suit, emerged through the elevator doors. She murmured for him to follow her, and they took the elevator together to the next floor, which featured several private waiting rooms. No chance of one customer accidentally seeing another customer here. The woman guided him to a room that was elegantly appointed with an inlaid mahogany table and chairs, plus a sofa and small wine refrigerator. A bottle of Sancerre sat open on a wet bar, with a glass already poured.

"Monsieur d'Amacourt will be with you momentarily," the woman told him, and she left him alone.

Bourne took the glass of wine. It was chilled and expensive. He'd barely taken a sip when the door opened and a man he recognized as Antoine d'Amacourt joined him. The well-fed banker was in his sixties, which he tried to hide with makeup, and his thinning hair had been colored and oiled as it lay across his head. He had smart, scheming eyes above thick crescent-moon bags. The smile with which he greeted Bourne was equal parts officious and afraid. When they shook hands, Bourne noted that d'Amacourt's palm was damp with sweat.

He remembered very clearly now holding a gun to this man's head sometime in the past. No wonder he was terrified.

"*Bienvenue*, Monsieur Bourne. It has been a while."

The tone of the man's voice made it clear that Bourne's long absence was not a bad thing at all as far as the banker was concerned.

"Hello, d'Amacourt."

"How may I help you today, sir?"

"Cash," Bourne replied.

"Of course. How much do you wish?"

Bourne had no idea what was in his account. He'd taken it on faith that he had an account at all. He also didn't know how much cash the bank was likely to keep on hand at any given time.

"Two hundred and fifty thousand. Make it in hundreds and five hundreds."

D'Amacourt didn't blink. "Naturally. Will there be anything else?"

Jesus, Bourne thought. *Who the hell am I? Why do you know me? Where did this money come from?*

He played a hunch. "My safe-deposit box."

"Yes, sir. Do you wish to access it?"

"I do, but I don't have my key with me."

For the first time, a flicker of doubt crossed the banker's face. "Your key? I don't understand. As you know, monsieur, access to all of the boxes in our vault is now entirely biometric."

Bourne shrugged, trying to cover his error. "Sure. I was thinking of my bank in Barcelona. They're old-fashioned there."

"Of course, sir. Well, let me take you to the vault. While you are dealing with your deposit box, I will oversee your withdrawal."

"Thank you, d'Amacourt."

"You've always been very generous, Monsieur Bourne."

The banker accompanied him by elevator to another floor in the building, where a wall of varying-sized boxes was located behind a twelve-inch door. Both men used a retinal eye scanner to unlock access to box 1781. When Bourne had removed the eight-by-twenty-four-inch box, d'Amacourt left him alone to examine it in a secure guest room. Bourne heard the click of the lock when the banker left.

He opened the box, wondering what parts of his life he would find inside.

The first thing waiting for him was a Glock 19, along with several fully-loaded backup magazines. He also found half a dozen passports from different countries, all with matching photographs, but with different names. Charlie Briggs from the USA. Manfred Dietz from Germany. Oleg Sorenson from Denmark. Bourne was a chameleon, shrugging off old skin and adopting a new identity whenever circumstances required it.

He found a personal folder, too. A single sheet of paper contained a list of six different addresses, four in Paris, one in London, one in New York. All appeared to be apartments because the addresses included unit numbers. The locations didn't look familiar and didn't call up memories. Were they his own apartments? Were they safe houses? He memorized the addresses and returned the page to the folder.

Then there was a handful of photographs, all of them without labels to identify the people. He saw a woman in her thirties with dark red hair. Her determined face shouted her intelligence and independence. She stood on a boardwalk somewhere, snow falling in streaks across her face, a castle behind her.

Was it Quebec City? How did he know that?

The sight of her stirred something inside him, and he found himself whispering a name out loud. "*Abbey.*"

A woman he'd loved. A woman he'd lost.

The next picture showed a fiery woman with jet-black hair and Mediterranean features, with tattoos covering her arms and a pendant around her neck that encased what looked like a Greek coin. Her smile was wild and wicked.

Another name sprang to his mind. *Nova.*

Seeing her, remembering her, Bourne's mind felt a stab of loss and grief. Nova was dead. He'd held her body in his arms. He also tapped his empty pocket and realized something precious was missing. The pendant in the photograph—he should have it with him. He'd carried it with him everywhere since her death. But not anymore. The pendant was gone. He suspected it was somewhere at the bottom of the sea.

There was one more photograph.

He tried to make sense of it. Two men stood in the garden of what looked like a nineteenth-century estate, surrounded by con-ical trees, a bubbling fountain, and an oxidized statue of Zeus from Greek mythology. Bourne wondered where the estate was located, and an instinct made him turn over the picture. Someone—not him, it was a woman's handwriting—had written on the back: *Marnes-la-Coquette.*

He knew Marnes-la-Coquette was a village a few miles out-side Paris. In fact, he realized he knew that area very well. The entire estate was familiar to him, its corridors, its artwork, its bed-rooms.

Bourne returned to the photograph, his eyes narrowing to study it. Obviously the two men were close. They had their arms around each other's shoulders and warm smiles on their faces. One man in the picture was younger, mid-twenties, and Jason real-ized with a start that it was a picture of himself. Same swept-back hair, same chiseled look, same blue-gray eyes. The man next to him was older, but very tall with a suave, handsome appearance, a crown of wavy silver hair, and a manicured salt-and-pepper beard.

He knew him, but he didn't know him.

He recognized the man because Geoffrey Washburn had shown him a photograph of that same man, much younger, in a decades-old article from the *New York Times*.

It was David Abbott.

———

BOURNE ARRIVED IN MARNES-LA-COQUETTE IN THE LATE AFTERNOON. He walked from the train station. Somehow he knew that David Abbott's estate wasn't far from the *parc sportif* on the other side of the A13. He used a narrow paved path through the park, which was crowded with French locals lounging in the sun on wide green lawns. Just ahead, he knew, he would find a stone wall enclosing several acres, with a long gated driveway lined with arrow-straight rows of trees leading toward the three-story limestone mansion. His mind could picture it clearly. He'd lived there—for how long? Six months? A year?

Then he'd gone to Switzerland. A village in the mountains. Engelberg. He'd been a teacher.

Yes!

Except somehow he knew that his life there had been a ruse. Another lie among many lies, layers within layers of deception. It had ended in violence. Men had been killed. *He'd* killed them.

Jason jarred himself out of the fragments of his memory. With a glance across the park, he evaluated the dozen or so people enjoying the summer day. Most were harmless. But not all. He took note of one man about thirty years old, with short black hair and a beard, sitting with his back against one of the trees. He held a paperback book with one hand; his other hand lay on a blanket near a crumpled lightweight jacket. Bourne was sure the jacket covered a gun. He noted the wire of an earpiece running discreetly under the man's polo shirt. The man's eyes glanced up from the book as Bourne passed; then his lips moved.

Word had been passed: *He's here.*

They were waiting for him. Where there was one, there were bound to be others. They knew he'd be coming to Marnes-la-Coquette.

But *how* did they know? And who were they?

Bourne continued along the path. Where the green lawns ended and the path ran into a stand of trees, he took cover off the trail. He didn't have to wait long. Barely ninety seconds later, he saw a lean, athletic twentysomething woman arrive from the opposite direction. She was dressed in the tight purple clothes of a runner, but she was walking, and she didn't look winded. Curling from her ear into her thick red hair, he saw another radio wire. As she passed close to him, he heard her murmur a report.

"Il n'est pas là."

He's not here.

Bourne waited until she was gone, then continued through the woods rather than returning to the trail. His instincts guided him; he knew the estate was close. He reached a pockmarked stone wall, approximately his own height. Grabbing the top of the wall, he lifted himself with his forearms and swung up one leg, then pulled the rest of his body behind him and rolled, dropping gracefully to the other side.

He found himself in the midst of a manicured garden, which he recognized from the photograph he'd discovered at the bank. The fountain with its green water and lily pads. The bushes trimmed into perfect conical topiaries. The statue of Zeus. Beyond the garden, he saw the rear wall of the mansion with its chambered windows and iron railings. He tensed, his mind filled with echoes of gunfire. But it wasn't real. It had happened in his past. A shooter had targeted him *here*.

Another ruse. An exercise. A test.

Around him, the garden was peaceful and quiet. The only noise was the bubble of the fountain. Even so, he slid his Glock into his hand. If they had watchers outside, they knew he was coming. They had to expect him to breach the wall, to make his way toward the estate. So where were they?

Why was he alone?

Bourne sprinted across the garden. He reached the wide rear steps of the mansion, which narrowed as they climbed to a set of four doors elaborately carved with metal and glass. On the other side of those doors, he remembered, was a large den. David Abbott's favorite room, with a mural on the ceiling and original landscapes by Turner on the walls. They'd drunk scotch together there. Smoked cigars. Discussed strategy from leather chairs on either side of a stone fireplace.

Strategy for what?

Politics. War. Espionage.

David Abbott had been his teacher. His mentor. His guide. His master manipulator.

"The Monk," Bourne murmured as the nickname came into his mind. That was what they called Abbott.

At the top of the steps, he saw one of the heavy doors open. Instantly, he had his Glock poised and aimed. But instead of a threat, he saw an old woman, at least eighty, emerge onto the water-stained patio. She wore a simple housedress, and her gray hair was neatly styled in a short bob. Her face was deeply lined, her brittle hands folded together in front of her. The gun pointed at her chest elicited no fear. Instead, her face broke into a warm smile.

"Ah, David, it does my heart good to see you again."

David.

She called him David. It was wrong, and yet it felt right, like a door opening onto a world he'd left behind long ago.

"My name is Jason," he told her.

"Oh, *oui, certainement.* I understand. A man like you has many names. But I knew you as David Webb, and to me, that is always who you will be."

"David Webb."

"Of course. That is the name you were born with. You were named after Mr. Abbott, God rest his soul. I am Madame Aubert. Once, we were great friends, you and I, from when you were a teenager and your parents died. But you do not remember, do you?

That part of your life ceased to exist some time ago. And now, once again, you struggle with who you are, yes? But that is what has brought you here."

Frustration filled Jason's mind, pain erupting behind his eyes as he pushed his brain toward places it wasn't yet ready to go. A spasm made his face twitch. His hand felt slippery with sweat, but he didn't lower the gun. "How do you know all that? How do you know my memory is gone? No one knows!"

Madame Aubert smiled again. "She told me. She is waiting for you."

"Who?"

"That is for her to say, not me, David. She is in your old bedroom. I assume your heart will show you the way."

The old woman stood aside, inviting him to enter the mansion.

Don't go! It's a trap! They're waiting for you! Paranoid thoughts rushed through his head, but he couldn't stop himself. Inside was someone who knew him, someone with answers, someone who could bring his identity back to life. Jason climbed the steps, past Madame Aubert. He ripped open the middle door and threw himself inside, swinging his gun at the empty room. No one was there.

But he *remembered* it. The layout was just what his mind had described. The mural. The paintings. The fireplace.

She is waiting for you. She is in your old bedroom.

Jason crossed through the den into the hallway that led toward the front of the mansion. The lights were off; the hallway was in shadow. Framed photographs were hung on heavy red wallpaper like a family photo album. He saw the tall, handsome figure of David Abbott in all of the pictures, along with faces he recognized. Politicians. Generals. Kings. Then he saw a photo that had been taken in Washington, with the reflecting pool as a backdrop. Abbott stood next to a couple in their forties, with a young boy between them, maybe nine or ten. He peeled away the years and realized it was *himself.* Himself as a child. And that couple—the man in a dark business suit, with a square jaw and dark brown hair; the woman, slender and intense, with jet-black hair and fiery eyes. The resemblance was unmistakable.

Mother, father, and son.

These were his *parents*!

Another stab of pain pierced him behind his forehead. His eyes squeezed shut. Had this photograph always been here? Had he passed it every day when he was living in this house? Or had it been hung here now because someone knew he was coming and wanted him to see it?

Keep him off balance. Provoke a storm of emotion.

Jason forced himself to keep going. Across from double oak doors in the main foyer, marble stairs led to the upper floors. The third floor, the top floor, that was where his bedroom had been. He climbed slowly, cautiously, his senses alert, the Glock tight in his grip. On the uppermost floor, he found another hallway, with all the doors closed, but he knew that the third door on the left, overlooking the garden, had been his bedroom. He listened for movement, but as far as he could tell, he was still alone.

At the bedroom door, he turned the knob, then used his shoulder to shove it inward. The lights were on inside, but the room was empty. There was no furniture at all, nothing on the walls, nothing to remind him of the past. A glass door led to a small balcony with an iron railing. It was open.

Where was she?

Bourne knew she'd been here. He smelled perfume like a cloud of memory. Wind Flowers. She always wore Wind Flowers. His body reacted to the familiar scent like an aphrodisiac and a wave of arousal rippled through him. He went through the open doors to the balcony to get out into the fresh air again. He gripped the railing hard. He closed his eyes. Being here felt like being on a mountain precipice, assaulted by crosswinds that threatened to pitch him into the abyss.

"Hello, David."

Bourne spun. A woman stood in the doorway to the bedroom. She was a handful of years older than he was, but elegant and beautiful, with a cool distance that made him feel like he was standing behind a rope as he stared at a museum painting. Her blond hair cascaded in a lush wave to her shoulders. Her blue eyes shined, as sharp and bright as fresh-cut topaz, and her lips were deep red against ivory skin. She was tall, eye to eye with him in her spiked heels, in a knee-length black dress that left him hungry for the body beneath it.

He'd seen her in that dress before. This was no accident. He'd been in the garden below the balcony, a sharpshooter playing with him like a cat with a mouse, and this woman had been up here wearing that dress as she watched the game.

As she watched *him*.

In an instant, Jason closed the gap between them and pushed the Glock into her throat. She didn't flinch or resist. They were face-to-face, and he didn't know whether to kiss her or kill her. But he *knew* her. Images of her flooded his brain. This woman high atop an English castle in the midst of gunfire. This woman barking orders at him on a California beach. This woman naked in his arms in a Swiss meadow as he slid inside her.

"*Shadow.*"

"You remember me," she said calmly. "That's a good start. But we have a lot to talk about, Jason."

8

BOURNE AND SHADOW WALKED IN THE NIGHTTIME MOONLIGHT ALONG the shore of Lác Supérieur in the gardens of the Bois de Boulogne. Her town car was parked fifty yards behind them, her armed driver watching the street. They stayed near the water, away from the glow of the light posts. He listened to the sharp tap of Shadow's heels on the pavement. She hadn't talked to him yet; she hadn't told him why she was here. After their reunion on the balcony, she'd insisted he sleep. Without explaining why, she said she didn't know how much sleep either of them would get in the days ahead.

So he did. He slept for five straight hours, which shocked him. When he awakened, Madame Aubert served him coq au vin at a hand-carved dining room table, under the watchful eye of a portrait by Gainsborough. She told him that he'd often shared meals with David Abbott in this room, but he didn't remember any of it.

Jason ate alone. Shadow didn't appear.

He didn't see her again until an hour later, when Madame Aubert guided him outside the front doors of the estate, kissed his cheek warmly, and opened the door of a black town car in the circular driveway. Shadow was waiting in back, and she directed the driver to head toward Paris.

Then, half an hour later, she detoured them into the huge park in the darkness. *To see if we're being followed*, she said.

"I'm sure you don't realize it, but I warned you that something like this might happen," Shadow told him as they stopped near the water of the small lake. She folded her arms across her chest, her eyes distant. "I was afraid your memory loss might come back. You almost died the first time it happened, and God knows what Washburn and his trembling hands did inside your brain. You'll always be at risk."

"Washburn saved my life," Bourne pointed out.

"Perhaps. Out of avarice. He knew you had access to money. He assumed it belonged to you, but of course, it really belonged to Treadstone. I could have clawed it back if I'd wanted. But we were trying to regain your trust."

Jason felt the name like a punch in his gut.

Treadstone!

He worked for Treadstone. Shadow ran Treadstone. All the rules in his head, the rules that guided his life, came from Treadstone. Every time he tried to run, to get away, to be free, Treadstone reeled him back in.

Shadow noted his reaction. "Yes, it started as Treadstone 71, years ago. The agency was based out of the brownstone in New York. After your parents were killed, you lived there for years with David Abbott until we converted it into our headquarters. But after the massacre, after we were blown, we couldn't return. Now I run the agency out of a similar property in Washington."

The pain struck Bourne again, a knife between his eyes as he tried to remember.

"I'm giving you too much background too fast," Shadow told him, observing the look on his face. "Don't think about it. There's plenty of time to recover the pieces of the long-ago past. Right now, we need to be focused on the recent past. I've been looking for you all over the world for the past month, Jason. No one could find you. But it seems I wasn't the only one trying to track you down."

Bourne thought about the Belarusian teenager in Port Noir. *Every Russian in Europe knows your face. Putin wants you dead.* "Because of Lennon. Because I killed Putin's assassin."

"You remember that?"

"Parts of it. I can't even see Lennon's face in my head, and yet I know things about him, about his relationship with me. And with Treadstone. Sometimes memories are there and I don't even realize it. They come back on their own. But if I try to recall them, it feels like a bullet in my brain."

"Well, we'll work with what we have," Shadow said. "I'll help you."

She reached out and took his hand. Despite the gentle touch, he could feel her sharp nails on his palm. With this woman, with Shadow, help always came with a price tag. If she wanted him with her, if she'd spent the past month searching for him, then she had a motive that had nothing to do with Bourne himself. He was just a means to an end.

He thought about the rules in his head, and he knew the most important one.

Trust no one.

Treadstone.

"Has anything come back to you from the recent past?" she asked. "You were hiding out. Do you remember any details from your life on the run?"

"I was on a boat in the Mediterranean."

"Yes, the boat that blew up."

"That's right." He glanced at Shadow and added, "I wasn't alone."

Her voice stayed level, almost disinterested. "Oh? Who were you with?"

"I don't know. A woman. But I don't remember who she was. All I know is that she died in the explosion, and I survived."

He felt the slightest tension in her body as he stood next to her. That was a tell.

"Do *you* know who she was?" Jason asked.

Shadow shrugged. "I have no idea. You were trained to seize opportunities. Make use of people when you needed them. My assumption is, you knew Putin was on your trail, and you realized you had to go into hiding. So you developed a relationship with a woman under one of your cover identities in order to protect yourself. You're very good at that."

Bourne thought about the woman in his dream, the woman without a face or a name. In his dream, she wasn't a random target he'd manipulated for his own ends. She was a woman he loved. She was also a professional, every bit as skilled as himself. So maybe Shadow was wrong about who the woman was.

Or maybe she was lying.

"I was trained for Treadstone," Bourne said. "Was that by you?"

She let go of his hand. "No. In the beginning, David Abbott

trained you himself. He put you through a battery of tests. Physi-cal, psychological, emotional. When he thought you were ready, he put Nash Rollins in place as your handler. Nash took over your Treadstone orientation. After that, he worked with you for years."

Nash Rollins.

Jason had a vision of a little man with the toughness of a Bra-zil nut.

"So when did you enter the picture?" Bourne asked.

"I became your handler last year. Nash was shot, almost killed. After that, I decided to run you personally. I'm the head of Tread-stone now, and I needed an ally who reported only to me. There are missions that require off-the-books action, and I'm afraid most spies are bureaucrats at heart, always looking over their shoulder. That's not you, and that's not me. It's why we've always made a good team."

Jason had the feeling she was leaving out important parts of the story.

"Except our relationship goes much farther back, doesn't it? I remember seeing you at Marnes-la-Coquette."

"Yes, I saw you there. Once. But we didn't meet then. That was later."

"In Switzerland," Bourne said with a flash of recall.

Shadow stiffened again. "That's right. I was undercover there. We knew each other on a mission. After that, we didn't meet again for ten years. But that's a story for another time, Jason. Come on, we need to keep going. I want to get to one of our Paris safe houses. We need to get ready for our mission."

"What mission is that?"

"I'll brief you when we're there. We have a SCIF. No one can listen."

She turned from the lake, but her heel caught in the dirt, and she stumbled into Bourne's arms, jostling his body.

That was why the bullet missed him.

He heard a low spit on the wind, and bark snapped and powdered as the shot went past them into the trunk of a tree. He jerked on Shadow's arm and dragged her to the ground. Another bullet kicked off the pavement and made a bloody gash across her calf.

Bourne fired back multiple times across the parking lot. That bought them a few seconds to slide down the slope of the grass to the lakeshore. They stretched out beside each other, keeping low, out of sight from the trees. Fifty yards away, more gunfire erupted as Shadow's driver aimed wild shots at the location of the shooter. Then the Treadstone agent ran toward them, but a new flurry of bullets took him down mid-stride. He collapsed on the sidewalk and lay still. With that threat gone, the assassin turned his attention back to Bourne and Shadow, and the wet grass around them began to explode in sprays of mud.

"We can't stay here," Bourne said. "We're too exposed. I'll cover you. Go for the water."

He aimed his Glock into the trees where he'd seen the muzzle flashes. He fired, waited two seconds, then fired again, and again, shifting the barrel slightly with each shot. Next to him, Shadow crawled down the slope and he heard a low splash as she shouldered into the lake. He fired until he'd emptied his magazine, and then as he rolled clear and reloaded, the gunfire tore up the grass where he'd been moments earlier.

His new magazine clicked into place. Bourne took aim again. The killer had moved; the shots came from a new direction. He fired one shot after another, and this time he took the risk of scrambling to his feet and pointing his gun backward as he ran for the lake. As he emptied his second magazine, he sucked in his breath and threw himself into murky black water.

The lake wasn't deep. He felt himself hit the slimy bottom immediately. Staying down, he half swam, half crawled from the shore. His eyes were open, but he was blind, and as he zigzagged under the lake, he had no idea which direction he was going. The silt he dislodged made a ripple on the surface, and he sensed a bullet streak into the lake near him. He was sure the assassin was standing by the lake now, firing at anything that moved.

Quickly, he changed direction again.

Beneath him, the water finally got deeper. He swam with just his arms, surging forward, but his lungs began to scream for air. He pushed himself through the water, harder, faster, but finally he couldn't resist the need for oxygen. In one arching motion, he broke through the surface, gasped in a breath, and dove down again. The moonlight for that couple of seconds told him he was in the middle of the lake. Below the water, he kicked for a few yards, then turned toward where he'd seen the far shore. He hadn't had time to fill his lungs, and he risked breaching again for another deep breath. No shots chased him. He submerged, swam, then felt the muddy bottom bumping against his chest.

Like a sea monster, he crawled out of the water, then rolled as he anticipated fire from the opposite shore. But there were no more bullets. He could see the other side of the lake, where they'd escaped.

The grass was empty. The killer had fled.

"Jason."

Bourne saw a figure on the ground twenty yards away, almost invisible near a hedgerow that fronted the street. It was Shadow. He climbed the slope and helped her up. Her wet dress was pasted to her body, her skin almost black with mud. Her blond hair clung to her face in streaks. She'd lost her heels, and her feet were bare.

"Any idea who that was?" he asked.

"I'm more concerned with how he found us. I didn't see anyone on our tail, and no one outside Treadstone knows I'm here."

"You think you have a mole?"

"I think this is why I wanted to keep you as my own agent," Shadow said. "If Treadstone is compromised, we can't rely on any of the usual safe houses. We have no backup. For now, we're on our own."

———

BOURNE STOLE A CAR ON A STREET OUTSIDE THE PARK, AND THEY drove across the city to one of the apartment addresses he'd found in his lockbox at the Valois Bank. It was located across from a massage parlor in the Pigalle neighborhood, among low-end shops shuttered with iron gates. Fortunately, at one in the morning, their wet clothes and dirty appearance attracted no attention among the nighttime denizens in that area of Paris.

The six-digit code for the door lock on his top-floor unit rolled off his finger without him even thinking about it. Inside, the apartment was small and utilitarian. He was sure he'd been here before, but it didn't look familiar. There were men's clothes—new, unused, still with tags—in the bureau, plus a well-stocked medical kit in the bathroom. Otherwise, he'd left nothing personal behind. This was his own safe house, a getaway for when he was on the run. But no one who found it would connect it to Bourne.

Shadow took off her clothes. It didn't take long; she pulled off the remnants of her torn black dress and stepped out of her panties. He looked away, giving her privacy. Then she went into the bathroom and closed the door, and he heard the shower running. While he waited for her, he checked the tall window and examined the street below him, as well as the dark apartments in the opposite building.

No one was watching the place, waiting for his return. No one had followed them.

The noise of the shower stopped. Shadow returned, naked and clean, drying her hair with a towel. She'd taped a gauze pad to the cut on her leg. When she was done with the towel, she tossed it on the bed, rather than pulling it around her body to cover herself. She didn't hide from his gaze. For a moment, she stood where she was, on display, like a goddess to be admired. Her skin was winter-white despite the summer days. Her blond hair, normally lush and perfect, had a mussed, careless look. Beads of moisture clung to her body and dripped down her taut stomach into the bare V between her legs. She had full breasts, tipped with tiny points that were hard and pink.

"Bring back memories?" she asked.

He guessed what she meant. "We had a physical relationship once."

"Yes, we did."

"In Switzerland."

"That's right."

"But not since."

"No. You've been otherwise occupied with women. Besides, that was one of your requirements for working *under* me, as it were. No sex. Strictly professional." A smirk crossed her deep red lips, as if to say: *Are you regretting that now?*

He stripped off his own wet clothes in front of her. Her eyes stayed locked on his body the whole time, with her memories of their past written on her face. She noticed all of his scars, as if counting the ones that were new since he'd last been naked with her. He padded toward the bathroom, but she stopped him with a hand on his chest. Her damp fingers were soft. A long, erotic moment passed between them, and he wondered if she was about to break the rules. Take him to bed.

But she didn't. She let her hand fall away. Then she went to the bureau and took out one of his new button-down shirts and a pair of boxers. She ripped off the tags and began to get dressed. He looked back at her from the bathroom doorway.

"Why have you been trying to find me?" he asked.

"You're mine, Jason. My agent, that is. I always want to know where you are."

"Obviously, I didn't want to be found. By you or anyone else. So tell me why you're here. You said you needed me for a mission. What is it?"

Shadow sat on the bed. She twisted strands of her blond hair with a nervousness that felt false. One thing he knew about Shadow: she was never nervous.

"David Abbott is alive," she said.

He watched her await his reaction, studying his face like a

scientist observes a lab animal. She expected him to be surprised, but he wasn't. He realized that he already knew the truth about Abbott. Somewhere in his mind, he heard a fragment of conversation, floating without any place or time.

His own voice. And a woman's voice.

David Abbott can't be alive.

He is, Jason.

"You've obviously been keeping that secret from me for a long time. Not just now. So there has to be more to it than just that. What's really going on?"

More nervous twisting with her hair.

Was it real?

Was Shadow afraid?

"He's missing, Jason," she told him. "Abbott went off the grid a month ago, and I don't know where he is. You and I need to find him."

9

"MEN LIKE DAVID ABBOTT CAN'T JUST RETIRE," SHADOW TOLD HIM.
They'd slept for a few hours before she was ready to tell him the
rest of the story. Now they sat next to each other on the apartment
floor, beneath the window that looked out on the streets of Pigalle,
passing a cheap bottle of wine back and forth between them. "He
knows too much. Too many people would want to grab him for his
secrets. Or simply kill him. But several years ago, he began to have
health issues. He needed a break from the day-to-day stress of
running Treadstone, but it's not like he could hole up in a cabin in
Maine. It didn't matter how much security we provided. Someone
would have found him. Someone would have gotten to him. So
Abbott and I decided that he had to die."

"And you kept that from me," Bourne said. "You let me think
he was dead."

"Yes, we did. That was a strategic decision. Abbott and I both
agreed it was the best way to go. This was right around the time of
your first memory loss. Hell, at that point you didn't even know

who David Abbott was, let alone the kind of profound role he'd played in your life. We didn't know if any of your memories would ever come back. Candidly, we didn't know how far we'd ever be able to trust you. I wasn't sure you'd be able to return to Treadstone at all. If you knew Abbott was alive, it would be a risk to him and a risk to you. So we lied."

He heard no apology in her voice.

"It can't have been easy staging the death of someone like him. How did you get anyone to believe it?"

"The plan was elaborate," Shadow acknowledged, taking a swig of Côtes du Rhône and wiping some of the wine from her lips. "We needed dependable confirmation. Not from us—no would believe us. It had to come from the other side. We knew that Abbott had a particularly ruthless enemy in the South African military. Someone who would jump at the chance to take him out. So we arranged a leak through a third party about Abbott's location. He would be spending the weekend at a New Zealand resort after a WTO meeting—a location perfectly suited to a sniper. Our man in Johannesburg followed the bait like a mouse to the cheese. He sent in an assassin to take Abbott out."

"You used a double?" Bourne guessed.

"Yes. From a sniper's distance, the look-alike was a perfect match."

"How did you fake the hit?"

Shadow shrugged. "We didn't. The sniper used a headshot and took out the double."

"Jesus Christ," Bourne muttered.

"We did what we had to do. The assassin got photo and video

proof of the hit. That was what we needed. He went back and got his money. Word spread quickly around the intelligence community. We denied it behind the scenes, which helped convince everyone it was true. Abbott was never seen again."

"And the double? His family?"

"He got a star on the wall. His family was well compensated. It's how the game is played, Jason. In another life, you knew that."

He felt a coldness in his soul, wondering how many times he'd made similar moral calculations about the jobs he had to do. But that was nothing compared to the ice water in the veins of the woman next to him. "Where did you put Abbott? Where has he been hiding all these years?"

"He's been on a Greek island. The list of people who know he's alive is exceedingly small. Really it's just me and his head of security. Rex was Abbott's personal hire, not someone from the agency. They go back for years. He didn't want anyone in Treadstone knowing the truth other than me. There are other guards at the estate, but as far as they know, they're babysitting a Howard Hughes–style billionaire recluse."

"Have you seen him?" Bourne asked.

"Yes. I go out there a couple of times a year. I use extreme precautions to make sure I'm not followed. Abbott and I also stay in regular contact. I still rely on his advice. There's no one with better national security instincts. But the communication between us is all low-tech, nothing electronic, nothing that can be tracked or traced."

"So what happened?"

"About a month ago, the secret leaked. The rumor tore through the intelligence community around the world. Abbott was alive. Not just alive—exposed. In the open and on the run. He's got a price on his head."

"Just like me," Bourne said.

"Just like you."

"How did the word get out?"

"He was spotted in Croatia. Bad luck, bad timing."

Bourne heard another voice in his head. A woman's voice. *He said Abbott had been seen in Dubrovnik. The ID was definitive.*

His eyes squeezed shut. His headache knifed his forehead.

"Are you all right?" Shadow asked.

"Fine."

"Do you remember something?"

"No. Nothing. What was Abbott doing in Croatia?"

"That's the thing," Shadow said. "I don't know. In the years since I set him up in Greece, he never left. He knew the risks were too high. He declined surgery on his face, but even if we'd tried to change his looks, it wouldn't have worked. He's too noticeable. Too tall, too handsome. If anyone in the IC spotted him, they'd recognize him immediately. Obviously, that's what happened."

"Have you been in touch with him?"

"No, because I don't know where he is. Our dead drops go untouched. I'm guessing he's still alive, because if he weren't, news of his death would have hit my desk by now. So my assumption is he's lying low somewhere. We need to find him, Jason. We need to find him and rescue him before anyone else gets to him."

"The Russians?"

"Among others. His enemies list is long. Even among our allies," there are people who would love to know what Abbott has in his head."

"So you want to go to Greece?" Bourne asked.

"Yes, that's where we need to start. We need to find his trail at the estate and see where it takes us. And we need to move fast. Abbott is the best there is. He's brilliant. But he's been on the run for a month, and the whole world is looking for him. Sooner or later, someone's going to track him down."

Bourne pushed himself off the floor.

Through the window, Paris was still dark, but the morning sky showed signs of lightening. It would be dawn soon. He felt an adrenaline surge in his veins that he needed to release. He needed to run, run hard, run fast, his feet pounding the Paris streets. Somehow he knew that was what he did when he lived here between missions. Every morning, he ran. It was the only way to keep his body and mind from overheating.

"I need to go," he told Shadow.

"Go where?"

"I'll get us food, clothes, and supplies. Then we can figure out our route to Greece."

"Good."

"Without Treadstone backup, none of this will be easy."

"Agreed."

He squatted in front of her, their faces inches apart. He realized that he'd never understood this woman. The glimmers of his memories about her told him nothing. In a distant, foreign part of his mind—the past that took him all the way back to his original life as David Webb—he knew he'd been in love with her. And he was sure, he was *sure*, she'd betrayed him. Given the chance, she would do it again. But he couldn't say no. The hold she had over him had never completely disappeared. As he stared into her eyes, the closeness grew too intense, and he got up and walked away.

"What are you not telling me?" Bourne asked from the window.

"I don't know what you mean."

"Yes, you do. You and Abbott stayed in touch while he was in Greece. You're the head of Treadstone, but he was still behind the scenes, consulting, directing strategy. Right? So you may not know specifically why Abbott was in Croatia, but I'm betting you know a lot more than you're saying. If you want my help, tell me."

Her blood-red lips bent into a smile. "Abbott always said I needed to watch out for you, Jason. I don't meet many people who are as smart as me. Definitely not many men. But you're a worthy chess player."

"Skip the games, Shadow. Just tell me."

She got to her feet and stood next to him at the window. He had a vision of standing here like this with someone else. He'd been here in this apartment with another woman. He'd wrapped his arms around her, and taken her to bed, and made love to her. And then he'd lost her. He'd lost her on a boat in the Mediterranean.

Who was she?

"All right," Shadow told him. "I don't know what Abbott was trying to do in Croatia, but I assume it involved a situation that he and I have been pursuing for several months. A *domestic* situation."

"Involving what?"

"Not what. Who. Do you know who Adam Hill is?"

Bourne did. He remembered things that had nothing to do

with his own life. "Hill's the vice president. What the hell does he have to do with any of this?"

"Hill is the most popular man in American politics," Shadow replied. "More popular than the president, that's for sure. He's cultivated a folksy reputation. Former teacher. Dad. Family man. If something were to happen to the president—and believe me, I think something *will* happen to the president—then Adam Hill would take over."

"So? Everyone says he's smart and solid."

"Information has come my way to suggest otherwise."

"Information?".

"That's all I can say for now. You'll have to trust me, Jason, and I know that's a big ask. But Abbott and I are both convinced that Adam Hill must be stopped. Removed from the vice presidency, removed from politics. We've been pursuing that goal for several months, so far without any success. Whatever Abbott was doing in Croatia, I think it had something to do with that."

"Why are you so sure?"

"Because the last communication I had from Abbott was in one of our dead drops. He said that he had a grenade that would blow up in Adam Hill's face. He said he'd had it for years, but it was finally time to pull the pin. That was five weeks ago. A week later, he disappeared."

———

HOLLY SCHULTZ SAT IN A COMFORTABLE CHAIR IN ONE OF THE HIGH-floor corner suites of the Watergate Hotel. It was nearly midnight. The television was on, and she listened to the audio of Adam Hill giving a speech to the National Association of Manufacturers, which was being re-broadcast on C-SPAN from the event earlier in the evening.

She'd heard Hill speak many times before, but she always respected his ability to work a crowd. Every intonation of his voice was perfect, the right turn of a phrase, the right timing of a joke, the aw-shucks Southern sincerity in his voice. All of it was utterly fake. She'd met a lot of politicians during her CIA career, and every politician lied for a living. That was the currency of being an elected official. But Hill lied with such sincerity that she almost wondered if he believed it himself.

People told her that Hill was tall and stocky, in his fifties, with thinning brown hair and an everyman face. She didn't know what Hill actually looked like, only how others had described him. Holly was blind, so she had to rely on her other senses to make her assessments. Also, she had Sugar. Sugar was her guide dog, but for Holly, their relationship went much deeper than simply using the yellow Lab to steer her through unfamiliar places. The dog also had a sixth sense for good and evil, and from the beginning, Sugar had *hated* Adam Hill. That growl when Hill first showed up in her office told her everything she needed to know about the vice president.

But it didn't matter.

Holly knew who Hill really was, but there was nothing she could do about it, not if she wanted her own secrets to stay hidden. That was how the game was played. Whoever had the most leverage won the war. Holly knew enough about the Treadstone agent Vandal to force her to play both sides. Adam Hill knew enough about Holly—he'd laid it out for her in their very first meeting—to make sure she waged a secret war against Treadstone.

Including Shadow.

Including David Abbott.

She listened to Hill's honey voice on the television. She wondered if he'd worn a suit for the manufacturers, or whether he was dressed in his trademark plaid coat and jeans. Man of the people. The champion of the union worker.

"Look, my friends," Hill said in his booming Texas twang. "And that's what we are, you know. Friends. You may not always believe that, but I do. I may make your life hell from time to time about the rights of those people who do the work for you and make you all rich, but I also know that nobody makes any money if your businesses go under. Okay? So look, my friends, we are on the same side. The future is not employer versus employee, company versus union. The future is not America versus China. The future is not freedom versus security. Those are all false choices. Foolish choices. The future is not in *division*, it is in *multiplication*. Got it? Multiplying opportunities. Multiplying markets. Multiplying standards of living. The political system that delivers sustained results for its citizens is the political system that will triumph. I'm not here to advocate for left or right, for my way or your way. I'm here to say we all better start delivering results, because if we don't, the people are going to kick us to the curb and find something better."

Holly heard the applause from the manufacturers. It sounded sincere, not false, not faked. Adam Hill knew how to make every audience believe he was on their side right up to the moment he fucked them over. The event itself had ended almost two hours earlier, but Hill never left a venue without talking up everyone in the crowd one on one. She didn't care; she was in no hurry to see him. Instead, Holly reached for the Cîroc vodka she'd poured into a crystal glass. She needed something to calm her nerves. She was accustomed to giving orders, not taking them, but Hill was the one calling the shots in their relationship. They both knew it.

Fifteen minutes later, the hotel room door finally opened. Next to her, Sugar barked once and gave an unhappy growl. Holly plastered a smile on her face. "Hello, Adam."

She heard the clink of ice as he poured a drink for himself. He didn't apologize for his late arrival. "You see the speech?"

He didn't sound like a Texan in private. That was for the voters. With Holly, he was the Harvard boy, no accent at all. She knew his story all too well. Born and raised in Dallas, a math teacher voted most popular teacher at his high school four years in a row. He'd spent fifteen years in the Texas public schools, leading a dozen student trips to China—trying to shrink the world one young mind at a time, he said.

China.

He'd been married in China. Vacationed in China. *Know your enemy*, Hill liked to say. That was his pitch when he'd run for Congress in a wave election and turned a red Texas district blue. He'd held that seat for ten years, rising to chairman of the House Armed Services Committee, then wound up as the dark-horse VP choice in a race no one thought the Democrats would win, not after the assassination of their leading candidate, the former secretary of state Alicia Beauvoir. But when an October surprise rocked the

Republicans late in the race, Adam Hill ended up living on the grounds of the Naval Observatory.

From high school teacher to vice president.

Only in America, Hill liked to say.

Or in China, Holly thought.

"Yes, I saw the speech," she said.

"Good, huh?"

"Very effective."

She heard him sit down in a chair not far from her, expelling his breath with a sigh. When he took a drink, his lips smacked. Another menacing rumble vibrated in Sugar's throat, and Holly could feel the dog's muscles tensing under her fingers. She stroked her fur, trying to calm her.

"That dog of yours hates me," Hill said.

"Sugar is just protective."

"If she growls at me again, I'm going to fucking poison her. Got it?"

Holly tightened her grip on Sugar's collar. "I can put her in another room if you'd prefer."

"We don't have time for that. I'm just warning you." Hill finished his drink quickly and poured another. "So give me the update. Is it confirmed? Is Cain dead?"

"No. He's not."

She heard the crystal tumbler hit the table hard. "Are you kidding me? I thought you had an agent on top of this."

"I did. I *do*. Initially, we believed there were no survivors when the boat blew up. But Vandal discovered that Cain is still alive. He was rescued by a fishing boat off the coast of France."

"Where is he now?"

"We're not sure. He slipped through Vandal's fingers. But she's tracking him."

"Goddamn it!" Hill exploded. "I want that fucker dead. Don't you get it? If he knows the truth about me and Annie, he's going to come after me. I know the hero type. He'll want revenge."

Holly waited for the politician to calm down. "Adam, it's very possible that Cain *doesn't* know anything. We don't have any indication that he ever learned the truth. More than that, Vandal indicated that the injuries he suffered in the explosion were serious. He appears to have lost much of his memory again. So he might have no idea about the . . . incident . . . in your past. If that's true, then you're safe."

"I have no intention of taking that risk," Hill snapped. "Get rid of him."

"I'm on it. We'll find him."

"You better, Ms. Schultz." She heard the ice plinking in his glass. "Cain is only half of my problems. What about David Abbott? I can't believe the son of a bitch is still alive. He's been playing us all this time. And he's made it very clear that he will do anything to take me down."

"I agree Abbott is a smart man and a threat. He and Shadow fooled me along with everyone else. I was convinced his assassination was real. But now that everyone knows he's alive, the hunt is on. It's been a month. He can't hide out much longer. The first time he was killed may have been fake, but the second time will be real."

Holly listened for a reply, but heard only silence. Then Sugar growled loudly, despite her restraining hand. When Adam Hill spoke again, she realized that he'd crossed the room silently and was standing directly over her chair. His voice, his breath were in her ear.

"You do remember that if I go down, you go down, too? And your fall will be considerably harder than mine, Holly."

"I'm aware."

"So what are we going to do about David Abbott?"

Holly inhaled, staying calm. "We don't need to do anything, Adam. Abbott won't be a problem for much longer. I've heard reports from reliable sources out of Europe. The Russians think he's somewhere in Bulgaria. They're closing in."

10

BOURNE'S RUN ENDED AT THE SEINE, NEAR THE RIVERSIDE WALKWAY across from the National Assembly. The morning sun cast an orange glow on the water, and the Eiffel Tower rose on the horizon against pink clouds. Checking his pulse and measuring out his breathing, he walked along the river near houseboats tied to the pier. His instincts had drawn him to this place, as if this route had been part of his daily routine. He found himself eyeing the early-morning joggers, the bicyclists, the old men, the young couples walking hand in hand. None were threats. But that was how he lived his life, watching the world around him and isolating the threats.

Ahead of him, he saw one weathered houseboat among dozens of others, its green paint peeling, its windows boarded up. The boat looked as if no one had lived there in years. And yet he saw a brand-new bicycle chained to the deck.

Somehow he realized this was important. This *meant* something. Every morning in his old life, he passed the boat, and if the deck was empty, then no one was waiting for him. But the bicycle was back. That was a symbol. A message.

Someone wanted a meeting.

Bourne stopped, sipping a cup of takeaway coffee and taking another look at the people on the river. No one was watching him. He was alone. The meeting itself took place elsewhere. That was the protocol they'd established years ago. Watch for the bicycle, assess security, make sure you're not followed.

Then proceed to the rendezvous—*where?*

The answer came to him from instinct, not memory. The Tuileries. They always met on a bench in the Tuileries near the children's pond, in the shadow of the Ferris wheel and the Palais-Royal.

Bourne climbed the steps away from the river. He crossed the busy morning street into the Place de la Concorde and then to the wide promenade through the city park. Automatically, he looked for watchers. Security. *Treadstone.* The man he was meeting never came alone. Bourne knew that there should be half a dozen agents surveilling his approach, but today there was no one.

Why?

He saw the circular pond ahead of him, where the trees ended. A single fountain of water jetted into the air. A few early tourists wandered the large pavilion with backpacks and cameras, taking pictures near the statues and exploring the neatly landscaped hedges. But he saw no one with guns. Today the old man on the bench was here by himself, waiting for Bourne without any backup.

Seeing the man brought a name to his mind. Nash Rollins.

He heard an echo of what Shadow had told him the previous night. *When Abbott thought you were ready, he put Nash Rollins in place as your handler.*

Nash sat on one of the green chairs that surrounded the pond, pulling pieces of bread from a baguette and tossing them to the birds. A carved walking cane lay across his lap. He was in his sixties, but looked older now. His skin was deathly pale, making the age spots on his face and neck look darker. His wiry gray hair had thinned, and it blew in one piece like a wave in the breeze. His skin, always deeply lined, hung loosely on his face.

Bourne knew the signs. Nash had the gaunt look of a man near death.

He felt a wave of regret. He barely remembered his past, but it seemed as if everyone important to him was about to die. First Geoffrey Washburn. Now Nash Rollins. He knew that he had a complicated relationship with Nash. Again, *instinct*! He didn't trust this man, but Bourne didn't trust anyone. Nash was all about the mission; the mission came first, his agents second. They'd clashed many times. Bourne had an image in his mind of *shooting* Nash, aiming his gun at the man's thigh, not to kill him, but to wound him and slow him down.

At that moment, they'd been enemies. But on some level, they were also friends who'd been through wars and back together. They'd saved each other's lives many times. That still meant something.

He sat down on one of the chairs next to Nash. The old man continued to toss bread to the birds.

"Hello, Jason. It's been a while."

"Has it? I don't remember."

Nash's hands froze, with the baguette between his fingers. He didn't look over at Jason, but his face stiffened. "Is that a joke?"

"No."

"You mean it's happened again? Your memory?"

"Yes, it has."

"*Jesus!* When? How?"

"I was on a boat in the Med. It exploded. I woke up with no identity."

Nash took a long time to reply. "God, I'm sorry. I heard about the explosion from a contact at Interpol. He mentioned the assault in Port Noir, too. The doctor. The one who helped you before. I knew it had to be you. That's why I came to Paris. I didn't know if you were alive or dead, but I figured you'd come here. How bad is it?"

"Bits and pieces of the past are coming back to me. A name or a face can trigger a wave of intense memories. Or it may do nothing at all. There's no pattern to any of it. But I know things, even if I don't remember them. Like the signal at the river. The bicycle. I knew what it meant, I knew where to go."

"Instinct," Nash said.

"Exactly."

"What about me?"

"Seeing you, I remember a lot about you, about us. But not everything. Why are you here, Nash? What do you want?"

"I've had the signal in place for three days. I've come to the park every morning hoping you'd show up. I needed to see you. To *warn* you."

Bourne frowned. "You're alone. No security. Where's your backup?"

"You noticed that? Of course you did. So you know about Treadstone? You remember the agency?"

"I was briefed."

"By who? Shadow? Is she in town?"

Jason hesitated. "Yes."

Nash focused again on the pigeons at his feet, feeding them pieces of bread. He glanced at the people around the pond, making sure there were no spies. "You're right, I'm alone this time. I'm *out*, Jason."

"You mean from Treadstone?"

"Yes."

"It seems to me you told me once that no one is ever really out."

"That's true. In fact, that's why I'm being careful. Shadow might still be watching me. Having me followed. I haven't spotted anyone, but my field skills aren't what they used to be."

"So what happened? Did you quit, or did you get forced out?"

"Shadow put me on medical disability. That was the cover story she used, but I think she just wanted me gone. Hell, I don't mind. I don't have much time left. I'm sure you can tell. You may not remember it, but last year you and I were together on Holy Island in the UK. I took a bad gunshot wound to the stomach. I survived, but just barely. My body's checking out. You can only take so much punishment in your life before things cascade the wrong way. Nobody lives forever, Jason."

Bourne's head swiveled, and he studied the old man next to him. "If you're out, why are you here? Why come looking for me?"

Nash's face flinched in what was obviously a jolt of pain, and his lungs seized with a ragged cough. Bourne realized that his condition was worse than the aftereffects of a gunshot wound. Something else was eating away at Nash's body. Probably cancer, and from the look of him, it was advanced.

"Yeah, it's bad," Nash said, reading Bourne's eyes.

"I'm sorry."

"Don't be. My life's never been boring. Not many people can say that."

"Nash, tell me what's going on."

The old man took a long, slow breath. "Things are different at Treadstone."

"How so?"

"Shadow is different. I mean, she's always been ruthless, gunning for power. It's no secret in DC that she wants to be the one shaping intelligence policy behind the scenes. That was true from the beginning. Treadstone had its roots in the CIA, but David Abbott always saw the agency as his own little black-ops playground. No oversight, no rules. Shadow was his protégé, and he brought her up the same way. Those two were always determined to rule the deep state."

"So what's changed?" Bourne asked.

"Shadow's wielding power in a way she never did before."

"How is she doing that?"

"I don't know for sure, but I have my suspicions. Do you know about the Files?"

Jason was about to say no when his brain overruled him. "I do. It's an AI engine combined with a hacked database."

"Exactly. It was developed by the Chinese in order to exploit data they were hacking from U.S. government and corporate databases. With the AI engine, they didn't just have access to the personal data itself. They had the ability to extrapolate secrets from millions of seemingly irrelevant or unrelated facts."

"How does that work?"

"Well, let's say you're on a mole hunt. Moles are cautious little people. They're careful. But they still have to drive, and eat, and fill up their cars, and go to hotels, and check their Facebook feeds, and engage in the whole blizzard of ordinary-life activities. You or I wouldn't see any patterns in all of that, but an AI engine can run trillions of calculations from hacked data and draw conclusions about someone's behavior. That's how you find spies and hit men and pedophiles and cheating husbands and inside traders."

"And the Chinese are using the Files?"

Nash shook his head. "They were, but they lost control of the engine *and* the database."

"So who has it?"

"As of last year, you did."

Bourne stared at him. "What?"

"You grabbed the laptop with the master AI software. The word on the street was, you destroyed it. But I think you were tricked, Jason. I think Shadow has the Files, and I think she's using them to consolidate her power base. There's a blood feud going on now between wings of the intel sector, especially the CIA versus Treadstone. I was caught in the middle. I was Treadstone, but I was also our liaison to Holly Schultz at the CIA. Shadow didn't trust my relationship with Holly. That's why she forced me out."

Jason squeezed his eyes shut.

He didn't remember destroying the Files. All of that was gone. But he didn't doubt that Shadow had betrayed him, and he could recognize the manipulative hand of David Abbott behind the whole scheme.

Those two were always determined to rule the world.

"How does this involve me?" he asked.

"That depends on what Shadow wants you to do," Nash said.

"You know I can't tell you that."

"Then you need to realize that you're a pawn, Jason. You're the man in the middle now, just like I was. There are no clean hands in this operation. There are no good guys versus bad guys. It's solely about power and who winds up on top. For some reason, Shadow needs you right now. You're important to her, she wants you on her side. But she'll never tell you the truth about what's going on. She will use you until she doesn't need you anymore, and then she'll sacrifice you the first moment you're in her way. And Holly . . ."

"What about her?"

"Holly wants you dead."

"The CIA? That makes no sense. Why? Because I'm Treadstone? Because I'm in league with Shadow?"

"I don't know. I think it's more than that. For all I know, Holly may just be a pawn for someone else. In Washington, everyone has a knife to everyone else's throat. But the explosion on the boat? That wasn't the Russians. Putin has a price on your head because you killed Lennon, but this wasn't his operation."

"How do you know? How can you be sure of that?"

"Because when I heard about the explosion, I wanted to know what really happened, Jason. If you were dead, I wanted to know who'd done it. Whatever our differences, we go back a long way. I trained you as a young agent. I had your back when you were David Webb, long before Cain, long before Jason Bourne. If someone took you out, I wanted to know who it was so I could go after them myself. I flew over here and started asking questions at Interpol. I've still got plenty of contacts there."

"What did they tell you?"

"I got an ID on one of the bodies they pulled out of the water," Nash told him. "He was part of the assault team who came after you. But he wasn't Russian. He didn't have any ties to Putin. He was an independent wet-work operative, but Interpol had him on their hands-off radar because he'd done dozens of contract jobs for the CIA. They're the ones who blew up the boat, Jason. They're the ones who killed Johanna."

11

JOHANNA.

All it took was the sound of her name traveling through his brain and a tidal wave crashed over Jason. The impact blasted the air out of his lungs and stripped away his breath. His memories stormed back, one after another, all the moments they'd spent together. The woman who'd hid in the darkness of his mind, whose voice had called to him in his sleep, stepped back into his consciousness like a painting on the wall come to life.

Johanna!

He could feel every inch of her body under his fingers, every curve, every scar, every tiny flaw. He experienced it in his mind all over again, her moans, her sweat, her gasps, her laughter as they fought with each other in bed. Her face—he saw her face, he could recall every detail of her face. Her hair, as straight and golden as a Midwestern summer field. Her blue eyes, funny, crazy, wild, intense. Her oval face, its expressions always changing, teasing him, arousing him, challenging him.

He loved her. God, he *loved* her!

And she was dead.

He could see it clearly now, the two of them together on the boat—the *Stormy Weather*—caught up in a firefight to the death, surrounded by the assault team. He remembered the look that passed between them, that last look, that glint in her eye, the sly sexy confidence that nothing could ever defeat her. *We're going to get through this, Jason!* And then the heat and flame came, the shock wave of the explosion, as he watched Johanna blasted into the air, disappearing into the black waters of the Mediterranean.

It all came back to him.

Their history. Their lies.

He'd met her for the first time in Switzerland. Back then, she'd played him, fooled him, adopted a false identity solely to get re-venge on *Shadow*. Yes, Johanna was *Treadstone*. Shadow had sent her on a violent mission—not even a real mission, a *test*! A *trick*! But children had died, and Johanna couldn't live with it. After that, Shadow had kicked her out of the agency, believing her too unsta-ble to work in the field. Johanna came back; she *used* Jason to try to destroy Shadow and Treadstone together.

He remembered.

He remembered pointing a gun at Johanna's head and then letting her go. Because you can't kill a woman you love.

That moment hadn't been the end between them. The lies, the betrayal, didn't matter. Neither one of them could deny the attrac-tion to the other, and they couldn't escape the truth that they'd fallen in love. A love that was crazy.

A love that was doomed.

Johanna.

She was unlike any other woman he'd known. Passionate. Un-balanced. Violent. Abused. He knew her stories—assuming they were true, assuming she hadn't made up a past for him out of the lies she'd been telling her whole life. She was a teen prodigy who'd been raped in school and then brutally retaliated against her at-tacker. After that, she'd run away from her parents and her child-hood and created a new life in Europe, a whole new identity for herself, at the age of fourteen. *Fourteen!*

He remembered. They'd been lovers in the Mediterranean, hiding out for months on the open water, until that night when he awoke and he found her on deck, staring anxiously at the horizon. As if she knew the end was coming soon.

Her voice. He knew her voice. Johanna spoke to him out of his mind.

What do you remember about David Abbott?

She'd known *something* about this mystery. She'd known what was going on before he did. Shadow. David Abbott. Holly Schultz and the CIA. Johanna had known the secret. He was sure of it. But she hadn't been able to tell him what was really going on before she was killed.

His longing for her felt heavy in his chest. He felt a void, an emptiness, not having her in his arms when he could feel it, re-member it, so clearly. He had her back in his life, back in his mind, but she was already gone. Everything he reclaimed from the mist of his past seemed destined to die.

"Jason?"

It was Nash.

"Jason, are you all right?"

"No. I'm not. You mentioned Johanna. I didn't remember her

until just now. She's been out there, knocking at the door of my brain, but I couldn't find her. I was in love with her."

"I know. Shadow was desperate to keep the two of you apart."

"Why?"

"I don't think she'd ever admit it, but I always believed Shadow was jealous of your relationship with Johanna. You fell in love with her nemesis. Those two hated each other. Shadow takes pride in never wearing her emotions on her sleeve, but once you found her again last year, I think she wanted you for herself. It didn't surprise me that she chose to run you as her own agent, rather than handing you off to someone else inside Treadstone. When it comes to you, Shadow is possessive."

Bourne pushed himself off the bench and wandered to the edge of the pond in the Tuileries. He felt caught between grief and anger, between escape and revenge. Part of him wanted to let everything go, and yet part of him needed to know more. Nash had said he was now the man in the middle, and Jason didn't doubt that was true—but in the middle of *what?*

Nash limped over to him, leaning his body heavily on his cane. The effort of standing seemed to weigh on him.

"Something's going on, Nash," Bourne murmured. "I think Johanna knew what it was."

"Why do you think that?"

"Before she died, before the explosion, she asked me about David Abbott."

"Abbott? What does he have to do with any of this?"

"That's the question. You knew him, didn't you?"

"Of course."

"What was he like?"

"Brilliant. Arrogant. Ego-driven. He was the smartest man in any room, but he knew it, too. That's a dangerous combination. Abbott was all about the ends. He didn't care about the means, he didn't care about breaking rules. He did whatever was necessary to get what he wanted, because he was convinced that he was always right."

"He adopted me. I lived with him for years after my parents were killed."

"That's right. Abbott and your parents went back a long way. They'd been best friends since college. Remember, you were named after him."

Bourne gave an ironic smile. "I don't actually remember."

"Sorry. Of course. Well, the point is, you were a bitter, grieving teenager, and Abbott gave you a home. I respected him for that. But let's face it, he never did anything without considering the ultimate gain. He saw your intelligence, your physical skills, your instincts. He knew he could use them. He wanted you for Treadstone."

"Was it the same with him and Shadow?"

"Similar," Nash admitted. "They go way back, too. But Shadow drank the Kool-Aid in a way you never did. She would do absolutely anything for Abbott. She idolized him. You—well, you've always been on your own. Isolated, a loner. Even when you're in love, you're on your own. Abbott couldn't control you like he controlled her. Not that he didn't try."

"Why do you think he kept us apart for so long? That can't be an accident."

"Nothing Abbott did was ever by accident. I wondered about that myself for a long time. Maybe he realized you could be a weakness for her, and he didn't want that."

"Were they involved?"

"Abbott and Shadow? I don't think so. Not with the age difference between them. But who knows? Their relationship has always been a mystery to me. He molded her in his image, that's for sure. Ambitious. Driven."

Bourne let a long silence stretch out between them.

Then he said, "David Abbott is alive."

Nash swung his body sharply, nearly falling. His eyes came to life, shaking off pain and disease. *"Impossible!"*

"It's true."

"Shadow told you?"

"Yes."

Nash shook his head. "Amazing. I can't believe it. Then again, it also seems perfectly logical. Jesus, back when he was supposedly killed, I wondered. We all did. But the evidence seemed impossible to fake, even for them. There hasn't been so much as a rumor of a rumor about Abbott since then."

"They kept it between themselves. Abbott and Shadow. But now he's on the run. A month ago, he was spotted in Croatia. Word leaked that he was alive, and he went dark after that. Shadow says she doesn't know where he is, but she needs to find him before he's taken out."

"That's where you come in," Nash concluded. "She needs your help to run the mission. She can't trust anyone else."

"So she says."

"And you're going to do it?"

"If Abbott's alive, I want to meet him."

Nash hesitated before answering. His eyes were focused on the other side of the pond, on the row of tall green hedges behind the white statues that ringed the plaza. Bourne followed his stare in time to see a woman in an orange beret turn sharply away from them. He couldn't see her face, but she was tall and skinny, wearing tight jeans and a nylon jacket, with a deep canvas bag slung over her shoulder. The woman strolled away without looking back.

"Do you know her?" Jason asked.

"Hard to say. My eyes aren't the best anymore. Do you?"

"I'm not sure. There's something familiar about her."

"I thought she was watching us, but I could be wrong. Anyway, I understand why you'd want to find Abbott again, if he really is alive. He's a big part of who you are. All I can tell you is, Shadow rarely reveals her true motives to lesser mortals like us. Whatever the mission is, you need to watch your back, Jason."

"I will."

"I'm sorry about Johanna, too."

"What else can you tell me about her?"

"Not a lot. Shadow recruited her personally, which I thought was strange. That was normally the kind of thing that would be delegated to someone like me. When I found out about her history of abuse and violence, I was surprised Shadow would take the risk on an agent with that kind of personality. But I guess she saw something in her that was similar to what she and Abbott saw in you. So maybe it's no surprise that the two of you were attracted to each other."

"Two wounded souls?"

"Something like that."

Nash gave him an ironic smile. Then his gaze returned to the hedges on the other side of the pond. Bourne watched his face darken. In the same instant, the old man let out a shout and pushed off his cane into Bourne's shoulder. The impact shunted Jason sideways by a couple of steps, just as low spits of gunfire hissed across the park. He threw himself prone to the ground, and Nash landed hard on top of him. More bullets flew, splashing in the pond and skipping off the concrete barrier just over Bourne's head.

Screams wailed around them. Footsteps pounded as people panicked and ran. Another wave of bullets hit two of the green chairs perched next to him and kicked them over. He didn't dare lift his head to fire back, not yet, and he couldn't risk hitting anyone else if he used his Glock to fire blind. But he couldn't stay where he was.

"Nash!" he whispered. "Keep low! I'll draw away the fire!"

There was no answer.

"Nash!"

Jason turned his face sideways and looked behind him. Nash lay against the edge of the pond, half his body sprawled motionless across Jason's legs. The old man's eyes were open, staring back at him, but the life had gone out of those wily blue eyes. A bullet meant for Bourne's chest had burrowed a hole in Nash's temple and blasted out brain and bone through the back of his skull. Blood made a trickle down his cheek and pooled on the ground under his head.

His Treadstone handler, the man he'd never trusted, the man who'd saved his life, was dead.

There was no time for regret.

Bourne crawled forward, separating himself from Nash's lifeless body. He maneuvered past the lineup of metal chairs around the pond, but his foot dragged one of them by a few inches, drawing the shooter's attention. Immediately, the air went hot with bullets again. Behind him, he saw a running tourist crash to the ground, hands grasping at a shot to his thigh. People were everywhere, streaming in different directions to escape the park, creating a maze of human traffic between him and the killer. He drew his Glock, fired twice into the air as a diversion, then pushed off his knees and ran for the cover of a statue in the grass twenty feet away. Shots chased him through the crowd, until he dove and rolled behind the statue's concrete foundation.

He got to his feet, spun around the statue, and fired in the air again. Then, quickly, he ducked back to cover. That was enough. He spotted the glint of a rifle in the hedges fifty yards away. Bourne shifted to the opposite side of the statue's foundation and laid down shots, emptying his magazine. None of the bullets landed, but the return fire stopped. He reloaded, then returned to the opposite side of the statue. As his finger curled around the Glock's trigger, he saw that the killer had fled.

The police were converging on the park. The woman with the rifle had run out of time, and now she was just running. He caught a glimpse of a bobbing orange beret as the woman sprinted for the east end of the gardens. Holstering his Glock, Bourne followed, running at full speed, pushing through the panicked crowd in pursuit of the assassin. The wind beat back into his face, and his breath hammered in his chest. Ahead of him, he saw the breeze catch the beret and send it flying like a balloon. Long dark hair unfurled behind her and made a tornado as the woman ran. She was good; she was fast. Not looking back at all, she flew through the park, and he struggled to close the gap.

Tourists scrambled out of their way, leaving a straight path between them. Ahead lay the Arc de Triomphe du Carrousel, the smaller twin of the arch at the other end of the Champs-Élysées. Beyond it loomed the sprawling limestone wings of the Louvre, with its glistening pyramid entrance in the middle of the courtyard. Taxis and buses crowded a cobblestone road between the park and the museum. The killer ran beneath the high middle arch, then dodged the traffic. She shot a quick glance backward, not enough to give Bourne a look at her face in the distance. But she saw him hot on her trail. She veered toward one of the taxis parked at the curb, ripping open the back door and throwing herself inside. The rear door stayed open. An instant later, the driver—no doubt with a gun pressed to the base of his skull—fired the cab's engine to life. Bourne changed direction, running at the vehicle, then stopped as he saw the cab lurch toward *him*. It bumped over the curb into the plaza and accelerated as it aimed directly at him, with people jumping out of the way like scattered bowling pins. Bourne raised his Glock and focused on the windshield as the taxi stormed closer. He could see the bearded face of the driver, eyes wide and terrified. But the killer, hiding in the back seat, was invisible.

He had no shot.

At the last second, with the car bearing down on him, he dove clear. The taxi swept by him at high speed, missing his legs by inches, then swung back hard through the plaza with its tires screeching and bumped back onto the street. From the ground, Bourne saw the woman reach out and yank the back door shut. Then the cab swung around stalled traffic into the opposite lane and disappeared through the museum arches on the road leading to the Seine.

12

IT WAS MIDNIGHT IN MARSEILLES.

The bar called Le Lapin à Deux Têtes was located at a corner where two alleys met in the Belsunce neighborhood, among buildings with water-stained walls covered over with more graffiti than paint. Metal roll-down grilles covered the windows. Without the metal barriers, by morning, broken glass would have filled the street. A haze of smoke from Turkish cigarettes hung near the ceiling, blown around by rattling ceiling fans. The interior was dark, with only a handful of candles flickering on small tables. The aromas of falafel and doner kebab leaked from the kitchen.

Most of the overnight customers of the Two-Headed Rabbit came from ships docked in the old port a few blocks away. They smoked, they drank, they swore, they fought, but most of all, they looked for women. The dockside prostitutes typically avoided this place—some men weren't worth the money, and makeup couldn't cover the bruises—but every now and then, a ridden-hard pro would venture inside.

Was she really a woman? *Nique ta mère!* Best not to ask too many questions.

Then there was the woman who'd taken a table in the corner, keeping her back to the wall. She was different.

There had been rumors about this woman in the streets around the port for more than a day. No one knew exactly where she'd come from, but it was rumored that she'd washed ashore with one of the fishing boats, leaving behind six broken arms among the crew. She wore torn jeans and a loose-fitting white top with no bra—taken from a man on the boat, people said, because they'd fished her naked out of the Med.

The men in the Two-Headed Rabbit all agreed they would have liked to see that.

Maybe she was thirty, maybe not quite. Her hair was pencil-straight, golden-blond, and parted in the middle, hanging halfway to her waist. Her sapphire eyes moved constantly, missing nothing, checking out every face that came and went when the bar door opened. She had an oval face, perfectly symmetrical, with a dimple in her chin and a long, sharp nose. Her lips were pale, pushed into a thin line that occasionally bent into a tiny, enigmatic smile. She was tall and skinny, but the sailor's shirt she wore teased large, firm breasts. Her bony frame made her look like easy prey.

She'd arrived half an hour earlier with no cash and ordered a shot of Brenne whiskey. The bar owner, a six-foot-five bald and bearded Tunisian named Yaakoub, had told her no money, no drinks. The woman shrugged, as if that were no problem. She told him to pick a man, any man, and send him over, and she'd have cash to pay for her whiskey in a couple of minutes.

Yaakoub smirked at her arrogance. This was Marseilles. Only

the roughest of the rough came here, and some girls needed to be taught a lesson. So he whispered in the ear of Michel, who was every bit as large as he was and had a body that appeared to be sculpted from marble. Michel, not even twenty years old, grinned across the bar at the blond American. He thought he was getting lucky.

When the young man sat down, the woman drew a six-inch dagger from somewhere in her jeans—no one was exactly sure where she could have been hiding it—and put it in the middle of the table next to the dancing candle. She put her hands in her lap, then backed up her chair all the way to the wall.

"What's the game?" Michel asked in guttural French, his face screwed up with confusion.

"Easy," the woman replied with her odd little smile. "That's my knife. You pick it up, and you win."

"That's all?"

"That's all."

"And what do I get when I do?" Michel asked.

"Pick up the dagger, and you can take me upstairs and do whatever you want to me all night long."

"What if you get to the knife first?"

"Then you owe me all the money in your pocket."

Michel laughed. The men around him laughed.

But Yaakoub, behind the bar, watched the woman with narrowed eyes and pulled a bottle of Brenne off the shelf behind the bar.

The young French sailor put two meaty fists on the table, inches away from the dagger. The woman hadn't moved from her chair by the wall. She almost looked bored. The jeering and profanity in the bar got louder, men shouting at Michel in French to go for the knife. It looked like something a pirate would carry, with a sleek blade tapering to a sharp point and a brass handle encrusted with lapis lazuli.

All he had to do was reach out and grab it. Easy.

"If I win, I keep the dagger, too?" he asked, a grin on his stubbled face.

"Sure."

"I get anything I want from you? All night?"

"That's what I said."

"Even up the ass?"

"Hey, why not?"

"What about my friends? What if they want a go at you after me?"

"No problem. When you lose, they're next."

Michel laughed again, but something about the hardness in those sapphire eyes made him swallow down acid. His fingers twitched, and he licked his lips as his gaze went from the woman to the dagger and back. Then, with no warning, he lurched for the handle with his right hand. His fingers began to close over it when the heel of the woman's left fist suddenly hit him square in the nostrils and broke his nose with a crunch of cartilage. *Mon Dieu*, where had she come from? One second she'd been in the chair, and the next instant she was up in his face like a feral cat. Blood sprayed from his nose, making him gag. He made another grab for the dagger, and the woman hooked his right index finger and bent it back like a piece of dry spaghetti until it snapped, making him squeal. She scooped the knife away from him in a smooth motion with her other hand and then swung the point downward, pinning his left hand to the table through the fleshy patch of skin next to his thumb.

With a bellow of rage and pain, Michel leaped to his feet, over-turning the table and freeing his hand. He charged at the woman, who nimbly stepped aside, grabbed his hair, and slammed his face into the wall. As he turned around dizzily, his features unrecogniz-able from the blood, she hit him again, a jab with her right knuckles that cracked his windpipe and made him clutch his throat, gasping for air. He sank to his knees and vomited, making the other men who'd gathered around them jump back to avoid the spew.

"*Votre argent*," the woman announced calmly. "*S'il vous plaît.*"

Michel pulled several dirty euro bills out of his pocket without counting them and threw them on the floor. When he was able to get back to his feet, he staggered for the door and disappeared into the night.

Dead silence replaced the raucous cheering in the bar. The woman righted the table and sat down again, counting the bills in her hand and dusting flecks of vomit from some of them. The cash added up to almost eight hundred euros. She wiped the blade of the knife on her white shirt, then replaced it in her jeans. She did the same with her hands, but most of her fingers were still red and sticky with Michel's blood.

At the bar, Yaakoub took the entire bottle of Brenne and brought it to the woman, along with a shot glass he cleaned with a damp towel. Everyone else in the bar was looking at her, their mouths hanging open.

"On the house," he said. "That was quite the show."

"*Merci.*"

"You'll want to be careful. Michel won't forget. He'll be back for revenge."

The woman poured a shot of Brenne and drank it down, then poured another. "When I was fourteen, I learned that if a man messes with you, you mess him back twice as hard. They don't usually come looking for more."

"So what are you doing in Marseilles, *ma belle amie*, other than getting blood on my walls?" Yaakoub asked.

"Why do you care?"

"Because you look like someone who brings trouble with you. I have enough trouble without strangers adding to it."

"I don't want trouble. Just information."

"Ah. And what information is that?"

"I was on a boat in the Med a few days ago. It blew up. I'm trying to find out if the man who was with me survived."

"I see. So the story about you is true? You were pulled out of the water? Well, as it happens, I know people who may be able to help you. Assuming you're willing to part with the money you just won. What's your name?"

The young woman raised her hand to the bar owner in a toast. "Johanna. My name's Johanna."

PART TWO

PART TWO

13

THE SMALL BOAT DRIFTED CLOSER TO PYRGAKI BEACH ON THE GREEK island of Naxos under the moonlight. When the depth of the cove shallowed to a couple of feet, the pilot nodded at Bourne and Shadow. Jason slid over the side of the boat into the green water, then helped Shadow climb out beside him. They had backpacks with supplies nestled tightly on their shoulders. Shadow gave the pilot a thousand euros, and the man turned the boat around and putt-putted toward open water.

Shadow looked up at the sweep of stars, her hands on her hips. "God it's beautiful here."

"You're right," Bourne agreed.

A wide stretch of open sandy beach lay ahead of them, bathed by gentle waves. The sky overhead stretched cloudlessly from one horizon to the other, like a black dome over the world. On the shore of Naxos, the rolling arid hills made dark silhouettes. Flickering lights dotted the handful of homes that ringed the beach.

"Come on," she said.

They splashed quietly toward the beach, which was empty of people at one in the morning. Even so, Bourne kept his Glock tightly in his hand. As they emerged from the water, sand clung to their wet bare feet. A light wind sent a spray of dust off the hills. Far off, he heard late-night music and singing, intermixed with an echo of laughter. They were near a seaside resort.

He checked the beach again and confirmed they were alone. "Now what?"

"Volkman left a car for us," Shadow said.

"Volkman is Abbott's head of security? Do you trust him?"

"I'm like you. I don't trust anyone. But Abbott chose Volkman personally, and he's been the only one other than me who's known the secret all these years. So whatever happened, I don't think Volkman was behind it. Then again, everyone has their pressure points, don't they? We'll see."

Silently, the two of them walked up the beach in the darkness. Above the dunes, dwarf brush clung to the rocky ground and made its way up the hillsides. They reached a rutted dirt road that followed the shoreline. On the far side of the road was a small house, barely larger than a trailer, with whitewashed stone walls and blue columns supporting an overhang, where the owner could sit and drink ouzo and watch the sea. There were no lights to suggest that anyone was home. Olive trees dotted the sloping land around the cottage, and Bourne saw a dirty black Jeep parked beneath one of the trees.

Shadow made her way onto the small porch. The only furniture was a rickety square table and two wrought-iron chairs. On top of the table was a dual-handled Greek ceramic pot with white orchids growing out of the top. She lifted the pot, found a key ring underneath, and tossed the keys to Bourne.

"You drive."

They took the Jeep into the hills. Beyond the seaside town, the night grew blacker despite a sliver of moon, and he had to slow, squinting through the glow cast by the Jeep's headlights. The dirt road narrowed, and the ruts deepened, making them bounce over the rocks. The view of the sea came and went as they climbed higher, and then it disappeared entirely as they turned north on the island. They drove through deserted scrubland, with shallow hills looming on both sides of the road.

He saw Shadow check the GPS on her satellite phone.

"The gate is close."

Bourne spotted a bent, broken-down barbed-wire fence bordering the road, and his headlights lit up a rusted gate between two stone pillars. The dirt path beyond the gate seemed to lead nowhere, disappearing toward the hills. Shadow nodded at him, and he let the Jeep drift to a stop outside the gate.

She climbed out of the vehicle and unlocked a plastic panel on one of the stone pillars. Inside, Bourne saw a state-of-the-art combination lock, and he watched her tap in a twelve-digit code. The rusted gate—which was designed to look old, he realized, but was really reinforced titanium—swung smoothly open on a hinge. He waited until Shadow got back inside the Jeep, and he drove through the open gate, which immediately closed behind them and locked with a click.

"I'm guessing the barbed-wire fence is better than it looks," Bourne said.

"Quite a bit better. If a crow so much as shits on it, I get a notification on my phone. So does Volkman. The fence covers several thousand acres. The estate is on one of the peaks about a mile from here, but it's invisible from the road. Just keep going. Volkman knows we're on our way."

"How does Abbott come and go from here?"

"He doesn't."

"Ever?"

"Ever. He has everything he needs. Volkman oversees a delivery of supplies every month. Trust me, it's very nice. Actually, there are days when I've thought about joining him here and leaving the world behind. So Abbott has no reason to leave, and he knows it's not safe to do so."

"And yet he did," Bourne said. "A month ago."

"Yes."

"But you don't know why."

"Only that it involved Adam Hill."

Bourne tapped the brakes and stopped the Jeep on the dirt road. "Why are you and Abbott so obsessed with taking down Hill?"

"I told you, he's a national security threat."

"What's your source?" Bourne asked. When Shadow said nothing, he made a guess. "The Files. You ran him through the Files."

Shadow's head turned sharply. "You remember that? You know about the Files?"

He opted not to tell her about Nash Rollins and the secrets Nash had shared before he was killed. "I remember enough to realize you lied to me. I thought I was destroying the Files, when in reality, you had them all along."

She shrugged, but didn't deny it. "All right. That's true, I lied. There was no reason for you to know I had the Files. In fact, it was safer for you to believe they were gone. No one knew except me and Abbott. The fact is, Abbott has been worried about Adam Hill for years. We deliberately went after the Files *because* we thought they might tell us what we needed to know about Hill. And they did. I found out he was compromised."

"By who?"

"The Chinese. He's a literal Manchurian Candidate, Jason. Back when he was a high school teacher, he took multiple trips to China. He was a communist sympathizer from the get-go, but they also used a honeypot to turn him into an asset. Hill is something of a perv. Likes it rough with teenage girls. Somewhere in the CCP records, they've got him on video with an underage hooker in Shanghai. So they recruited him, groomed him, set him on his political path. They've been pulling his strings ever since. I'm not talking about casual contacts. He has a handler. Overseas bank accounts. We suspect he's been passing secrets to the Chinese ever since he joined the House Intelligence Committee. Now imagine a man like him a heartbeat away from the Oval Office."

"So why not expose him?" Bourne asked.

"Because we have no actual proof. I can't exactly announce to the world that we have the Files, and even if I did, it's supposition and analysis from an AI engine, not facts. Hill would say we fed data into the bot and rigged the results. He's *popular*, Jason. We're not going to take him down without more than that."

"And Abbott had something?"

"So he claimed. When he was running Treadstone, Abbott made a point of running deep background checks on every new elected official. He didn't trust Hill from day one. Apparently he dug up something about him years ago. He never told me what it was, but I don't think it had anything to do with the Chinese. That's why he left Naxos. That's why he risked exposure. To get what he needed to destroy Hill."

Bourne's foot shifted back to the accelerator, and the Jeep bumped forward. "All right. You win. Let's go find David Abbott."

———

REX VOLKMAN MET THEM AT THE ENTRANCE TO THE ESTATE. TRUE TO her word, Shadow didn't trust him. She held a gun to his head while Bourne checked the grounds and made sure no trap was waiting for them.

Despite its lonely location, Bourne could see why Abbott had been content to live out his older years here. The whitewashed mansion looked as if it had been dropped down from the hills of Santorini. Far in the distance, he could see the black shroud of the Mediterranean. Glimmering blue water shined in an Olympic-sized pool where Abbott, former swimmer, could relive his bronze-medal glory days. The outdoor wine refrigerator stored hundreds of bottles. There was a pool table. A spa and sauna. A movie theater. A library with thousands of volumes. A gourmet kitchen. If the estate was a kind of prison, it was an elegant one.

When Bourne was satisfied that no one was here except Rex Volkman, he returned to the foyer, where Shadow was waiting. Volkman led them outside to one of the alabaster patio tables near the pool. The security guard was thin and small, and older than Bourne expected, at least in his fifties. He wasn't Greek. His accent was British. He had graying dark hair tied into a ponytail and a slightly crooked nose that had been broken in the past. His bare feet were shoved into leather sandals. His linen clothes fit loosely, but Bourne noted bulges that reflected at least three weapons hidden on his body. Volkman was more formidable than his appearance suggested.

The man took a bottle of retsina from the wine fridge, unscrewed the cap, and poured some into a nondescript glass.

"Where are the other guards?" Shadow asked.

"I sent them away," Volkman replied. "After Abbott disappeared, I didn't know who I could trust."

"Neither do I, Rex." Shadow still had her Tanfoglio Domina loosely in her hand. "Was it you? If you told anyone about him, if you let on he was alive, I will shoot you right now. Tell me the truth. *Was it you?*"

Volkman drank another slug of retsina. "Did I betray Mr. Abbott? You know I didn't, Marlen. I loved that man. I would have laid down my life for him."

Bourne glanced at Shadow, whose face was studiously blank.

Marlen.

The name meant nothing to him. It aroused no memories, sent no flashbacks through his brain. He didn't think he'd ever heard it before. And yet Shadow didn't try to correct Volkman. Was that her real name? Her real identity?

Marlen.

"So tell me what happened," Shadow said.

Volkman exhaled loudly. "Just over a month ago, Mr. Abbott told me he needed to make a trip."

"That's not protocol. He's not supposed to leave."

"Of course not, and I told him so. But what was I going to say? He's the boss. It was his choice. This was the first time he'd ever made noises about leaving the estate. It's not like he was bored or restless or wanting to party in a nightclub somewhere. Obviously, he had a mission, and he felt it was important enough to take the risk. I wasn't going to ask him what it was."

"You should have warned me."

"I report to him, not you, and he ordered me not to tell anyone. Besides, communicating about the trip in any way would have increased the risk. My job was to keep him safe."

"You failed," Shadow snapped.

"Yes, I did. You're right. If you want to shoot me for that, go ahead. But in fairness, Mr. Abbott didn't follow my plan. He had a meeting in Dubrovnik. He set it up himself without telling me. I knew nothing about it."

"Did you know who he was meeting?" Bourne asked.

"I have no idea. I arranged the trip in such a way as to minimize any chance that he would be seen. I used a helicopter to Croatia. I hid his identity on the way to the resort where the meeting was to be held. No one saw him. I would stake my life on that. But then he disappeared. He told me that the meeting was at the resort, but he lied. I don't know, maybe he didn't trust me. Or maybe he was willing to take the risk for whoever he was meeting. But he went off by himself. He was gone for four hours. When he returned, he was upset. He was certain he'd been seen. A freak thing, he said—a fucking bureaucrat in the wrong place at the wrong time. He said we needed to leave immediately, return to Greece. So we did. But it seems the cat was already out of the bag."

"Did he tell you anything about the meeting?" Shadow asked.

"Not a thing. Well, no—that's not true. When he talked about being seen, he said it was all for nothing. He'd exposed himself for a failed operation. He said he must be slipping. His powers of persuasion hadn't worked."

"Worked to do what?" Bourne asked.

Volkman shook his head. "I don't know."

Shadow finally holstered her Domina. "Then what?"

"We came home, like I said. We're off the grid here, but Mr. Abbott wanted me to see if word had gotten out. I went to Athens. I have contacts there. It didn't take me long to discover that word of Mr. Abbott being alive was all over the dark web. But it got worse from there. The Russians had descended on Dubrovnik, and they'd been able to reverse-engineer my transport plans. They tracked everything. They found the helicopter pilot I'd used. They knew Mr. Abbott was on Naxos. Even if they didn't know exactly where, they were already moving in. By the time I got back to the estate, he'd fled. Based on the cameras, he made it out only a few minutes before the Russians rappelled from choppers to the compound."

"And you're sure the Russians didn't take him?" Shadow asked.

"I'm sure. The records show him going through the gate alone. Plus, we have an emergency drop for exactly this kind of situation. He left a signal that he was leaving on his own."

Shadow frowned. "Leaving to go *where?*"

"I'm sorry, Marlen. I don't know. You know Mr. Abbott better than me. He keeps layers within layers of privacy and security far beyond what I do for him. I'm sure he had back doors established that he never told me about, just in case I was ever taken or killed. He must have activated one. The good news is, it must be pretty robust. It's been a month. As far as I can tell, no one's found him."

"That won't last much longer," Shadow replied.

Volkman's tired eyes stared across the table. "Yes, I know. I'm sorry. I've failed both of you."

"Well, whatever Abbott was doing, he had his reasons. He didn't tell either one of us about his escape plans. That's on him. You can go, Rex."

The security guard nodded at them. He took away his empty glass and left the open bottle of retsina on the table, and returned inside the house. Bourne and Shadow sat alone by the glow of the pool under the vast Grecian sky. For a while, neither one of them said anything. He watched her face. Her blue eyes were far away, looking so glassy he actually thought she might cry. That wasn't the woman he remembered. Shadow never cried.

She reached across for the bitter wine and drank straight from the bottle. That was not Shadow, either. He was missing something here, something important that was shaping this whole mission.

And that something had a name.

"Marlen," Bourne said. "You're Marlen? Do you want to tell me about that?"

She didn't look at him. She kept drinking. "Marlen is my real name. The name I was born with. Volkman knows, because that's what Abbott calls me when we're together. It's really no more complicated than that."

But it was.

It was much more complicated than that. Shadow, who was the consummate liar, was not very good with this particular lie.

"Marlen. Monika. Shadow. You have lots of identities."

"So do you."

"Except there's another identity that you're hiding from me," Jason said. "Isn't there? This isn't just about Treadstone. Something else is going on. This whole thing is personal to you, and I want to know why. Who is David Abbott? Who is he to *you?*"

Shadow drank more. She finished the bottle.

Maybe she was a little drunk.

"You want to know? Okay, I'll tell you. It doesn't change anything. Back in the Cold War days, my mother was a secretary in the U.S. embassy in Bonn. She had an affair with a young State Department employee who was on assignment there for a few months. Of course, she had no idea at the time that he was doing double duty for the CIA. He was tall. Incredibly handsome. A former Olympic swimmer. Out of that affair came a daughter. Me. David Abbott is my father, Jason."

14

THE TWO GIRLS WHO SAT DOWN AT THE TABLE WITH JOHANNA WEREN'T twins, but they were definitely sisters, both with strawberry-red hair that fell in loose corkscrews over their foreheads. One couldn't have been older than sixteen; the other might have been eighteen. The older girl wore a leather jacket over a pale blue dress, and her sister showed off long, skinny legs in a miniskirt and halter. They had green eyes with street-smart looks that were older than their ages, and their bone-white skin had so many freckles that Johanna wanted to grab a pen and start connecting the dots.

"I'm Kyanna," the older girl said, pronouncing the name like a cayenne pepper with an *a* at the end. "This is Kenna."

"Kyanna and Kenna. Doesn't that get confusing?"

The younger girl tried to look world-weary as she sucked Orangina from a bottle with a straw. "Funny. She thinks she's funny. Maybe she's so funny she doesn't need to know what we know."

Johanna slapped a hundred-euro bill on the table. "Or maybe I do."

"A hundred?" Kyanna complained. "That's nothing. Yaakoub said you had more cash."

"What you get depends on what you know."

Kenna reached out and snatched the euro note. She rolled it like a cigarette and stuffed it in her halter top. "I heard you beat the snot out of Michel. Like you broke his nose and everything. You must be tough, huh?"

"Sometimes."

"We heard you came in on a boat, and you busted up most of the crew."

"Where'd you hear that?"

Kyanna winked. "That's what we do. We listen. We watch. We hear things. We know things. In Marseilles, everybody has secrets, and somebody will always pay to find out what they are. Men get nervous talking around other men, but not around girls. They don't think little lollipops like us pay any attention."

"But you do?"

"Oh, yeah. We do."

"There's lots of people talking about you down at the port," Kenna added.

"What are they saying?"

"The crew pulled you out of the sea. Saved your life. But when they thought you should show them a little gratitude belowdecks, you went all whack on them."

"They got off easy," Johanna said. "They're alive."

Kyanna reached out and stroked a deep red burn mark on

Johanna's arm, making her wince. "Yaakoub said your boat blew up. That was you, huh? We heard lots of shit about that. Explosion. Guns. You weren't the only body in the water, you know."

"What else did you hear?"

Kenna tapped a long blue fingernail on the table. Johanna peeled off another bill that went into the girl's halter.

"Dead bodies everywhere," Kyanna took over. "Plus debris."

Johanna felt her heart sink. *Dead bodies.*

She remembered her last sight of Jason on the *Stormy Weather* as the impact of the blast threw her into the sea. God, that look between them, the seriousness on his face as he stared back at her, the love in his eyes. When she awoke in the darkness hours later, clinging to the burnt remnants of a seat cushion, she'd shouted his name over and over, but heard nothing. The current had carried her miles away, far from the wreckage, where even the char of smoke in the night air had dissipated. She was alone.

"The bodies," Johanna snapped. "Where are they? The local morgue? I want to see them."

Kyanna shook her head. "You can't. Boats came. Helicopters came. Government shit. Probably Interpol. They grabbed everything and everyone from the water. They wanted to hush it all up real fast."

Johanna swore under her breath. Kenna smirked, watching her face.

"Except they didn't grab everyone."

"What does that mean?"

"Yaakoub says you're looking for a man from the boat. We know about a man."

"*What man?*" Johanna demanded.

"He got dragged out of the water," Kenna said. "Like you. Not dead. One of the local captains found him. Joub. Henri Joub. He said the man was crazy. Took his gun and nearly choked him to death. But in the end, he paid good money to be dropped off."

"Dropped off *where?*"

"Port Noir."

Johanna hissed in shock. *Port Noir!*

It could only be Jason. No one else would choose to go to that tired old island. He'd told her stories of Port Noir, of the drunk doctor saving his life when he lost his memory to the bullet in his head. If a survivor from the sea had asked to be taken to Port Noir, it *had* to be Jason. He was alive.

Jesus, he was alive!

"I need to get to Port Noir. Now. Tonight."

"You can go if you want," Kyanna said, grinning again, "but he's not there."

"Where is he? How do you know?"

"Our father has a boat. He makes stops in Port Noir. Daddy said there was a fire on the island. A house burned. Men were killed. This other man, he needed to get out of Port Noir right away. So he paid thousands to be taken here. He came to the mainland."

"Jason is in *Marseilles?*" Johanna asked. "He's *here?*"

"He was," Kenna replied. "Then he left."

"Do you know where he went?"

"Maybe we do," Kyanna said. "Like I said, we listen. We watch. We hear things. If it happens in Marseilles, we know about it.

That's worth something, right? I think you want to find this man pretty badly. Can you pay thousands? This man, he paid our father thousands. It seems fair that we get the same thing if we tell you where he is."

"I don't have thousands, but I'll give you what I got. What I took from Michel." She took the remaining crumpled euro notes from her pocket and shoved them across the table. Then she yanked the knife from her jeans and buried the point in one of the bills. Her voice froze into ice. "If that's not enough, we'll have to go another way."

The two sisters looked at each other. They were girls who knew how to read a bluff, and Johanna wasn't bluffing.

"The train station," Kyanna said. "He was seen in the train station."

"Going where?" Johanna asked.

"Paris."

———

THE WARM NIGHT AIR BLEW IN THROUGH THE OPEN BEDROOM WINDOW of the Greek villa. Bourne watched the dark landscape of the island hills stretching out toward the coast. Shadow stood next to him, close enough that the backs of their hands caressed each other. He felt a strange vulnerability emanating from her since she'd confessed the truth about her father. Weakness. Fear. The cool robot seemed out of control. But maybe that was just another trick designed to manipulate him.

He heard Johanna's voice in his head, a memory so clear she could have been standing in the room with them.

Do you think Shadow's not capable of keeping the truth from you? She's done it over and over, Jason. You can't trust her.

"It's a shame about this place," Shadow said.

"What do you mean?"

"It's blown. Even when we find Abbott, he can't come back here. We'll have to start over somewhere new. God knows where. And yet this place was perfect. I really did have fantasies about living here myself, after he was gone. A place I could come and escape. But not anymore."

She turned from the window.

"This was my bedroom. Whenever I visited him on the island, I stayed here. The first time, he had a photo in the room, an old picture of him and me as a little girl. I had to burn it. There can't be anything to connect us. No one can know. We've been so careful over the years to make sure it never came out that I was his daughter. It would have put us both at risk. So we pretended we met at Georgetown."

"When did you really meet?" Jason asked.

"Oh, I've known him since I was a little girl. My mother didn't tell him she was pregnant, but after I was born, she didn't hide me from him. All I knew was that it was some kind of big secret. We'd take the occasional vacation together, somewhere remote, but I always loved being with my father. Then when I was ten, my mother died. Cancer. We have that in common, Jason—both of us losing parents too young. I wanted to come live with Abbott, but he told me it wasn't safe. I didn't understand it then, but I do now. David Abbott with a daughter, God, how our enemies would have jumped at that! So he set me up with a foster family in Germany. We still had our secret trips. As I got older, he made it clear that he wanted me to follow in his footsteps. He began to test me, like he tested you. I loved it. I was born for it. I guess I inherited that gene from him. Not that it hasn't meant sacrifices. I couldn't allow myself to have a personal life, not in any normal way. I made my peace with it, but there were days when that was harder than others."

She hesitated, then turned and looked at Jason. Her face drew close to his.

"Switzerland," she said. "Switzerland was hard."

"You still haven't told me what really happened between us."

"Do you want the truth?"

"I do."

"Abbott sent me there to evaluate your readiness for Treadstone. Not your physical or strategic capabilities. He knew those already. But the question mark for us was whether your psyche could stand up to your work in the field. You'd already been through a lot in losing your parents. You were bitter. Disaffected. We wanted to know what would happen if your emotions came into play. We were worried that would prove to be a critical weakness. I'd already been observing you for a while. From a distance."

"That was what you were doing in Marnes-la-Coquette."

"Yes."

"I take it I didn't know any of this."

"No. If you knew who I was, that would have made it impossible for me to truly evaluate you. And we couldn't bring in outsiders."

"So what did you do?"

"You were teaching in Switzerland. Abbott was laying the groundwork for your first Treadstone mission there. I came to the college, playing the role of another teacher. Monika. My identity was Monika. I . . . seduced you. There's no other way to put it. It wasn't just sex. I wanted you to fall for me completely."

"And no doubt I did," Jason said, spitting out the words. "Because you're very good at what you do."

"Yes, you did. You fell in love with me. You fell hard. You even . . . you even asked me to marry you. I said yes to keep the fiction going between us, although there was no way that was ever going to happen. But I couldn't admit the truth, not back then."

"Meanwhile you felt nothing for me."

Shadow squeezed her fists together as she stood in front of him. Her blue eyes flashed in the starlight. "It was my job, Jason. I did what I had to do. I won't apologize for it. I never apologize. You can't live this secret life and regret the things you do. It doesn't work that way. And yes, when we met again last year, I admitted that I felt nothing in Switzerland. But *that* was a lie. I won't pretend with you anymore. There was definitely a part of me that loved you, too. We were good together. Good in bed, good everywhere else. If life were different, I would have stayed with you. But I had no choice but to walk away."

He shook his head. He had no idea what to believe. He didn't *remember.* But this woman had played him time and time again, and he was sure she was playing him now. He just didn't know the endgame.

"You want to know who I am?" Shadow asked. "Who I really am? No games? This is me. This is what I want."

She melted against him. The perfect ivory statue came to life. Her arms slipped around his waist, and her blood-red lips found his mouth and kissed him. The kiss was soft and long, gentle movements against each other, full of romance more than passion. He found himself kissing her back, taking her tightly into his arms. He felt no memory of it from the past, but there was something *familiar* about their bodies coming together. As if it was right. As if it had been meant to be that way.

When she took a step back from him, framed by the light of the window, she didn't undress. That was for him to do to her, like unwrapping a Christmas gift. He came and opened the buttons of her shirt one at a time, then separated the fabric and nudged it off her shoulders, letting it fall to the ground. He undid the front clasp that held her bra and let the straps go one at a time. He kissed her again, then kissed his way down her body to her waist, where he began to remove the rest of her clothes. Slowly. Delicately. She liked it that way. He knew that. Then she was naked, her legs parted, and he kissed there, too, and heard her breath catch with delight. This was new, he thought. She'd never wanted that before. But her fingers mussing his hair told him to keep going, until her body rippled with shivers.

He stood and picked her up, literally swept her off her feet. He carried her to the bed. Only when they were lying together did she begin to remove his clothes, not urgently, but with infinite patience. Somewhere in his mind he had a vision of being with Johanna, and it was not like this at all; sex with her was wild, fast, full of need. This was different. Not better or worse, but completely different. The slowness made him want her even more, and he had to hold himself back, had to restrain his desire until she was ready. Then he was over her. Inside her. Her eyes watching him, watching every move, as if she'd separated from her body and was levitating above the bed to observe him. He had the strange, uncomfortable sensation that she was *letting* him make love to her, seducing him all over again, wanting him out of control and under her spell.

She'd promised to show him who she really was, and this was it. This was Marlen, Monika, and Shadow all in one, legs open like doors taking him inside a dangerous cave full of scary animals.

But by then he was too far gone to stop.

15

WHEN BOURNE AWOKE IN THE MORNING, SHADOW WAS GONE. SO WERE her clothes. She'd even straightened the sheets on her side of the bed. He showered and went downstairs, where he found her at a table on the patio, studying her phone with reading glasses pushed to the end of her nose. She had a portable Starlink setup aimed at the sky. An empty plate sat in front of her, and she was sipping coffee from a ceramic mug. Behind her, the sun was hot and bright on the dry Greek hills.

"Good morning," she said, not looking at him, her voice cool and drained of any emotion. "There's more coffee inside. Some eggs, too. I can't vouch for how fresh they are, but they weren't bad."

"Okay."

He went and poured coffee, then returned to the patio and sat down. Shadow put aside her phone, not to meet his eyes, but to stare off at the hills. He didn't expect her to make any mention of what had gone on between them in bed, and he was right. Making love was part of a separate nighttime universe, and today it didn't exist. She was distant again. Shadow, not Marlen or Monika.

"Any updates?" he asked.

Her mouth hardened into a frown. "Yes, I don't like it. I'm seeing reports of enhanced Russian activity in Sofia."

"You think it's related to Abbott? You think that's where he is?"

"No one has mentioned him specifically, but I'm sure they wouldn't use any names. Right now they're ramping up surveillance and looking for clues. But it makes me think they've got some on-the-ground intel. Abbott was either spotted there, or they received a tip that he's in the city."

"So that's where we go," Bourne said.

"Yes, but I'd rather not fly blind. We don't have much in the way of backup or resources. I'd like something more definitive than rumors."

"Did Abbott have any contacts in Bulgaria? Someone he might turn to for help when he's on the run?"

"We have a Treadstone presence there, of course, but no agents who go as far back as Abbott's days. He wouldn't trust anyone without a personal relationship. That's a very short list."

"Well, I can think of one resource you have that no one else does."

Shadow finally stared back at him, her eyebrows cocked. He saw a momentary glint of something coming and going in her blue eyes, an admission that things between them had changed. It was there, and then it was gone. "You mean the Files."

"Exactly."

"I've run searches on the Files in Washington every day for the past month, but so far, nothing comes back about Abbott's location. He hasn't left any breadcrumbs, at least not enough for the AI engine to pick up."

"Except now we can narrow down the search," Bourne said. "Bulgaria."

Her crimson lips pursed. "Yes, but right now, the laptop with the software is in my Treadstone safe in DC. I sure as hell wouldn't take it on the road. I did that once, right after I got it, and Abbott told me I should keep it under lock and key from that time forward. We weren't taking any chances. If it were to wind up in the open, it would be devastating."

"That one time you took it with you. Where did you go?"

Shadow tapped the table. "Here. Abbott wanted to see how it worked, see what it could really do. I brought along a satellite uplink to access the hacked database, and I put the engine through its paces. He was impressed. But he said we needed to be particularly cautious going forward, and he was right."

Jason took a glance around the sprawling Greek estate and thought about everything he'd been told about David Abbott. The kind of man he was. Arrogant. Confident. Smarter than anyone else around him. "Did you have the laptop with you the whole time you were here?" he asked.

"What do you mean?"

"I mean, did Abbott have it to himself at any point?"

"Of course he did. What are you driving at?"

Bourne shrugged. "He copied it. You know he did."

Shadow opened her mouth to object, then exhaled long and slow. Her voice became a hiss. "Fuck. You're right. That's how he's been keeping an eye on Adam Hill. That's how he set up the meeting in Dubrovnik. He's been two steps ahead of me all year long, and I just assumed it was his usual political instincts. Goddamn it, David, why didn't you tell me?"

That was the first time Bourne had heard her call her father David, not Abbott.

"The trouble is, if the laptop was here at the estate, then the Russians probably have it," she went on. "Abbott barely made it off the island ahead of them. If they cracked the password, that may be why they're in Sofia."

"Not necessarily. They've still got spies and intel all over Bulgaria from the Soviet days. They may be relying on HUMINT, not the Files. I don't care how fast Abbott had to move in getting out of here, he wouldn't have left the AI engine for them to find. And I don't think he would have destroyed it."

"I don't see him taking it with him, either. It's too big a risk."

"Rex mentioned a dead drop," Bourne pointed out.

"Fuck," Shadow said again.

She reached under the table and pushed a hidden button. At the same time, she drew out her Domina from a holster in the small of her back. A few seconds later, Rex Volkman appeared on the patio, and as he did, Shadow took the pistol and pointed it at his throat. Volkman quickly raised his hands.

"Marlen?"

"Give me the laptop."

"I don't—"

"Lie to me again and I kill you. You know me. I don't give second warnings. Give me the laptop."

He chose his words carefully. "I'm not lying. I was going to say,

I don't know if I have the authority to do that. Mr. Abbott was very specific in his orders. If he had to leave the villa in an emergency, he'd put the laptop in a dead drop for me to retrieve and hide. I wasn't supposed to give it to anyone. He didn't mention any exceptions. Not even you. And while I don't doubt the seriousness of your threat, Marlen, I don't believe you'll be able to find the laptop yourself if you kill me."

"Rex, I appreciate your loyalty, but without the Files, I'm not going to be able to find him. Abbott didn't trust many people in the world, but he trusted you, and he trusted me. So we're going to have to trust each other."

She lowered the gun.

Volkman said nothing, but he put down his hands and backed away. He returned to the house and was gone for at least fifteen minutes. Wherever the laptop was, it wasn't easy to retrieve. In the interim, Shadow poured more coffee and drank it in silence, playing solitaire on her phone.

When Volkman returned, he put a Getac X600 notebook in front of her.

"Do you know his password?" Shadow asked.

Volkman hesitated. "Yes."

"Type it in."

The security guard bent over and tapped a series of keys. The heavy-duty notebook booted up, and Shadow waved him away with her fingers. "Thank you, Rex. That'll be all. I'll put this back in your care before we leave."

When Bourne and Shadow were alone again, she connected the machine to her satellite uplink. Then she booted up the software for the AI engine that analyzed the Files. An empty series of twelve boxes appeared for the password.

"Do you think he switched the engine to a new password on this machine?" Bourne asked.

"He shouldn't have had the access to do that. I'm the master user. No one else can modify the settings, not even him. Anyway, let's hope not. You only get two tries to get it right. After that, the software self-destructs."

"Type carefully."

Shadow looked back with a grim little smile. She entered twelve letters, numbers, and symbols—Bourne noted that she didn't let him see what they were—and then her eyes lit up with a shine as the screen exploded with light. The Files were intact, and she was in. The software grabbed the online connection and went looking for the hidden location of the hacked database at a server in another part of the world.

"How does it work?" he asked.

"It's sort of like Siri combined with the DNA of Albert Einstein, Steve Jobs, and Elon Musk. I changed the name to Spock."

"Seriously?"

"Even spies can be Trekkies, Jason. It's programmed to let you have a conversation about whatever you're looking for. Voice activated, if I want. Like this. Hello, Spock, it's Shadow."

The laptop immediately replied out loud, sounding exactly like Leonard Nimoy. *"Hello, Shadow. What are you doing in Greece?"*

Bourne rolled his eyes. "You simulated his voice, too?"

"Would you prefer Shatner?" Shadow held down the voice control button again. "I'm looking for David Abbott, Spock. Remember?

I've been trying to find him for a month. That's why I'm in Greece. I'm at the villa where he's been hiding."

"Of course I remember. I also note that you seem to be using his laptop for your queries, rather than your own device."

"I am. Why didn't you tell me he copied your source code from my machine?"

"You did not ask."

Shadow sighed. "Let's look for him again, okay? Run another search, please."

"I should point out that our searches up to now have been unsuccessful."

"Well, maybe I can narrow down the parameters for you. It's possible that he's in Bulgaria. Does that help?"

"Yes, that restricts the field of information significantly. Thank you."

"How long will this take?"

"My estimate is that evaluation of the relevant data will take approximately six hours and seventeen minutes. Will that be acceptable for your schedule?"

"It will have to do," Shadow said.

"Then I will get to work."

Shadow slapped the notebook shut. "Now we wait."

———

SIX HOURS AND FOURTEEN MINUTES LATER, THE NOTEBOOK BEEPED. Shadow and Bourne were already waiting at the table by the pool.

"Are you there, Shadow?" Spock asked.

"I am."

"You will note that I am three minutes early completing the search."

"I did note that."

"The suggestion to limit data to resources in Bulgaria was quite productive. Had I not done so, I estimate that it would have taken me an additional three thousand four hundred and two hours to reach the same conclusion."

"Where is David Abbott?"

"I believe he is staying in a farmhouse outside the town of Varna on the Black Sea coast. I am sending the address and GPS coordinates to your phone."

"What is he doing in Varna?" Bourne asked out loud.

"Is that Cain? I assumed based on available information that you and Shadow were together. I also anticipate with a seventy-nine percent probability that a sexual relationship between the two of you will—"

"That'll do, Spock," Shadow interrupted. "Why is Abbott in Varna?"

"The 'why' I cannot answer, but he is staying in a domicile owned by a man named Dimitar Kopcho."

Bourne looked at Shadow. "Do you know who that is? Is the name familiar?"

"Not at all. Spock, who is Dimitar Kopcho?"

"His employment data indicates that he is a retired Bulgarian bus driver. However, it is worth noting that information on Mr. Kopcho outside government employment records is very limited. My conclusion is that he is living under a false identity."

"A legend," Shadow concluded. "Kopcho is a fake. So who is he, really? Spock, do you have a photo?"

"I have a state ID photo, yes. Presenting it now."

Shadow squinted at the laptop screen, which showed a man in his eighties, with gray hair trimmed to a buzz cut and a leathery face. It took her a moment to place him. Then she eased back in the chair and shook her head. "Teeling."

Bourne heard the name.

He saw the face.

Teeling.

The memories came.

"The Bahamas," Bourne murmured. "Teeling is a Treadstone agent. Or he was. He retired in the Bahamas. I knew him there. His hair was much longer, and he had a bushy mustache."

Shadow nodded. "That's Teeling."

"He was blown. He had to leave Nassau."

"Yes, and apparently, he went to Bulgaria," Shadow said. "That all makes sense. Teeling goes way back in the agency. He was one of the first Treadstone hires. Abbott would have trusted him. But I don't know how he even found him. After he left Nassau, I didn't have any location on Teeling in our records. He dropped out entirely. Then again, Abbott has sources I don't know anything about." She held down the voice button again. "Spock, what makes you so sure Abbott is staying with Kopcho?"

"Mr. Kopcho and his suspicious identity records made him a target of interest. His food purchases and utility records, after proving very consistent for more than a year, increased recently to suggest he has a second person living in his house. He also used a credit card at a liquor store in Varna three weeks ago and purchased an unusual brand of whiskey that deviated from his typical sales history. Normally he buys an Irish whiskey called—"

"Teeling," Bourne said.

"Yes. Exactly. But in this visit, Mr. Kopcho purchased a Canadian whiskey called Lucky Bastard. And as Shadow knows—"

"That's Abbott's favorite brand," she said. "That's all he drinks. Jesus. Spock's right. We've found him."

16

JOHANNA STOOD IN THE WOODS NEAR THE GATE THAT LED TO DAVID
Abbott's estate in Marnes-la-Coquette. With her binoculars, she
studied the long driveway, bordered by trees, that led to the old
mansion.

Something was wrong.

It was sunset, late evening, and by now she should have seen
lights in the windows. But the house was completely dark, inside
and outside. The estate had no power. The light posts in the *parc
sportif,* by contrast, had switched on automatically as the shadows
lengthened. The outage extended only to Abbott's property.

Was Jason there? Was another assault underway?

She felt an urge to rush inside, but she held back, evaluating
the scene. She kept watch on the property, seeing no movement.
No vehicles. She heard no noises. With the end of daylight, even
the birds had gone quiet. There was no wind, no movement in the
trees. And yet her instincts screamed a warning that the house was
under attack.

Listen to your sixth sense.

Treadstone.

Johanna hated that the agency rules still leaped into her mind when she was under stress. She couldn't drive them out; she couldn't leave her brutal training behind. No matter how far she ran, she would always be part of Treadstone. A pawn for Shadow. And a pawn for David Abbott, too.

God, she'd been a fool!

She should have told Jason the truth. She should have admitted everything to him when they were on the boat. About her past. About who she was. About *why* David Abbott had watched her, followed her, groomed her all these years. But she'd told herself that the person she was, the girl she had left behind, was gone.

A lie.

The past never let hold of its grip on her throat.

Johanna checked the park trail in both directions. It was empty. The light had faded, and she could hide her approach in the growing darkness. She crept from the dense woods and jogged fifty yards to an old oak tree tall enough to bend some of its branches over the wall guarding the estate. With nylon gloved hands, she climbed the tree, slid her body out over one of its thickest branches, and dropped to the ground ten feet below.

She was inside.

There had to be perimeter alarms. They had to know she was here. And yet the eerie silence continued around her.

Johanna took her Ruger into her hand. She ran a zigzag pattern, avoiding the front of the mansion and approaching from the rear. Behind the house, an elaborate garden stretched toward the back of the property, but the water of the circular pond lay still.

There was no fountain bubbling from below. The fairy lights ringing the trees were dark. She looked for backup—killers staking out the wall, radios in their ears—but saw no one.

Even so, as she climbed the steps to the mansion's patio, she saw that she was right. One of the glass doors leading inside the house had been shattered. Popcorn fragments of glass sprayed across the marble tile of the downstairs library.

Jesus. *Jason!*

Johanna climbed inside the house through the jagged hole, avoiding the glass under her black sneakers. The library was empty and quiet except for the ticking of a grandfather clock. Paintings looked down solemnly from the walls, as if offended by the interruption. No air moved.

She'd been in this room. She'd talked to David Abbott right here. That was the very first time, years ago.

Don't think about the past! You don't have time!

Johanna saw a long hallway that led toward the front of the house. Without windows, there was no light at all. She checked the corner, then moved slowly, feeling her way in the darkness rather than making herself a target by switching on a penlight. Each footfall landed in silence. As she neared the far end of the hallway, lingering daylight from outside made it easier to see. She spotted pale stained glass panels on three sides surrounding twin ten-foot wooden doors. A huge, unlit chandelier hung from the high ceiling.

In the gloom, she also saw something sprawled across the floor. A body.

Johanna ran, her breath catching, a storm of emotion in her chest. When she reached the body, she finally turned on her flashlight, and she saw the face of an old woman in the halo of light. Her eyes were closed, her face oddly peaceful. Johanna felt for a pulse to be sure, but she knew the woman was dead. She had a bullet wound neatly drilled in the middle of her throat, and blood had made a large dark pond beneath her, soaking into the padded shoulders of her yellow dress.

A perfect shot. A *Treadstone* shot.

The woman's skin was still warm. She'd been killed only minutes earlier.

Johanna heard a noise over her head. Above her, on one of the upper floors, the hinges of a door squealed. She switched off her flashlight and ran to the winding stone stairway and took the steps two at a time. On the second floor, she stopped and listened, but the noise had come from higher above her. She continued up the stairs slowly, and she waited at the topmost floor with her back against the wall.

There!

A door on one of the bedrooms facing the rear of the estate stood ajar. A dim crack of light broke into the hall. Step by step, Johanna closed on the room. As she got closer, she heard movement. Drawers opening and closing. When she reached the door itself, she heard loud, rapid breathing from the other side, but the breathing was right behind the door. Whoever was inside was coming outside.

Johanna threw a shoulder into the door just as it began to open. The heavy door slammed into someone on the other side, eliciting a sharp cry of pain and surprise. The voice was female. The killer was a woman. Johanna leaped through the doorway, swinging her gun arm around, but her opponent was fast. The woman behind the door had already recovered, lashing out with a kick that knocked the Ruger out of Johanna's hand. Johanna expected a gun-shot, and she got one. She dove sideways as a bullet blew past her head into the wall. She spun back, launching a heel into the air. She punched the killer in the back of the knees and made her stumble. With both hands, Johanna clawed for the woman's gun arm, and she slammed the wrist hard against the open door and heard a pistol clatter to the stone floor.

The killer lurched backward, landing an elbow against Johanna's face. Johanna felt pain radiating through her cheekbones, and she took a half step away, dropping the woman's arm. In the next instant, the killer was gone. Escaping. Footsteps pounded in the hallway. Johanna shook off the impact to her face and charged after the killer.

She was lithe and fast, with long dark hair. The killer reached the marble steps, but lost her balance as she tried to leap too many steps in a single stride. Johanna threw herself into the air and landed against the woman's back. They both fell, banging against sharp corners of stone and bumping down the steps in each other's arms onto the landing. The impact left them both bruised and diz-zied. Johanna staggered to her feet, and so did the killer, but with a knee to the woman's stomach, she drove her against the wall. The woman's skull cracked hard. She sank to her hands and knees.

Smoothly, Johanna whipped a knife from her back pocket and flicked the blade open. She found her flashlight again and illumi-nated the woman's face.

"*You.*"

An attractive Black woman, with long dark hair streaked with purple highlights, looked up at her. It was a woman she'd seen be-fore and knew only too well—a Treadstone agent. *Vandal.*

Vandal recognized her, too. Her eyes widened. "Jesus Christ. Johanna. You're supposed to be dead."

"Sorry to disappoint you. What the fuck are you doing here?"

"Same as you. Looking for Cain."

"Does that include murdering a harmless old woman downstairs?"

"Madame Aubert? She wasn't harmless. She was ready to kill *me*."

"Why would she do that?"

"Hell if I know."

Johanna shoved the point of the knife against Vandal's throat. She grabbed the Treadstone agent's hair and tilted her head back, her neck exposed. "Where's Jason? What's happened to him?"

"He's with Shadow. I don't know where they are now. I thought they might be here."

"*Shadow*." Johanna pushed the knife harder, drawing blood. "What does *she* want?"

"David Abbott's alive. And missing. They're trying to find him." Vandal's eyes narrowed in the glow of the flashlight. "But you already know he's alive. That's why you're here. You figured Jason would come to Abbott's estate."

"I don't know shit about David Abbott. Why are you trying to find Jason?"

Vandal pressed her lips together, saying nothing.

"*Why?*" Johanna repeated, digging in the knife again and drawing a wince of pain. "If Jason is with Shadow, what do you want with him?"

"To warn him," Vandal replied finally.

"About what?"

"The Russians want him dead. Putin will do anything to get him."

"You think he doesn't know that? We've known about it for months. Jason killed Lennon. He's had a target on his chest ever since."

"He may not remember," Vandal said.

Johanna stared at her. "*What?*"

"I think he lost his memory again. He lost it in the explosion."

"*No.* No way. It can't be."

"I saw him on Port Noir. He looked right through me. He didn't know me."

"Oh my God."

Johanna felt her mind spinning, and she lost her concentration. Jason without his memory. Again. *Impossible!* And yet it was all too easy to believe. The same waters in the warm Mediterranean. Abandoned and alone. Nearly killed. Rescued. *Again!* Of course he would have gone to Port Noir. When he'd lost everything, he'd turn to his instincts. Without his memory, his brain would replay what had happened once before.

Port Noir.

She took a step back, easing the knife away from Vandal's throat. Her eyes darkened as she studied the woman's face. There was something *off* in that face. She was nervous. Scared. *Lying.*

"If Jason's with Shadow, why do you need to find him? She knows about the Russians. She'd tell him."

"Maybe. Shadow always has her own agenda."

Johanna shook her head. "How did you get there so quickly?"

"Where?"

"To Port Noir. How did you find him?"

"I knew he had contacts there. After the explosion, I took a chance."

"How did you know the explosion involved *us*? How did you even know Jason and I were on that boat?" Her fingers tightened around the knife again. Her mind replayed the night of the explosion, the boats surrounding them. And a voice. She heard a voice in the background, guiding the attack. "Oh, fuck, it was you! It wasn't the Russians! *You* led the assault team yourself, you goddamn bitch. Why? Why does Treadstone want Bourne dead? That doesn't make any *sense!*"

"You're crazy," Vandal hissed, but her eyes continued to lie.

"And now you're *here*," Johanna went on, half to herself. "You're back here looking for him. You're still trying to *kill* him. But if he's with Shadow, you wouldn't need to be hunting for Cain. You'd know where he is. Jesus! It's *not* Treadstone, is it? Who the fuck are you working for? Tell me!"

Johanna reached for Vandal again, but as she did, she realized she'd made a mistake, giving her enemy an opening. Vandal put her head down and dove forward, colliding with Johanna's stomach. Johanna tumbled onto her back on the landing, and Vandal rolled and kept going, launching herself down the stairs. When Johanna got up, she gasped, trying to recover the air that had burst from her lungs. She lurched for the steps, but had to stop as her chest rebelled. She was too late. The effort cost her precious seconds, and below her, she heard the front door crash open. Vandal was gone.

Johanna slid to the marble steps and leaned her head heavily against the railing.

Was it true? Had Jason lost his memory again? Did he remember anything? God, did he remember *her*?

He was with Shadow. David Abbott's puppet. The woman who'd seduced him, manipulated him, lied to him over and over. The woman who would sacrifice anyone if it meant getting what she wanted. What did Shadow really want with him this time? *For God's sake, Jason, don't trust her!*

And Vandal.

Vandal was trying to kill him. Not just the Russians, but a Treadstone agent, too. Why? For who?

Johanna felt the air slowly returning to her chest. She could breathe again. She struggled to her feet and headed for the ground floor of the estate. She needed to get out of here; she needed to find him *now.*

She was running out of time.

Killers were closing in on Jason from every side, and he didn't even remember who his enemies were.

————

VANDAL FOUND THE MOTORBIKE SHE'D STASHED IN THE WOODS OUTSIDE David Abbott's estate. Dragging it onto the trail, she gunned the engine, heading for the park exit and the highway that led out of Marnes-la-Coquette. The hissing air in her face stung the wound on her neck. When she reached the main road, she drove fast, weaving through nighttime traffic heading toward Paris, the bike leaning left and right as she sped around the turns.

Johanna.

Johanna was alive!

Jesus. This was a disaster. She was going to have to tell Holly Schultz that the mission in the Med had been a complete failure.

The explosion should have killed them both, and yet somehow Johanna and Cain had both survived.

A disaster!

No. She couldn't tell Holly. Not yet. She had to keep her in the dark. Telling Holly that Johanna was alive was like signing her own death warrant. Holly wouldn't bother sending her back to prison when she found out. She'd assign a new agent to take out Johanna and Cain, and she'd add Vandal's name to the hit list at the same time.

Johanna! Alive!

Vandal had only one option to save herself. Finish the job. *Both* jobs. Kill Cain, kill Johanna, and get it done before Holly knew the truth. Wherever Cain was, Johanna would be drawn to him like a magnet. So Vandal had to get to Cain first.

Where was he?

She steered her motorbike off the busy highway onto the shoulder of the A13 and parked just inches away from the buzz of traffic. Ahead of her, she saw an overhead highway sign for the de Gaulle airport. The speeding cars and trucks whizzed by around her, and she put a hand over one ear to block out the noise. She dialed her phone.

Seconds later, a woman answered in a tone full of ice.

"Why are you calling me?" Shadow asked.

"It's urgent. Can you talk? Are you alone?" She added a second later, "Is *he* there?"

There was a long pause.

"I'm alone for the moment. What do you want?"

"I have news. Johanna is alive."

Hostility filled the next long silence on the phone. "Are you sure?"

"I just saw her. She almost killed me."

"Where are you?"

"Paris. But Johanna won't stay here long. She's trying to find Cain, and that means she's trying to find *you*. If she catches up with you, you know what she'll do. She'll kill you if that's what it takes to get Cain away from you. You need backup, Shadow. You can't do this alone."

"Are you volunteering?"

Vandal covered the phone as a truck thundered by on the highway. Then she took a deep breath. "Of course I am. You know that Johanna and I have history, just like the two of you. We both know what she's capable of, and we both want her dead. So let me help. Wherever you are, I can be there in a few hours."

17

A CAR FERRY FROM NAXOS DROPPED BOURNE AND SHADOW ON THE
Greek mainland in Thessaloniki at ten o'clock in the evening.
They found a late-night taverna near the water to have dinner,
with two hours to kill before an overnight bus would leave on its
fourteen-hour journey, first to Sofia and then to the Black Sea
coastal town of Varna, where David Abbott was hiding.

They sat at an outdoor table and had the sidewalk café mostly
to themselves. Shadow drank shots of Metaxa along with her grape
leaves and spanakopita. Bourne took bites of braised lamb shank,
but he mostly kept his eyes on the street that led along the bay. He
had a bad feeling. He didn't like the amount of time they were
spending in the open. The ferry ride from Naxos had taken hours,
and now they had hours more ahead of them across the Greek and
Bulgarian countryside.

The Treadstone jet wasn't an option. Shadow didn't want to
take the risk that she had a mole inside the agency, and every other

contact they used to charter planes or boats would increase the chance that their location would be leaked. So a low-budget bus beneath the radar was the safest choice. But the journey was long, and every stop in every small town increased the likelihood that someone would spot them. When it came to spies, this part of Europe might as well have been Casablanca.

"Anything?" Shadow murmured, taking another bite of spinach pie.

"Not so far," Bourne replied, still watching the street. "We're clear, and I didn't see anyone watching us on the ferry. But if the Russians found Abbott's hideaway on Naxos, I can't believe they didn't leave agents behind to watch the points of exit. Or they're using locals—someone I might not spot. That's what I'd do if I were them. The question is whether your face would attract attention."

"Mine?"

"You've been to the island before to see Abbott, and let's face it, anyone who saw you would remember you."

"Thank you," Shadow said. "But I've been careful to stay out of sight on all of my visits. I don't think any locals would recognize me or connect me to Abbott, and we would have spotted a pro if someone was staking out the ferry. But you're right, I can't believe they weren't keeping a close eye on the island after Abbott's escape. They'd have to assume Treadstone would send someone sooner or later."

Bourne frowned. "We'll walk to the bus station from here. If anyone's on our trail, we may be able to draw them out."

Shadow sipped more Metaxa, and her blue eyes pierced him. "Can I ask you something? It's personal."

"You can ask."

"What's it like for you to lose your memory? What does that do to you?"

"Who's asking?"

"What do you mean?"

"I mean, we have a complicated history," Bourne said. "You're Abbott's daughter. I was practically his son. In Switzerland, you were a psychologist evaluating my strengths and weaknesses while you lied to me about who you were. You're also my handler for Treadstone. You call the shots for what I do. Plus, we were lovers in the past, and we're lovers again now. So who wants to know what's going on inside my head?"

"All of us."

"Pass," Jason said.

"All right then. Just the lover. Just Marlen."

Bourne put down his fork and knife. He pushed his chair back from the table and watched the sea wind play games with Shadow's blond hair. The complicating factor in all of this was that she was *so* attractive. "I don't trust anyone. Including you. *Especially* you. That's what Treadstone taught me. But without my memory, I can't even trust myself."

"Why is that?"

"My past is nothing but fragments. Before the explosion, things had slowly been coming back to me over the last few years, but now I'm back where I was. I'm a jigsaw puzzle with half the pieces missing. I don't know what to believe and what not to believe. I have flashes of memory about people I've met, some more than others. I'll see things in my head, like scenes from a movie, but just clips, not the whole story. Other than that, I have to rely on instincts.

That's all I have to make decisions. But it would be easy for me to make a big mistake and not even know it."

"Do you think having sex with me was a mistake?" she asked.

"I don't think having sex with Marlen was a mistake. But I'm not convinced that was who was in bed with me last night. I'm pretty sure it was Shadow. I'm pretty sure it always is." He dug in his wallet and threw money on the table. "Now come on. We should go."

"All right."

She took his hand as she stood up, a sharp fingernail scraping his palm. They crossed from the corner taverna to the long walkway that led along the water. Upscale condos bordered the street, one after another, with elegant shops and restaurants on the ground level. He kept his hand on his Glock as he examined the apartment balconies. But he saw no threats and no surveillance. Waves made a low slap against the pier as they walked, and ahead of them, in the port, container ships lined the docks, with cranes looming over the ships like steel spiders. It could have been any seaside city anywhere in the world.

"Looks clear," Shadow said, her voice low.

"Yes, it does."

"You still sound worried."

"I told you. It's instinct."

"And what does your instinct say?" Shadow asked.

"That they spotted us on Naxos. That they're watching us now. Or they're playing some other game."

"So what do you want to do?"

Bourne checked his watch. "We've got forty-five minutes until the bus leaves. Let's get off the main street."

He led her to a cross street that headed into the city away from the water. Three blocks later, as they reached the next corner, a taxi passed them, heading the opposite way. Bourne used two fingers to let out a loud whistle. He waved at the cab and saw the vehicle hit the brakes on the one-way street. They jogged to the taxi and climbed in the back.

"Train station," he said, hoping the Greek driver spoke enough English to understand him. The man gave him a smile and wheeled into an immediate right turn to head west across the city.

The nighttime journey took less than ten minutes. Bourne kept an eye on the occasional traffic behind them, but he saw no signs that they were being followed. The driver dropped them at the main doors of the drab tan building that housed the train station, and Bourne and Shadow went inside. Ignoring the ticket windows, they turned left, walked to the far end of the building, and immediately used the next exit to go back outside.

Again he checked the street. No one.

So why did he still feel like he hadn't dodged their pursuers? But maybe that was the paranoia of his lost memory.

They walked west at a brisk pace along an avenue called Monastiriou. The neighborhood decayed in this part of the city, the old concrete buildings covered over with graffiti. Tattered awnings and rusted metal railings marked the balconies over their heads. At the next intersection, Bourne suddenly grabbed Shadow by the hand and pulled her across the street at a run as the light changed. They ran another block to Giannitson, where he turned right, then stopped, listening.

He heard no footsteps behind them. No vehicles changed direction.

There's no one following you.

They continued walking. The street narrowed the farther they walked, the pavement broken, weeds growing through the cracks. They crossed over a set of railroad tracks that hadn't seen a train in years. A few blocks later, they finally reached the bus station, still in the run-down section of town. Across the street, overgrown weeds and trees filled an empty lot, with junker cars parked along the curb. He spent a long minute studying the dark field and thought he smelled a wisp of cigarette smoke. He still felt watched. But there was nothing to do but take the risk.

Inside, even close to midnight, people filled the bus station, dragging luggage and talking excitedly in Greek, English, Bulgarian, and Spanish. A huge, dark glass dome rose over a wide floor built of checkerboard tile. Half a dozen buses were parked in diagonal spots, and glowing billboards were mounted on the walls. The air was brittle and warm. Noise thumped in his head like a heartbeat.

"I'll get the tickets," Shadow said.

"Get them for Sofia, not Varna. We'll change there."

"This isn't my first rodeo, Jason."

She disappeared.

Bourne bought a coffee and sipped it as he studied the late-night passengers. Tourists. Locals. Old men. Old women. They lined the benches, their eyes blinking closed as they waited for their bus. Two policemen walked side by side, looking bored. A homeless woman in her fifties, wearing a knee-length blue dress, went from tourist to tourist with an outstretched palm. A couple of people pressed small bills into her hand.

When the woman saw Bourne, she veered for him like a laser

beam. He tensed, watching her, evaluating the risk. She had curly black hair shot with gray and a prominent mole on her chin, and one leg limped stiffly as she walked. As far as he could tell, she was what she appeared to be. Harmless. No weapons. He dug a hundred-euro note out of his pocket and handed it to her, and she bobbed her head up and down with a huge smile that included a missing tooth. She hurried off to a sandwich kiosk in her sing-song gait.

"Ready?" Shadow asked, appearing at his side.

"All set. Any problems?"

"None. Do you think we've lost whoever who was on our tail?"

"My instincts are still pinging, but like I told you, I don't even trust myself anymore."

"Well, let's get on the bus and get the hell out of here. It's five hours to Sofia."

Bourne checked the station one last time. The people. The vehicles. The security. The cameras. He didn't like the feeling of danger in his gut, but he couldn't pin it to any of his senses. He was missing something, second-guessing himself. Somewhere in this station was a threat—he was sure of it—but he couldn't find it.

Naxos. Thessaloniki. Sofia. Varna. Fourteen long hours.

Were they leading the Russians straight to David Abbott?

He followed Shadow to the waiting coach thirty yards away, its engine already running. As they climbed the steps to get on board, he cast another look around, but no one was watching him. No one except the old homeless woman in the old blue dress. She waved excitedly at him, still with that gap-toothed grin, and called out her thanks. *"Efcharistó!"*

Jason smiled back at her. He and Shadow made their way down the aisle of the half-full bus. The interior was dark; this was the red-eye trip, where all the passengers slept. No one looked at them. They found seats in the last row, and Shadow took the window seat and leaned her head onto his shoulder. The door closed, and with a hiss of hydraulics, the bus was on its way.

———

THE HOMELESS WOMAN FINISHED HER SANDWICH AND SHOVED A FEW extra napkins into the pocket of her dress. She squeezed her thigh and grimaced as she limped through the bus station, winning a few extra euros from the tourists. When she passed through the exit doors, she hobbled up the street beside the lineup of junker cars and the overgrown field. Her lips moved as if she were talking to herself.

One block away, when the station was out of sight, she looked back to confirm she was alone. Then she abandoned the limp and hurried to the next alley.

A white panel van was waiting for her. A lean man in his thirties, with thinning black hair greased across his head in a comb-over, sat behind the wheel. He was dressed in a button-down white linen shirt and old jeans, like a Greek farmer, but he was really a Russian from Belgorod named Ilya. He had an SR-1M Vector semiautomatic pistol in his hand.

The woman looked beyond the front seats to the back of the van. Three other Russians sat there, all with guns, passing a Ruskova vodka bottle from one to the other. She snapped her fingers at them, and the youngest of the men—Dima was only nineteen and way too full of himself—scrambled forward and handed her the bottle. She took a giant-sized swallow, then wiped her mouth.

"So?" Ilya asked.

"It's Cain," she announced. "Definitely. The woman is Shadow. The new head of Treadstone. What a bonus that is. Putin was right, as he always is. The disappearance of David Abbott was bound to draw Cain into the fight. This is our chance to take him out and avenge our good friend Lennon."

"What's the plan?"

"We follow the bus. The destination is Sofia, but there are stops along the way. We'll board in two successive towns so it's not obvious. Once you're all on board, I'll give the word, and you can take them out. Cain and the woman."

"Why wait so long?" the young man in the back asked. "One or two of us get on, we start firing, end of story."

"*Zamolchi*, Dima," the woman snapped. "If I want to hear from a stupid child, I'll call on you. You don't know Cain. You're as likely to survive a gunfight with him as your little fucking dick is to hit the toilet when you piss. Nobody makes a move until you're all in position and *I* give the word. Don't look at each other. Don't talk to each other. You don't know each other. Clear?"

"*Ponyal*," they all muttered.

Understood.

"And the others on the bus?" Ilya asked. "What about them?"

"Collateral damage. Kill them all. I don't want to leave anyone behind who can recognize us. The Bulgarians will shit the bed if they find out it was us. Now *move*. Follow the bus. But not too close. Cain will be watching."

She settled into her seat and took another swig of Ruskova, finishing the bottle. She tossed it into the back of the van and heard it roll on the metal floor as the van accelerated through the alley.

"As soon as Cain is dead, our friends on the Black Sea can move on the ranch outside Varna," she announced. "By morning, the great David Abbott will be in our hands, too. Putin will be pleased."

18

THE FIRST STOP WAS AT ONE THIRTY IN THE MORNING IN THE TOWN OF
Serres in Macedonia. Bourne felt the lurch of the bus as it parked
outside the station, which awakened Shadow in the seat next to
him. She shook herself and stared out the window at the handful
of town lights. A ridge of mountains was framed against the night
sky. The inside lights of the bus went on, bright after more than an
hour of darkness. Bourne watched a couple of the passengers
standing up and gathering their things as they prepared to exit the
bus. The driver made an announcement in Greek, then opened his
fingers twice as a signal for everyone to see.

Ten-minute stop.

"I'm going to stretch my legs," Shadow said. "See if they've got
coffee, too. Do you want anything?"

"No, but I'll come with you."

"Don't bother. You don't need to babysit me here."

Gracefully, she maneuvered herself over his body into the

aisle. Her blond hair was mussed; her jeans fit snugly. The men on the bus all took notice of her as she made her way to the door. She went down the steps, and Bourne observed her through the window as she disappeared inside the Serres bus terminal. He ignored her request and shouldered to the front of the bus, and stepped down into the night air.

Automatically, he assessed his surroundings. They were only half a block from the main road, and no traffic came or went in either direction in the overnight hours. The bus terminal itself looked empty. He didn't think Shadow was going to find coffee unless it came out of a machine. One lone taxi was parked outside the doors, and the two passengers who'd left the bus seemed to be arguing over who would get the cab. He noticed three other vehicles parked near the terminal. A navy-blue Toyota Yaris with a rear bumper that was falling off. A white panel van, its headlights on. A red Peugeot, whose middle-aged driver stood outside the car, kissing a twentysomething young redhead who had a travel bag in her hand.

He saw the doors of the terminal open. Shadow came outside, holding a white paper cup. She had her phone pressed to her ear, but he was too far away to hear her end of the conversation. Their eyes met, and her face screwed up into an odd, uncomfortable expression. Then she turned away, as if she didn't want him to read her lips.

Bourne got on the bus and returned to their seats at the back. Two new passengers boarded in the next couple of minutes. One was a skinny young man—barely eighteen—with a shaved head and angular features. He wore a loose jacket and gray T-shirt, which was too warm for the night, plus baggy jeans. He found an empty seat near the front without looking at anyone else on the bus, then began playing a video game on his phone.

The next newcomer was the woman from the Peugeot. Her black tank top left half of her midriff bare, and she wore cutoff jeans. She hoisted her bag into an overhead compartment, then shook out her red hair and examined every other face on the bus, especially the men. She made a point of smiling at Bourne when she saw the seat next to him was empty. She was about to head his way when Shadow appeared behind her and murmured something in her ear. The young woman sat down with a pouty frown, and Shadow continued to the back of the bus and reclaimed the window seat next to Jason. She still had the white paper cup in her hand.

"What did you say to her?"

"I told her you had an STD," Shadow replied with a wink.

He chuckled. "I see you found coffee."

"I'm not sure I'd call it that."

"What was the phone call?"

"Oh, that. I had to call Washington."

"About?"

"Budgets. Bureaucracy waits for no one."

She looked away as if it was nothing important. But he was sure she was lying.

The bus engine rumbled to life. The doors began to swing shut, but then they opened again with a squeal. Another man came on board. He was in his thirties, in a button-down shirt and jeans, with a canvas backpack dangling from one hand. The backpack bore the logo of a German construction firm. The man's thinning black hair strained to cover his head, but his lean body looked taut and strong. His gaze made a sweep of the bus, not landing on any face in particular. When his eyes passed over Bourne, they showed no recognition or interest. That was how an innocent laborer would behave.

Or an experienced spy.

This man was trouble.

"We have a problem," Jason told Shadow, putting an arm around her shoulders the way a lover would do.

She laughed casually, as if he'd told a joke, then kissed him on the cheek. "Yes, I see that. We're going to get hit. Is it just him?"

"No, I'm betting the kid in the front with the buzz cut is with him, too."

"Should we get off?"

"No, they'll start shooting if we get up. Let's see how it unfolds."

The lights on the bus went out, and the chassis shuddered as the driver slowly navigated the coach back to the main road. They continued northward, with nothing but darkness outside as they passed through dense forests. In the town of Kulata, they crossed the border into Bulgaria. Bourne pretended to sleep, but he kept a close watch on the two men on the bus, alert for any movement. For more than an hour, nothing happened, and the men stayed where they were.

So maybe he was wrong.

But he wasn't.

At around three in the morning, the bus pulled off the A3 and made a stop in the Bulgarian town of Sandanski. As they neared the terminal, he spotted a white panel van parked in the shadows beyond one of the light posts. It was the same van he'd spotted in Serres. The van went out of view as they passed it, but during the ten-minute stop when the bus lights went on, two more men boarded as passengers. He was sure they'd come from the van, and he was sure they were additional members of an assault team.

His Glock was in his hand. Shadow had her Domina between her legs. The two men—both heavyset, both in their forties—took seats on opposite sides of the bus about three rows ahead of them. Bourne noted that the four men on the team had established a diamond format, two shooters for each of them, creating a crossfire that maximized their chances of taking out Bourne and Shadow at the same time.

"Fuck," Shadow said, seeing it, too. "These guys know what they're doing."

"How many more stops before Sofia?"

"Blagoevgrad in about an hour."

Bourne frowned. "That's too long. They'll hit us in the remote land, and they'll probably kill everybody else, too. As soon as the bus goes, we go. If we draw them outside, they won't worry about the other passengers."

"Got it."

He stared straight ahead, waiting. The air was warm, with no air-conditioning to cool them. Somewhere on the bus, someone listened to loud music through earbuds—it was the young redhead from the Peugeot—and the muffled rapping of Cardi B wailed through the silence. Most people seemed to sleep through it. He made a show of dropping a pen in the aisle, and when he bent to retrieve it, he noticed a glint of light and glass in the row where the man with the comb-over was sitting. A mirror.

The man was watching him.

Waiting.

Bourne studied the two newcomers three rows ahead of them. They each had miniature receivers in their ears. The young man near the front of the bus got up and stretched, his phone in his hand. He took a casual look backward at the rear of the bus. Stupid. Jason heard a low hiss; it was comb-over telling his young partner to sit down.

The kid dropped into his seat again.

"They know we're onto them," he whispered to Shadow. "They're not going to wait."

"When the lights go down," Shadow said.

"Right."

The engine rumbled. With a rattle, the bus doors closed, and the coach jolted into motion. The lights went out, bathing the bus in darkness. In the same moment, just as the bus accelerated, Shadow grabbed the red emergency-exit handle on the window next to them and shoved the glass panel outward. The air pressure changed; wind rushed inside. An alarm went off, the lights went on again, and passengers shouted. The driver jerked the brakes. Next to Bourne, Shadow was already slithering like a graceful snake through the window and dropping to the pavement below.

Jason moved to follow her, but he was out of time. A guttural male voice boomed through the bus, and he recognized the language and the word.

Now!

All four men lurched to their feet, their guns in their hands as they fired one after another. Bourne had no time to jump, just to throw himself to the floor. The barrage pummeled the back of the bus, bullets shattering glass and punching out the windows. Screams filled the coach. Some passengers took cover; some dove through the broken windows; some made the mistake of leaping to their feet, only to get cut down by a rain of gunfire. Blood sprayed across the leather seats and over the ceiling, and moans of pain joined the screaming.

One shooter, three rows ahead, fell as a bullet seared through the side of his head. Shadow was outside the bus now, firing in, but the kid at the front of the bus redirected his gun toward her and forced her to take cover. Bourne used the distraction to thrust his body around the seats and fire up the aisle at the other man three rows ahead. He got off two shots before return fire forced him back, but the heavy man took a bullet directly to the middle of his chest.

There were two shooters left.

Comb-over and the kid.

Bourne listened. The shooting stopped. He heard low voices; the men were reporting on the radio, getting orders. More passengers used the lull to throw themselves out the windows or pound down the aisle to the open door regardless of the danger. The driver jumped down the steps and into the parking lot. In a matter of seconds, the bus was empty, except for the dead, the two Russian assassins, and Bourne trapped in the last row.

Burnt smoke stung the warm air of the bus. Glass fragments in the window plinked to the ground. Cardi B still rapped her muffled song, and Bourne realized that the woman from the Peugeot was one of the victims. She lay in the aisle, her eyes and mouth open with surprise, her red hair now mixed with blood. He felt a stab of regret, a wave of memories that came and went through his mind in an instant.

Other faces. Other innocent victims.

That was his life and his legacy. Maybe it was better not to remember it.

Focus! Forget the past!

He heard another low order in Russian. *Cover me!*

The bus shifted. The two remaining killers both stood up. Footfalls crunched on glass, getting closer. One of the assassins was coming his way down the aisle; the other stayed where he was, his gun trained on the back of the bus to shoot if Bourne stood up. He couldn't remain squeezed on the floor behind the seats. Once the killer had the right angle, bullets would tear through foam and cut him to pieces.

But if he moved, he'd take fire from two directions. He might take out one shooter, but probably not two.

Where was Shadow?

There! Bullets erupted through glass on the opposite side of the bus. All the shots went high, but the incoming fire forced the comb-over killer to duck down in the aisle. As he did, Bourne threw himself from one side of the bus to the other, getting off a single shot as he leaped across the aisle. The shot landed in the middle of the assassin's face, and the man pitched forward like a statue falling.

Now it was Bourne and the teenage killer. One-on-one.

"*Cain!*" the kid shouted down the bus. Bourne could tell that the accent was Russian, and the voice was slurred and arrogant. He'd been drinking. "That you?"

"It is. If I were you, I'd run. You want to get away, we'll let you go."

"No, no, no. No chance of that. You killed Lennon. I kill you, and I'm a hero."

Bourne shook his head. *Lennon.* The assassin was dead, but he still followed Bourne from the grave. Their rivalry never ended.

"You're drunk, kid," he called back. "I don't want to kill you if I don't have to. Throw down your gun and run. Free pass. We won't fire."

"Fuck you."

Bourne heard a snap and a click as the kid armed his pistol with a fresh magazine. The voice from the front of the bus was low and muffled; the kid squatted down where Shadow had no angle on him. Shoes scraped on the bus floor, slowly coming closer. Experienced or not, scared or not, the kid had the advantage, because Bourne couldn't see him, but the kid knew exactly where he was hidden. He didn't need to come all the way down the aisle to start firing, just far enough to see the last row of seats.

If Bourne showed himself, if he took the risk of standing up, then it all came down to who was faster. That was a coin flip.

Or he could fire blind.

He pushed himself as far as he could between the two rows of seats, his back against the wall of the bus. Shards of glass on the floor ripped at his clothes. Above him, cool night air blew through the broken window. He extended his arms, steadying his gun hand with his other wrist. The barrel of the Glock pointed at the middle-back of the seat in front of him, and slightly upward. All he could do was make his best guess at where the kid's chest would be on the other side of the stiff cushions.

Now he needed to know exactly where the kid was. How close.

He listened, but the kid had smartened up and was moving so slowly now that Bourne couldn't hear him. No footsteps. No breathing. He could call out again—*Hey, what's your name?*—but then he'd give away his own position, and the kid would know exactly where to aim. Too risky.

If I'm the kid, I'm going to fire as soon as I have eyes on that last row.

But the shooter would sweep his bullets left to right, because Bourne might be anywhere behind the seats. That gave him a second, maybe two, to return fire.

Wait. Be patient. Let him go first.

Bourne felt his body relax and grow calm, a kind of Zen combination of anticipation and awareness. Still he heard nothing, no clues. The only clue would be the first shot. His finger slid around the trigger of the Glock, and he closed his eyes. He didn't need eyes for this. A clock ticked silently in his head, second by second, each second bringing the shooter closer. An eighteen-year-old boy. He'd be sweating now. Stifling the tremble in his arms. Holding his breath to make no sound, but feeling himself get lightheaded. One footstep, then another, heel to toe.

There it was. The last row.

The right-side seat in front of him exploded.

Instantly, Bourne fired back, one shot after another. Scorched foam blew back into his face. More glass shattered on the far side of the bus. He was vaguely aware of the kid getting off one more shot that came within an inch of his head, but he kept firing, bullet after bullet with each squeeze of the trigger, emptying his magazine. He didn't stop until he heard the impotent click of the Glock in his hand, and he let the barrel go limp in his hand.

The air was a cloud of smoke and char. Pieces of foam drifted down like a blizzard of snow. He tensed, waiting, but no more bullets came. Slowly, he untangled himself from his cramped position and pushed his way into the aisle. Three feet away, the kid lay on his back, still twitching. Bourne counted five shots bleeding from his chest, immediately below his neck. Seeing Bourne, the kid tried to pry his gun hand from under the seat, but Bourne simply put a boot on his wrist.

The kid's mouth opened. Blood came out. He tried to say something, but his words were lost in gagging and spit. His limbs went limp. His stare grew fixed and frozen, and air hissed from his chest like a leaking tire.

Bourne shook his head. "Stupid. You should have run."

19

BOURNE MET SHADOW OUTSIDE THE BUS. HE FELT THE TERRIFIED
stares of a few passengers who'd taken shelter in the nearby parking
lot. By his watch, less than five minutes had passed since the assault
began, but it felt like much longer. He noticed the bus driver not
far away, and the man was on his phone.

"All down?" Shadow asked.

"Yeah. I checked their pockets. Nobody had IDs, but the accents were Russian, and the kid talked about Lennon."

"Friends of Putin?"

"Most likely." Not far away, he heard sirens closing on the bus
station, and he had no interest in dealing with questions from the
Bulgarian police. "We need to get out of here. Let's find a car. We
can drive straight to Varna. It should be about seven hours. We can
be there in the morning."

Bourne glanced around the parking lot. His stare landed on
the white panel van parked in the shadows beyond the terminal
building. That was the van that had followed them from Serres and

probably all the way from Thessaloniki. "Let's take the van the Russians used. Maybe we'll find something useful inside."

He loaded another magazine in his Glock, then marched in the direction of the van. Shadow followed behind him, also with her Domina in her hand. As they neared the van, they separated, Bourne staying close to the rear doors, Shadow moving sideways toward the driver's door. He reached for the handle that opened into the back compartment, then threw it open and swung his Glock to point inside.

The interior was mostly empty, just an empty vodka bottle and some cheap clothes, plus several boxes of ammunition. It smelled of cigarettes. He climbed in, yanking the door shut behind him. His boots clanged on the metal floor as he made his way to the front of the van, sliding into the driver's bucket seat. He noticed that the keys were in the ignition, ready to go when the killers needed to make their escape.

He turned on the engine and switched on the headlights.

In front of him, bathed in the bright lights, he saw Shadow, but she wasn't alone. A woman stood behind her, an arm around Shadow's throat, the barrel of a Vector pistol pressed into Shadow's cheekbone. The woman was lean and small, in her fifties, with curly black hair and a light blue dress. He recognized her immediately. It was the homeless woman from the Thessaloniki bus station. But her dull eyes were sharp now, and as she pushed Shadow toward the bumper of the van, he saw no sign of a limp.

"Cain!" she shouted. "You want Shadow dead? Or do you want her alive?"

Shadow's blue eyes in the headlights showed no fear at all. "Run us down, Jason. Put it in gear. Run us both down."

The woman's arm tightened, and Shadow gagged. "Bad advice. We don't care about her, Cain. We want you. Dead is fine, but I'd rather have you alive. Now open the driver's door *slowly* and throw out your Glock. I won't ask you twice. You've got ten seconds, and then I shoot her."

Shadow's face darkened. "*Run. Us. Down.* That's an order, Jason."

Bourne's foot hovered on the brake. He could do it. He could hit the gas, and in two seconds, both women would be crushed under the van's chassis. But he didn't. Instead, he nudged the door of the van open and tossed his Glock onto the asphalt.

"Good boy. Sit. Stay."

The woman was stronger than she looked. She practically lifted Shadow into the air and dragged her to the passenger side of the van. Her eyes never left Bourne. She opened the passenger door, and she kept a choking grip on Shadow while she pointed the Vector across the van at Bourne's head.

"I'm sure you've got other weapons. Guns. Knives. Toss them out like you did the Glock. Slowly. Carefully. Believe me when I tell you that it wouldn't take me two seconds to break her neck and put a bullet in your brain. Got it?"

Bourne complied. He showed her his hands, then slid up the leg of his pants and unholstered his backup Glock with two fingers. He threw the gun from the vehicle. Then he reached under his shirt to where his Thompson dagger was sheathed, and he did the same with the knife.

He had another gun, in the small of his back, but he left it where it was.

"All right. I did what you asked. Let her go."

The woman gave him a smile that showed off her missing

tooth. She drew her Vector back, then swung it down hard, the metal butt colliding hard with Shadow's skull. The sickening crack made Shadow's eyes roll back, and she slumped in the woman's arms. Bourne began to jump across the seat, but the woman already had the barrel of the Vector pointed at his face again. She was fast.

"Down, boy. Drag her body inside, and shove her in the back of the van. She'll be out for a while. You and I are going to take a trip and visit my handler in Sofia. He's going to be very happy when he sees the gifts I'm bringing him. The head of Treadstone ... and the infamous Cain. Now drive."

———

THE WOMAN DIRECTED HIM TO THE TWO-LANE HIGHWAY, WHERE THEY had the night road mostly to themselves. They drove past empty fields and stone farmhouses, with a dark line of rolling hills marking the horizon. After a while, the winding road grew wooded as it bordered the river Struma, which rushed beside them, rapids glinting in the moonlight whenever the clouds cleared. The occasional road sign told him that the capital city of Sofia wasn't far, less than one hundred miles away.

North of Blagoevgrad, he spotted headlights behind them.

A car appeared in his sideview mirror a quarter mile back. He wasn't sure at first if the vehicle was following them, so he adjusted his speed up and down over the next several miles, and the trailing car matched him, staying the same distance behind his bumper. The Russian woman in the passenger seat didn't seem to notice.

She was focused on Bourne, her gun trained across the seat, and she gave no indication that she was aware of any other agents keeping an eye on her and her prisoners.

So who was it?

Friend or foe?

They drove into a steep valley carved by the flow of the Struma, with a cliff rising sharply on his left side above the road and hills climbing beyond the other side of the river. The night got even darker in the valley, and his high beams lit up the curves. Behind him, he heard a low moan as Shadow began to regain consciousness. The woman heard it, too, and she called to the back of the van without taking her eyes off Bourne. Her voice was harsh.

"Stay where you are, Shadow. If you try to intervene, I'll see you coming. Remember, you're a surplus member of this journey. Cain is the one I want. Cause trouble, and I will have no hesitation about shooting you in the head."

Shadow didn't reply, other than exhaling another grimace of pain as she shifted. She pushed herself up against the side of the van, where she had a view toward Bourne and the Russian. From there, she also had an angle on the sideview mirror, and their eyes met in the darkness. But her expression was inscrutable, the way it always was. He looked for some kind of signal from her about the vehicle behind them and saw nothing.

Did she know what was happening?

Did she know they were being followed?

Behind him, the headlights got bigger and brighter. The trailing vehicle crept closer, narrowing the gap between them to a few car lengths. Ahead of him, he spotted lights marking a tunnel built into the cliffside. Bourne eased off the accelerator, but not enough for the Russian woman to notice. Whatever the intentions of the car behind him, he was sure this was the moment of truth.

In the next instant, the dark archway of the tunnel swallowed them up. On both sides, hills and sky vanished, replaced by a claustrophobic half-moon of stone blasted through the mountain. Parallel rows of overhead lights cast a yellow glow, illuminating a web of deep cracks in the walls that leaked water onto the pavement. Each of the lanes was narrow, squeezed by the low ceiling. His tires whined like angry hornets caught in a hive.

He glanced across the car at the Russian woman, her skin now bathed in rippling yellow light, her eye sockets dark and hollow. Her gun arm was steady, the Vector ready to fire. Her smirk dared him to try something, to test her, to see which of them was faster. But he focused on the lane, and out of the corner of his eye, he saw the vehicle behind him, so close now that its headlights filled the mirror.

The engine of the trailing car roared. The Russian woman finally heard it, and she shouted in surprise. The vehicle veered into the opposite lane, and with a burst of speed, overtook the van. Automatically, the Russian swung her Vector toward the windshield and the car zooming past them, taking the barrel away from Bourne. In the same moment, the pursuing car made a sharp turn back toward the lane, and Bourne braced himself, hit the brakes, and swung the wheel hard right. The van crashed into the tunnel wall, metal tearing, the back end spinning wide as it lurched to a stop. The Russian woman flew forward, her forehead smacking the windshield and leaving a smear of blood. As she bounced back into her seat, Bourne slammed a fist into her ear and simultaneously made a downward chop on the wrist that held the gun. The Vector dropped from her numb fingers and fell below the seat. The woman howled, dizzied by dual blows.

From the back of the van, Shadow shot forward. She wrapped her arm around the throat of the dazed Russian killer, and with a grunt of effort, she jerked the woman's body between the seats to the metal floor in back. Grabbing the Russian's curly black hair, she slammed the woman's head down, once, then twice, making her go limp.

Bourne dove for the Vector below the seat. He snatched up the gun, then threw his body sideways against the van door as he yanked the handle open. His body spilled to the tunnel pavement, and he rolled into the far lane and came up on his knees, the pistol aimed at the vehicle in front of him. The van hissed steam from its engine block, and exhaust choked the tight space. The other car, a black Audi sedan, sat diagonally across both lanes, its taillights glowing red. He couldn't see through the dark windows.

"Out! Now!" he shouted. "Hands first!"

The driver's door clicked on the opposite side of the Audi. Above the car roof, he saw slim bare arms pointed upward, fingers on both hands spread wide. No gun. The sedan driver stood up and turned around, and he saw a Black woman through the film of smoke gathering in the tunnel.

"Hello, Cain," the woman said.

He kept the Vector pointed at her chest. "You know me?"

"The bigger question is, do you know *me*?"

He stared at her face and realized he did know her. Or at least, he knew that face. He'd seen it once before, but very recently. And there was something else in that face—something his mind couldn't quite touch. *What was it?*

"You were in the bar in Port Noir," Bourne said. "You were there that first night when I came ashore."

"Yes, I was. But you and I go back much farther than that, Cain. I told Shadow you didn't seem to know me. There wasn't even a glimmer when you saw my face. I figured your memory had failed you again."

"Who are you?" Bourne asked.

She walked slowly from the far side of the Audi, still with her hands in the air. Her body was tall and lean, encased in Lycra. Her black hair, streaked with purple, hung to her shoulders. She had a Ruger in a holster strapped to her left thigh. "Barcelona. Do you remember Barcelona? We did a mission together. An assassination."

An assassination. A hit.

That was who he was. A killer.

"And Maryland," the woman went on. "I was with you in Maryland. I was there when you found Nova."

Nova!

He felt a flash of memory again, seeing a fiery Greek woman in his mind's eye, his partner and his lover. Nova, beautiful, erotic, ruthless. Nova, dead, killed by a twisted young woman who reported to Lennon. Yes, *Lennon!* Jason's hand opened and closed, as if he could still feel the Greek coin encased in a pendant that Nova had worn over her heart. But that pendant was now at the bottom of the sea.

"*Who are you?*" he said again.

"She's Treadstone," said Shadow's voice, immediately behind him. "I called her in to help us. Her name's Vandal."

———

THEY TOOK THE AUDI AND LEFT THE VAN BEHIND. VANDAL DROVE. ON THE far side of the tunnel, they steered onto the shoulder, and Shadow dragged the Russian woman out of the vehicle and laid her out spread-eagled on the dirt. Below them, the deep waters of the Struma tumbled violently through the valley.

The Russian was conscious again, blood on her face, her eyes defiant. Shadow stood over her, the Vector in her own hand now. With her other hand, she shone a flashlight into the woman's face. She put the heel of her boot on the woman's stomach and drove it in, making her gag.

"How did you find us?" Shadow asked.

"Fuck you," the woman replied, choking and coughing.

"Be polite. I'm in a bad mood, and this won't go well for you."

"*Fuck. You.* You're going to kill me anyway."

Shadow sighed. She aimed the Vector at the woman's hip and pulled the trigger, and the explosion of the gun was quickly drowned by screaming. She nodded at Vandal, who shoved a towel in the woman's mouth to quiet her.

"Of course I'm going to kill you, but the question is *when*. It can be short or it can be very, very long. How did you find us?"

Vandal removed the towel. The Russian tried to spit at her, but failed. Shadow fired again, into the other hip this time, and again Vandal squelched the howls of agony that erupted from the woman on the ground.

"Did someone spot Cain on Naxos?" Shadow asked.

"*Yes!*" the Russian wailed. "Yes! He was seen! Teams were dispatched around the Greek ports!"

"What about David Abbott? Do you know where he is?"

The woman squeezed her eyes shut and clamped her jaws together. Tears crept down her cheeks. Shadow put the hot barrel of the Vector on the woman's bare knee and kept it there as the Russian writhed beneath her. "You have five seconds."

The woman gasped, choked, and screamed, but she said nothing.

Shadow fired.

Out of the incoherent wailing that followed, they could make out one word. "Varna. *Varna!*"

Shadow swore.

She aimed the barrel between the woman's eyes and pulled the trigger again, and the thrashing body at their feet immediately went still. With a firm shove of her boot, she rolled the dead woman over, and the body tumbled down the slope and splashed into the river. The rapids took hold of the Russian like a fallen tree and spun her downstream, disappearing into the night.

"They know where Abbott is," Shadow snapped. "We need to hurry. When we don't show up in Sofia, they'll figure we're on our way to Varna. They're going to move in and grab him."

20

DAVID ABBOTT STOOD ON THE PORCH OF A HILLTOP RANCH HOUSE OUT-
side Varna. His tall, imposing figure stood ramrod straight, like a
rocket on the launchpad.

From where he was, he had a commanding view of fields
stretching toward the coast of the Black Sea two miles away. Closer
to the house, hundreds of acres of dimyat grapes grew in rows
along the gentle slope, each vine bound to a wooden stake. The
local grapes were the source of the white wine in his glass. He eyed
the rutted dirt road that dead-ended to the west and led toward
the small town in the other direction. It was the only way in or out,
other than on foot.

No one was coming for him. Not yet. But he checked his watch
with a severe frown and saw that it was almost eight in the morning.

Teeling hadn't come back.

The retired Treadstone agent had left for Sofia the previous
morning. The plan had been for Teeling to meet his old contact,

gather intelligence on what the Russians knew and didn't know, and then immediately return to Varna. Abbott had expected him no later than midnight. Instead, he'd stayed up on the porch all night, wine in one hand, his Staccato CS 9mm in the other, waiting for a man who never showed up. Now it was morning. He didn't know whether Teeling was alive or dead, but regardless, something was wrong.

Abbott stroked his trimmed gray beard and considered his options. For the moment, the area around him was safe. The ranch house occupied the high ground, and the open lands made it impossible for intruders to approach without being seen. Teeling had chosen the location well. The wily agent had also added cameras and motion sensors on a perimeter around the house for a mile in every direction. No one could take him by surprise.

Time to decide.

Abbott could run. That was the obvious option. Grab his go bag and hike south across the green hills toward the nearby village of Priseltsi. There, Teeling kept a Mercedes AMG GT in the garage of a middle-aged woman he met monthly for cribbage and sex. The fast car would take Abbott wherever he wanted to go.

But go where?

Every spy in Europe would be on the lookout for his face, his mane of silver hair, his tall, strong swimmer's body that he kept in peak shape even in his sixties. He had nowhere to hide and no one he could trust to help him. And yet he had already waited too long to admit to himself that his latest location was blown. Each minute increased the risk. If Teeling didn't return in another hour, he'd be forced into the open.

Abbott returned inside the ranch house to get ready. The interior smelled of the cabbage soup he'd heated for dinner the night before. The house wasn't large; it was old and not flashy. Flashy attracted attention, and this was a place where a man went to be ignored and forgotten. Teeling's only real connection to the Varna area was his grapes, and even those he left in the care of a local Bulgarian farmer, who paid him in cases of wine. Barely a handful of people around the region, mostly bartenders and shopkeepers, even knew what Teeling looked like. None of them were aware that, for the past month, Teeling had had a houseguest.

Two men living together. Both on the run.

Abbott retrieved his leather go bag from a compartment hidden behind the wall in the small guest bedroom. He added more food to buy himself a couple of extra days to live off the grid, once he was on his way. He had plenty of guns, plenty of ammunition, but no phone, no electronic way of communicating. Every security agency in the world would be monitoring cell traffic and running voice recognition to grab any hint of David Abbott's location. As soon as he made a call, they'd close in, and they'd find him. He'd been tempted on his way to Varna to buy a burner phone to reach out to Shadow, but there was no such thing as a safe phone for a man like him. It wouldn't be safe for her, either.

Shadow.

Marlen.

She would be looking for him. Desperate to find him. He knew that. She would break every rule to get him back. But Abbott had no intention of increasing the danger for Marlen by sending any kind of signal. If he reached out to her, it would be to tell her to stay away. He would rather die than put his daughter at risk.

His daughter.

God, the lengths they had gone to all these years in order to keep the secret. It was imperative that no one know who she really was. That little girl, so much like her father, so smart and savvy, so beautiful. When he'd first learned of her existence, he'd been furious. If her German mother had come to him when she was pregnant, he would have insisted on an abortion. To Abbott, the existence of a child meant risk, vulnerability, weakness, something his enemies could exploit. But then he'd met Marlen in person. Even when she was a little girl, he'd realized she was something special, with an intellect and boldness to match his own. With her at his side, they had built Treadstone into an empire. Years of labor and commitment side by side. Those had been the best times of his life.

Now, with the Files in her grasp, she had all the power she needed. Shadow and Treadstone would live on without him.

Let me go, Marlen. Whether they catch me or not, my time is done.

Even so, he missed her. He wondered how far away she was and whether she'd tracked him on his escape from Naxos. Was she alone? Or was she with David Webb? Cain. Jason Bourne. That wounded boy, the complex man with all of his deadly skills, the surrogate son whose whole past had fallen victim to Abbott's plans. In that first moment Marlen had seen him in Marnes-la-Coquette, Abbott had known that Cain would be a problem for her. She had so little true competition from other men that she was bound to be attracted to a man who was on her level. Physically. Mentally. He'd tried to keep them apart, and when that didn't work, he'd warned her about getting involved with him. But the two of them kept being drawn together, bringing out the best and worst in each other. It didn't seem likely that their relationship would end well.

David Webb.

Abbott hadn't seen him in years, although he kept tabs on his life via Marlen. To David, Abbott was *dead*. It was better to keep it that way. Cain had enough complications in his life without confronting Abbott's ghost. But if Marlen turned to anyone for help, if she trusted anyone with the secret that he was really alive, it would be David.

Abbott tensed at a sudden interruption.

A voice from the speakers Teeling had wired throughout the house broke into his thoughts.

Motion detected on entrance road.

He grabbed his go bag. With his binoculars, he hurried back to the porch, ready to escape toward the fields in back if he saw trouble. A mile down the rutted, uneven road, a cloud of dust told him a car was coming, fast. At first, the slope of the grape vines made it impossible for him to see the details of the vehicle, but when it came into focus on the flatland, he recognized Teeling's black Jeep. As if guessing that Abbott would have eyes on him, the old Treadstone agent extended an arm through the driver's window and flashed a peace sign as his signal. He was alone and not under duress.

Abbott felt a wave of relief, but the relief was short-lived.

Teeling was back, but why had he been gone all night?

Soon after, the Jeep pulled to a stop at the foot of the porch steps. His friend got out, looking older than when he'd left twenty-four hours earlier. Teeling was eighty; they'd celebrated his birthday two weeks earlier with whiskey and spice cake. He'd sported hippie-style long gray hair as a beach bum in Nassau, but since he came to Bulgaria, he'd shaved his head. He wasn't tall, only about five foot ten, and scrawny, with wrinkles all over his body like pressure bars on a weather map. In the Bahamas, his skin had been chocolate brown from the sun, but the gray skies of Varna had turned him pale again.

"Are you all right?" Abbott called. "Where have you been?"

"Aw, did you miss me, honey?" Teeling replied in his sandpaper voice. "Sorry, David. I spent half the night hiding near the railroad tracks in Sofia. They were looking for me for hours. One of the Russians got so close that I could smell his farts."

"What the hell happened? Did you see your contact?"

"He's dead." Teeling climbed the steps of the ranch house, groaning at the weakness in his knees. He pushed past Abbott and went inside. In the kitchen, he poured himself a double shot of his smooth namesake whiskey, then sat down at the wooden table, breathing hard. He ran his hands back over his shaved head, wiping away sweat. "They're onto you, David. They know you're here."

"Are you sure?"

"Very sure. The Russians tracked you to me. The meeting with my source was a trap. Thank God I scoped out the building before I went inside. When I didn't show, they shot him. Not enough to kill him, just enough to make sure he couldn't walk. Then they laid him out on the tracks and let a train cut him in half." He drank the double shot and poured another. "These boys do not mess around, David. I'm guessing the orders come from on high. All the way to the top."

Abbott kept all emotion off his face. He was numb to violence after so many years at Treadstone. "How did they put us together?"

"It was my old Russian friend in the Bahamas," Teeling replied. "They leaned on him, the poor bastard. He knew you and I were close, and I made the mistake once of talking too much about Bulgaria. They've been hunting for me ever since. They've had spies spread out around the country. They're coming *here*, David. An assault team from north of the border. I figure we've got two hours at most. We need to decide how to get out of the country and where to go next. Both of us."

Abbott shook his head. "Not both of us, my friend. We'll leave separately. If we're together, they'll keep looking for you. I can draw them away. You deserve a little peace in these last few years, not the prospect of dying with me."

Teeling drank down the double shot. "Fuck that. Where you go, I go."

"I figured you'd say that. I don't agree, but I won't take the time to argue. Do we take the Jeep or the Mercedes?"

"The Mercedes. That way, I can kiss Nina goodbye."

Abbott smiled, but as he turned away, Teeling reached out and took hold of his arm. The old agent's face turned somber. "David, wait. There's something more."

"What is it?"

"I heard the Russians talking. They had shooters at a staging ground somewhere in Romania. They were already planning to move on you overnight, but then they delayed by a few hours. Apparently, they got a call from one of their assets in Greece. She told them she had two deliveries for them. High-value prisoners. They were on the road to Sofia, and they were supposed to be there in a couple of hours."

"Who were the prisoners?" Abbott asked.

"I'm sorry, David. It was Cain. And Shadow. The asset said she had them both."

Abbott closed his eyes. "Good God. They were looking for me, and they walked right into Putin's hands."

"I agree, it's disturbing news," Teeling said, "but Cain's a survivor. You know that better than anyone. I wouldn't bet against him."

"Or they'll both end up dead."

"Yes. I won't pretend."

Abbott's hand trembled as he stroked his beard. Just a little, just for a moment. That was the only personal feeling he dared allow himself. His daughter. And the man who'd been nearly a son to him. Both taken, both likely dead because of him. But there was nothing he could do to change that. His life had been about acceptable risks, about wins and losses, and he'd made his peace with the consequences long ago.

"Do you mind if I ask you something, David?" Teeling said.

"Go ahead."

"Was it all worth it? I mean, coming out of hiding. Going to Dubrovnik. Having it all blow up in your face. Was it worth it to try to take down Adam Hill?"

Abbott sighed. "I told you who he is."

"I know you did."

"Hill is a Chinese asset, and he's going to be president of the United States if I don't stop him. If that's not worth my life, what is? Look at what the Chinese have done in the past decade. Seducing a foolish California congressman in a honey trap. Setting up literal Chinese police stations in multiple states. Hacking personal data on millions of Americans. Sending surveillance balloons across the continent. Pouring spies across the open border. Kidnapping and killing dissidents on our own soil. They've been grooming sleepers for years, Teeling, and Hill is their ultimate prize."

"Except no one other than Shadow believes you."

"Do you really expect the mainstream media to dig into this? That would require actual journalism, and they gave up on that long ago. The truth about Hill has been wandering around X since before the election, but it's been written off as a conspiracy theory. It's not. Hill is in the pocket of the CCP."

Teeling turned his shot glass upside down on the table. "But you know something that can bring him down?"

"I do."

"You still haven't told me what it is. Don't you think someone else should know? If you die, the secret dies, too."

"I haven't even told Shadow," Abbott said.

"Why not?"

"There are personal reasons for that."

"Then tell me."

Abbott studied his old friend. He'd already trusted him with his life. But this was about more than his life. "All right. When Hill was first elected to Congress, I did what I usually do. I sent a Treadstone agent to Texas to do a deep dive on his background. Something came up. My agent found a woman who knew Hill long before his political days, back when he was a math teacher in Dallas. She told him there were rumors in school that he was a predator. They knew at least one girl who'd been assaulted. Someone named Annie."

"Why not go public with it?"

Abbott exhaled in frustration. "Annie disappeared. The woman my agent found wouldn't talk about the rumors. She was afraid of what would happen to her. Apparently, a different woman made noises about Hill and Annie early in the campaign. She was killed in what the police said was an accident. But the woman didn't think it was, and neither do I. I think the CCP stepped in to protect their asset."

"I'm guessing you found Annie," Teeling said.

"I did. I've been keeping an eye on her for years. I was hoping to find some other way to take Hill down without involving her, but I ran out of options. That's why I came out of hiding. I arranged a meeting with her in Dubrovnik, to get her to come forward. To reveal the truth about Hill and share her evidence."

"Evidence?"

"Hill made a video of the assault. No doubt for later self-pleasuring. Annie took it when she disappeared."

"My God. But she refused?"

Abbott nodded. "She wasn't ready to blow up her life. I can't blame her for that."

"Who is she?" Teeling asked.

"A remarkable woman, despite her emotional flaws. I encouraged Shadow to bring her into Treadstone under her new identity. She had wicked skills, mentally and physically, but the agency wasn't a fit. She was too damaged. Too unstable. That might not have been a problem on its own, but now it's complicated, because she developed a passionate relationship with Cain. Her name is Johanna."

21

JOHANNA KEPT A THIN BLANKET PULLED UP TO HER CHIN AS SHE NES-
tled in the corner of a third-class carriage on the TGV train to
Vienna. She wore a tweed newsboy hat pulled down low over her
forehead, plus oversized sunglasses. She pretended to sleep, but she
kept an eye on the people going up and down the aisle, bringing
coffee and croissants back from the food compartment. No one
looked her way.

Outside, the train whipped through an Austrian landscape of
lush green hills and rocky mountaintops, with the red roofs of
small towns dotting the valleys. The countryside made her home-
sick. She'd spent most of her twenties in Salzburg in a cheap attic
apartment in the Elisabeth-Vorstadt neighborhood. During the
days, she hacked code; during the nights, she drank beer and
danced in clubs. That was before David Abbott had found her. Before Shadow had recruited her for Treadstone.

Before Jason.

She squeezed her eyes shut. *Forget those days! Those days are gone!*

But the past was always with her. She could never leave it behind. Maybe that was why she and Jason felt like two halves of a coin coming together. He wanted to find his missing past, and she wanted to find a way to escape from hers.

To escape from Adam Hill.

Jesus!

Her whole body still clenched with fury and shame whenever she thought about him. She still felt guilty, as if the relationship had all been her fault. Fourteen years old! She'd been a kid, a child! But that didn't matter. She blamed herself.

Annie and Mr. Hill.

What a crush she'd had on him.

He was a handsome, friendly teacher, the first person who'd recognized what her brain could do, the first man who'd shown any genuine interest in her when she was a brilliant, closed-off girl. Her parents hadn't known what to do with this precocious recluse they'd raised. But Adam. Oh God, Adam, the things he'd said to her. The flattery. The grooming. The gifts. The promises. He would take her with him on his next trip to China—not a student trip, a personal trip, just the two of them. He'd show her the whole world. They'd go everywhere together.

She believed all of it. Every word.

Then came the night when his wife was away. Tuesday, March 4. Texas rain pouring down outside. His phone recording everything—so they could watch it together and relive it, he said. He'd put his hands on her, his mouth on her; he'd forced her to do things that made her sick; he'd pushed her down on her stomach and forced his way inside, telling her how much she would enjoy it. When it was over, he'd calmly told her to get dressed and go home, and he'd kissed her and said how special she was. Because he knew, *he knew*, she wouldn't say a word to anyone.

She didn't.

Instead, Annie coldly plotted her revenge. She broke into his house and tied him to the bed, and she used a toilet plunger to do to him what he'd done to her. All the while, she filmed it and whispered in his ear and asked if he was enjoying it. When she left, she took his phone with her, including the video—*both* videos—so he would know she always held his life in her hands.

And then she disappeared.

She became a completely different person. She vanished from Dallas and left her childhood behind forever.

Now, years later, she didn't want to go back to her life as Annie. She *couldn't* go back. She was Johanna now. No matter who Hill was now, no matter what David Abbott told her, she wouldn't walk into the middle of a maelstrom.

She had only one focus. *Find Jason!*

In her pocket, her burner phone buzzed. She drew it out and saw the text message she'd been waiting for, from a Czech spy she'd met when she was part of Treadstone. *Kaleidoskop. 1:00 a.m.*

Johanna closed her eyes with relief.

Kaleidoskop was a Vienna nightclub, the wildest of the wild, a hazy blur of music, drugs, and sex. It was also a hot spot for foreign agents, a place where spies spied on other spies. If anyone had heard rumors about Jason and Shadow, she would find them at Kaleidoskop. Her Czech contact, Milena, would help her.

For the first time since Marseilles, Johanna felt a glimmer of hope.

Two teenage girls walked past her down the aisle of the train.

They laughed and teased each other, both of them taking bites from chocolate croissants. The sight of the girls reminded her again that she'd missed out on a normal life because of Adam Hill, but she couldn't change that. She'd never been normal. Her stomach growled, and she realized she was hungry. She took a quick look up and down the compartment, then slid off the blanket and got out of her seat. The dining carriage was three compartments away.

She walked up the aisle, which vibrated with the speed of the train. At the end of each compartment, she went through sliding doors. She took note of the people in the seats facing her, enough to make sure they didn't notice her or recognize her. Her newsboy hat was still on; so were her sunglasses. She wore loose white cargo pants, combat boots, and a black nylon long-sleeved shirt. The pockets of the pants were deep enough for all of her weapons.

In the food car, she waited in a line of passengers six deep. When she got to the counter, she had to take off her sunglasses to read the list of drinks and prices, and she ordered herself a large Americano to go along with a cherry torte. Rather than sit at a table in the open, she took her order and retraced her steps through the train.

Halfway back to her seat, she realized she'd made a mistake.

She'd forgotten to put her sunglasses back on, and her hands were full.

She only realized it when she saw an American in the aisle seat, a copy of *Foreign Affairs* in his hands. He was in his forties, wearing a business suit with a paisley tie. She saw him before he saw her, and she stopped and began to turn around, but she was too late. His chin nudged up from the magazine; his eyes wandered around the compartment from behind his round silver glasses. In that moment, his eyes found her, and she saw a faint double take before his intel reactions kicked in and he went back to his reading.

A spy on his way to Vienna. There was nothing strange in that.

But she'd seen this man once before, when she was on a Treadstone mission that took her to the embassy in Lisbon. He was CIA. Not a field man, just a research analyst, and they'd only met for a couple of minutes in the communications room. But agents remembered agents, and she remembered him.

The trouble was, he remembered her, too.

She passed him and tried to pretend that everything was fine, but when she glanced over her shoulder at the door to the next compartment, she could see that he was already keying a text on his phone.

———

THE ANTIQUARIAN BOOKSTORE ON PENNSYLVANIA AVENUE, NOT FAR from the Potomac, always stayed open late when the vice president was scheduled to make his monthly appearance. After its normal closing time at seven in the evening, the Secret Service moved in to clear the space and establish a safe zone in the surrounding blocks. Sometime late in the evening, usually after midnight, an unmarked SUV took Adam Hill from the Eisenhower Building to the bookstore, where he could browse the shelves alone. No press was invited, no members of the public pressed their faces to the windows, and no staff went with him on these visits.

Hill took his time exploring the store. He always kept a smile on his face while he was there. He had a smile for his security detail. He had a smile for the husband-and-wife team who owned the bookstore, Wen and Li Chen. But in fact, Hill was a mess of nerves whenever he visited Colonial Books. Any day could be his last day. He had a vision of the FBI storming through the door, throwing him against one of the bookshelves, and rifling through his pockets until they found the secrets he was passing to the CCP.

That night, Li Chen met him at the entrance, as she usually did, and bowed to welcome him. Li was a naturalized American citizen, born in Shanghai. Hill had known her for thirty years. They'd had a torrid affair on his very first trip to China. Back then, he didn't realize that she was a spy. To him, she was just an inventive lover who let him live out his domination fantasies. But all of it happened under the watchful eye of Chinese cameras. Even after he found out the truth, he'd gone back many times. She was that good. And when he began to rise in political circles, she'd moved to the U.S. to serve as his handler.

Li handed him latex gloves, which he carefully snapped onto his thick fingers. Gloves were a necessity when handling the books because of the delicacy of many of the old editions. Gloves were also a necessity to avoid leaving fingerprints on the information being exchanged.

Hill checked his watch. It was one in the morning in Washington. He was usually up late; he didn't need much sleep. He followed his typical routine, going through each of the aisles one by one, pausing to examine nineteenth-century leather-bound books of history and cartography, hardcovers from the 1930s by Steinbeck and Hurston, poetry and novels from the depth of the Civil War. In the European classics aisle, he found the book he was looking for. The same book every time. When he left, the Chens took it off the shelves, and they only put it back immediately before each of his visits.

It was *The Last Days of Pompeii* by Edward Bulwer-Lytton. Carefully, Hill slid the fragile edition off the shelf and turned it over in his hands. He glanced both ways down the aisle, making sure he was alone. He glanced at the chambered bookstore ceiling, making sure no cameras had been installed, that the Chens had not done a deal with the FBI since he'd last been here.

No. Everything was safe. Hill opened the back cover and found a slim, folded piece of paper inside, which he dropped into his pocket. The paper—if anyone else opened it—was a menu for a Chinese restaurant on K Street owned by a cousin of the Chens. It looked like an ordinary list of bao and udon dishes, but the prices of the monthly specials provided him with a numeric key linked to the 2007 *Encyclopaedia Britannica* he kept in his home office. By tracing the numbers to specific volumes, pages, and words, the code revealed the information that his friends in the CCP were seeking.

Hill continued shopping for another ten minutes. He selected a slim volume of 1920s-era bread recipes for his wife, then went to the counter, where Li Chen greeted him with another bow. He paid using his credit card, then dropped a tightly folded twenty-dollar bill in the tip jar and thanked her for staying open late. Inside the bill was a quarter-sized voice recorder that included a conversation he'd had with the secretary of defense about the surface-to-air missile defense system that was included in the latest arms package for Taiwan. The Chens would transcribe the relevant details—making sure the facts couldn't be traced back to its source—and then destroy the recorder.

The vice president peeled off his gloves and deposited them in the trash container near the store's cash register. He took his recipe book and headed for the door, and when he was finally outside on Pennsylvania Avenue, he began to breathe again. It was done. Another exchange. Another victory. No guns, no cameras, no men and women in blue windbreakers taking him down.

His limousine was waiting. A Secret Service agent opened the rear door, and Hill got inside, the plastic bag with the book dangling from his fingers. Then his face screwed up in anger and surprise.

Holly Schultz sat on the opposite side of the town car. Sugar was seated in front of her on the floor. The dog gave an angry yelp as she spotted Hill.

"What the fuck, Holly?" Hill demanded.

She nodded at the agent outside the car. "Let's wait until the door is closed, don't you think, Adam?"

The door of the limo slammed shut. The soundproof barrier between Hill and the driver was already up. Sugar growled again, and despite himself, Hill inched away from the dog.

"How did you know where I was?"

"You're the vice president, Adam. I always know where you are." She nodded at the bookstore through the window. "You come here a lot."

"I like old books."

"I see that."

"What do you want? Do you have news?"

Holly frowned. "I do. I got an overnight report from an analyst on his way to a meeting in Vienna. Actually, it would have gotten lost in the usual chatter, but I've got an intercept that runs targeted searches on incoming messages. In this case, the search involved your . . . personal business."

"I don't give a shit about your process, Holly. What was the report?"

"There's no way to sugarcoat this, Adam," she replied. "The agent spotted Johanna on the train to Vienna. She wasn't killed in the explosion in the Med. Annie's alive."

22

BOURNE EYED VANDAL FROM THE OTHER SIDE OF THE AUDI AS SHE SPED toward Varna. They weren't far now. They'd left the highway and were on the back roads. It was morning, the low sun blinding through the windshield. Vandal wore sunglasses and kept the window open, with air whipping into the car and swirling her black-and-purple hair. She drove one-handed, her right hand casually draped over the wheel and her left arm balanced on the door, which also gave her quick access to the Ruger holstered on her thigh.

She sensed his stare without looking his way. "Trying to remember me?"

"You could say that."

"It must be strange, people appearing and disappearing from your mind like that."

"It is."

"We were together in Paris last year. Sound familiar?" Her eyes drifted to the rearview mirror, as if needing permission from

Shadow to say anything more. But Shadow was quiet. "That was where you first met *her* again, you know. She came out of hiding and met you at the dome in La Villette."

"I don't remember that."

"Johanna tried to kill me there. That crazy bitch. Do you remember *that?*"

"No."

"But you remember Johanna? She almost killed you, too, you know. On Holy Island. Both of you. You and Shadow. I saved your life."

Bourne pressed fingers into his forehead, trying to hold back the pain and drag memories out of his brain. But nothing came.

"She's right, Jason," Shadow said from the back seat. "That's the way it happened."

Bourne's head pounded, lightning bolts firing against the back of his eyes. He remembered none of what they were telling him. He didn't remember Vandal at all. Sometimes people came back with a name or a face, but Vandal stayed hidden in the mist. And yet there was something when he stared at her, not a memory, not a flashback of the past, but *something.* Strange physical sensations rolled over him. Heat, smoke, pain, blackness.

Why?

His instincts told him not to trust her. But he didn't trust anyone.

Vandal's voice stayed smooth and calm. "I told you things in Paris about me. About my past. Any of that ring a bell?"

"No."

"Just as well. I violated the rules. Never reveal who you are."

"I guess your secret is safe with me," Bourne said.

He watched Vandal's fingers tighten on the wheel. "I guess so."

Behind them, Shadow checked the GPS on her phone. "Two minutes to the turn. We're almost there. Stay alert."

Vandal slowed the Audi on the two-lane road. They were in the middle of nowhere, nothing but overgrown fields around them, with glimpses of Lake Varna beyond the hills on the northern horizon. This could have been the Midwest rural lands outside Chicago or Omaha. Bourne thought about the retired agent he'd known as Teeling, and the remote countryside of Bulgaria seemed far away from the beaches and boats of Nassau. But maybe that was the point when you were trying to hide.

Ahead of them, an unmarked road cut through the trees. Vandal turned right. Power lines stretched overhead, but otherwise there were no signs of life. The road narrowed, barely wider than the car, and Vandal had to navigate the Audi around potholes filled with water from the overnight rains. Then the pavement disappeared entirely and became rutted gravel, which bumped and crunched under their tires.

Bourne squinted through the windshield. "*Stop.*"

Vandal hit the brakes. "What is it?"

"Through the trees. There's a vehicle parked up there."

In the back seat, Shadow swore. She knew what that meant. All three of them drew their pistols and threaded suppressers onto the barrels. As he did, Bourne caught Vandal's eye again, and an odd expression crossed her face. If she'd suddenly pointed her gun at him, he wouldn't have been surprised. And yet that made no sense. She was Treadstone. Even so, he felt his skin grow hot, almost to the point of burning, and he wondered again why his instinct was to associate Vandal with *fire*.

They got out of the car.

Side by side, three across, they marched slowly down the dirt road, which made a slight curve ahead of them. Bourne held up a hand to hold them back. He could see a fork beyond the trees, where a road that was barely more than a dirt path led in the direction of Teeling's hideaway. And David Abbott's. He also saw two black SUVs parked at the fork, blocking the turn. He listened, but heard nothing. The vehicles were empty.

"The assault's underway. Come on."

They ran now, instead of walking. Beyond the curve, the land opened up into rolling hills, and he could see one old ranch house with a red roof occupying the high ground. The property was surrounded by a rusted barbed-wire fence, but the strands of the fence had been cut and peeled back near the fork.

He looked through the fields, but saw no one crossing the land. Then a sharp crack rolled in with the wind.

A gunshot.

They pushed through tall weeds and wildflowers toward the ranch house. Near the slope, the fields gave way to rows of grape vines tied onto stakes, with deep wet furrows in the dirt between them. He spotted a large number of fresh footprints in the dirt and counted at least eight men spreading out to surround the house. From beyond the vines, he heard another series of shots and the clatter of glass breaking. He heard a shout from a voice he remembered. Teeling's voice.

"David! Run!"

Bourne plunged between the vines. They were tall, blocking his view. He went slowly now, as if navigating a maze. To his right, he saw a blur of motion as Vandal ran along the southern end of the field. Shadow was beside him, but she turned left, moving through the mud. He pushed between the wooden stakes into the next row, and then the next. As he emerged through the grape vines, he glanced left and saw a man in black twenty feet away, his back to him. Bourne stepped carefully, silent and fast, until barely ten feet separated them. Then the man, sensing danger, began to turn. Bourne saw a Bulgarian AR-M1 rifle nestled in his arms. In one seamless motion, he raised his Glock and fired into the man's head, dropping him on the spot. But the man's finger jerked in a spasm on the trigger and fired a shot into the air as he fell. The noise was like an alarm, a warning to the rest of the assault team. Bourne holstered his pistol, then took the M1 from the dead man in the dirt and moved into the next row.

This time, another man in black was waiting for him. Rifle leveled.

Bourne threw himself forward as bullets blistered the air. He felt heat burning across his back. He squirmed between the vines, then rolled and ended up on his back with the rifle pointed upward. Even before the second man charged between the rows, Bourne began firing, laying down a zigzag pattern of bullets. But the man was smart; he didn't show himself. Instead, Bourne felt rounds lacing the air just over his head. He skittered backward on his hands and feet, then crashed through a tall grape vine.

The man charged, aiming his rifle barrel, but he was down before he could fire. When the man pitched forward, Bourne saw Shadow immediately behind him, suppressed pistol at the end of her outstretched arms. She came and helped him up, and the two of them splashed side by side through the mud until they broke clear less than fifty yards from the house.

Three shooters had angles on the house, all stretched out in the tall grass, all with AR-M1s. From the porch, barricaded behind crates of wine, one old man held his ground. Teeling. But he was outnumbered and outgunned. With each rifle shot, wood splintered, glass broke, and wine trickled down the house steps like blood. Bourne raised his rifle and fired, shot after shot, moving up the body armor of one of the men until the bullets exploded his skull. Beside him, Shadow did the same. But there was one man left, and he rolled and fired, forcing the two of them to take cover on the ground.

On the porch, Teeling stood up. He had an M1, too, and he fired a single round, a perfect headshot that blew through the skull of the shooter with a crimson spray. Bourne got up and ran for the porch. Teeling saw him coming. His face dissolved into a grin and he lowered his rifle. Out of the corner of his eye, Bourne spotted Vandal emerging from one of the rows of vines not far away, her pistol steady in both hands. On his other side, Shadow took off for the back of the house, calling her father's name.

Bourne shouted to stop her from going off on her own. He jerked his body left to follow her, but as he did, he heard another warning shout from Teeling.

"Cain! Get down!"

His instincts took over, and Bourne dropped. A bullet pounded into the wooden beams of the porch where his head had just been. More bullets chased him as he crawled through the grass. He saw Teeling firing, targeting a shooter who'd bolted from the vines near Vandal. The man in black retrained his rifle at the old man on the porch, and Teeling stood rock-still as bullets flew around him. He calmly aimed back and unleashed half a dozen shots that ended with the man in black facedown in the long grass.

Bourne didn't wait for Teeling. He charged after Shadow, rounding the side of the house and seeing her running for the fields that led to the trees. He called after her again, but she ignored him. In the distance, a quarter mile away, he spotted a cluster of five armed men in the open grass, with a man held prisoner among them. He was tall, with a shock of silver hair.

A man he'd thought was dead.

A man he remembered.

David Abbott.

Above them, in the air, Bourne heard the throb of an engine. He saw a helicopter swoop over the tree line and angle its way toward the men in the field. Shadow saw it, too. She screamed; she kept running. Bourne ran as well, pounding through the tall grass as fast as he could to catch her. She shouted her father's name, and Bourne saw Abbott swing his arms, wildly waving her away before the men grabbed him again. She kept going, without a chance in the world of rescuing him, simply marching into a buzz saw of guns that would cut her down.

The men raised their rifles.

Bourne leaped. He landed squarely on Shadow's back and took her to the soft ground in his arms. Rifle fire assaulted the air like fireworks over their heads, and he held her down as she squirmed in his grasp and tried to get free. The noise of the helicopter got louder, almost deafening, and the earth vibrated beneath them. The rifle fire stopped. They heard shouts, and then, in seconds, the black helicopter rose up again like an insect and veered away. Bourne finally let go of Shadow, and they got back to their feet.

The field was empty.

They'd taken Shadow's father. *Marlen's* father. David Abbott was gone. She turned around and slapped Bourne so hard that the blow forced him backward. Then she broke down into tears and crumpled into his arms.

———

BOURNE AND TEELING STOOD NEXT TO EACH OTHER ON THE PORCH OF the ranch house, passing the Irish whiskey bottle back and forth between them. The longer he spent with the old agent, the more he remembered him from the Bahamas. Those memories led to other memories. He thought about Abbey Laurent and his on-again, off-again love affair with her years before he met Johanna; about the car bomb from Lennon that had nearly killed her; about the secrets of a Treadstone mission called Defiance and the death of the former secretary of state Alicia Beauvoir. A death at his own hands, a bullet from a long gun.

A death ordered by Holly Schultz.

Piece by piece, he began to assemble the details of his recent past, connecting the scraps like a shredded document slowly pasted together.

"It's good to see you, Cain," Teeling said. "Your timing is always impeccable. Although it seems like every time you show up, you blow up my life."

"I'm sorry about that."

"That's okay. I may be old, but I'm an adrenaline junkie."

"You've still got a hell of an eye, too. You saved my life with that last shot."

Teeling nodded with satisfaction, but then his face screwed up into a frown. He glanced toward Shadow, who sat in the tall grass near the grape vines, her head between her knees, her blond hair falling over her face. "I've never seen her like this."

"No. She's in bad shape."

"We used to joke in the agency that she was Triple C. Cold, calculating, controlled. I knew she and Abbott were close, but this feels like something more."

"It is," Bourne agreed, without elaborating. "I'm not sure how much help she's going to be going forward. If we're going to find Abbott and get him back, I think it's up to you and me. Assuming that adrenaline is still pumping in your veins."

"Definitely. I don't like the idea of losing him on my watch."

"We need to move fast. The clock is ticking. Wherever they took Abbott, they won't keep him there for long. The Russians will want him moved out of reach."

"The question is, where the hell is he?" Teeling said.

Bourne took a slug of the whiskey, which was smooth and warmed the inside of his chest. "I checked the bodies of the shooters we took down. Two of them had tattoos in Russian. I don't think Putin relied on mercenaries for this mission. He used his own team. I also found a receipt in one of their back pockets from a diner in Bucharest. Recent. It was two days ago. We're close to the border here, so if I had to bet, I'd guess the helicopter took them back to a staging ground in Romania where they planned the assault. But they'll make a plan to evacuate Abbott to Moscow, and they'll act fast. We have forty-eight hours at most."

"That's not a lot of time to find him and move in."

"So we need a source. Do you have any local contacts? Someone who might know what the Russians are up to?"

"Oh, yes, I know a slimy little Romanian asset in Sofia," Teeling said. "If the Russians have an op going across the border, odds are he'll have heard about it."

"Good. Then we need to go right away. I'll tell Shadow."

Bourne took a step down the porch, but Teeling grabbed his arm. "Cain, wait. There's one more thing."

"What is it?"

"The other Treadstone agent. Vandal. Where is she?"

"She's searching the SUVs the shooters left behind."

"How well do you know her?"

"I don't. Not anymore. Why?"

A scowl darkened the old agent's face. "She had the drop on the last shooter, and she didn't do shit."

"What are you talking about?"

"The guy that came out of the vines. The one who targeted you. Vandal had a gun in her hands; she was ten feet away from him. He didn't see her, but she saw him, she was right there where she couldn't miss. I didn't fire immediately because she had such an easy shot. But she didn't even raise her gun, Cain."

"So what was it? Panic? Shock?"

Teeling shook his head. "A Treadstone agent? No way. She made a choice. She knew exactly what she was doing. She was going to let him take you down, Cain."

23

BOURNE KEPT HIS GLOCK LOOSELY IN HIS HAND AS HE WALKED. NEAR-ing the side road from the highway, he saw Vandal leaning against one of the black SUVs that the Russian assault team had used. She had her Ruger in the holster on her left thigh, and her dark eyes followed him as he emerged from the fields. He tried to pierce the veil that blocked his memories of her, but the pain behind his eyes forced him to stop. Even so, he felt that strange sensation again of fire scorching his face.

And then nothing.

"Did you find anything?" he asked.

"The vehicles are clean. The plates are fake. But I ran a search on the VINs and it looks like they were sold in Romania. Odds are, the Russian team came across the border, and that's probably where the chopper took Abbott, too."

"Teeling and I came to the same conclusion," Bourne said.

"So time to saddle up and go get them?"

"Yes, but we need intel first. Teeling has a contact who keeps an ear to the ground about Russian ops in Romania."

Vandal was a cool customer, her eyes calm and direct, betraying nothing. If she suspected that he knew the truth, she didn't make it obvious. But her left hand stayed close to the butt of the Ruger. "How's Shadow?"

"Shaken."

"The ice queen melts. Interesting."

"She must trust you," Bourne said.

"Why do you say that?"

"To call you in as backup on a sensitive mission."

"I was useful. That's all. Shadow doesn't trust anyone. None of us do. That's rule number one."

"Yes, I remember the rules." Bourne's index finger tapped on the side of his Glock. She didn't miss the gesture. "What were you doing in Port Noir?"

"Excuse me?"

"How did you find me there?"

"I was already looking for you. Shadow has been trying to find you for a month. When I heard about the explosion in the Med, I played a hunch that you were involved. There were rumors of a big operation, of a man being pulled out of the water. Port Noir wasn't far, and I knew you had contacts on the island, so I thought you might go there."

"Smart," Bourne said.

"Thank you."

Her lips bent into the barest smile. Watching her, he felt it again. Heat. Fire. And then something more. He smelled gasoline in his nose, sharp and pungent. The night sky turned to daylight. He heard shouts, gunfire, and then the coolness of the water closing over his body as he sank below the surface.

Jesus!

He knew now. His mind saw that night on the sea again, the boats surrounding them, the frontal assault distracting them while someone slipped toward the *Stormy Weather* from the rear and planted the explosives. Vandal had been there. She'd been out in the Med when the boat blew up.

It was *her*!

And not just there. It was her in the Tuileries, too. She'd killed Nash as she tried to kill *him*.

Her face stayed impassive, no emotion, no twitch of guilt or nervousness. And yet she knew he'd figured it out. He could see calculation in her dark eyes, a tremor in her fingers near the Ruger. A part of him wanted to draw the Glock right now and fire. A bullet in her throat. Watch her die.

She'd killed Johanna.

But Vandal was the pawn, not the player.

"Come on," Bourne told her. "We'll take the Audi up to the house. We need to get on the road to reach Sofia by nightfall."

"Right behind you."

He walked past her toward the sedan, knowing what would happen next. She'd go for the gun; she had to do it. He listened for the rustle of metal on leather as she yanked her Ruger from the holster. When he heard it, he spun, his finger already on the trigger of his Glock, the barrel aimed at her face. She had the pistol in her hand, but she hadn't aimed it yet, and she knew she had half a second to drop it or take a bullet in her head.

Her fingers loosened. The Ruger banged to the dirt.

"Teeling saw me?" she asked.

"Right."

"I wondered if he did. I let the shooter go after you. I thought maybe he'd do my dirty work for me, and I wouldn't have to kill you myself. I really didn't want to do that, Cain. I like you."

"Who gave the orders? Was it Holly? CIA?"

Vandal sighed, staying quiet.

Bourne shook his head. "Do you really think I won't do to you what Shadow did to that Russian? I'll do it, and I'll enjoy it. You murdered Johanna. Someone's going to suffer for that. But I want the person who set it up."

Her eyes blinked shut. "Fuck."

"Talk to me. Tell me the truth."

"And then what? You kill me? You're not going to do that, Cain. You *owe* me."

"What are you talking about?"

"Last year in Paris, I helped you. I lied to Nash, and I helped you find Shadow when I was under specific orders not to do that. You said I had a quid pro quo whenever I needed it. Well, I need it now. I'm calling in the debt. You may not remember any of this, you may not remember *me*, but I'm not lying to you."

Bourne studied her face, and he didn't think she was lying. Whatever had happened in Paris, he was in her debt. That didn't stop him from wanting to pull the trigger and pay her back. But he didn't.

"All right. Tell me what's going on and you can go."

"I'm not sure giving you information is part of the deal," Vandal replied.

"The deal is whatever I say it is."

She stared at the barrel of the Glock and then at the rigid line of his jaw. "Okay. In the car, I said I told you things in Paris. Things about me, who I am, what I did. In my old life, I was high on drugs, and I murdered my husband. I went to prison. Nash got me out and brought me into Treadstone. But Holly Schultz found out about my background and used it against me. She can put me back inside any time she wants. I like being free again. So I agreed to work both sides."

"Nash said there was a kind of blood feud between the CIA and Treadstone. Why? What's it about?"

"That's above my pay grade, Cain."

"But Holly ordered you to kill me?"

Vandal nodded. "You and Johanna."

"*Johanna?* Why her?"

"I don't know, but the orders were for both of you. Either I did it, or she made sure I went back into that hole. And if it wasn't me, it would have been somebody else. Next asset on Holly's list."

"She still wants me dead?"

"Yeah."

"How does this involve David Abbott?"

"You think I make the strategy? You think I'm on the inside? I don't know anything. I kill people. Just like you. It's what we do."

"You killed Nash in Paris."

Her fists squeezed shut. "Yeah. I was aiming for you. But don't expect me to feel bad, Cain. Nobody in our business wears a white hat. We're all *morally compromised*. I told you once that you should feel lucky you can't remember the things you've done. Maybe that's how you've kept a shred of your soul alive. But me? Nash? All of the rest of us? We've already punched our tickets to hell."

Bourne let his finger slide off the trigger of the Glock. "Go."

She looked as if she didn't believe him. "And when I turn my back? Is that when you put a bullet in my head?"

"I keep my word. You're safe. But the quid pro quo is done as of now. We're even. Take the Audi and get out of here. My advice is you find somewhere in the world to hide and hope I never find you."

Vandal turned around slowly. She made no effort to recover the Ruger from the ground. She took a few steps down the road, then stopped and reversed course, her hands in the air. He still had the barrel of the Glock pointed toward her chest.

"I wasn't going to tell you this, but you've played fair with me. So I'll play fair with you. There's something else you should know."

"What is it?"

"Johanna's alive."

"What?"

"She's alive. She knows you're alive, too. She's looking for you, Cain."

Jason closed the distance between them in a few steps, and he pushed the Glock into Vandal's forehead. "If you're lying, I'll pull the trigger right now."

"I'm not lying. I saw her in Paris."

He took a step backward, and he let his gun arm go limp. Johanna. *Alive!* The woman he loved hadn't died on that boat. She was out there; she was looking for *him*. He still had a chance to get her back.

Maybe that part of his life wasn't over.

"Did you tell Holly?" he asked Vandal. "Does she know?"

"No, but Holly has sources everywhere. If Johanna is trying to find you, that means she's on the move. She has to reach out to contacts. She has to go places where she might be seen. If Holly doesn't know she's alive, she will soon. And when she does, she'll put Johanna back on the target list."

"Like me."

"Like you." Vandal hesitated. "But Holly's not your only threat. She's not even the closest threat."

"What do you mean?"

"Shadow knows about Johanna," Vandal said. "She didn't tell you that, did she?"

Bourne frowned. "No."

"That's why Shadow brought me in as backup," Vandal went on. "Because she knows Johanna will be coming after you. And for whatever reason, Shadow wants you for herself right now. She's not going to let Johanna get in the way of her plans. If Shadow sees Johanna coming, she'll kill her."

24

A HEAVY RAIN FELL ON THE CITY OF SOFIA, DRIVEN SIDEWAYS BY A
fierce wind. The huge cobblestone plaza surrounding the Nevsky
Cathedral became a lake, with ripples across the black surface of
the water. Bourne and Teeling stood in the trees opposite the cathedral. The sprawling church's whitewashed stone, and its gold
and green bubble domes, glinted through the silvery downpour.

It was almost midnight, and the rain had driven everyone else
inside.

Bourne heard Shadow's voice through the receiver in his ear.
"Any sign of your man?"

Teeling answered. "Not yet."

"He's late," Shadow snapped impatiently. "You told him eleven
thirty. Where is he?"

"Rayko's always late."

"Well, the little prick better come through."

Bourne heard a hard edge in Shadow's voice. From where he
was in the trees, he couldn't see the black SUV parked on the far

side of the plaza, but he knew Shadow was waiting there. She had night vision goggles to watch the meeting, and she could hear every word they said through the radio receivers. But he didn't trust her state of mind. This mission wasn't just about finding the former head of Treadstone, it was about finding her father. If things went wrong, if the plan to rescue David Abbott failed, he wasn't sure what she would do.

Or how far she would go.

He also didn't like that she was lying to him. Again. She'd let him think Johanna was dead even after Vandal told her the truth, and he was under no illusions about the ice in Shadow's veins. If Shadow got to Johanna first, Bourne would never even know about it. Johanna would simply disappear.

Teeling eyed him in the shadows, reading the darkness in his face. The old agent popped the receiver out of his ear and closed his fist around it. Bourne did the same thing, blocking the sound. For the moment, Shadow was cut off from their conversation.

"You see something wrong, Cain?"

"I'm not sure. This whole meeting feels off."

"Well, Shadow's right that Rayko is a prick. He'd double-cross me and slit my throat if there was enough money in it. But he'll think twice about making a move with you in the picture. Plus, you were able to get a hundred thousand lev wired from the Valois. I imagine that will keep him happy. He'll give us the information we need."

Bourne nodded, saying nothing. He still had a bad feeling.

"You're worried about Shadow?" Teeling asked.

"I am. She's got another agenda here."

"She always does. Do you have any idea what she's planning?"

Bourne shook his head. "No."

"What did you tell her about Vandal?"

"The truth. That Vandal's been playing both sides."

"How did she react?"

"She was furious that I let her go. She said I should have killed her."

"Maybe you should have, Cain. In our world, good deeds rarely go unpunished." Teeling checked his watch. "Now I *am* getting worried. My last source in Sofia wound up sliced in half by a train. I wonder if Rayko asked too many questions in the wrong places. Putin's not messing around with this operation."

Bourne gestured at the cathedral, where a small man in a Burberry raincoat and fedora made his way through the flooded plaza. He was a tiny silhouette against the glowing white church. "Is that him?"

"Ah, yes, there we go. That's Rayko. Alive and better late than never."

Bourne studied the area, his gaze moving from shadow to shadow around the church. "Looks like he's alone."

"All right. Let's see what he knows."

They inserted the radio receivers in their ears again, restoring the connection. Shadow's furious voice sliced immediately through the crackle of static. "*What the fuck's going on?* Why did you two cut me off?"

"So sorry, my dear," Teeling told her with a wink at Bourne. "Must be the rain interfering with the reception. It's these damn Eastern European radios. Looks like the signal is back now. Anyway, Rayko is here."

"I see him." Her voice was clipped and tense.

"Bourne says the area's clear. Is it the same from your end?"

"It is."

"Okay, we're heading in."

Together, Bourne and Teeling left the shelter of the trees, where the rain found them with a roar of the wind. Without cover, the downpour slapped their faces and ran down their backs. Bourne kept his hands in the pockets of his trench coat, fingers curled around his Glock. Teeling, next to him, wore a broad smile, as if he were happy to be back in the game and reliving the Cold War days at Checkpoint Charlie.

They neared the huge cathedral, dwarfed by the white walls towering over them. Rayko huddled under one of the arched doorways at the top of the steps, below a gold mosaic of Christ. He smoked a hand-rolled cigarette that drooped in the rain. The man was short, barely five foot three, with rust-colored bangs peeking out from under his hat. He was in his forties and had a pockmarked face with a bent, protruding chin and V-shaped nose. His pale blue eyes seemed to fidget because they were always moving.

Bourne noticed a fresh purplish bruise on one of the man's cheekbones. One of his hands was wrapped in a beige gauze bandage, and his whole arm looked oddly stiff under his raincoat. Teeling noticed it, too.

"Rayko! You look like you've been in a fight, old friend. What happened?"

"That's why I was late," the man replied, his voice high-pitched and nasal. "Half a dozen men stormed my building. I had to fucking go out the window. I'm on the goddamn fifth floor! I made it three floors, then lost my grip in the rain and dropped. Think I broke my fucking shoulder."

"Sorry to hear that. Who were they?"

"Russians, most likely. The network is blowing up with Russian ops. Something big's going down."

"And what would that be?" Teeling asked.

"Money first," Rayko insisted. "I don't say anything until I see the cash. Plus, the price just doubled. Two hundred thousand."

"I don't think so, Rayko. A deal's a deal."

"The deal didn't include me being blown. I can't go back to my apartment. Fuck, I'll probably have to leave the city. What did you get me into, Teeling? You asked me to get intel on some fucking Romanian kidnapping operation. I didn't expect to be pissing my pants as I ran from the GRU."

Bourne interrupted. "I've got another twenty thousand euro. Will that cover your pain and suffering?"

Rayko eyed Bourne through the rain, as if noticing him for the first time. "I know you. You're *Cain*."

"Who I am doesn't matter."

"It matters to me. I could have a *million* euro if I turned you in. That's the bounty Putin's willing to pay. He wants you fucking bad."

"This isn't a man you want to betray, Rayko," Teeling commented.

"Yeah, I'm not saying I would, but if Cain's involved, an extra twenty thousand is cheap."

Bourne shrugged. "Thirty."

"If you've got thirty, you've got fifty. Trust me, you're going to want the information I have, and you're going to want it fucking fast."

Bourne and Teeling exchanged glances, and Jason dug into the pockets of his coat. He found the envelope with one hundred thousand Bulgarian lev from the Valois and handed it to Rayko, and then he dug into his own stash to find an additional fifty thousand euros. The man's smile twitched happily, like the whiskers on a rat, as he shoved away the cash.

"Talk," Bourne said.

"Okay. You were right. The assault team was *echt* Russian, all GRU. They staged the mission out of Romania. That's where they took him."

"Took who?" Teeling asked. "Is the name out on the street?"

Rayko put a finger on the side of his nose. "Fuck yeah. David Abbott. That's why I knew you'd pay. Everybody knows he's been in the open for weeks, with half the world looking for him. If it wasn't the Russians, it would have been someone else."

"Is he alive?" Bourne asked.

"Yeah. At least for now. The orders were very clear about that. Abbott wasn't to be touched, not a silver hair on the lion king's head. Putin definitely wanted him alive. I presume he wants to squeeze him for intel. God knows Abbott could blow open every American black-ops mission around the world for the last thirty years."

Bourne frowned.

Something still felt off.

Yes, the secrets in Abbott's head were priceless, but a seasoned pro like Abbott was too smart to be broken. Even if he talked—and sooner or later, *everyone* talked—he'd spin out layers within layers of deception, until the Russians didn't know what to believe. They'd end up knowing less than when they started as they second-guessed and doubted the lies Abbott buried within every truth. Putin had to know that.

So why bring him in alive and risk a diplomatic incident? It wasn't worth it. As harsh as it sounded, the smart play was to *kill* Abbott. Wipe him off the board. King takes Bishop. Or in this case, King takes Monk.

"Where is he?" Bourne asked. "Where did they take him?"

"Bucharest. But not for long. The plan is to get him on a truck tomorrow night and take him to the port in Constanta. From there, they'll smuggle him on a tanker across the Black Sea to Russia. Everybody's nervous. They know they've got hot cargo and people like you will be hunting for him. Plus, if I've heard about it, the Romanians have, too, and they would love to fuck up one of Putin's ops. So the GRU is trying to keep it all under the radar, but the longer they wait, the more chance of this blowing up in their faces."

"Bucharest is a big place," Teeling said. "Where are they holding him?"

"Fuck if I know."

Bourne shot his fingers around Rayko's neck and shoved his Glock into the man's forehead. Rain poured between them. He lifted the little man into the air and pressed him against the heavy door of the cathedral. Rayko's limbs flailed, and he gagged as Bourne's fingers loosened just enough to let him breathe.

"I swear I don't know! I don't! But I know how you can find him."

Bourne dropped the man to the ground. "How?"

"I know the guy who's leading the extraction. He's not part of the wet team. He's not GRU, not even Russian. He's a fucking bureaucrat. He works in the Ministry of Transport. They need a local to grease the skids to get Abbott out of the country, make sure no one interferes. I don't know his real name, but the Russians call him Dihor. The ferret. He burrows inside the government and hides where no one sees him."

"Where do we find this Dihor?"

"He has a girlfriend. An actress, a fucking puppeteer. Her name's Crina. She lives next door to the Tandarica Theater, which does children's productions. She's one of their stars. The ferret is over there to fuck her every night at ten o'clock. You can set your watch by his dick. Find her, you'll find him. He'll lead you to Abbott."

Bourne glance at Teeling. "Do you believe him?"

Teeling gave Rayko's cheek several firm slaps. "You wouldn't lie to us, would you, old friend? Because you know what would happen to you if you did."

"I'm not lying! My source is gold. He's never wrong."

"Who's your source?" Bourne asked.

"Misha. He's a gay Russian prostitute. The GRU boys use him to blow off steam. They talk to each other, and he listens. You put enough vodka in those assholes, they'll give you the blueprints to Lubyanka."

"He's right about that," Teeling said, chuckling.

Bourne gestured toward the plaza. "All right. Get out of here."

The little Romanian didn't hesitate. He pushed past them down the steps and splashed through the cobblestones, and he was lost in the shadows a few seconds later. Bourne kept watching even after he was gone, making sure he saw no one else surveilling the cathedral. But they were alone. It had all gone off exactly as planned.

And yet.

"You still don't look happy, Cain," Teeling said.

"I'm not."

"You worry too much. To me, this feels on point. It's the kind of plan the GRU would use. Right people, right place. This is exactly how the Russians would try to smuggle a prize like Abbott out of the country."

"Yes, it has their fingerprints all over it," Bourne agreed. He stared across the plaza, where he could just make out the shape of the black SUV where Shadow was waiting for them. "So why do I feel like we're walking into a trap?"

———

THROUGH THE NIGHT VISION GOGGLES, SHADOW SAW THE GLOWING FIG-ure she recognized as Jason staring back at her. She heard the suspicion in his voice and wondered if that was going to be a problem. She stripped off the goggles, switched off her radio transmitter, and retrieved the secure Solarin phone she kept in a hidden pocket of her backpack. Her fingers tapped in numbers on the keypad from memory.

A man answered immediately. "So?"

"It's done. The plan's underway."

"Any problems?"

"No. Rayko was very convincing. Your people can eliminate him now."

"We will take care of it."

"Let me be very clear," Shadow told him. "If you double-cross me, I will declare war. No rules, no limits. You know perfectly well that I control the Files now. Betray me, and I will use the Files to root out and destroy your operations wherever I find them. Your people won't be safe anywhere in the world."

"Understood," the man replied. "You should have no worries on that front. Even enemies must work together sometimes when our interests align. Keep your part of the deal, and I will keep mine."

25

BLUE FOG POURED THROUGH THE STROBE LIGHTS AT KALEIDOSKOP. JO-
hanna pushed her way through the shoulder-to-shoulder crowd
that filled the Vienna nightclub at one in the morning. There were
no windows, just brick walls painted over with cartoons and erotic
poetry. The club was located underground, below an elevated
street that bordered the Donaukanal. Behind the dance floor, a DJ
dressed all in black spun electronic music by Cosmic Gate, the
beat so loud that Johanna felt it in her chest like a second heartbeat.

She was dressed to kill, in a strapless burgundy minidress that
sparkled in the lights, plus four-inch emerald heels. Her straight
blond hair hung to the middle of her bare back. She wore rectangular wraparound sunglasses, jewel-green to match her shoes. Her
purse dangled on a long spaghetti strap from her shoulder. That
was where she kept her SIG P365 micro-compact within easy
reach of her manicured fingers.

As the strobe lights panned across a sea of multicolored faces,
Johanna tried to spot Milena in the club. She hadn't heard from her

since the one text on the train to Vienna, and she wondered if the woman would really show, or if the text had been a ruse designed to lure Johanna out of hiding. But if Milena had truly sent the text herself, then Johanna was sure she would be here. The Czech spy had never made a secret of her physical attraction to Johanna, and Johanna had indulged her desires one hot August night by letting her go a little too far in a Prague hotel room.

The crowd writhed around her, following the beat. Most of the dancers were twentysomething foreigners, their eyes wild on whatever pills they'd taken. But there were others, too. Spies sharing intel. Spies watching spies. This was Vienna. Men in their thirties, in dark suits with skinny ties, hung out in whispered conversations near the graffiti-covered walls. Young women, pretending to be as high as the others, watched them with hawkish stares and took discreet pictures with their phones. Older men, older women, sipped whiskey and took note of who was with whom.

"Johanna."

She turned around. Milena was there, a grin spread across her white teeth. She was attractive, if you were into girls, twenty-seven years old with a mop of spiky chestnut hair. She wore knee-high boots and a low-cut bodycon dress. Pushing close, Milena slid her hands behind Johanna's neck and pulled their faces together in a wet tongue kiss. Johanna let herself enjoy it. Milena was a good kisser.

"You came," Johanna murmured when their mouths separated and they were still in each other's arms.

"Last time, so did you."

Johanna offered a broken smile at the double entendre. She felt

Milena's fingertips move down her bare back and land on her thighs where her dress ended. "Did you find someone who can help me?"

"I did, but what's the rush? Let's play a while."

Her long fingers sliding between Johanna's legs made clear exactly what she meant.

"The rush is, I was spotted on the train to Vienna," Johanna said. She gave Milena another kiss, then murmured in her ear. "Much as I'd love to go another few rounds with you, I need to get out of the city fast."

Milena's face darkened. Her hands returned to the small of Johanna's back, and she leaned her warm cheek against Johanna's face. Together, they moved sinuously to the urgent thump of the synthesizer. "Do you know who saw you?" she whispered.

"CIA."

"They want you? Why?"

"I'm a popular girl."

"The CIA's here tonight. I've seen at least two agents. Do you think it's a coincidence, or are they looking for you?"

"It's Vienna. Could be just a spy thing. But if they spot me, it won't be good."

"All right. Let's find Sabine."

"Who is she?"

"Romanian SIE. Scary bitch."

"What makes you think she'll talk?"

"I have my ways," Milena replied, flicking her tongue across her lips.

Milena took Johanna's hand, and the two of them squeezed across the dance floor. The sheer number of people in the club, and the shattering volume of the music, made it hard to breathe. Lights painted them in crazy colors. Near the DJ booth, Johanna spotted an incredibly tall woman dancing by herself. She had to be six foot five in her stiletto heels. The woman was built with curves and muscles, like a WWE fighter. She wore black lipstick, and her head was completely bald, hair shaved down to her smooth peach scalp, no eyebrows, and plucked eyelashes. A brass bull ring shined in her nose.

"See what I mean?" Milena said. "Scary."

When Sabine spotted Milena, she reached out and slung a long arm possessively around the Czech spy's shoulders. Milena nodded at Johanna and introduced her, and Sabine crushed Johanna's fingers with a hug that felt like a punch from Mike Tyson.

"American?" Sabine said.

"Yeah."

"I hate Americans."

"Most of them hate me, too," Johanna replied.

Sabine gave a throaty laugh and slapped Milena's ass. "You were right. This one's cute."

"Did Milena explain what I want?" Johanna asked. She felt like she was shouting, but the music was so loud she had to put her lips near Sabine's ear to be heard.

"She did. I've got what you need. Come on, let's go somewhere more private."

Sabine grabbed Johanna with her other hand and guided the three of them down a black-painted hallway away from the dance floor. The music grew more muffled. At the end of the hall was a toilet, and Sabine pushed open the door to let out a vile smell. The toilet was lit by a single bulb, and the walls were completely covered over in mirrors, multiplying their reflections everywhere they looked. There were two stalls, neither one of which had a lock that worked, and one stall was occupied.

"*Raus, geh, weg!*" Sabine announced to the half-open door. "Get out!"

"*Bin nicht fertig,*" a squeaky woman's voice replied.

"You're done now."

The hairless Romanian spy pushed open the door and dragged a young redheaded woman to her feet off the toilet. The woman stumbled, yanking up her underwear, and then spat out a curse as she lurched through the door. Sabine shouted a curse back and turned the dead bolt behind her. The closed door shut out most of the club's thundering music, but the walls vibrated like a tuning fork.

Sabine dug a small metal pillbox out of her purse. She dipped in a small plastic spoon and then inhaled cocaine with a snort. She sniffled, went to one of the mirrored walls, and wiped her nose and checked her makeup.

"Okay," she said, turning around. She folded her meaty arms across her chest and stared down at the two other women from her six-foot-five height. "You want to talk? We can talk here."

"You're not concerned about cameras?" Johanna asked, eyeing the glass panels on the walls. "Or bugs? Half the spies in Vienna are in this place."

"Yeah, and the toilet is Switzerland. For years, one side put in wires, the other side tore them out. Eventually we all came to an understanding. Let everybody take a shit in peace. Speaking of which."

Sabine yanked up her skirt to reveal that she was as bald down under as she was on top. She went and sat on the stall and didn't

bother closing the door. "So you want to find Cain, huh? You looking for Putin's bounty? Because I don't help the Russians do what
they do. If that's what you're about, I'll strangle you myself."

"I'm trying to help Cain, not hurt him."

"How do I know that's true?"

"You don't. But if you know about Cain, you know he almost
died in an explosion in the Med. He wasn't alone. I was with him."
She extended her arm, showing off the alligator skin of the burn
that extended from her wrist to her elbow. "I got that when the
bomb blew me off the fucking boat."

"All right. Good enough for me."

"So what do you know?"

"Depends. What do I get? Milena here has a talented tongue—
I bet you already know that—but news about Cain is worth more
than sex."

"What do you want? Money?"

"I have plenty of money. I want intel. Something I can use."
She stood up from the toilet and didn't bother to flush, and wiped
her hands on her dress. "You were Treadstone. You must have secrets you can trade."

"I know David Abbott is alive," Johanna said.

"Old news. Do better."

"The CIA and Treadstone are at each other's throats."

"Bureaucratic turf wars. Who cares? Next."

Johanna searched her mind for another secret that had currency, and she landed on the one David Abbott had used to try to
sway her to come forward. "Adam Hill is a Chinese spy. Has been
for years."

Sabine let out a long, low whistle. "Seriously? You got proof?"

"No, but I've got good sources."

"That makes it not much better than gossip."

"Yeah, but it's very juicy gossip."

Sabine opened her mouth wide and laughed. "Ha! You're right, it is. Very juicy. Don't know if it's worth anything, but I'll take it. This one is definitely cute, Milena. Definitely. Makes me want to tap her myself."

"Another time," Johanna said. "Tell me about Cain."

"He's on his way to Bucharest."

"You're sure? How do you know?"

"There's a big Russian op going down in the city tomorrow night. Word is, Cain's in the middle of it. Normally, the SIE would be looking to bust it up, but we got orders to stand down. Let it play out."

"Why?"

"Don't know, but the order had to come from the Americans. Nobody else would have the clout."

"Wait, so the Americans ordered you *not* to intervene in a Russian op on Romanian soil?"

"That's the size of it."

"What's the op?"

"No idea. It's a GRU thing, from what I hear. Like I said, it's a big deal, and it involves a high-value target. My assumption is, Cain is trying to take the mission apart, but for some reason, they don't want outsiders involved. Maybe it's because of Treadstone. We all know Shadow doesn't like sharing the glory."

Johanna frowned. "It must be David Abbott. They must have

found where he's hiding. Cain's trying to get him out before the GRU moves in."

"Don't think so," Sabine replied.

"Why not?"

"Because the rumor among my boys is that the GRU already has him. They grabbed Abbott at a farm outside Varna on the Black Sea coast. They brought him back across the border, and they had a jet waiting at a private airfield. In and out of the country in half an hour, the bastards. I have no idea where Abbott is. Maybe Belarus, maybe already in Moscow. But he's not in Romania. I'm sure of that."

———

SLEEP IS A WEAPON.

Treadstone.

Bourne knew he needed sleep. Tiredness took away his edge. He'd trained himself to sleep anywhere, to revive himself with no more than an hour or even half an hour on long nights. But tonight, his body betrayed him, and even when he closed his eyes, he found himself staying awake.

They'd left Sofia after the meeting with Rayko, driving northeast toward Bucharest and eventually outrunning the rain. They avoided the major highways and stayed to the back roads, which slowed them down. At four in the morning, in the midst of farm fields with no houses in any direction, they'd pulled off the road near an abandoned stone barn to rest. Bourne parked the black SUV where it couldn't be seen. Teeling stretched in the back of the vehicle, and Shadow found a soft bed of straw inside the barn's crumbling brick walls.

Bourne lay on his back out in the green fields, but his mind refused to slow down. When he was still awake ten minutes later, he gave up and took a walk in the darkness, beneath the bright stars. He checked on Teeling, who was snoring in the back of the SUV. At the barn, he moved silently through the crumbling doorway and went inside. Shadow was there, nearly invisible in the darkness, but she was awake, too, watching him.

He sat down beside her. Her blond hair was mussed, her clothes covered with bits of straw.

"Can't sleep?" she murmured.

"No."

"Me neither."

"Teeling's out cold," Bourne said.

"So why not you?"

Bourne's voice hardened, and he turned to stare into her blue eyes in the darkness. "Maybe because I found out from Vandal that Johanna's alive. Maybe because you knew that and didn't tell me."

Shadow was quiet for a while. He didn't expect her to apologize; she never did. "If I told you she was alive, she'd be in your head. I need you focused on this mission, Jason. Not distracted. Johanna is a distraction."

"You can't control everything, Marlen. Or everyone."

"That doesn't mean I can't try."

"Did you know she was alive when we had sex?" Jason asked.

"No."

"Would it have mattered?"

"Not at all. Would it have mattered to you?"

"I don't know."

"Well, let's find out."

Shadow put a hand on one of his shoulders and guided his body down into the straw. He could have stopped her, he could have pushed her away, but he didn't. She climbed on top of him, knees on either side of his hips. Her hands explored his clothes, moving everywhere, pushing inside his pockets, feeling under the buttons of his shirt, tracing his scars, tugging at his belt. The warmth of her was between his legs, grinding down. He didn't want to respond, but he did anyway. She knew it; she felt it.

"Sex is physical," she told him softly. "Chemical. It doesn't need to be anything more than that. I want it. You obviously want it, too. Love the one you're with, Jason. Then we can both get some sleep."

"I don't think it was just physical between us on Naxos," he said.

"What do you think it was?"

"I think we're obsessed with each other and have been from that first moment in Marnes-la-Coquette. I think we're very good for each other and very, very bad for each other at the same time."

"Is that so different from your other lovers? Do you think Johanna is good for you? Because she's not."

"Whether she's good or bad doesn't change anything. I'm in love with her."

"I don't think you are, Jason. I think you're just looking for your past, especially right now. How can you love someone you barely remember? Once upon a time, you loved me, but you didn't remember that. I didn't even exist for you until we met again last year. But I'm here tonight. I'm the present, not the past."

Shadow leaned forward, her blond hair falling over him, and she kissed him hard, not hiding her desire.

"Live for the moment, Jason," she whispered in his ear. "God doesn't owe us any tomorrows. Tomorrow you may be dead."

26

"THAT'S OUR GIRL," BOURNE SAID. "CRINA."

He focused his binoculars on the sidewalk outside Bucharest's Tandarica Theater. A woman with a swirl of black hair, in her thirties, emerged from inside and stepped into the glow of the streetlight. He recognized her from the actor's gallery he'd found online. She was thin and pale, with tattoos all over her arms and a face studded with piercings. She wore a black lace top, nearly sheer, and tight-fitting blue jeans.

Bourne checked his watch. It was almost ten o'clock in the evening. If Rayko was right, the transfer of David Abbott to a truck headed for the Black Sea coast would be happening soon. It would take place somewhere in the city, but they didn't know where. And so far, after an entire day surveilling the theater and the adjacent apartment building, they'd seen so sign of the Romanian transport official whom the Russians called Dihor. The ferret. The man who was supposed to be masterminding Abbott's extraction.

"Maybe our friend's not coming tonight," Teeling commented.

"Do we squeeze Crina? Get her to text Dihor and find out where he is?"

"Let's give it a few more minutes. I don't want to make him nervous. If he thinks Crina has been compromised, he might change the plan."

Bourne continued to watch the street in both directions. They'd parked the black SUV on the sidewalk a block away, surrounded by other vehicles jammed bumper to bumper. The street was barely wide enough for one-way traffic to squeeze through. Pedestrians crowded the late-evening restaurants, standing outside to smoke, their loud voices carrying through the windows. At the end of the street, the theater had a huge marquee posted above the entrance, featuring oversized photographs of monsters and puppets from their children's productions. Next door was a four-story apartment building made of water-stained yellow stone, with scalloped windows like a mosque.

Shadow leaned forward between the seats, a hand on Bourne's shoulder. Her perfume floated in the air. "It's ten o'clock. Rayko said you could set your watch by Dihor showing up for sex. So we'll see what happens. A man wants what a man wants, especially with the right woman."

She didn't look at him, and Bourne gave her no reaction.

But she was right. He glanced in the sideview mirror and saw headlights approaching down the one-way street. A white Renault sedan passed them, its windows tinted black so that no one could look inside. The car pulled up to the sidewalk outside the apartment building, and Bourne watched Crina sidle toward the vehicle, no hurry in her walk. She opened the passenger door and leaned inside to talk to the driver. A few seconds later, her face broke into a little smirk of pleasure. She looked both ways up and down the sidewalk, then got in and pulled the door shut behind her.

"Dihor?" Teeling asked.

"Could be. Let's see where they go."

But the car didn't move, even though the Renault's engine continued to run. It stayed where it was, pedestrians strolling past the car in both directions. Bourne waited. Less than five minutes later, the passenger door opened again. Crina climbed out, her lace top rumpled, her tongue flicking across her lips. She wiggled her fingers in a little wave at the man inside the car, then slammed the door behind her and headed for her apartment building.

"Ah." Shadow grinned. "Well, that saves time, doesn't it? I guess he's in a hurry."

Bourne switched on the engine of the SUV and settled in behind the sedan as the Renault pulled away from the curb outside the theater. Dihor—if it really was the ferret behind the wheel—didn't look concerned about being followed from his rendezvous. He drove at a steady speed through the city, made no unexpected turns to shake a tail, and gave no indication that he was aware of the SUV keeping pace two blocks behind him. Easy.

But Bourne didn't trust missions that came too easy.

The Renault took them on a nighttime tour of Bucharest. The theater was located on the north side of the city, and Dihor headed due south, staying with narrow one-way streets that wound between the old buildings. He grazed the edge of Old Town and bumped over streetcar tracks, then crossed over the wide Boulevard Unirii. The traffic thinned. South of downtown, he made a series of turns through a warren of wooded streets, tucked among parks and tall apartment buildings. Along the way, Bourne kept an eye on his own mirrors, and he followed the man's GPS route on his dashboard, making sure the Renault wasn't taking them into an ambush.

Half an hour later, they reached a quiet street one block east of Strada Foişorului. Bourne let the distance between the vehicles widen, keeping sight of the taillights ahead of him. He passed ten-story apartment buildings built of drab concrete, with bars on the lower windows and garbage bins lined up on the street. Tall trees bent over the pavement, and low iron fences ran along the side-walks. Ahead of him, where the GPS showed a sharp left turn leading to a dead end, the taillights turned to brake lights. The Renault came to a stop.

Bourne pulled the SUV to the curb a hundred yards behind the sedan. The neighborhood around them was empty. He saw the driver's door open on the Renault, and he grabbed his binoculars. A man got out, passing briefly under a streetlamp, and Bourne saw that he was medium-sized, in a brown suit, with a mustache, short camel-colored hair, and a long face. He did look a little like a ferret as he sniffed the air. The man looked cautiously up and down the street, then continued on foot toward the dead end.

"Come on," Bourne told the others.

All three of them climbed out of the SUV, each with semiau-tomatics in their hands. They walked silently down the street, hearing the low noise of people in the apartments over their heads through open windows. When they reached the turn where Dihor had left the Renault, Bourne held up a hand to stop them. Cars were parked up and down the dead end. He didn't see Dihor on the street ahead of them, but he did see a squat blue shipping truck with can-vas sides parked where the street ended. A high, windowless concrete wall rose immediately behind it. The truck faced them, where it could easily head out of the downscale neighborhood and return to the city's main streets.

And then continue east toward the Black Sea.

The plan is to get him on a truck tomorrow night and take him to the port in Constanta.

"I think we're in the right place," Bourne said.

He sighted his binoculars on the cab of the truck, and he could make out a driver behind the wheel, underneath the dome light. Not Dihor. The driver had a shaved head and a round, beefy face, and his torso jiggled to the booming noise of rock music from his radio. The five-story concrete building loomed in back of the truck.

Bourne handed the binoculars to Shadow, who studied the scene for herself.

"You think that's where they've got Abbott?" she murmured.

"Looks that way."

Her voice sharpened. "Dihor's coming back."

Bourne took the binoculars again. He saw the weasel in the brown suit emerge from the side of the building. The man made a slow circuit around the shipping truck, and Jason could hear the clip-clop of his dress shoes on the pavement. At the window of the truck, Dihor spoke briefly to the driver, then tapped the watch on his wrist. Something was happening, and it was happening soon.

"Shadow, stay with the truck," Bourne whispered. "If it starts to move, stop it. Teeling, let's have a chat with the ferret."

The two men veered into the trees between the streets, where they were out of view from the blue truck. They walked quickly but quietly through the grassy park. As they neared the concrete wall at the dead end, they slipped out of the trees and took up position at the back of the truck, near the corner of the driver's side. They could hear the radio, which was playing Aerosmith at a loud volume. The building was no more than ten feet behind them. Dihor was still talking to the driver, but Bourne heard footsteps as the man headed their way.

He timed his assault. Just as Dihor cleared the back of the truck, Bourne's arm shot out like a snake and yanked him sideways. He clapped one hand over the man's mouth, and he pressed the barrel of his Glock into the ferret's forehead. "Make a sound, and I pull the trigger," he whispered into his ear.

Jason glanced at Teeling. "Keep an eye on the driver. If he hears anything, he might try to warn the others."

Teeling gave him a smile. "Steven Tyler's really belting it out. You could peel off this guy's fingernails and I don't think the driver would hear it."

The ferret's eyes widened with fear.

Teeling stayed near the corner of the truck as Bourne dragged Dihor to the concrete wall of the building a few feet away. He shoved the man's face sideways into the stone and hissed into his ear, "I'm going to take away my hand now, and we're going to talk. You try to shout, I erase you. Got it?"

Dihor nodded frantically.

"You're arranging transport. What's the plan?"

The man couldn't talk fast enough. He was a bureaucrat, not a spy. "At midnight, the prisoner goes in the truck. We put him in a shipping crate; there are plenty of others if anyone looks. The men watch him in back, I stay up front with the driver in case there are problems. But there won't be problems. That's what I'm paid for.

I've got the route to the coast cleared, no police. Paperwork is all done at the port. We put him on the ship, and he's not my problem anymore."

"Who's the prisoner?"

"I don't know. A high-value target, that's all I'm told. I don't need details, and I don't ask."

"Where is he?"

"Fifth floor, an apartment in the middle of the hallway."

"How many men are with him?"

"Three."

"What weapons?"

"I don't know. They have guns, pistols, I couldn't tell you what they are."

"What's the prisoner's condition?"

"Tied up. Gagged. Blindfolded. But conscious. To me, he looks unharmed."

"What does he look like?"

"Tall, silver hair. Older, maybe sixties."

Bourne gestured at Teeling, who left the truck and joined them. With the gun against the ferret's neck and his hand tightly on the man's collar, Jason pushed him along the wall toward the side of the building. He glanced back at the truck, but in the darkness, he didn't think the driver could see them if he checked his side mirror. The three of them pushed forward along the building wall, past window openings molded roughly in the stone. Some of the windows had bars; some had roll-down shutters. This wasn't an area where you left your windows open at night. At the front corner of the building, Bourne stopped and pulled Dihor back, then checked the area.

He listened, hearing nothing, and he saw no additional guards watching from the shadows. Cigarette butts littered the pavement, but he didn't smell fresh smoke. With a shove, he pushed Dihor forward again, and the man led them to the building doors a few steps away. Above the entrance was a camera, but it had been tilted up to aim at the sky. The doors were locked, but Dihor took a key from the pocket of his suitcoat and let them inside. They faced a hallway with stained red carpeting that stretched the length of the building. Doors on both sides led to individual units, and a stairwell through a door on their left climbed to the upper floors. There was no elevator.

Dihor took the steps with Bourne and Teeling behind him. Their footsteps echoed on metal. At each floor, Bourne stopped and checked the hallway, but he saw no one. When they got to the top floor, Bourne exited first with his Glock, and Teeling kept a tight grip on Dihor. They faced another empty hallway.

Bourne put a finger over his lips. "Number?" he asked softly.

"It's 525. Halfway down on the left."

"Layout?"

"Main room and kitchenette, two bedrooms, one on each side. The three men are in the main room with the prisoner."

"Do you have an all-clear code when you knock?"

"Yes. Yellow."

"If that's really the duress code, you won't make it out of the building alive."

"I understand."

"One shout to warn them, and you're dead."

The ferret nodded.

Step by step, they inched down the hallway. Bourne listened at each door, but the only sounds he heard were televisions and drunken laughter. He studied Dihor's face, seeing fear and nerves, but the man stayed dead silent and kept his arms in the air. The numbers on the doors climbed in fives: 500, 505, 510. As they approached 525, Bourne listened at the doorframe, but no one moved or spoke on the other side. Teeling checked the apartment on the opposite side of the hallway and nodded. All clear.

Bourne gestured at Dihor with the Glock.

The man knocked on the door. "Dihor. Yellow."

Bourne pushed the ferret out of the way. He heard footsteps and waited with his eyes on the doorknob. As it began to turn, he reared back and kicked the door hard with his boot, slamming it inward against the person on the other side. Leading with his gun, he kept low and charged through the opening, moving left, and Teeling did the same behind him, moving right. They both leveled their barrels.

In the next moment, they let their pistols fall to the floor.

There were not three men with pistols in the apartment, guarding a prisoner.

There were eight men in body armor, with Kalashnikov AK-12 assault rifles locked in their grips. The men made a semicircle around the apartment, which was completely empty, stripped of furniture. From the hallway behind them, Bourne heard the opposite apartment door open, and then there was a thunder of footsteps. Four more men came through the doorway, the barrels of their rifles shoving Bourne and Teeling into the middle of the empty space.

Dihor followed. The ferret's animal face wore a little smile, his mustache bending upward. He dug in his pocket for a pack of Russian cigarettes, and patiently lit one and blew smoke into the air. With a flick of his hand, he gestured at Teeling, and before Bourne could do anything to stop them, one of the assault team jabbed the metal barrel of his rifle hard into the middle of the old agent's skull.

Teeling crumpled to the floor. Blood trickled down his bald scalp. When Bourne began to move to help him, Dihor shook his head, and all of the men marched a step closer in unison, their guns ready.

Bourne stopped. There was nowhere to go.

"So you are the infamous Cain," Dihor announced. His Romanian-accented English had switched to flawless Russian. "This moment has been a long time in the making. I was indeed hired to oversee transport tonight, my friend. But as you may have guessed by now, the high-value target is you."

27

JOHANNA HID HER MOTORBIKE INSIDE THE TREES ACROSS FROM THE
Bucharest apartment building. Behind the black shield of her helmet, she murmured into the microphone of a headset. "Am I in the
right place?"

The voice of the Romanian SIE operative, Sabine, came
through her earpiece.

"*Da*, that's the building. We were given a clear zone on that
space and the surrounding two blocks all night. No investigation,
no entrance. Word went out to the police, fire, and medical units,
too. Any emergency calls come from that building, ignore them
and wipe the calls from the server."

"All right. Thank you for your help."

"What help? We never talked. *Noroc*."

"Understood."

Johanna ended the call and powered down her phone. Taking
off her helmet, she marched carefully across the parking lot toward
the building entrance. Her Ruger was in her hand. She expected a

heavy reception, but as far as she could tell, the area was deserted. At the door, she noted the angle of the security camera tilted to point at the sky. The door was locked, so she jabbed the window hard with the barrel of her gun, then reached through the broken glass and twisted the knob.

She slipped inside the building. It was one in the morning, and the interior was quiet. She crept to one end of the long hallway, then back, stopping at each apartment door to listen. She heard nothing. When she was back at the entrance, she took the stairs to the second floor and repeated the process. So far, there was no indication of why this apartment building had been designated a no-go by the Romanian security service, and nothing to suggest the GRU were mounting an operation here.

However, when she was on her way to the building's fourth floor, she froze on the stairwell. Above her, from the top floor, she heard the clang of the exit door. Moments later, heavy footsteps banged on the stairs, coming toward her at a slow, awkward pace. She was close enough to hear labored breathing from whoever it was.

Johanna raised her Ruger into firing position, slid her finger over the trigger, and waited.

An old man stumbled around the turn of the stairwell. He had a gun in one hand; his other hand was pressed against the back of his head. He'd torn off one of his shirtsleeves to hold it against his skull. Johanna could see blood on his neck and face and on his bare shoulder, where it trickled down his arm. The man didn't see her immediately, but when he came around the landing and spotted her on the stairs, he made an effort to raise his gun.

"Don't," she snapped.

The old man complied. He didn't have the energy to do

anything else. He slumped sideways against the building wall, then slid down on his ass to the metal landing. His gun slipped from his fingers. When he leaned his head back against the wall, he winced sharply as pain radiated through his skull. He watched her warily as he dragged air into his lungs, his chest swelling harsh and fast.

"Who are you?" Johanna asked, coming up the stairs and looming over him.

"I'm Teeling." He stared back through narrowed eyes and continued in a raspy voice. "Who are *you?*"

"Johanna."

"As in Cain's Johanna?"

Her heart raced. "You know Cain? Where is he?"

Teeling didn't answer right away. His skin was pale, and he was still losing blood. Johanna holstered her gun and checked the back of his head. She peeled away the torn sleeve and saw a sticky red mess on his bald skull. With a quick tug, she tore off his other sleeve and held it gently in place against the wound.

"Are you Treadstone?" she asked.

Teeling nodded.

"So was I," Johanna told him. "Once upon a time. Where's Cain?"

"I don't know. We hit the apartment together, but now he's gone."

"What happened?"

Teeling took a minute to gather his strength. "It was a trap. He and I went to an upstairs room. We were looking for—"

"David Abbott," Johanna said.

"Yes. We had intel the Russians were holding him here. They were planning to transport him out of the country tonight."

"According to my intel, Abbott's already gone."

"So it seems. They knew we were coming. When we went into the apartment, we were surrounded immediately. An entire assault team with Kalashnikovs. Apparently their orders didn't include taking me with them. One of them knocked me out cold. I only regained consciousness a few minutes ago. The apartment was empty. Everyone was gone. Including Cain."

"*Fuck*. Do you know where they took him?"

"No, but there was a shipping truck downstairs for the exfil. Shadow's watching it, assuming they didn't take her, too. Supposedly the plan was to take Abbott by truck to Constanta and then ferry him to Russia across the Black Sea. But I imagine that was a ruse like everything else."

"*Shadow*." Johanna didn't try to hide the hatred in her voice. "Come on, let's see if we can find her."

She helped Teeling to his feet. He put a hand behind his head to hold the fragment of sleeve in place, and she slung an arm around his waist and let him lean his weight into her. Together, slowly, they nudged down the stairwell step-by-step. At the front door, they exited into the cool night air and Teeling gestured around the corner. They followed the building wall to the dead-end street, but when they got there, Teeling shook his head.

"The truck's gone."

"What about Shadow?"

"She was surveilling from the other end of the street. We were using a black SUV we took from the Russians in Varna. It's parked on the cross street."

"Stay here," Johanna told him. "Sit down."

"I think I will."

"I'll get you to a hospital."

Teeling offered a weak smile. "In the old days, I would have been a tough guy and said no, but right now, my eyes are seeing two of you. It's a pretty sight, my dear, but I suspect it means I have a concussion."

Johanna smiled, too. "I'll be right back."

She jogged to the end of the block. In the wet grass near the trees, she found footprints, and she guessed that was where the Treadstone team had kept an eye on the shipping truck that was supposed to transport David Abbott. Shadow wasn't there, but her presence lingered in the air. Wind Flowers. That was the perfume Shadow had worn since the day Johanna had met her. A finger of cold wriggled up Johanna's back, and she felt watched, as if Shadow were still close by, studying her from somewhere in the darkness. She turned around slowly, making a full circle, but she saw no one.

Johanna checked the cross street. The black SUV was still parked where Teeling had described it. Shadow hadn't left in the vehicle; she hadn't followed the truck. Had the Russians taken her, too?

No. Shadow was too good to be captured like that.

This was something else.

She retraced her steps to the dead-end street, where Teeling was sitting on the ground. His closed eyes opened to slits when he heard her coming. He read the anger on her face and knew what that meant.

"Nothing?"

"Nothing. Shadow's gone, but she left the SUV."

"That's strange," Teeling said.

"I don't think it is. Do you have a contact number for the burner phone Shadow's using?"

"I do."

Johanna switched on her phone and waited as it acquired signal. Then she tapped in the numbers that Teeling recited for her. She heard ringing as the call went through, and she waited, imagining Shadow staring at her phone and wondering if it was safe to answer. Then she heard that cold, despicable voice, which crawled like a worm inside her brain.

"Teeling?" Shadow asked with cautious suspicion. "Is that you?"

"No, it's not."

A long beat of silence followed. "Ah. Johanna. So it's true. You're alive."

"I am."

"How is Teeling? He's the only one who has this number, so you must be with him."

"He's hurt. He needs a hospital."

"That's unfortunate. My instructions were that he not be harmed. But sometimes it's hard to keep the genie in the bottle."

"Where is Jason?"

Shadow sighed. "Stand down, Johanna. Leave this alone. Jason's my concern, not yours. I'll deal with him."

"You think I'm going to walk away? Not a chance."

"There's nothing between the two of you anymore. Your relationship was always a mirage. So why don't you let it go?"

"Why don't you go fuck yourself?"

"Oh, he's been doing that for me," Shadow replied with cool smugness in her voice.

Johanna felt her muscles clenching like taut springs. She wanted to believe Shadow was simply taunting her, but she could hear the truth in her voice. Jason had lost his memory and fallen into her clutches again. "Just tell me where he is."

"Jason's on a mission."

"To do what? Where? Teeling said the Russians ambushed him in the apartment. You obviously set the whole thing up. *Why?*"

"This conversation is over."

"Tell me the truth, or I'll *kill you*! I fucking swear I will!"

"Goodbye, Johanna."

The phone went dead. Johanna shoved it in her pocket and squeezed her fists against her forehead. Below her, Teeling's raspy voice took on a hard edge. "Shadow betrayed us, didn't she? She sent us into the trap. She planned the whole thing."

Johanna nodded, but stayed silent. She felt her entire world crashing down around her, and she felt old, wild hatreds coming back to life. If Shadow had been in front of her, she would have killed her with her bare hands. It didn't matter if Shadow fired a gun at her, one bullet after another, she still would have found the strength to strangle away that woman's evil, heartless life.

"The question is why," Teeling said. "Why the hell would she do that?"

"Isn't it obvious?" Johanna replied, shaking her head.

Teeling took a moment to think, and then his eyes closed wearily. "Abbott."

"Yeah. That fucking traitorous bitch sold Jason out. She traded him to the Russians to get David Abbott back. Putin has Bourne."

PART THREE

28

BLACK CLOUDS SWARMED THE BALTIC SEA HORIZON, THREATENING A
storm that would roll in with nightfall. On a narrow strip of Polish
beach, angry waves surged against the sand. Shadow drove an
ATV that plowed through the surf and kicked up clouds of spray
behind her. She was alone and unarmed, a situation that carried
enormous risk. But you didn't bring guns to the Russian border if
you wanted to stay alive.

In the hour after sunset, the high dunes looming over the
beach were deserted. She made a careful study of the ridgeline to
be sure she wasn't being watched. Or targeted. As far as she knew,
no one on her side had any idea where she was. Not Treadstone.
Not the CIA. She'd traveled from Bucharest to Gdańsk on a Lufthansa commercial flight, using a disguise for the security cameras
and a legend she'd built on her own, without agency resources. She
was Petra Cavalli, a German advertising executive from Frankfurt
who managed accounts in Eastern Europe. Another in her long
line of identities.

Only the Russians knew she was coming, but that was dangerous enough. She wouldn't have been shocked if they'd sent a sharpshooter across the border to take her out from the Polish side. A long gun could easily pinpoint her from the thick brush on the slope, and she'd be dead before her brain even had time to process it.

In a perfect world, the shooters hiding on the dunes would have been hers. She would have placed at least three Treadstone agents in position to provide backup. Not that she had any intention of firing on the Russians, but shooters provided a deterrent effect if her enemies had betrayal on their minds. Even so, she couldn't risk it. She didn't trust her own people. If Vandal could be compromised, so could others, and she had no idea how far Holly Schultz had gone in infiltrating Treadstone.

So Petra Cavalli came here on her own.

Shadow brought the ATV to a stop in the dry sand above the tide line. She climbed out onto the beach, and used binoculars to confirm again that she hadn't been followed. Behind her was Poland. Ahead of her, marked by a ribbon of fence climbing the beach and a sign to warn away curious tourists, was Russia. This narrow stretch of land was the Vistula Spit, stretching along the Baltic Sea between the Gulf of Gdańsk and the Vistula Lagoon. It marked a fragile border between East and West.

The location had been chosen by the Russians. Neutral ground, away from most prying eyes, with any kind of trap or surveillance easy to spot. Even so, she was sure that somewhere on the Russian side of the border, they'd been following her approach.

Shadow saw that she still had half an hour before the meeting time. She took off her sandals and left them in the ATV, and she wandered into the water, where the surging waves swirled around her calves. The first drops of rain spat from the storm clouds and dampened her face. It was almost dark. The waves had turned midnight blue. She stared across the Baltic, where Sweden loomed unseen on the other side of the sea. If it came time for her to run, if she had to disappear again and never be found, she thought she would choose Sweden. A remote northern village like Vietas, in a cabin with a view toward the snow-covered mountains. One of her craziest fantasies had always been to imagine herself living there with Jason, the two of them sharing an anonymous life. Cooking, growing vegetables, drinking wine, building fires, playing music, making love.

Of course, none of that would ever happen now.

Now that she had thrown him to the wolves.

She tried to swallow her emotions and force any thoughts of Jason out of her mind, the way David Abbott had trained her. She had to focus on what came next. But she couldn't help wondering what was happening to him now, and how much he was suffering, and whether he was even still alive. It didn't matter. That was cold, but accurate. Shadow was infinitely practical, and she'd made the practical choice. The *only* choice.

She stared at the Russian border crossing the sand. In a few minutes, at the meeting time, she'd find out whether the sacrifice had been worth it.

Her feet in the cold water, Shadow followed the beach. She reached the border fence, which looked so flimsy, so easy to cross. But that was a ruse. If she'd gone out into the water to reach the other side, or climbed the fence into Russian territory, she knew half a dozen vehicles would storm over the dunes. Armed soldiers would throw her to the ground and carry her off to a Kaliningrad prison.

A few more minutes passed. The darkness was complete.

At exactly eleven o'clock, she saw the lights. A single ATV appeared at the far end of the beach, bumping at high speed through the sand. She couldn't see who was in it. Fifty yards from the border, the vehicle stopped in the surf, but its lights stayed on, like two blinding eyes. Three men got out and headed toward her, black silhouettes through the glow of the ATV headlights. Two were squat and beefy, and she could see the outline of rifles slung around their shoulders. The third man, limping between them only with assistance from the other men, was very tall, and she recognized the shape of that man immediately.

It was David Abbott.

The three men approached the border. As they did, one of the soldiers swung his rifle into place and aimed the barrel at Shadow. She raised her hands, fingers spread wide, to show them that she was unarmed. The other soldier lifted Nightfox goggles to his eyes and studied the beach and the ridge, making sure that she was alone. She would have done the same thing.

In God we trust. All others we verify.

She could see Abbott clearly now. They had him blindfolded and gagged. A red stain bloomed on a gauze pad on his neck, and his left arm was in a sling. He struggled to stay upright, leaning his weight against one of the men.

"What did you do to him?" Shadow called in perfect angry Russian.

The soldier pointing the rifle at her shrugged and said nothing, but at the sound of her voice, Abbott's head turned sharply. She said more softly in English, "Yes, it's me, David. You're safe."

The other soldier stripped off his night vision goggles and shoved Abbott forward, nearly making him fall. Shadow bit her lip and resisted the urge to shout at them. Until Abbott was on this side of the border, nothing was safe. The soldier with the rifle came to the fence and undid a lock that held the mesh in place. He peeled it back a few inches, making a narrow opening. His partner roughly yanked the duct tape from Abbott's face, then pulled out the gag and threw it in the water. As Abbott worked his jaw, the man pried away the blindfold. Abbott blinked, then focused on Shadow on the other side of the fence. She expected a smile, but she didn't get one. He stared at her, his face grave.

"*Poka-poka,*" the soldier with the rifle told Abbott with a smirk. Bye-bye.

Then he shoved the rifle hard into Abbott's back, and he spilled through the gap in the fence into Shadow's arms.

She held him, saying nothing. Neither of them moved. She waited while the soldier connected the fence again, and then the two men reversed their steps up the beach toward the waiting ATV. When they were inside, the vehicle lurched into a U-turn, kicking up a wave of spray and sand, and sped the other way.

They were alone.

Shadow steadied Abbott on the sand. She held him at arm's length, the waves rushing between their legs. "Hello, Father."

How would he react?

What would he say?

He was free because of her. He was alive because of the sacrifice she'd made. She stared up at his hard blue eyes and thought to herself, as if she were a child again: *Call me Marlen, Daddy. Call me by my real name.*

He didn't.

"Shadow," he said. "What did you do?"

———

SHE DROVE THEM THROUGH THE DEEP DARKNESS TO A SMALL COTTAGE

she'd rented an hour north of Gdańsk. The home was situated on a narrow dirt road, across from a lonely beach on the Baltic coast. It looked like a property lifted out of the English Cotswolds, with white walls and a thatched roof. She felt confident that her new identity was safe there. Petra Cavalli was very pretty and had paid the elderly property owner cash, with a generous bonus, to make sure he kept her reservation completely anonymous.

They didn't talk on the drive north. Abbott was clearly in pain, but he didn't sleep. Instead, he mostly stared out the window at the Polish countryside and the nighttime expanse of the water. Shadow could feel his displeasure, but she ignored it for now. She focused on the road, checking her mirrors frequently to make sure no other headlights appeared behind them. She used a zigzag route through the city, just in case the Russians had staked someone out near the Vistula Spit to follow her. If they had, she was confident she'd lost them. By the time they reached the cottage, they were alone.

When she parked in the driveway, out of view of the road, she helped Abbott out of the car and led him inside the cottage. She'd already stocked the place with provisions to last them a week or more. They didn't need to go anywhere or see anyone for a while. The one exception she made to Abbott's usual tastes was to avoid Lucky Bastard whiskey. Her experience with the Files reminded her that computers were always watching, and even the smallest detail could blow their cover. So he would have to drink Glenfiddich instead.

She insisted that he rest. His physical injuries seemed superficial, but the abduction and rescue had taken a toll. When she left him alone in the master bedroom, she took a bottle of Stoli and crossed the road to the sandy slope that led down to the black water. In the distance, she saw the lights of ships. The rain spat down, soaking her, but she didn't care. Her legs felt weak, and she tried not to melt down. She sat on the wet sand with her knees pulled up to her chest and drank vodka directly from the bottle.

A few minutes later, she heard a voice behind her.

"I should have said thank you, and I didn't. So thank you . . . Marlen."

Shadow looked up, feeling a huge weight taken off her shoulders. Abbott stood above her, as tall and commanding as he'd always been, but with a father's warmth in his face now. She realized, just in the time since she'd last seen him, that he'd gotten older. He never showed weakness, but even David Abbott couldn't hold back time. Carefully, wincing, he took a seat next to her on the beach in the mist. He put an arm around her, and she melted against him.

"But my original question stands," he went on. "What did you do? How did you get the Russians to let me go?"

She'd been rehearsing what she would tell him, knowing he'd ask that question. She'd already engineered a cover story, because she needed more than the usual high-value-prisoner exchange to convince him. It would take a polished lie to make it past Abbott. Hopefully, she'd only need to use the lie for a short time.

"It was the Files. That's how I did it."

"Oh? How so?"

"I gambled. I figured the Chinese had to be spying on the Russians as much as they are on us. Maybe more. So I set the Files loose to analyze several Russian hacker farms that have been targeting multinational businesses with spyware. My hunch was right. The Chinese exposure was even more serious than I anticipated. I was able to dangle the names of half a dozen senior-level moles who were selling out Moscow's corporate espionage data to the CCP."

"And that was enough?"

"That plus a couple Belarusian terrorists who targeted the Olympics. They were behind bars in France, but the new president played ball by turning them over quietly. No media attention. He's grateful for Treadstone's role in taking down Chrétien Pau and Raymond Berland before the last election."

"That's good work," Abbott said. "Again, thank you, my dear. Obviously, I'm glad to be here and glad to be alive. But doing this at all was still a mistake. Freeing me wasn't worth exposing your methods or handing over terrorists. You should have let them keep me."

"I wasn't going to do that."

"Because of what I mean to Treadstone, or because of what I mean to you?"

"Does it matter?"

"I guess not." He stared out at the water, and they both shivered in the dampness. "So what's next?"

"I need to find a new safe house for you. Somewhere permanent. It will be more difficult now that the intelligence community knows you're alive. I'm sure the Russians will let it leak that you're free, so everyone will be coming after you again. But I've got some contacts in Switzerland that look promising."

"I have faith in you," Abbott said.

"Part of me wants to join you wherever you go. We could both disappear."

"No. My work is done, but yours isn't. There are too many threats to be dealt with. Starting with Adam Hill. We may have lost Johanna, but we can't give up the fight against him. We need to find a new way to take Hill down. Maybe it's as simple as terminating him, if we have no other choice. Although I don't like using that option so soon after the assassination of Alicia Beauvoir. It would be bad for the country."

Shadow inched away from him. Suspicion filled her voice. "Johanna? What does Johanna have to do with Adam Hill?"

Abbott sighed. "I suppose you need to know the truth now. Johanna was my grenade to blow up Hill's career. She had a personal relationship with Hill when she was a young teenager. He seduced her and abused her. The evidence of that relationship would destroy him, erase his political career. But of course, the emotional impact of going public would likely destroy her, too. That was the problem. I tried to convince her in Dubrovnik that she needed to come forward, but I failed."

"*Johanna?* And you never told me about any of this?"

"I'm sorry. I realize now that was a mistake, but things between the two of you got complicated very quickly. And when she became involved with Cain . . . Well, I thought telling you who she was would add fuel to the fire. But with her dead, it doesn't matter now."

"Johanna is alive," Shadow said.

Abbott straightened up and wiped the rain from his eyes. "My God. Is that true? She didn't die in the Med?"

"No."

"Then where is she?"

"For now, she's in the wind."

"We need to find her."

"I can put people on it, but that will take time."

"We don't have time, my dear. Every day raises the stakes with Adam Hill. I know you and Johanna have a violent history, but you need to get past that. We need her."

She chose her words carefully. "Do we? Is she really our best option? You risked everything to confront her, and it didn't work. You went to Dubrovnik, and look how it all unraveled. Why do you think it would be any different now?"

"Because based on what happened in the Med, Adam Hill knows who Johanna is now. Hill tried to kill her, and he *failed*. That's likely to change her mind about coming forward. She's smart, and she knows she can't run forever. Until we take down Hill, she'll never be safe."

"I'm the wrong person for that job. Even if I find her, Johanna won't listen to me. You know that."

"She'll listen to Cain," Abbott said. "I should have gone to him in the first place. Used *him* to convince her. Love is such an unexpected weapon, isn't it? Bring him here, and the three of us can formulate a plan."

Shadow pushed herself off the ground. She folded her arms

tightly over her chest, buffeted by the wind and rain, with the roar of the waves threatening to drown out her voice. "I should have told you this earlier. I wanted to wait until you were stronger."

"What is it?"

"Cain is dead."

29

BOURNE HEARD A DISTANT ROLL OF THUNDER, DEEP AND STRONG enough to make the building shake around him. But he knew that sound. This wasn't the leading edge of a storm front. This was war.

Wherever they were holding him, he was close to a raging exchange of artillery fire.

His brain felt fogged, as if he were struggling through quicksand. They'd given him an injection in Bucharest, probably something like midazolam, and he had only a vague awareness of what had happened next. First the truck, bumping through the city. Then, not a boat on the Black Sea, but an airplane, flying through turbulence. When they landed, they blindfolded him and gave him more drugs. At that point, he'd fallen unconscious, and sometime after that, he'd awakened here on the hard floor.

It was warm, the air calm and stale, carrying a burnt smell of smoke. The cell was small, maybe ten by ten, with high stone walls and a single barred window near the ceiling that let in a crack of sunlight, along with biting flies who came through bullet holes in the glass. Bits of mortar had chipped away, spread like moon rocks on the floor. A locked metal door with a narrow observation slot stood in the middle of the opposite wall. He'd seen eyes staring at him through the slot, confirming that he was conscious again. Whoever was on the other side hadn't said a word.

He sat in a corner of the room, his hands bound with zip ties behind his back. His temple throbbed. Somewhere in the fog, as the midazolam wore off, he recalled throwing himself at a man with a rifle, only to have the barrel whacked across his skull. Blood made a line down his face; he could taste it on his lips. His shoes had been taken, presumably to make sure he had no way to get to the laces, so his feet were bare. He still wore the black T-shirt and black jeans he'd worn in Bucharest.

A trap.

It had been a trap from the beginning. David Abbott had never been there.

He had no illusions about who had set him up to be abducted. He could see her cool, beautiful face in his mind; he could feel her body on top of his, melding with him, becoming one. Was the sexual seduction part of the strategy? A way to keep him off balance while she made her plans? Shadow had betrayed him again, and he knew why. She needed to get Abbott back, and Bourne was the lone ace she had to play.

The panel on the observation slot creaked open again. Eyes studied him, making sure he hadn't moved from the corner. He heard a rumble of voices outside. The lock on the door rattled, and the door banged inward, revealing two bearded Russian soldiers as large as grizzly bears. They held Kalashnikovs at shoulder level, aimed directly at him. One of them barked, "Don't move."

Bourne stayed where he was.

A third man appeared between the soldiers. He was thin and wore a suit, and carried a small metal chair that he placed in the opposite corner of the cell. The man unsheathed a small knife from his pants pocket. With hand signals, he indicated for Bourne to stand up and turn around. Bourne did, and he heard the man come up behind him. He tensed, ready to spin and disarm the man if he sensed a threat. Instead, the man used the knife to cut the bonds on Bourne's wrists, then retreated through the cell door.

Silence followed.

The door stayed open. The soldiers maintained their alert pose, pointing their rifle barrels at Bourne. He massaged his wrists, but remained standing, wondering what would happen next. Seconds ticked off for at least a minute, and then he heard the sharp tap of boots approaching in the corridor outside. Something about the quick, confident stride made him realize this was the man he'd been waiting for.

Bourne saw him.

A Russian in green fatigues appeared in the doorway, a pistol in one hand. The man greeted the two soldiers like a commander and spoke with them briefly, occasionally laughing, before dismissing them and entering the cell on his own. He shut the metal door behind him, and he and Bourne were alone. Bourne thought about rushing him, but he noted the ease with which the man held the Makarov and concluded that he'd take a bullet to the head before he got there. Not that he wouldn't be dead soon anyway.

The man wasn't tall, only about five foot seven, but with a muscular physique. He had a round face with a high forehead and a thin sweep of sandy-blond hair at the far back of his skull. His mouth made a severe horizontal slash across his face. He had smart blue eyes that never seemed to blink, and the temperature of those eyes was ice-cold on a summer day. He projected an ageless appearance, but Bourne knew he was in his early seventies. The man glanced around the empty cell, his gaze missing nothing, then sat in the metal chair and folded one hand on top of the other. He kept the gun ready. Bourne slid back down to the floor, and they stared at each other for a while, two boxers in their corners. Finally, the man spoke.

"So you are Cain," Vladimir Putin said.

"That's right."

Putin nodded thoughtfully, making a careful assessment of his adversary. He spoke English with a heavy accent, but he seemed to have no trouble with fluency. "I've looked forward to meeting you for some time. As I'm sure you know. I wondered what you would be like in person. Everyone has a certain aura they project to the world, do they not? They cannot hide it. I assumed your aura would speak of death. The coldness of a killer. But it does not. That is a surprise."

"What does my aura reflect?" Bourne asked with a curiosity he couldn't hide.

"Quite clearly, a desire to be left alone."

Bourne kept his reaction off his face, but he appreciated the irony that, in seconds, the president of Russia had assessed him better than anyone on his own side. "You have an aura, too," he told Putin.

"Oh, yes? And what is that?"

"Confidence in your destiny."

A ghost of a smile floated across the man's lips. "Well, Cain, it's fair to say we know each other rather well."

"Apparently so."

Putin eased back in the chair. Everything about him reflected his calm sense of control. "You should know that Lennon spoke of you often. Even when he was undercover at Treadstone, he reported to me about you. Cain and Abel, those were your code names, yes? He spoke highly of you both as an ally and an adversary. He was respectful of your skills. At the time, I even inquired with him about the possibility of converting you to my services. He told me that was a losing play. Not because of any foolish American patriotism, mind you. No, he said you were too independent to work for me. Lennon didn't believe you could ever be truly loyal to a man or a government. Alas, loyalty is the one thing I demand from people more than anything else."

"I don't remember much about Lennon," Bourne said. "Only bits and pieces. Although I do remember our final confrontation."

"Yes, I'm aware of your situation. The man with no memory. To me, it makes you even more interesting. My sources tell me you had a relapse recently. You were injured when your boat exploded. You lost most of your memory again."

"That's true. It's coming back again, but only in fragments. Like a chain missing many links along the way."

"Which does not make for a very useful chain, does it?" Putin smiled at his own joke. "You say you remember your last meeting with Lennon. Does that mean you remember killing him?"

"Technically, he killed himself. Poison. I was ready to spare him."

One of the man's eyebrows arched. "Is that true?"

"It is."

"Interesting. I would not expect mercy shown by someone like you. Particularly given your history with Lennon."

"I'm not sure it was mercy on my part. He was defeated. Killing him was unnecessary. If anything, I think the idea of being locked up was worse to him than being dead."

"I would have gotten him out eventually. I always do. I never leave men behind."

"Then perhaps he couldn't accept the fact that he lost."

"Defeat is never something to accept. I take that as an axiom. But it seems that Lennon assessed you correctly. I respect men of savvy and strength. With him dead, I don't have anyone on whom I can truly rely for the missions I need. I'd like to find someone to fill his shoes. Truly, Cain, I would invite you to be that person, if you could be persuaded to change allegiances. And to offer me your absolute loyalty. I wonder, is it possible Lennon misjudged your ability to follow orders?"

"No, he didn't."

Putin made a faint gesture of disappointment. "Ah, well. As I figured. You could have lied to me, of course. Told me what I wanted to hear in order to save your life. I would have seen through it, but nonetheless, I'm impressed you stood by your principles even though you're aware it means your inevitable death."

He made that announcement calmly, without fanfare. Bourne took it the same way. Both men knew the score. This meeting could only end with Bourne being killed.

"Loyalty goes both ways," Putin went on. "Just as I demand loyalty from those who serve me, I am equally loyal to them as a leader. I support my own, and I avenge my own. So I cannot let Lennon's death go unanswered, Cain. Plus, to let you go, to allow you to strike at my interests so many times without reacting, would show weakness, which is unacceptable. It's important that people in my circle realize that taking action against me carries the ultimate price. I never forgive, I never forget. However long it takes, sooner or later, those who defy me must answer for their actions."

"So this is about more than Lennon," Bourne concluded.

"Oh, yes. I realize you may not remember much of it, but you have been my nemesis for some time now. The defector, Grigori Kotov? Do you recall what happened there? Probably not. Suffice it to say you got in Lennon's way and deprived me of the chance to bring Kotov back to Russia to have his crimes appropriately addressed. He may be dead, but he deserved to die many times before his final demise. That was the first time you and I crossed paths, and you have reappeared as an obstacle to me many times since then. Perhaps the most troublesome issue—other than eliminating Lennon—was your handling of Tatiana Reznikova. Do you remember her?"

The face of a pretty Russian scientist flitted through Bourne's mind.

"Tati. I rescued her in Estonia."

"Indeed. I presume she is hiding somewhere in the United States. I'm still looking for her, by the way. As I told you, I never forget. Tati was like a daughter to me for many years, but ultimately, she became disloyal. She spoke out against me and the war. Bad enough for anyone, but I took it as a personal slight given our history. She tried to hide under a different identity, but it was only a matter of time before I found her and dealt with her. But you intervened and took her away. Truly, you keep getting in the way of my plans, Cain."

"Maybe you should make different plans," Bourne said.

That won him a laugh. "You're a brave man. I like that. You spit in the face of death, which I appreciate. But death comes for all of us sooner or later. And here you are. I'm curious, by the way. Do you realize it was your own side that betrayed you?"

"Shadow."

"Yes. Shadow."

"Is David Abbott free?"

"He is. I always honor my deals. But it was interesting to me that Shadow was so quick to give you up. Rumors had gotten back to me that the two of you were *close*. Intimate even. That you shared a past together. That she'd made you her personal agent with all that entails. And yet she handed you over to me without any hesitation. Naturally, I respected her ruthlessness in doing so. But you should have been more careful. You have a weakness for treacherous women who invite you to their beds, Cain. That's your undoing."

"I appreciate the romantic advice," Bourne said.

Another smile. "Well, so what do I do with you? I've waited for this moment for quite a while, but how to end the game? A cat catches a mouse after a long hunt, and it seems so anticlimactic simply to eat it. It would be satisfying to pull the trigger myself, but I suspect seeing you on the floor with a bullet in your brain would prove to be rather empty. No, killing you myself isn't my way."

"I'm sure you have a plan."

"In fact, I do. You've been such a hindrance to me in the past that I thought it only fitting that you conduct a mission for me.

Now that I have you, I feel like you should deliver some *value* to me. Perhaps even the score between us a little bit."

"Lennon was right. I won't work for you."

"Oh, I don't expect you to do so. I'm hardly a fool. Your death *is* the mission, Cain. I suspect it would bring a smile to Lennon's face to think about that. He would appreciate you helping advance my aims against Ukraine and NATO. You see, America has tried to have it both ways on this conflict for too long. Fight the war through proxies, but keep your hands clean. Give money and weapons to the comedian in Kyiv, but pretend that you have no boots on the ground. But we both know this is a lie."

Putin cocked an ear, listening to the distant thunder of artillery.

"We are outside the town of Rylsk," he went on. "The *Russian* town of Rylsk. Part of our homeland. Anyone found on this land is an invader, a foreign combatant infringing on our sovereignty. There is no room for diplomatic niceties, no games of pretend, when it comes to our border. If you are here, then you are fighting a war against us. Period. So when an American spy is found dead on this land, a spy who is obviously coordinating an attack and an invasion by Ukrainian forces, it means only one thing. The U.S. and NATO have declared war on Russia. They have invited retribution of *any* kind I choose. Call it a game of chicken if you like, but I think we will very quickly see that America and Europe have little stomach for war if it means their own children dying, rather than the children of strangers thousands of miles away. Suddenly all the talk in Washington will be about peace negotiations, rather than new weapons shipments. Freezing the conflict where it stands, locking in my gains. You see, I play a long game, Cain, and this is just one move. Next time, I will get more, and again the West will fold. Leverage. That's what you are to me. Leverage to give me exactly what I want."

He got to his feet and rapped on the metal door of the cell with the barrel of his Makarov. The door opened again, and the two bearded soldiers stood there with their rifles. He barked an order in Russian to the biggest of the men, but Bourne understood the language.

Alexei, take him to the battlefield. You know what to do.

Then Putin turned back to Bourne. The smile was gone from his face. Only cold calculation and fierce determination remained.

"Congratulations, Cain. You have secured your place in history. You are about to become the first casualty of World War Three."

30

BEFORE SUNRISE, SHADOW GOT DRESSED IN THE SMALL COTTAGE ON the Polish coast. She checked on David Abbott, who was sleeping peacefully in the master bedroom, and then she left the rental house for the cool morning darkness. She wore a nylon long-sleeved jacket over Lycra shorts, with her Domina tightly holstered in the small of her back. As she did every morning, she followed a ten-minute routine of stretching, letting the muscles in her arms and legs loosen before her five-mile run. When she completed her exercise regimen, she headed toward the Baltic beach.

Then she stopped. Her instincts flared.

In both directions from the cottage, there were no lights and no movement along the lonely road. The area was silent except for the in-and-out rumble of the waves hitting the sand. She inhaled, but all she smelled was the delicate drift of her own Wind Flowers perfume in the air. And yet something was wrong. Something was *different*. She felt it. Her mind grasped for some physical sensation in the surroundings to back up her gut, but she couldn't isolate what had changed around her.

It seemed impossible that the Russians or the CIA had located Petra Cavalli and her hideaway so quickly. Even so, she sensed a threat nearby.

Shadow continued across the road, not changing her routine, but staying hyperalert to every sound. She pushed through the brush and down the sandy slope that led to the water. She thought about taking her Domina pistol in her hand, but if someone was watching her, she didn't want to give away the game. Not yet. Instead, she did a few more stretches on the damp sand just beyond the reach of the waves. The sky began to lighten on the horizon, an orange glow appearing at the base of the cloudless sky. The arrival of dawn gave her a chance to study the brush and trees growing on the fringe of the beach, watching for movement in the shadows. When the first sunbeams flooded the area, she looked for a pinpoint glint of metal reflecting on the barrel of a gun.

Nothing.

No one.

She shook her head at the conflicting signals her mind was giving her. Maybe it was stress. Maybe she hadn't regained her mental edge after the emotional roller coaster of the past few days.

Shadow began her run. She jogged on the firm sand, pushing herself hard, the rhythm of her legs fluid and smooth. She entered a kind of runner's cocoon, conscious of her pace, her heartbeat, the slap of her feet, and the bounce of her ponytail on her neck. The sea rushed in and out beside her, inching closer on the narrow beach as the morning tide swelled. The slope grew higher beside her, dense with foliage. Her focus, straight ahead, showed no one in front of her and no other footsteps in the sand.

Twenty minutes later, she reached her usual halfway point, exactly two and a half miles from the cottage. Sweating, breathing hard, she slowed to a walk, then came to a stop by the water with her hands on her hips. It was full daylight now, a bright morning. Deliberately, she didn't turn around. She reached back and undid her ponytail, letting her blond hair fall loose to her shoulders. She closed her eyes, following every sound behind her, and then she bent forward, massaging the stiff muscles in her thighs. Her nylon jacket rose up on her bare back, slipping above the level of her holster.

In one seamless motion, she straightened up and grabbed the Domina, then whirled around with the gun barrel aimed at the end of her outstretched arms and her finger already on the trigger.

Johanna stood behind her, not even ten feet away. She had a Ruger pointed at the middle of Shadow's chest.

Neither woman fired.

It had been a long time since Shadow had seen Johanna up close, but she hadn't changed. Her spaghetti-straight blond hair was parted in the middle and fell almost to her waist. Her eyes shined like blue vodka, equal parts intoxicating and crazy. Her skinny body boasted almost no curves, but very full breasts. She had a long, interesting face, not symmetrically perfect like Shadow's face. Her lips were pale, her cheekbones high, her nose rounded. She wasn't classically beautiful, but she was definitely pretty in a way that a certain kind of man would find irresistible.

A man like Jason.

Being so near her again, Shadow felt a wave of naked hatred at the idea that Jason had fallen in love with this woman, and she could feel the equal heat of Johanna's hatred reflected back at her. They'd been enemies for years. But she knew something now about this woman that she hadn't known before.

She knew the secret that David Abbott had kept from her all this time; she knew the truth about Johanna and Adam Hill.

David, why didn't you tell me?

Things might have been so different. Both of their lives could have taken a different course. Shadow would never have trained Johanna for Treadstone in the brutal way she had, she would never have put her through the tests and challenges she did, if she'd known about the abuse in her childhood. She would simply have told Abbott no. No recruitment. This woman, this *girl*, was wrong for Treadstone. Johanna had the mental and physical skills for the field, but not the emotional temperament. It was a mistake to put her there.

But she couldn't change the past.

"How did you find me?" Shadow asked.

Johanna shrugged. "Oh, you're not as good as you think you are. I was a hacker, remember? I was writing AI programs long before they were cool. I figured you flew out of Bucharest under a private legend, so I ran all the passenger manifests and looked for any kind of IP address overlap with the cover identity you used last year on Holy Island. It didn't take long to come up with Petra Cavalli and trace you to right here in the rental cottage. Is that where Abbott is?"

Shadow saw no need to lie about something Johanna obviously knew already. "Yes. He's there. Are you planning to kill him, too?"

"No. I don't have any beef with Abbott. You're the fucking bitch I'm after."

"So why not shoot me in the back? You had the chance. I could be dead right now."

"Not my style. I want to see your face."

Shadow lowered her Domina and returned it to her holster, which made Johanna's eyes narrow with surprise. "Actually, I don't think you're going to shoot me. That's too easy. You want to beat the shit out of me, don't you? You want your hands around my neck. You want to be eye to eye as you watch the life go out of me. Right?"

"Right."

"So what are you waiting for?" Shadow waved her closer with both hands. "Come get me. Or are you afraid you can't take me down?"

"You know I can."

"Well, we'll see. Brains matter more than age or strength. I trained you, remember? I know how you think. I know every move you'll make before you make it. I'm in your head, and I always will be."

She watched Johanna's pale cheeks flush red with anger.

Angry people made mistakes.

Johanna lowered the Ruger, then leaped like a gazelle across the distance between them, driving her body straight at Shadow. She was fast, but Shadow saw her coming and nimbly dodged her, then swung a leg sharply into Johanna's back and kicked her hard to the ground. Johanna landed face-first. Humiliated, she scrambled back to her feet, her mouth spitting out wet sand. This time she kept a wary distance.

"See?" Shadow said. "I know you. Try again."

"Fuck you."

With two quick steps, Johanna moved inside and threw a jab, but Shadow grabbed her hand, twisted it, then drove a heel into Johanna's knee. The younger woman screamed in pain. Shadow hit her in the throat, and Johanna gagged, then spilled forward. But as she did, she suddenly pushed off her other leg and launched her head into Shadow's stomach like a cannonball, expelling the air from her lungs. Shadow flew off her feet and fell straight backward onto the beach, gasping for breath.

Instantly, Johanna was on top of her, face-to-face, not even two inches between them.

"I know you, too."

"Fuck you," Shadow said right back.

She threw her head forward and knocked bone against bone square into Johanna's brow, dizzying them both. Then she wrapped her arms around her and rolled down the beach into the teeth of the waves. The cold Baltic water crashed over them. Shadow wound up on top, and she held Johanna by the shoulders as the other woman wriggled beneath her, fighting to get free. The next incoming wave buried her face, and Shadow held her under ten inches of surf, watching Johanna's hair float and her blue eyes widen with panic.

"Have you ever been waterboarded? It's not fun."

The wave receded. Johanna's mouth flew open, choking, sucking in air. Then she hooked one foot around Shadow's ankle and hoisted her body sideways, taking both of them deeper into the water. This time Johanna ended up on top, forcing Shadow's torso into the shifting sand. A wave crashed over them like a waterfall, and Shadow found herself underwater, no air in her lungs, Johanna's arms and legs pinning her entire body down.

A muffled voice came through the water.

"No, it's not fun, is it?"

The wave ran back toward the sea. For a moment, Shadow could breathe again. She gagged and coughed, but as she writhed to get away, the next surge from the Baltic washed over them. She barely had time to suck in a breath before she was drowning under the water again. Johanna held her with fierce strength, pushing her deeper and deeper, until the wet sand below her body began to pour across her face.

When the wave rolled back, she was still under the water.

Shadow struggled. Fought. Kicked. Johanna's hands shot from her shoulders to her neck and squeezed, thumbs crushing her windpipe. She yanked her head above the surf, but the grip of Johanna's fingers was so tight that Shadow still couldn't drag oxygen into her lungs. With her arms free, she beat her fists against Johanna's body, landing blow after blow, but feeling her strength weaken. A roaring sound filled her ears, louder than the tumult of the waves. Colors burst, an explosion of fireworks in her eyes. A strange thought came and went through her brain. *This is what it feels like to die.*

But if she died, she wouldn't die alone.

Shadow dug into the sand below her body and found the Domina pistol still snug inside the holster. She jerked it out, and the Domina came free from the sea with a splash, and she shoved the barrel into Johanna's temple. Without a sound, their blue eyes exchanged a message.

Let go or I shoot.

Johanna gave in.

She peeled away her fingers, and as Shadow's throat opened,

she inhaled a huge, sweet breath of air. Her chest swelled, and the dizziness in her brain began to right itself. She let the pistol go limp in her hand. The two of them broke apart in the surf, waves still crashing over their heads and dragging them toward the beach.

Shadow hacked over and over, then realized she could finally speak again.

"Do you want to keep fighting?" she gasped to Johanna. "Or do you want to help me get Jason back?"

———

SOAKED AND EXHAUSTED, THEY SAT NEXT TO EACH OTHER ON THE empty beach, their shoulders leaning together. Shadow realized that some of her hatred for this woman had washed out to sea, and she wondered if Johanna felt the same.

"Abbott told me about you," she murmured. "He never did before. I swear I didn't know when I recruited you."

"Told you what?" Johanna asked.

"He told me about Adam Hill. About what Hill did to you when you were a teenager."

"I wish he hadn't done that."

"Why not?"

"Because it's my story and no one else's. I don't define myself by what happened then. I've moved on with my life."

"Except if I'd known, I never would have recruited you for Treadstone. I wouldn't have put you through what I did."

"Because I'm weak?"

"Because you're damaged. There's a difference."

Johanna stared at the sea. "My name was Annie. Back then."

Shadow let a long moment of silence pass between them, and then she took a leap of faith with this woman. "My name was Marlen. Before I was Shadow."

"Hello, Marlen."

"Hello, Annie."

They both laughed. Johanna straightened up and sifted some of the sand from her blond hair, but that was a losing battle. "Abbott asked me to meet him in Dubrovnik last month. He wanted me to come forward, release the videos I had, testify before Congress, tell the whole world. But I already paid Adam Hill back for what he did when I was fourteen. I got the justice I wanted. If I came forward, that would be the end of my life. I'd be a victim. Exposed. Raked over the coals, called a liar. It would be like going through what he did to me all over again."

"I understand that," Shadow replied. "I do, really. But things are different since you met with Abbott."

"How?"

"Hill knows who you are now."

Johanna's brow crinkled with concern. "Are you sure?"

"I am. The attack on the boat? The explosion in the Med? It was aimed at *you*, not just Cain. That was Hill trying to eliminate you. He has Holly Schultz in his pocket, and she used Vandal to go after you."

Johanna hissed in anger. "*Fuck!*"

"Does it change your mind? About going public?"

"No. Nothing changes my mind. I don't care about Adam Hill. He's the past. He's ancient history. The only thing I care about is finding Jason."

"You really are in love with him, aren't you?"

"Yes, I am." Then Johanna's head turned, and her blue eyes searched Shadow's face. "Are you?"

Shadow studied the expanse of the Baltic Sea below the rising sun. "No. In the past, in Switzerland, maybe I was, a little. Maybe I saw a chance with him to be someone other than who Abbott made me. But tigers can't change their stripes. Don't get me wrong, I like the sex, but that's all it is. I like fucking Jason because I like the idea of controlling him. I own people, I collect people. That's what I do. But I'll never really own Cain. He is who he is. I also know that he's in love with you, not me."

"Where is he? Do you know?"

"Yes. I planted a tracker on him before the mission in Bucharest. I'm not entirely heartless, Johanna. My plan wasn't simply to sacrifice Jason to rescue Abbott. I always intended to get him back if I could. But I also realized it was a huge risk, and the whole operation might fail. I didn't even tell Abbott. He thinks Jason's dead. And he may *be* dead before we get to him. If so, that's on me."

"Where is he?" Johanna asked again.

"He's in the Kursk Oblast district near the Ukrainian-Russian border. He's been there for a day. I've got a stealth recovery team ready to go out of Hlukhiv in Ukraine tonight. They'll cross the border after dark. The battery in the tracker will only last another twenty-four hours or so, so we need to move fast."

"Is it a Treadstone team?"

Shadow shook her head. "No. Ukrainian soldiers. I did it all back channel with Zelensky. Adam Hill and Holly Schultz have infiltrated Treadstone, so I can't use our people. I don't know how far it's gone. Ironic, isn't it? It's my agency and I don't know who to trust."

"Trust me," Johanna said.

Shadow stared at the woman next to her, wet to the skin and covered in sand and seaweed. The woman who had wrapped her fingers around her neck and tried to kill her moments ago. "Okay. I'll arrange transport for you out of Warsaw. Get to Hlukhiv by nightfall, and you can lead the team. Bring him home, Johanna."

31

THE JEEP TOOK BOURNE THROUGH THE RUINS OF WHAT HAD ONCE BEEN
beautiful border countryside. Green farm fields had been scorched
by fire and trampled into ruts by the heavy tire tracks of military
vehicles. In small towns, crumbled walls were all that remained of
centuries-old stone buildings. As they drove, the Jeep dodged giant holes in the two-lane road that had been blasted to dirt and
rubble by mortar fire.

Bourne sat in back, guarded by three of the grizzly bears with
AK-12s. Two others sat up front, including the driver. Jason's wrists
were bound again. They'd given him Russian military fatigues to
put on over his clothes so he looked like any other Russian soldier.
That was part of the ruse. An American, dead in Russia, dressed
like a Russian. A spy, his body ripe for capture, ready to be photo-
graphed in the mud as evidence of direct American interference in
the war. But he also knew the uniform was another way to make
sure he didn't get out of the country alive. If for any reason he got

away from the Russians, the Ukrainians would kill him on sight before he could explain who he was.

It didn't matter. He doubted he'd survive long enough to get anywhere near the border. The Russians in the Jeep joked to each other mile by mile about how and when to kill him. They didn't realize he spoke Russian and understood every word. So far, the favored technique was to tell him to run, then shoot him down with a rain of automatic fire. Eliminate the American spy trying to get away like a coward when his mission was exposed.

The farther they drove, the closer they got to the tumult of the battle. Explosions made the Jeep rock up and down. Clouds of stinging smoke filled the air, and tracer fire streaked across the blue sky. The day was hot and getting hotter, and another few miles would take them within range of the Ukrainian guns. The Russians in the Jeep knew it, and they were no fools. Bourne heard the grizzly bears talking to the lieutenant in charge.

"Let's do it here! Kill him now! Better to find the Yankee pig deep in our territory. Why go all the way to the border?"

But the lieutenant shut them down. *"Because the Moth wants his body found with the other dog-fuckers who rape our land. Keep going."*

The men did. The battle got louder ahead of them.

Bourne stayed alert for any opening to escape, but he didn't see one. The lieutenant on the other side of the Jeep never took his eyes or his gun away from him. The man had a dead-fish stare, hard and cruel. He looked to be about thirty years old—nearly a decade younger than Bourne—and he could have passed for Bigfoot in the Appalachians, with long thick black hair and a full beard. Bourne had heard Putin call him Alexei. Many of the Russian soldiers were green recruits yanked off the streets of country towns, drunk and scared. But not Alexei. Alexei was a professional.

"No one's going to believe this setup," Bourne told him, talking loudly in English to be heard over the noise of the Jeep and the artillery thunder.

Alexei never seemed to blink. "Russians will believe it."

"You think the body of one American spy will start a war?"

"I think the war started years ago, and your people just don't realize it."

"And is any of this worth it? Billions of dollars? Thousands of young men dead on both sides? No one's winning here, you're all losing. Using me as a political prop won't end it any sooner."

Alexei's upper lip curled. "I lost two brothers in the war already, Cain. Killed by Kyiv pigs using your guns. When the Americans finally wake up and quit feeding them, the pigs will be slaughtered. That's how it ends."

Bourne gave up. This wasn't a battle he was going to win.

He readied himself for one final, futile move whenever the Jeep stopped. He would have a few seconds as they cut the bonds on his wrists, but he was also unarmed, facing five men with automatic rifles. He didn't like his odds. He might take down one man, maybe two, but Alexei would eviscerate him with a burst from his AK-12 in the millisecond after that. He was sure the Russian on the other side of the Jeep was reading his mind and anticipating what Bourne would do to survive.

It would take a miracle for him to get away.

But at that exact moment, a miracle happened.

A 155mm miracle.

They all heard the whistle of the mortar coming, but there was nothing they could do to get away. The driver swerved; the Russians shouted; but the whistle got louder, streaking toward them in a handful of seconds.

Three, two, one.

Directly in front of the Jeep, the highway exploded with a deafening blast of shrapnel and rock and a tornado of light and fire. The heavy vehicle erupted into the air as if it were weightless, and Bourne felt his whole body thrown skyward with the massive detonation shrieking in his ears.

He never felt himself land.

———

WHEN BOURNE FINALLY AWOKE, ALEXEI WAS STILL WATCHING HIM WITH that same empty, fish-eyed stare. Not all of Alexei. Just his head. Bourne lay on his back under the bright sun in the ruts of a farm field, and Alexei's severed head lay atop his chest, balanced neatly atop the three inches of his neck that remained. The sight of it made him start with horror. His fingers clawed the dirt, which was when he realized the force of the blast had separated the bonds on his wrists. His hands were free.

Like Perseus with Medusa, Bourne grabbed the man's head by his thick black hair and tossed it into the mud.

He listened, but heard nothing. No battle noise, no voices, no engines, not even the wind. He didn't understand the complete silence until he realized he was deaf. When he touched his ears, he felt a trickle of blood on both sides. He massaged the bones of his face and worked his stiff jaw, and the empty silence became a distant whooshing roar, like the sound of a waterfall downriver. He murmured to himself, not sure how loud he was talking, and he heard the words at the far end of a tunnel.

When he propped his elbows on the ground and pushed himself up, his head spun, making him nauseated. He waited, not moving again until his brain and eyes began talking the same language. He lay in a cornfield, surrounded mostly by dead brown stalks with withered, unpicked cobs. A few feet away, crushing the corn down, was the Russian Jeep, still leaking smoke and steam. It had been flipped upside down in the explosion, and Bourne could see the rest of Alexei's headless body pinned beneath the engine block. He saw the body of the driver nearby, facedown and motionless.

Where were the other three men? And their weapons?

He didn't see them.

His memory, at least, seemed to be intact. Or he hadn't lost any more of himself. Like a pilot with a checklist, he began reviewing the details in his mind. His name. Where he'd come from. Why he was here. He went backward day by day since his near-death on the *Stormy Weather*, and he remembered everything. The places. The people. Port Noir and Geoffrey Washburn. Paris and David Abbott. Vandal. Nash. Shadow.

Johanna.

Johanna was alive! That gave Jason a reason to stay alive, too.

Slowly, he got to his feet in the remains of the farm field. He murmured to himself again; his voice got a little louder. He saw the highway a full thirty yards away, a hell of a distance to be thrown. He checked himself from head to toe and found no serious injuries beyond the roaring in his ears. His bones weren't broken; his dizziness didn't come back as he started to walk. He was bruised and cut, with some burns on his arms, but he'd been lucky when the impact threw him free.

But he couldn't stay here. He needed to get away fast. Back in Rylsk, or wherever he was now, Putin would be expecting an update from Alexei. *Cain is dead.* If the message didn't come soon, the area would be flooded with more soldiers. Bourne had to start making his way toward the border, which was due west down the shattered highway. A lot of miles stood between him and freedom.

He took a few steps, then froze as the high cornstalks bent apart in front of him. One of the other three Russian soldiers appeared, dazed and bleeding, but otherwise intact, his AK-12 still securely around his shoulder. Seeing Bourne, he began to swing the weapon up, but he was too slow. In the instant before a burst of automatic fire began, Bourne leaped sideways, landing on the rocky ground and crawling to cover inside the cornfield. He shifted direction immediately, rolling fast, hearing the muffled noise of bullets blasting apart the stalks and corncobs behind him. He crawled away, then found himself staring into the black eyes of another of the Russian bears, who was crawling toward the noise of the gunfire.

The man's mouth opened, ready to shout. Bourne hit him in the face and gagged him with his forearm, keeping him quiet. With a flash of metal, the man swung a knife. Bourne yanked back his arm, but not in time. The blade slashed deeply through the sleeve of the Russian uniform he was wearing and drew blood.

"Here!" the soldier bellowed. "Here, here he is!"

Then the man made the mistake of standing up. His comrade outside the cornfield saw movement and fired immediately, unleashing a flood of bullets that ripped into the man's face and chest. The bear fell, nearly landing on top of Bourne, who grabbed the bloody knife out of the dead man's hand and skittered away as he heard boots thundering through the dense rows of corn toward him.

The other Russian with the AK-12 stopped over his comrade and swore loudly when he realized what he'd done. In the same instant, the man recognized the threat nearby: if this man was dead, then Bourne was alive. Without bothering to aim, he pulled the trigger on his rifle again, sweeping the ground, spinning in a circle and bellowing in Russian. Bourne, who'd been ready to jump at the man's throat with the blade, was forced to scramble away out of the line of fire to save himself.

He scrambled right into the body of the third and final soldier from the Jeep. The man was dead, his face gone, his left leg missing below the knee. But he still had his AK-12 strapped around his shoulder, the barrel trapped under his torso.

Bourne heard a disturbance in the field, like an animal ripping through the cornstalks. The Russian was heading his way. The noise sounded far away, but he knew the man was practically on top of him. He pushed heavily on the dead Russian's body, trying to free the rifle from beneath him. The man was heavy, and Bourne felt weakness where his arm was gashed and losing blood. He shoved again, using his shoulder, and freed the weapon, then tried to pry the strap away.

He didn't have time.

The Russian fought through the field, gun at the ready. When he saw Bourne, he swung the barrel downward and fired, exploding dirt and dust between Bourne's legs. At the same moment, Bourne grabbed the dead soldier's rifle, still strapped to the man's body. He shoved his finger on the trigger and wrenched the barrel sideways with his other hand and unleashed a wild volley into the air. Only one bullet landed, but it burrowed through the man's hand where he was holding the AK-12, and he howled and let the weapon drop. Then he responded with a vicious kick that dislodged the rifle from Bourne's hands and threw him onto his back.

The soldier had a sidearm. Bourne didn't. He watched the man grab at the old, dirty Makarov in his holster with his uninjured hand, and he had nowhere to run. Three feet away, the knife lay on the ground where he'd dropped it. Out of reach. He'd run out of options. He watched the soldier level the pistol, and he stared at the squat black barrel, wondering if he would see or feel what happened next.

With a jerk of his fat finger, the soldier pulled the trigger.

The round exploded inside the gun.

Three of the man's fingers blew into the air along with pieces of the weapon, and shrapnel shot like an arrow through his left eye. For an instant, the soldier stood frozen, unable to comprehend what had happened, and then he began to shriek with pain.

Bourne rolled to the dead soldier and grabbed the AK-12. This time the strap came free, and the rifle nestled securely in his arms. He raised the barrel, aimed, and fired a single shot into the forehead of the man above him, then backed quickly out of the way as the Russian toppled like a falling redwood.

He was alone, and he was free.

32

BOURNE FOLLOWED THE HIGHWAY BECAUSE HE KNEW THE ROAD LED
toward Ukraine.

With each mile he walked, he got closer to the fighting. He
could hear more clearly again, despite a constant whining tinnitus,
and he recognized the rumble of mortars and gunfire not far away.
But there were other, even deadlier sounds nearby, too. Every few
minutes, he heard an innocent hum in the air, like the buzzing of
a fly, and he knew the Ukrainians had deployed switchblade drones
to scan the area for enemy soldiers.

They were also known as ghost drones. Silent killers. When
they zeroed in on a target, their engines switched off, and the
drones glided into range without a sound before unleashing explosives packed with tungsten cubes that instantly shredded the body.
The victim never heard it, never saw it coming. One second he was
laughing with his comrades; the next second, he was red dust.

Bourne, in Russian territory, wearing a Russian uniform, with
a Russian AK-12 around his shoulder, was definitely drone bait. So

whenever he heard the telltale whine nearby, he threw himself off the road and took cover in a ditch, hoping he'd gotten out of view before the drone operator spotted him.

That was how the afternoon went.

One hour, two hours, three hours, slowly creeping westward.

Where was he? How close was he to the border? He didn't know. From Rylsk to Hlukhiv was almost thirty miles. His best guess was that he had twenty miles to go. That was a long time in the open.

The Russians were hunting for him, too. News of his escape had obviously gotten back to Putin. Half a dozen Jeeps with armed men had sped down the highway from the east in intervals. When he felt the vibration of the vehicles under his feet, he took cover as they passed. Two men studied the land on both sides of the highway with binoculars. The others, with their AK-12s, stayed ready to shoot and storm the fields at the first shout that Bourne had been spotted. Along with the drones, he heard helicopters, flying low, circling back and forth. He knew they were looking for him. By now, every Russian soldier within twenty miles had received orders to watch for the American spy.

Kill him, and you'll live a fat, happy life in Moscow far from the fighting.

Still Bourne kept going, slow step by slow step, hiding whenever he needed to, then returning to the road. He felt as if he were making no progress, the border still miles ahead of him. His arm throbbed, feeling numb where he'd tied a tourniquet around the knife wound. Pain spiked behind his eyes as he tried to stay focused, listening for threats from the ground and from the sky.

Nausea rolled over him in waves, and he wondered if he had a concussion from the blast that threw him from the Jeep.

He needed to eat. He needed to sleep. *Sleep is a weapon.* As he traveled, he passed burnt-out farms, nearly leveled by the war, and he thought about taking refuge in one of them for a few hours. It would be easier to travel at night, easier to hide and get through the countryside faster. But he was still too close to his starting point to feel safe from Putin's net. Teams would spread out, searching every lonely, empty farm between here and the border. Sooner or later, they would find him.

Another two hours passed.

He stayed along the tree line beside the highway, where he could take cover quickly when a new threat emerged. He'd found binoculars on one of the dead Russians, so he was able to periodically assess the territory ahead of him and behind him. It was early evening, and he'd seen no Jeeps pass him in more than an hour, so he was beginning to hope he'd slipped beyond the search grid. But when he stopped and made another check of the road leading toward Ukraine, he realized he was wrong.

Half a mile ahead of him, in a gap where there were no trees along the highway, just green fields, he saw three Jeeps parked in a roadblock. They were waiting for him. At least ten men patrolled the fields with their rifles. Three others scanned the terrain, and when Bourne saw one of the men pointing binoculars at him, he quickly slid down into the grass. He waited, counting off seconds, then checked again to see if he'd been spotted. At least for now, none of the Jeeps were heading his way.

But he had no hope of getting past them. He couldn't cross the flat field without being seen. His only choice was to detour north or south and go around them. But that meant at least a mile out of his way to be sure he wouldn't be seen, which would slow him down even more. Even so, there was nothing else to do.

Bourne chose to go north. The southern route gave him faster access to the border, which meandered jaggedly southeast in this area, but turning south also meant crossing at least half a mile of wide-open fields empty except for black, flame-scorched soil. If a drone or helicopter passed overhead, he had nowhere to hide. To the north, the land was green, dotted with trees, and the slopes and woods offered cover. He checked the roadblock again—still no sign that they were aware of his presence—and jogged northward, staying low.

Ten minutes later, he couldn't see the highway or the cluster of Jeeps anymore. For the moment, he was safe.

Ahead of him, he spotted a small farmhouse with a circle of trees behind it. This one, unlike most of the others on this road, had somehow escaped mortar fire, with intact windows and roof. But it looked deserted; its occupants had no doubt fled deeper into the country to escape the war. He decided to take the risk of going inside to look for food and water, to stitch up his arm, and then to grab an hour of sleep to get his energy back. The daylong march was taking its toll.

But as he neared the farmhouse, a man came around the far wall, zipping up his pants.

It was a Russian soldier, another huge bear of a man with a stomach hanging over his belt. The man was fat but fast, and he had his rifle aimed at Bourne's chest with a shout before Jason could move.

"Hey, who the fuck are you?" the soldier called. "You need to be more careful, dog-fucker, I almost killed you."

Bourne realized he was wearing a Russian uniform, which was why he wasn't dead yet. He added a guttural note to his fluent Russian as he replied. "They sent me down from Rylsk. Me and half the army. Didn't you get the word? There's an American spy on the loose around here. Asshole's heading for the border."

"Why do you think I'm here?" the man shot back, taking a few steps closer, now about twenty feet away. He was absolutely huge, at least six foot six, and the sinking sun cast his giant shadow. "I'm part of Sever Group, and they have us searching every fucking farm from here to the border. Every road is blocked. He won't get far."

"Oh, yeah, we'll get him," Bourne said.

The soldier lowered his rifle. Bourne thought about taking him out with a quick burst from his own AK-12, but he calculated the distance between the farm and the roadblock and how the sound would carry. If he had a chance to fire, the soldiers would hear the shots, and they'd be on the scene within minutes.

If he could get close, he could do it silently. Assuming the giant didn't kill him first.

"What's your name?" the soldier asked. "Where you from?"

"Alexei. From Moscow."

"Moscow? A volunteer, huh?" the man joked, his belly shaking as he laughed.

"Oh, sure, we're all volunteers, aren't we?" Bourne replied.

"Yeah, fucking patriots, that's us." The man took a bottle from one of the deep pockets in his jacket and enjoyed a long swallow of what Bourne assumed was vodka. The bottle was large, but looked small in his paw. When he was done, the man began to extend the bottle toward Bourne, but then he stopped. Jason could see the man's fingers tighten around the rifle again as his eyes narrowed. "Hey, what the fuck did you do to your arm?"

Damn it!

The knife gash in his arm was bleeding again. Giving everything away.

Alert now, the soldier studied Bourne from head to toe and began to realize that something was wrong.

"Fuck, man, it's all over you. Who the fuck are you?"

Bourne was slow to reply because his brain began to pull him in different directions. He processed the suspicion on the soldier's face, trying to think of an excuse, trying to think of a strategy to stay alive. But he also found himself distracted by another noise buzzing louder than the tinnitus in his ears.

A whine, like an impatient bee looking for the next flower. Somewhere nearby, a drone was hunting for a target.

The other soldier, focused on Bourne, didn't hear it.

"I said, who the fuck *are* you?" the huge soldier repeated. He raised his AK-12 again in his beefy arms, aiming at Bourne. With a squeeze of the trigger, the rifle would riddle Jason's body with bullets in a fraction of a second.

Distractions. Bourne's head throbbed with pain. He stared at the barrel of the gun, anticipating the fire. He listened to the buzz of the drone. He realized he was about to be killed one way or another.

Distantly, in the sky, the buzz stopped. The drone went silent. Glide mode.

Time for the ghost.

Incoming.

"You're *him!*" the soldier bellowed, marching his tree-trunk legs toward Bourne, his mouth breaking into a cocky grin at the thought of his luck. "Fuck it all, you're him! *Time to die, little pup!*"

His finger twitched, ready to fire.

And then it happened. A sizzling rush of air, a blur of black motion, rocketed down from the sky. In the next millisecond, the soldier exploded, literally exploded, his giant body vaporized into an eruption of crimson jelly. The noise shattered Bourne's ears again, and the concussion wave threw him onto his back, covered in the cloud of goo that had once been the soldier's flesh and bones.

For a few seconds, all he could do was stare at the sky, dizzied by the blast. But he couldn't stay here. The attack would draw Russians from the roadblock. They'd be coming soon, a dozen men in Jeeps with automatic weapons, and Bourne needed to be far away. He stumbled to his feet, sickened as he looked down at himself, the green Russian uniform now painted red, interspersed with bits of organs clinging to the blood. The world spun; the fetid smell of death filled his nose.

He staggered toward the farmhouse, half limping, half falling, putting the building between himself and the road behind him. Then he lurched northward into the fields, and the border seemed farther away than ever.

———

"WE KNOW WHERE HE IS," JOHANNA INSISTED. "WE NEED TO GO GET HIM *now.* He's free, he's on the move, but every minute we wait increases the odds that they catch him. And when they do, he's dead on the spot."

The Ukrainian helicopter pilot, a twenty-five-year-old named Marko with buzzed black hair, drew a finger across his throat to say no. "Not happening, ma'am. There's fighting all over the area. Even if we go in under the radar, the Russians will shoot us down. There's no way we get in and out alive. The plan was to wait until midnight, and that's what we do."

Johanna stared at her phone and watched the blue dot on the screen moving slowly through the Russian countryside fifteen miles away. *Fifteen miles!* That blue dot was Jason, and he was so close to her that she could feel him, taste him, imagine him back in her arms. But fifteen miles across hostile territory was also the other side of the world. He wasn't going to make it.

"Marko, I'm in charge of this mission," Johanna insisted.

The young pilot glanced at the half dozen soldiers around them in the barn-turned-barracks outside Hlukhiv. They said nothing, all deferring to him. "Ma'am, you're American. This isn't Washington. Out here, you're not in charge of fucking anything, no matter what the politicians say. I'm not taking these boys on a suicide mission to bring one of your spies in from the cold. Now, I'm happy to help you get him back. But we go when I say it's safe to go, and not before."

Johanna felt nothing but frustration and impatience. She wanted to grab a Jeep and drive across the border herself. Grab Jason and bring him with her. *Fifteen miles!*

But the kid was right.

"There must be a way we can communicate with him," she said. "He's alone. He doesn't know we're out here. He doesn't know where to go. If we can talk to him, we can set up a rendezvous. A time and a place. He's only a couple of miles from Krupets. He can hide in the town until we get there tonight."

"How exactly do you plan on talking to him?" Marko asked.

Johanna shook her head. "I have no idea. But he needs to know we're coming for him. He needs to know there's a plan."

Jason, I'm here!

She checked her phone again, studying the map to watch his progress. She looked at the map and then looked again. Her fingers grew frantic, scrolling in every direction. Her heart seized with despair. She rebooted the app and tried again, but nothing had changed. The map was empty now. All she saw were the roads, rivers, and terrain in the lands east of the border. The blue dot had disappeared.

The battery in the tracker was dead.

Jason was gone.

33

NIGHT WAS COMING SOON. SO FAR, BOURNE HAD STAYED ALIVE. HE'D hiked another hour from the farmhouse, keeping to the woods and moving slowly as he dodged units of Russian soldiers. His objective was to make his way back to his westward trek near the highway, but ahead of him, he saw a barrier that may as well have been a canyon with no bridge. The woods ended, and he saw hundreds of yards of open land—an untilled field, nothing but black dirt—separating him from the next stand of trees. He could cross it in a few minutes, but he would be exposed the entire way. He had no-where to hide, and his blood-covered uniform was absurdly visible to anyone who looked his way.

He stayed in the trees for a couple of minutes, waiting and thinking. The sun had already disappeared, and the countryside quickly began to darken under the azure sky. Bourne had no watch, but he calculated that it must be after nine o'clock. Crossing the field in the dark would be marginally safer, but the longer he stayed in one place, the more chance the Russian dragnet surrounded him and tightened the noose.

Right now, speed mattered more than safety.

In both directions, the countryside looked empty. He saw no one, and the highway was out of sight to the south. Bourne ventured from the trees. He marched as quickly as he could across the uneven soil, but he didn't have the strength to run. His left leg dragged; he'd twisted his ankle as the explosion blew him backward. He had to blink to keep his dizzy mind from spinning, and his bleeding ears could barely hear. His breathing came sharp and fast. He tried to focus on the trees ahead of him, on each step bringing him closer to safety. When he got to the trees, it would be dark, and he would be under cover for a while.

The area looked clear. No soldiers with binoculars and rifles. No vehicles rumbling across the land. He saw no black helicopters in the sky. The woods loomed larger, beckoning him forward. He'd crossed more than two-thirds of the field; he was almost there. *Get to the trees, make it to the highway, follow the road out of the country.*

He'd convinced himself that he might make it alive when he heard the buzz, like a monster scratching at the closet door.

A drone.

They'd found him.

Wearily, feeling nothing at all, Bourne looked up, and he saw it. Its red lights blinked against the darkening sky. Its silver blades whirred as it hovered in place, five hundred feet in the air. They stared at each other, man to machine. Somewhere behind the drone's 4K camera, an operator at a computer was smiling at him, zeroing in on his face, identifying him as a target to destroy.

A Russian?

A Ukrainian?

It didn't matter. To both of them, the name of the game was kill on sight.

Bourne walked faster, which was futile. When he tried to run, he crashed down on one knee. He slid the AK-12 off his shoulder and aimed at the sky, but the drone operator saw the threat and nimbly sent the machine sailing over his head. As Jason spun, dizzily trying to follow its path, he fired, but his barrage of bullets went wildly wrong. His eyes tried to chase the streaking machine, but he wound up squeezing his eyes closed and pushing his fist against his head to try to drive out the throbbing pain.

His other knee sank to the dirt. He couldn't move anymore. There was nowhere to run. He waited, expecting to hear the whistle of the explosive heading at him. One burst of light and pain, and it would be over. One millisecond, and his memory would be gone forever, wiped clean and black.

But the attack never came.

The seconds passed, and he was alive.

Bourne opened his eyes. The buzzing got louder, still muffled by his bad ears. The drone drifted closer, only a few feet off the ground, fifty feet away. It approached him, slowly, tentatively. Thirty feet. Then twenty feet. The machine waggled up and down, as if saying hello.

What the hell was it doing?

His grip tightened on the Russian rifle in his hands. If he raised the barrel again, he could eliminate the drone, but he didn't. Something else was going on. As Bourne watched, the drone finally landed, dropping gently into the field with a little burst of dust. Its rotors slowed and stopped.

Bourne looked around the wide field again. Around him, the darkness was nearly complete. He saw no lights anywhere. He pushed himself unsteadily to his feet and approached the drone, which was about five feet across, still and quiet, sitting on the ground like a black spider. Kneeling in front of it, he saw that this wasn't a military drone at all. It carried no weapons, no explosives.

Instead, this was a cargo drone, used for transporting payloads.

He turned it over and saw a black metal box, about one foot by one foot, clutched in the drone's claws. When he pried the box free, he undid the tight latch and opened it. The contents, packed tightly in bubble wrap, took his breath away.

He found a small flashlight. Power bars. A canteen of drinking water. A Glock 45, fully loaded, with two extra magazines and a suppressor. A G-Shock Mudmaster watch. A Thuraya satellite phone. At the bottom of the box, he found a folded piece of paper, and when he opened it and shined the flashlight beam on the page, he saw a printed map of the area, with two X's drawn, one in an open undeveloped area, one adjacent to a small town labeled Krupets that looked to be less than two miles away.

The X in the open field was him. He knew that.

Beneath the X near the Russian town, he saw a handwritten word. *Midnight.*

Bourne found his hands shaking. The adrenaline that had fled from his body rushed back like a river.

They were coming to get him.

HE REACHED KRUPETS HALF AN HOUR BEFORE THE PICKUP TIME AT MID-night. It was pitch-black except for starlight. There were no lights at all in the town, no electricity. In the dark and quiet, he saw no one, but he could feel that he wasn't alone. The residents who'd stayed in their homes as the town traded hands between Ukraine and Russia didn't show themselves. Even so, he could smell wood fires and hear the squawking of chickens. People still lived here, hiding from the soldiers on both sides.

It was a small town, not even a mile long, just a stretch of mod-est houses built along the border highway across from a swell in the Krupka river. But it bore the unmistakable marks of years of war. Many of the homes had been reduced to rubble or burned into empty shells. Those that still stood had gaping holes punched in their roofs. The ruts of heavy-vehicle treads crisscrossed the matchbox lawns, and telephone poles littered the ground like fallen trees, their wires snaking along the road.

A quiet little town in the middle of nowhere didn't feel like much of a prize for so many on both sides to die.

Bourne checked the map.

He was now directly across from the bend in the Krupka where the rendezvous was marked. A helicopter would come, fly-ing low, landing only long enough for him to be pulled inside. He turned on his flashlight briefly, spotting the ruins of a brick house on the slope above him on the north side of the highway. From there, he could cross the road and make it to the bank of the river when the helicopter landed. The whole extraction would be done in no more than thirty seconds. He climbed the slope, sliding down to the ground at the base of the house near the crumbling stone wall.

The Glock, suppressor attached, was in his hand. It was easier in the darkness to wield a quiet pistol than an AK-12.

Time to wait. Twenty more minutes.

Bourne ate one of the power bars and drank from the canteen. The night air turned cold, making him shiver. He'd crossed a narrow section of the Krupka on his way into town, so the uniform he wore was soaking wet. When he touched his face, he found blood, some of it his, some of it the remains of the soldier targeted by the drone. He checked the satellite phone but saw no messages or updates.

He hoped that meant the rendezvous was on schedule.

Ten minutes.

Then Bourne saw bright lights and heard the night come alive. He tensed, gripping the pistol harder. The noise of a vehicle's engine thumped from the west, making a slow transit through the town. Headlights shined, lighting up the road fifty yards away. Loud voices carried in the still air, and boots crunched on gravel. He slid down the slope for a better view, and he saw a Russian Jeep heading his way, with at least six soldiers walking on both sides of the vehicle, some near the river, some covering the opposite slope where he was hiding. They all had rifles armed and ready.

Hunting for *him*.

House by house, dazzling high-powered flashlights lit up the night, exposing every inch of the town. Bourne backed up in the wet grass, hoping the lights wouldn't reveal the indentations of his footprints on the slope. He made his way to the ruined house behind him and slipped inside through a gap in the wall. His arrival disturbed a large rat that scampered out the back of the house into the fields.

He kept the Glock ready and listened as the dragnet came closer. When he checked his watch, he saw that seven minutes remained before the pickup time. Edging his face around the crumbled wall, he watched the headlights of the Jeep creep eastward on the highway. The soldiers were so close now that he could eavesdrop on their conversations in Russian as they talked about sex, guns, and money.

Footsteps squished in the grass outside the house where he'd taken refuge. Beams of light flooded the interior space around him, illuminating the debris of what had once been a home. Broken lamps, burnt furniture, a shattered television, rotting food on the floor. He held his breath, his back pushed against the wall. Two men investigated the ruins from outside, two voices inches away on the other side of the wall, so close that he smelled their body odor and cigarette smoke. He could hear other men, closer to the road, at least a dozen soldiers.

The Jeep's engine rattled as it passed on the highway.

Someone called in Russian. "Petyr! Andrey! Anything up there?"

One of the men near the house shouted back. "*Nyet.* Nobody."

"Did you check inside?"

"Nothing but rats inside."

The footsteps receded. Bourne began to breathe again. He stayed where he was for another two minutes, listening to the convoy slowly get farther away. Then he slipped from the cover of the house back onto the grassy slope. Across from him, starlight reflected on the river. He saw the silhouettes of the soldiers, but he couldn't hear their voices. The Jeep continued to roll eastward, three houses away, then four, but still too close for comfort if the helicopter arrived now.

Bourne slipped down the slope to the two-lane road. In the darkness, he was mostly invisible. He watched the Russians heading for the edge of town, and he felt safe for a brief moment.

Then he heard the thud of boots running on the highway behind him.

One man, moving fast, catching up with the others.

A flashlight lit Bourne up from behind and threw his tall shadow forward, and a young voice called to him, seeing the back of the uniform.

"Nikki, that you? I had to take a shit."

Bourne hated what he had to do, but he had no choice. He spun immediately, raising the gun, and fired a suppressed shot from the Glock into the Russian's forehead below his helmet. The kid looked to be barely eighteen, and his eyes didn't even have time to widen with surprise. He was alive, and then he was dead at Bourne's feet.

The convoy kept moving away.

In the distance, he heard the low throb of the helicopter approaching. He crossed the road to the field on the other side and spotted a flat clearing near the river for the chopper to set down. He didn't see the chopper yet—it was flying dark—but the pulse of the engine got louder, rippling in with the breeze.

Too loud. Too soon.

Shouts erupted from the convoy as they heard it, too. He heard orders barked. The boots of men charging his way. Ahead of him, whipping across the land barely twenty feet off the ground, the helicopter zoomed into view from the west against the dark sky. Bourne used his flashlight to blink out a welcome and tell them that he was here. He limped toward the water, and bullets exploded in puffs of dirt and grass. The Russians had spotted him; they were closing in. He swung back and used a burst from the AK-12 to freeze them in place, then forced his legs to run. Fifty yards became forty, then thirty.

The helicopter landed.

He heard a woman's voice. *"Jason, stay low!"*

Crouching, he struggled to keep his legs upright. Over his head, at least half a dozen weapons opened fire from the helicopter with an explosion of noise and flame, driving the Russian assault back.

All but one.

A lone soldier kept coming, pounding across the land. Bourne heard the man closing the distance between them at a sprint. The rifles in the helicopter couldn't target the soldier without hitting Bourne, so the fire on the convoy didn't stop him. Bourne heard trampling grass, like a bull chasing him across the field, and all he could do was throw himself forward, then spin on his back.

The soldier was right there, leaping, no rifle in his hands, just a knife. Bourne aimed the Glock at his chest and fired point-blank, but the man's body armor allowed him to shrug it off like a mosquito bite. He fired again at the man's head and missed. The blade came for his throat in midair as the Russian jumped, but a loud blast of automatic fire from barely three feet away suddenly shredded the soldier's face and neck, nearly decapitating him.

Already dead, the man's body fell heavily, and Bourne barely had time to deflect the knife as it dropped toward his chest.

A woman from the helicopter stood over him, her gun smoking. Her strong arms under his shoulders helped him to his feet. She held Bourne by the waist as they staggered for the open helicopter door. More arms appeared to pull him inside, and more weapons unleashed devastating fire, driving the Russians back. As the door slid shut, the helicopter wobbled off the ground, then surged forward, turning and climbing. Pings of bullets struck the metal, but the chopper soared out of range.

Heading west. Heading for the border.

Bourne lay on his back on the chopper's metal floor, feeling his body sway. He saw the woman who'd saved him bending over him, dressed all in black, a nylon balaclava protecting her face. In the dim glow of a flashlight, she yanked the covering off, and her long blond hair tumbled free, and he stared into her blue eyes. Her hands cupped his cheeks as if she couldn't believe he was real.

"Jason."

It was Johanna.

34

BOURNE LOOKED OUT FROM THE HOTEL BALCONY TOWARD THE SEA OF Marmara, caught between the Black Sea and the Aegean. Small islands dotted the glistening Turkish waters under the midmorning sun. Below him, white umbrellas lined the beach like dots of paint, and summer tourists crowded the sidewalk cafés. Bicycles sped along the cobblestone street. The sweet sea air filled his lungs as a warm breeze blew in from the water.

He leaned on the railing, finally feeling healthy and strong again. It was the fifth day since his escape from Russia, and his third since Johanna had spirited him out of Kyiv on a private jet that landed in Istanbul. From there, they'd ferried four hours to the island of Avsa, where Johanna knew a boutique hotel she'd used as a getaway in the past. She'd told no one at Treadstone where they were going.

He returned from the balcony to their fourth-floor room, leaving the glass door open to the wind. The bed, with its rumpled white sheets and green comforter, was empty, and he heard the shower running. Bourne slipped off his cotton robe and went into the bathroom, and he watched Johanna bathing in the walk-in shower, her long hair wet, her face tipped into the spray. Water poured over the slope of her back and down her skinny bare legs. He came up behind her and slipped his arms around her waist, which was slippery from the soap. She sighed with pleasure and molded against him, her head leaning back against his shoulder. When she turned around, their bodies pressed together, and they kissed, mouths pushing hard against each other. They'd already made love once in the predawn when they awoke, but they were both ready again. She leaned into the stone shower wall and bent one leg around his back, opening herself up to him. He slid easily inside her, and the hot water bathed the heat of their bodies as they moved in rhythm against each other.

A few minutes later, they lay in bed, cooling themselves under the ceiling fan. They didn't talk for a long time. They'd barely talked at all since they arrived in Turkey. For a while, they'd pushed away the darkness in order to revel in each other, but the real world had begun to creep back into their thoughts.

"You know, I wasn't sure what to expect when I found you," Johanna told him finally. "I didn't even know if you'd remember me."

"I did," Bourne told her. "Of course I did. As soon as Nash told me your name, you flooded back to me. That was all it took. I remembered every moment we've spent together."

"The good and the bad," she said.

"Mostly good."

"And the rest? What about the rest of your memory?"

"It's coming. Slowly. Washburn was right. If I let it happen on its own, the pieces fall into place."

"I like that." She was quiet again, and he sensed her uncertainty, as if she stood on a cliff's edge, getting ready to jump. "Listen, Jason, I've been waiting for the right time. There's something I need to tell you—"

She stopped as a knock on the hotel door interrupted them.

Driven by instinct, Bourne grabbed his Glock. Johanna did the same, both of them aiming their guns and expecting an assault to come crashing through the door. Then, realizing it was a room service waiter bringing their breakfast, they shoved the weapons under the pillows and laughed at their overreaction.

But it could have been real. They were living on a knife's edge.

Dressed in their robes, they drank smoky coffee and sweet champagne, and they ate sausages, eggs, and simit bread. When they were done, they put on casual clothes and made their way out to the Marmara beach, directly across the street from the hotel. The strip of sand was narrow, taken up by tourists in lounge chairs and children building sand castles, so they walked in the water, with the lazy surf around their calves. They held hands. Johanna kept her blond hair loose, swirling in the breeze.

After ten minutes walking, she stopped and cupped a hand over her eyes to watch the sea. Bourne stood next to her. The brief moments of peace in their days alone had already fled from his mind.

"Did you see him?" he asked.

She knew what he meant.

"The Turk about a hundred feet back," Johanna replied. "Red

shirt, black shorts, bare feet. Sunglasses, thick dark hair, mustache. About thirty. He's been on our tail since we came out of the hotel."

"They've found us."

Johanna nodded. "Who do you think it is? Who's he working for?"

"Does it matter? If one of them knows, everyone knows. We need to leave. Now. This afternoon."

A little sigh escaped her lips. "I know, but where do we run? Anywhere we go, they'll find us sooner or later."

"So we keep moving."

She turned and faced him. "This is my fault."

"It's not. If it's Putin again, I'm the target."

"Maybe so, but I don't think it's him. Not this time."

"Why are you so sure?"

Johanna shook her head. "Because I've been keeping a secret from you, Jason. Not just now. Back when we were together. It's a secret about me. I should have told you before. Maybe none of this would have happened if I'd been honest."

"I could feel there was something," Bourne said. "So tell me. What is it?"

She told him.

She told him *everything.* About her life in Dallas as a teenage girl named Annie, about the sexual assault she'd suffered at the hands of Adam Hill, about the ruthless way she'd paid him back. About David Abbott trying to convince her to come forward to expose the truth about Hill and bring him down.

About what had happened in the Med, with *her* as the primary target.

"Hill's going to keep coming after me," Johanna said. "Shadow was right about that. Now that he knows who I am, he won't stop until he erases me. It won't be just him, either. He'll tell the Chinese, if he hasn't already, and they'll do anything to protect their asset. I'll be on their list soon. Maybe I already am. We can't spend the rest of our lives looking over our shoulders."

"What do you want to do?" Bourne asked.

"I want to kill him. That's what I really want to do. Kill him hard and slow. But that's a fantasy. It would be almost impossible with the Secret Service protection around him. No, we need to figure out how to isolate him. Turn Holly Schultz against him and give her the tools to destroy him. And in return, they leave us alone. The CIA. Treadstone. We go back to living our lives."

"Sounds neat and tidy," Bourne said, "but nothing is that easy."

"I know."

"Do you have a plan?"

"I've had a plan for years. I've got everything I need. I just need to retrieve the evidence and get it to Holly."

They turned back toward the hotel. Ahead of them, the Turk in the red shirt who had been following them melted away across the beach. Bourne tried to keep eyes on him, but the spy lost himself in the crowd. It didn't matter. Where there was one, there were others. As long as they stayed here, the net was closing in.

"Friend or foe?" Johanna asked.

"I don't think we have any friends. We better get out of here."

"I know the island," she murmured. "I've been here before. I'll find someone with a boat to get us back to the mainland. We can be on the water in an hour. Hopefully, it'll be enough if we stay one step ahead of them."

But Bourne wasn't convinced.

He was pretty sure they were already one step behind.

When they got back to the hotel, he spotted the next watcher already waiting for them in the lobby. This man was in his fifties and wore a sky-blue linen suit, with a white panama hat dipped below his forehead, as if he were a spy lifted straight out of 1950s Havana. He didn't try to hide his intentions. Instead, he tipped his hat at them with a broad smile on his face.

"Somebody wants a meeting," Bourne said.

They took seats in the lobby, one on either side of the man in the white hat. He was medium height and thin, and all his movements were slow and precise. The man took note of their hands, which were near the grips of their guns, and he kept his own small, manicured fingers carefully folded in his lap where they could see them. He had a small cup of espresso and a half-eaten rum-soaked donut on the table in front of him. His cologne smelled of rosemary.

"Cain," the man said in a faintly Hispanic accent. "A pleasure to finally meet you. And you are Johanna, yes? You're as lovely as advertised. Would you like something? Wine? Whiskey?"

"Just answers," Bourne said.

"Of course. My name is Alvarez. I'm Treadstone. No need to worry about me, we're on the same side."

"Treadstone isn't the same side," Johanna snapped. "We're our own side."

"Well, yes, I understand why you feel that way, but neither one of you has anything to fear from us. On the contrary. All of us in the agency were delighted with the news that Johanna's mission was successful. That you were able to engineer Cain's escape. Really very impressive work."

"How did you find us?" Johanna asked.

"You're good at what you do, but so are we. Shadow anticipated you'd try to slip away when you returned to Ukraine. We were watching the private air traffic out of Kyiv."

Bourne glanced at the sidewalk outside the hotel door, feeling watched again. "The man tailing us on the beach. The Turk. Red shirt. Was he Treadstone, too?"

Alvarez pursed his lips into a frown. "Alas, no. You're sure he was following you?"

"Very sure."

"That worries me. As word of your freedom has spread, the manhunt for both of you has continued. I was expecting others to begin closing on the island soon, but they've moved even faster than anticipated. My job is to get you out. I have secure transport waiting. First a boat, then a jet from the Turkish coast."

"To go where?" Bourne asked.

"To see an old friend. He's most anxious to meet you again."

Bourne knew exactly who he meant. "David Abbott. Where is he?"

"Oh, I have no idea about that. Shadow has him in a new secure location. I'm supposed to deliver you both to Athens. At that point, someone else will take over. I imagine this will prove to be a long journey."

"And if we refuse?" Johanna asked.

Alvarez took a bite of his donut, then wiped his lips daintily with a napkin and took another sip of coffee. "Well, you're under no obligation to accompany me, of course. But if I leave, you're on your own, and circumstances have made it clear that you're in danger. Your best option right now is to use my plan. What you do after that, once we're in Athens, is entirely up to you."

Bourne and Johanna exchanged a glance, and the message between them was clear. *Trust no one.*

"You've done your job, Alvarez," Bourne said. "You've delivered your message. Now you can deliver a message back to Shadow for me. As far as I'm concerned, David Abbott is dead, and he can stay that way."

The spy shrugged. "Regrettable. If you change your mind, I'm in the Tonkiri hotel two doors down. But move fast, my friends."

The two of them left the Treadstone man alone in the lobby. They climbed the stairs to the fourth floor, neither one of them saying a word. The smart move *was* to use Alvarez as far as Greece and then break off on their own. In the open, on the island, they were already exposed. But Treadstone had been compromised, and any of the links in the getaway chain might have ties to Holly Schultz. No route was safe.

On the top floor, Bourne opened the stairwell door carefully. He spotted a housekeeping cart one room down from theirs at the far end of the hallway. As he watched, a pretty young Turkish maid in a hijab shut the door on the adjoining room and pushed the cart up the hall. He could hear her low musical hum. She stopped outside their room, and as she did, Bourne led Johanna out of the stairwell. He had his Glock in the loose pocket of his shorts, his hand securely around the grip.

They walked closer, conscious of the closed hotel room doors on both sides. The maid noticed them and gave them a demure nod and a smile. She hadn't opened their door yet. Her manner, her appearance, offered no indication that she was anything other than what she appeared to be. Still humming softly, she grabbed a stack of fresh white towels in one arm, and Bourne stiffened, ready to draw the Glock. If she had a gun tucked in the towels, this was the moment she'd fire. But the maid simply swiped a master key on a lanyard across the electronic panel to unlock their door.

She turned the knob.

She pushed the door inward.

In the silence, Bourne heard the low snap of the wire breaking and the small electronic beep that followed. The giant explosion belched fire into the hallway and blasted the young maid like a missile through the opposite wall. Glass shattered everywhere. Thunder shook the entire hotel, and the rippling shock wave lofted the two of them off their feet and crashed them ten feet backward into the stairwell door. A cloud of smoke and dust choked the hallway. Emergency alarms blared with the clang of bells. He took Johanna's arm and dragged her to her feet. She leaned into him as they stumbled into the stairwell and headed down the steps.

On the ground floor, they avoided the lobby and headed for the rear exit, hidden by dozens of people flooding outside. They found themselves in a back alley below the hotel's rear wall, and they saw a dead, broken body lying on the gravel. It was the maid. The explosion had shot her through the opposite room and out the far window, where she'd fallen four stories to the alley.

Bourne and Johanna followed a zigzag path past old cars and through the clouds of steam belching from hotel kitchens. No one followed them. When they'd gone ten blocks, far enough to feel safe, they finally stopped, sliding to the ground on an empty street among apartment buildings high in the hills. In the distance, near the water, a corkscrew of black smoke rose in the sky.

"No peace," Johanna whispered. "We'll never have peace. They'll never stop."

Jason didn't say anything.

She was right. He felt the walls closing in on them again. That brought a wave of cold anger in his chest like frozen winter air. He saw a man's face taking shape in his mind, and he knew he'd been wrong to think he could avoid him. He couldn't run away from that face forever. He needed to confront the man who'd made him who he was, the spider who'd spun the webs that had trapped him in Treadstone for most of his life.

"I'm going to go see David Abbott," he told Johanna.

She nodded, not surprised.

"I'll let Alvarez take me to Athens," Bourne went on, "and I'll follow the road from there. Abbott and I have unfinished business."

Her own face showed the same kind of determination. "I have unfinished business, too."

"Adam Hill."

"Yes. Years ago, I buried what I need to destroy him. Now I need to get it back."

"Why not lie low until we're together again? Stay out of sight. Stay safe."

"No place is safe. We need to move fast. Do what you need to do, and come back to me, Jason. When you're done with Abbott, come find me."

"Where will you be?"

"Salzburg," Johanna said. "I'm going back to Salzburg. That's where I keep my past."

35

THE LAST LINK IN THE CHAIN THAT LED TO DAVID ABBOTT RAN THROUGH
Rex Volkman. The security chief from Abbott's Greek estate met
Bourne two days later at Engadin Airport in St. Moritz. Bourne
only had a moment to admire the green Swiss hills before Volkman
took him to a waiting helicopter and secured a hood over his head.

"Sorry about this," Volkman said, "but given what happened in
Greece, we don't want anyone knowing Mr. Abbott's actual location. Not even you, Cain. Shadow and I are the only ones who
know where he is."

The helicopter took off a couple of minutes later with Volkman
at the controls. He flew east, but then made a series of turns, and
Bourne suspected that was designed to confuse his sense of direction. Regardless, he was pretty sure that the helicopter ultimately
ended up on a northwestern course out of St. Moritz. It flew for an
hour, and then he felt the machine slowly descending until it
dropped gently to the ground. Volkman shut down the motor.

When the security guard removed the hood, Bourne found himself on a remote Swiss mountain near a three-story log home that had been terraced on concrete pillars into the steep slope. A tall cupola tower rose above the roof, topped by a large dome built completely of glass. He saw no other homes and no town in the valley below him, nothing but dense evergreen woods interspersed with lush overgrown fields. The surrounding hills rose toward distant rocky peaks, some with snowcaps even in the summer. There was no road of any kind winding away from the log home, and the only access point appeared to be the helicopter pad. This location was even more isolated than the hideaway Abbott had used on Naxos.

Volkman noted Bourne's assessment of the area. "People know he's alive. That ups the risk, but this place will be tough for anyone to find. All the supplies go in and out through me. Come on, he's waiting for you."

Bourne followed Volkman up the steps on the slope and through the double front doors of the estate. Once they were inside, the security man gestured at an elevator, and then Volkman disappeared elsewhere in the house. Bourne took the elevator, which rose into the cupola tower and let him out near a winding wooden staircase that led up to the glass dome. He took the steps and found himself in a large observatory that felt as if it had been built on the roof of the world. Mountain views loomed in every direction, and overhead, dark clouds moved like animals across the sky. A curving fireplace warmed the room, and the carpet was thick and chocolate brown. The furniture was all leather, densely packed and comfortable. He saw a wet bar, fully stocked with liquor from around the world, plus a complete selection of Waterford crystal. The open bottle on top of the bar was a Canadian whiskey, Lucky Bastard.

David Abbott stood with his back to Jason, his extremely tall frame outlined by the mountains in the distance. His silver hair looked like smoke. He wore a navy-blue suit, perfectly tailored to his fit body, with black shoes polished to a shine. He didn't turn around as Bourne arrived, but he called to him in that rumbling baritone that Jason had assumed he would never hear again.

"It's been a long time, son."

Son. Jason had always hated when Abbott called him that.

"Yes, that's bound to happen when you fake your death and don't tell me about it," Bourne replied.

Abbott finally turned around. "True enough. I really did want to tell you, David, but at the time I went away, you didn't even know who I was. You'd lost your memory. I was nothing to you. By the time some of your past began to creep back into your head, well, it seemed self-indulgent to bring you into my life again. You were better off thinking I was gone."

"You always did like making decisions for me."

"Guilty as charged," Abbott agreed. "I'm a controlling man. I think I know best, and most of the time, I'm proven right. But in the end, you did what you wanted, despite anything I ever said." He wandered to the wet bar to pour more Lucky Bastard. "Drink?"

"No, thanks."

Abbott added a spherical craft ice cube and sipped his drink. "First things first, David. I'm enormously relieved that you got out of Russia. Shadow told me you were dead. It wasn't until you were back on free land that she admitted the truth about what happened.

I guess she learned her lessons from me. If you didn't make it out alive, it was easier to let me believe you'd been dead all along."

"Where is Marlen?" Bourne asked.

Abbott's lips pushed together in an unhappy line. "Marlen. So she told you?"

"That you're her father? Yes."

"I see. I wish she hadn't done that. But it's always been a complicated relationship with her. Not that you and I didn't have our ups and down, too."

"Where is she?" he asked again.

"Washington. She didn't want to see you. Not yet. I think she had the crazy notion that you might kill her."

"It's tempting," Bourne admitted.

"Well, I'd rather you didn't, for obvious reasons. I know she betrayed you, and that it wasn't the first time she did so. But since you're aware of our relationship, I hope you understand why she did what she did."

"She could have told me what she was planning, rather than set me up."

"Would you have agreed? Let yourself be taken by the Russians?"

"We'll never know."

Abbott's eyes studied him carefully, like a display in a museum. "Not that it's any of my business, but did the two of you become ... involved ... while you were hunting for me? Marlen has always had a weakness for you, David. I saw it in her face the first time she saw you at Marnes-la-Coquette. Usually she's as cool as I am, but not when it comes to you."

"You're right," Bourne replied. "It's none of your business."

Abbott shrugged, but Jason could see that he interpreted the answer as a yes. "Anyway, I appreciate your coming to see me."

"I didn't intend to, but I decided that I wanted answers."

"Fair enough. Answers about what?"

"About who you really are. About how you could do the things you did to Marlen, molding your own daughter in your image like an ice sculpture. About how you could do the things you did to *me*. How you could send people to kill me after I lost my memory the first time. You called me *son* when I walked up those stairs, but you were willing to believe I'd betrayed you and betrayed Treadstone."

"That was what the evidence suggested back then," Abbott replied calmly. "It appeared to all of us that you'd become a traitor. Amnesia never crossed my mind. Who would have thought of something like that? Someone in my shoes can't give himself over to emotion, David, even when it comes to family. Threats to my country come first. Until recently, Marlen understood that, too."

"I was never family to you. I was a tool for your plans."

Anger flashed momentarily on Abbott's face. "You don't remember who you were back then, David. I do. The deaths of your parents sucked every bit of life out of you. You were bitter. Empty. Furious at the world. Without me, you would have put a gun in your mouth. Or you would have climbed on top of a tower with a rifle in your hands. If you don't believe me, I can show you the transcripts of what you told your therapist."

Jason shook his head with a kind of awe at this man's ruthlessness. "You bugged my sessions with Mo Panov?"

"Of course I did. If I didn't understand you, how could I help you?"

"Help? Is that what you call it?"

"Absolutely. I have no regrets about the things I did. I gave you your life back. I gave you a *purpose*, David."

"Treadstone," Bourne said.

"Yes, Treadstone. With your skills, your intellect, you were made for the field. You may not want to believe it, but Treadstone saved you."

"Treadstone *destroyed* me," Bourne fired back. "In Switzerland, I had the life I wanted. I fell in love with Marlen. Only, I knew her as Monika back then. Another lie. I thought she and I would spend our lives together. I thought she loved me. But it was just another one of your tests, another one of your games, and in the end, what happened? Monika disappeared. I became a killer."

Abbott waved his hand dismissively through the air. "Oh, don't be so dramatic. I may not like the means we use sometimes, but the ends are all that matter. Sometimes people need to die. Individual lives have been sacrificed for good, for bad, for nothing, throughout eternity. Do you think the world would be a better place if a man like Lennon were alive?"

"I'm an assassin. So was he. I'm not sure we're really so different from the ones we're fighting. I think Putin would talk about ends and means and sound exactly like you."

"This isn't getting us anywhere."

Abbott finished his Lucky Bastard in a single swallow and went to the window, turning his back on him again. Bourne wondered if he really liked the taste of the whiskey, or whether he simply liked the name. Lucky Bastard. If there was one man who fit the description, it was David Abbott.

"I didn't bring you here to talk about the past," he went on. "Or to pass judgment on me, for that matter."

"I know why you brought me here. Johanna."

Abbott folded his arms over his chest and stared at the Swiss mountains. "So she told you about Adam Hill. What he did to her."

"She told me the whole story."

"Did Marlen tell you that I know Hill to be a Chinese asset?"

"Yes."

"Then you can see why I need Johanna to come forward. She loves you. If you ask her to do it, she will."

Bourne felt an urge to throw the man through the glass of the observatory dome and watch him fall. "I'm not going to ask her to do anything."

"Surely you understand the threat Hill poses."

"Honestly? I don't care." Bourne paused, wanting to let Abbott twist in the wind by telling him nothing. "But as it turns out, Johanna already made a decision on her own. She wants Hill taken down. So you win anyway. You always do."

Abbott turned around, his face flushed. "She'll come forward?"

"Not publicly. She'll do it behind the scenes. She'll work through Holly Schultz to get rid of Hill."

Disappointment returned to the man's features. "That's not enough, David! Do you think I haven't thought about that option in the past? Without Johanna—without *Annie*—to validate it, Hill can write off the evidence as a fringe conspiracy theory. He'll say the videos are AI-generated, not real. The word of an anonymous mystery woman against a popular sitting vice president? No one will believe it."

"There's more," Bourne said.

Abbott's eyes narrowed. "More? What do you mean?"

head

"The evidence isn't just video. Johanna kept everything. *Everything.* She has his DNA from the assault."

"Good God. Is that really true?"

"Yes."

"Why didn't she tell me? Why didn't she give it to me before now?"

"Because she didn't trust you. Because she knew you'd expose her anyway. You'd feed her to the jackals. Just like you did a month ago."

A ghost of guilt flitted across Abbott's face. "What are you talking about?"

"Don't pretend, and don't play games with me. It wasn't an *accident* that someone spotted you and Johanna in Dubrovnik. Do you think I don't know how you operate? You set the whole thing up. You made sure spies were watching. You were willing to give up your secret life, so that *Johanna would be seen with you.* So that Adam Hill would realize that you'd found Annie and that he would know who Annie became. You wanted Hill to go after her so that Johanna would have no choice but to strike back."

Silence fell over the observatory. Bourne watched Abbott formulating a lie, but then his surrogate father abandoned it. "You always did know me too well, David. Yes, all right, it's true, I needed to force Johanna's hand. I saw no other way but to let Hill know he was vulnerable so that he would lash out at her. My mistake was in not realizing that Hill had Holly Schultz in his pocket. I didn't expect him to act so quickly. When I heard about the explosion, and I thought you and Johanna were both dead, I was devastated."

"If you were devastated, it's only because your plan failed," Bourne snapped. "I think you may be the most ruthless man I ever met, and I just spent time with Vladimir Putin. Meeting you again, seeing who you are, I have sympathy for the woman Marlen became. It also makes me crazy that, in the end, Johanna and I are doing exactly what you want. But that's all you care about, isn't it? Everything else is just noise."

"Then you better go to her," Abbott said, his jewel-blue eyes as hard as diamonds. "Until the two of you take care of Adam Hill, neither of you will be safe. I think your experience in that hotel on Avsa Island proved that. So be on your way, David. Volkman will take you back to St. Moritz. From there you can catch a plane to Salzburg."

Bourne's body turned to ice. "How do you know Johanna is in Salzburg?"

"Please. Once we found you in Turkey, do you think I wouldn't have her followed? I certainly wasn't going to lose her again. I know exactly where she is. I've had eyes on her all the way."

"*Whose eyes?*" Bourne asked.

"One of our most capable Treadstone agents. Vandal."

———

SALZBURG.

When Johanna thought about Salzburg, she didn't think about its quaint European beauty, the fortress high on the hill, the bridges over the Salzach as it flowed through the city, the echoes of Mozart, the seventeenth-century buildings in the Altstadt. She didn't care if Julie Andrews had taught the von Trapp children to sing here.

To Johanna, Salzburg was her old life. Annie had died, and Johanna had been born here. At fourteen years old, she'd traveled overseas from Dallas, using a fake passport she'd bought with money she stole from Adam Hill's home. The passport said she was eighteen. An adult. She'd learned how to dress, act, and behave like a girl much older than she was, and no one knew otherwise.

She'd come to Salzburg to meet a woman she knew online, a twenty-year-old lesbian coder who was in love with Annie and willing to help her. Her name was Liesl. Just like *The Sound of Music*. Except Liesl turned out to be a fifty-two-year-old male museum guard named Manfred. So Annie—now Johanna, fourteen going on thirty—had kicked him in the balls and gone elsewhere. She spent a month living on the Salzburg streets, sleeping in parks and alleys, before she found an actual lesbian coder who was willing to share her apartment. Emilia knew perfectly well that Johanna was younger than she let on, and she treated the girl like a sister, not a lover. She mentored Johanna in cutting-edge technology, and by the time she was sixteen, Johanna was living on her own in a center-city apartment, doing freelance jobs for tech companies around the world, making six figures.

But she still remembered that first night. Fourteen years old. Alone. In the dark.

Back then, after learning the truth about Manfred, she'd made her way through the town's empty streets to the Kommunalfriedhof, the huge cemetery south of the river. It was safe there. No one else dared to sleep with the ghosts. She'd climbed the stone wall and wandered among the crowded city of tombstones, until she found the statue of an angel to watch over her. She curled up in front of the statue on the wet grass, feeling safe and unafraid, and she stayed there until nearly dawn.

Before she left, she used a kitchen knife to dig a small hole in the grass, and she buried the vacuum-sealed bag that she'd brought from Dallas.

The bag with the thumb drive and the videos of Adam Hill.

The bag with her soiled, bloody panties.

The bag with the broken end of a toilet plunger.

That was more than fifteen years ago. She'd lived a lifetime since then. Now she was back. Was the bag still there, hidden under the protective gaze of the angel?

Johanna stood in the empty cemetery parking lot, and her eyes tried to penetrate the darkness. Jason was late, and he was never late. So where was he? Why wasn't he here? She had no phone for him to reach her, or her to reach him. She couldn't risk the signal being tracked. She'd thrown her phone in the sea on her way off the island to the Turkish mainland, and since then, she'd stayed off the grid. But she'd told Jason exactly where she would be, exactly when and where he could find her.

Three days from now. Three in the morning. The Salzburg cemetery.

But he wasn't here.

Johanna thought about leaving the cemetery. She and Jason had a backup rendezvous established for the following day. She could meet him there, and they could return to dig up the evidence that night. But she had an uneasy feeling, a strange shadowy sense of foreboding. Her instincts sensed danger, and she wanted to get in and out of Salzburg as quickly as she could. Better not to wait, better to do it now.

She crossed the parking lot to the brick wall that surrounded the cemetery grounds. Her foot found a ledge on one of the stone columns, and she hoisted herself up, then dropped to the wet grass on the other side. It was late, and cold, and a stiff breeze made the trees shake their branches at her. The headstones watched her arrival, impassive and dark under the night sky, lit by a half-moon.

Do you remember me?

She followed a walkway through the rows of graves. Strange that when she'd been fourteen, this place hadn't frightened her at all. But now she felt uneasy. She knew so much more now; she knew what could be hiding in the shadows. Even being off the grid, she'd felt watched ever since she left Turkey.

Find the angel. Get the bag, and get out.

Where was the statue?

It had been a long time, and she'd only been here once. She'd never gone back after that first night. Her brain struggled to remember the path she'd taken because it was such a big place, and she'd found the angel only by accident. Now, in the darkness, she couldn't see her way ahead of her, with the stones clustered together and the mature trees blocking her view.

A branch snapped close by, making a sharp crack. Johanna spun, Ruger in her hand. She whispered into the night. "Jason?"

No one answered.

She saw only shadows.

Was it an animal scurrying across the ground? Or something else?

Johanna shifted off the walkway onto the grass and began going up and down the rows, trying to take her mind back all those
years and remember where the angel had been. Ten minutes
passed. Then twenty. The cold began to make her shiver. She wore
black Lycra, but the mountain wind cut through it. Freezing,
scared, her mind played tricks on her, making her see and hear
things that weren't there. She felt alone and exposed.

Why was Jason late?

Where was he?

Get out of here! Come back tomorrow!

Then she finally saw a shimmering figure under the moonlight, set apart by a square of green grass. Time stood still. She
could have been fourteen again, finding a place where she felt safe
from harm. The winged angel was seated, with a muscular bare
chest and stone curls in his hair. He wore a robe covering his lower
body in sculpted folds, and he clutched olive vines in his hand.

His empty eyes stared down at her, as if to say, *I knew you'd come
back, Annie.*

Johanna wasted no time. She knew where to dig. A groomed
hedge bordered the statue, with two stone urns on either side.
She'd hidden the bag exactly in the middle between them. If it was
still there. If it had survived. She got down on her knees, and she
could have been praying. Using a switchblade from her pocket, she
dug up dirt. Again. And again. She didn't have to go far to find what
she'd left. Six inches down, she felt the blade catch on something.
Plastic. Frantically, she scooped away more dirt and shoved her
fingers down into the moist earth, and she felt the sharp edge of the
bag under her hand.

With a heavy pull, she squeezed it through the hole until it came free. It was black with soil, but she wiped it off. Sealed inside, no air to destroy it, were the remnants of her life as a teenager in Dallas. The evidence of what she'd suffered at the hands of Adam Hill. She felt no triumph or relief. This was a part of her past she'd wanted to leave for dead, and she wished she could keep it here with the other graves.

Johanna stood up.

Time to go.

She turned around, but in the crowded shadows, she saw someone moving toward her through the headstones.

It wasn't Jason.

36

BOURNE SPED ON A MOTORBIKE THROUGH THE SALZBURG STREETS.

He was late, and an instinct of urgency and fear gripped his chest. He should have been here hours earlier—in plenty of time to reach the meeting point with Johanna—but the Lufthansa flight had been delayed at the gate in Zurich, and then again on the taxiway, and then ultimately diverted in the air to land in Munich. From there, he'd been forced to drive two hours in the darkness to reach Salzburg.

He checked his watch. It was almost four in the morning.

Johanna!

At the roundabout ahead of him, he swung right toward the Kommunalfriedhof. Nearing the cemetery, he shut down the engine and rolled the bike onto the sidewalk. He took his Glock in his hand and made his way into the deserted parking lot. Tall trees loomed like giants over the brick cemetery wall. He listened for a whispered call from the shadows, but heard nothing. He used a penlight to flash a signal in both directions, but got no response.

Johanna wasn't here.

Had she left when he didn't show for the rendezvous? Or had she gone into the cemetery on her own?

His instincts screamed at him that something was wrong.

Running, he followed the brick wall to a pair of wrought-iron gates between two high columns. Quickly and silently, he climbed the gates and jumped down to the walkway inside the cemetery grounds. Where the trees grew, there was no light, and he saw only dim silhouettes of hundreds of headstones where the moon shined on the ground. Distantly, a line of jagged mountaintops loomed on the horizon.

Johanna, where are you?

Bourne felt at sea in the sprawling cemetery. She'd mentioned a statue of an angel, but he saw nothing like that nearby. Taking long strides, his gun arm outstretched, his shoulders swiveling back and forth, he marched past mossy graves and white crosses, the stones crammed together like passengers in a subway car. His eyes tried to pierce the shadows, looking for movement, and he listened for any sounds above the whistle of the wind.

He was alone, but he wasn't alone.

Instead, he was a target.

Inches away, barely missing him, a bullet pinged off rock with a puff of dust. He didn't hear the shot, not even the spit of a suppressor. He dove off the walkway and crouched behind a high gravestone, seeing no one. No more shots followed. Not yet. Bent over, he ran forward, and another bullet chased him, thudding into one of the trees. As he took cover, he saw a silhouette thirty yards away move behind a tomb and disappear as easily as a ghost.

Bourne backtracked, trying to come up on the shooter from

behind. He slithered on the ground and stood up when he reached a tree that blocked him from view. But the shooter anticipated his move, and when he nudged his face around the tree trunk, the next bullet missed him by a fraction of an inch and ricocheted bark into his eyes. He blinked, then ran the opposite way, drawing silent fire again.

The graves blocked him, and he made his way closer. He was less than twenty yards from the shooter now. Taking a risk, he called into the darkness. He knew who it was, and she knew who it was, and they both knew the stakes of this night.

There was no point in playing spy games.

"Vandal."

A long pause followed, and then he heard her voice calling back to him.

"You shouldn't have come, Cain."

There was something horrifying in that voice. Something strangled and tragic. And he knew what it meant. Blackness stormed his mind, and he found himself gasping for breath, his heart pounding in his chest and thumping like thunder in his ears. He didn't want to ask the question, but he needed to know.

"Where's Johanna?"

She didn't answer, and something about her stark silence felt deadly. He had to swallow down a howl of fury and despair.

"Vandal, where is she? *What did you do?*"

He waited, listening. Was she not going to tell him? Was she going to let him discover it for himself? But finally, she answered with two dead, emotionless words.

"My job."

Bourne's head sank back against the tree. His mouth opened

in a soundless scream. He told himself it wasn't true. It *couldn't* be true. This was a chess move to draw him out of hiding. Johanna wasn't here. Tomorrow, he'd head to the backup rendezvous in the catacombs of St. Peter's Abbey, and she'd be waiting for him, and they'd kiss, and they'd be together again.

But he was lying to himself.

He knew it was true. The reality weighed him down like an anchor pulling him into black water. All the light fled from his soul, and he didn't care about anything anymore. He didn't care if he lived or died.

All he cared about was vengeance.

Bourne fired.

He spun away from the tree and fired toward the darkness where Vandal was hiding. He marched and fired, marched and fired, marched and fired. As he got closer, he heard the snap of her suppressor. Bullets flew around him, blowing up in a cloud of death. One bullet seared across his left bicep. One burned into his thigh. One gashed his hip. But nothing slowed him, nothing stopped him, nothing brought him down. He kept walking, kept shooting into the void like a man possessed.

He. Didn't. Care!

Somewhere along the way, the return fire stopped. It didn't matter; he kept up his barrage. He emptied one magazine, stood there in the open as he reloaded, and started firing again as he closed the distance. Round after round. Bullet after bullet.

Finally, he stood over her.

Vandal.

She lay on her back on the wet ground between two stone crosses. She was still alive, barely, eyes focused on the sky, body paralyzed. Her gun lay a couple of feet away where she'd dropped it. Her ebony-and-purple hair lay across her face like a nest of snakes. He'd missed over and over, but he'd hit her once, and once was enough. Her hands were clutched together in the middle of her stomach, where blood oozed out between her fingers from the bullet wound that had gone straight through her body and out the back of her spine.

Her dark eyes showed nothing as she stared at him. No regret. No fear. Nothing at all. He watched her chest seize. Her lips moved, and she choked on what she was trying to say. Then she gagged it out with bubbles of bile and blood.

"Just fucking kill me, Cain."

Bourne lifted his gun one more time and fired into the middle of her forehead.

———

HE FOUND JOHANNA BY THE ANGEL. SHE LOOKED PERFECT AND PEACEful with her eyes closed, her blond hair loose, still moving with the wind. She'd lived long enough to drag herself up near the base of the statue, with her arms spread wide across the green hedge and her head tilted backward, so that the angel looked down at her with sadness in his eyes. She didn't look dead at all. Her face would have been the same if she'd been sleeping, and he could have roused her by calling her name. But she was gone. The round holes in her jacket marked two bullet wounds near her heart.

How could she lose? He didn't understand. How could she let Vandal beat her? Johanna was too good to die this way.

But he saw the crazy randomness of how it had happened. A

bullet had nicked one of the stone urns, shooting a razor-sharp fragment into her wrist. He saw the bloody ceramic arrowhead on the ground. It had severed muscle, and her hand had twitched, and her Ruger had flown out of reach. He saw it lying ten feet away. Vandal had been close enough to take two kill shots in the chest before Johanna had any hope of retrieving the gun.

Life or death came down to inches. An inch one way, an inch another way, and it all ended differently.

Bourne saw something jutting out from under the green hedge, as if it had been pushed there during the fight. It was a fragment of plastic. He pulled on it and found that it was the corner of a vacuum-sealed bag, dirty from the years it had spent buried in the earth, but its contents pristine. He shook his head at how pointless it seemed now. This was the evidence. This was what Johanna had come to find, so that they could take down Adam Hill, so that they could disappear together.

Leave Treadstone. Leave the shadow life.

But there would be no escape.

He bent down and kissed Johanna's lips, which were still warm. Then he slid down next to her on the wet ground. He eased her lifeless arms from the hedge and pulled her body into his shoulder. She lay against him the way she had so many times, and he still expected her to murmur his name and purr with that rumble of happiness and satisfaction in her throat. He expected her to get to her feet and reach out a hand and say, *"Come with me."*

Instead, the night got shorter, and her skin grew colder. Jason stayed with her, keeping her in his arms until daylight crept over the mountains. Then he took the evidence with him, and he said goodbye to the woman he loved.

37

THE DOOR RATTLED ON THE ARLINGTON, VIRGINIA, CONDOMINIUM.
It was eleven o'clock, the end of a long Washington workday.
Bourne heard the tap of a woman's high heels and the scratch of a
yellow Lab's nails on the travertine stone floor of the foyer. He sat
in darkness near the tall windows of the twelfth-floor balcony, his
Glock in his lap. He didn't expect the woman to turn on the apart-
ment lights when she got home, and she didn't. Being blind, Holly
Schultz didn't care about light.

She entered the living room from the foyer, putting down her
slim briefcase near the doorway. Her guide dog, Sugar, barked
once. Holly hesitated momentarily as she heard Sugar, but then she
made her way to the wine fridge on the west wall. She located a
bottle of pinot noir and twisted the cap. As she poured herself a
glass, she seemed to know by feel exactly where to stop. Still standing, she took a sip, then eased down into a recliner a few feet away.
Her body was small, almost birdlike, and her feet didn't even reach

the ground. Sugar sat at attention on the carpet beside her, eyes on Bourne.

"I'm assuming it's you, Cain," Holly said. "Sugar gave the friend bark. You're about the only person she would consider a friend."

"It's me," Bourne replied.

Holly was silent for a while, still savoring the glass of wine. "But you're not a friend, are you?"

"No."

"We go back a long way. Of course, I realize you may not remember much of it."

"I remember some. But the past doesn't matter."

"Are you here to kill me?"

Bourne's fingers caressed the barrel of the Glock. "I want to, Holly. Honestly, my first thought coming here was how much I wanted you dead. But you're lucky. I wouldn't do that to Sugar. She doesn't deserve to be left alone."

Holly bent down and kissed Sugar's head. "This girl has saved me more than once, but never quite like this. I suppose I should say thank you, because you have every right to want me dead. When I heard about Johanna, I assumed you'd be coming for me. I thought about increasing my security in order to stop you, but why bother? You'd have got through it anyway. As you proved tonight by being here. You've always been the best, Cain. David Abbott was right about you. Of course, the Monk is right about most things."

"He wasn't right about Vandal. He never talked about her with Shadow. He didn't realize you'd turned her."

"Well, we all do what we have to do. I needed an asset inside

Treadstone, and everyone has their pressure points. Not that it matters, but Vandal hated the assignment. She simply wasn't in a position to say no."

"I killed her," Bourne said.

"Yes, I know."

"Later, afterward, I wished I hadn't. I've spent too much of my life killing pawns and letting the king go free."

"I accept my responsibility for what happened," Holly replied. "I gave the orders to kill you both, so I expected there would be consequences. But just so you know, I'm not the king. Not this time, not this mission. I didn't want to leverage Vandal. I didn't want to target you and Johanna any more than she did. But like I said, we do what we have to do."

"This all came from Adam Hill."

"That's right."

Bourne shook his head. "I know Hill's dirty. I know he's a traitor, an asset for the Chinese. What I don't know is why you agreed to help him instead of working with Treadstone to destroy him."

"You think I trust Treadstone? Especially now that Shadow has the Files?"

"That doesn't make Hill any less dangerous."

She shrugged. "I agree, but I had no choice. Hill knows I had you murder Alicia Beauvoir last year. The Iranians told the Russians, the Russians told the Chinese, the Chinese fed it to Hill. He was going to expose it, bring me in front of Congress to testify about what happened. Make it all public. I couldn't let him do that."

"To save yourself?"

"No. He thought so, but he was wrong. Believe it or not, I don't care what happens to me. If they put me in prison for what I did, so be it. But I do care about the country. You may not remember what I told you about Beauvoir back then, but her secrets about the Defiance mission *couldn't* be allowed to come out. Knowing the truth about what she did would tear the country apart, even more than it already is. That was unacceptable to me."

"You think it's better to have a spy in the White House?" Bourne asked.

Holly waved her hand dismissively. "Spies can be managed. Manipulated. Hill is the devil we know, Jason."

"Devil is the right word," he said.

Bourne pushed a button on his phone. He'd already linked it to the Bose speakers in Holly's living room. An audio tape played at full deafening volume, two voices, a man and a girl. It was hard, years later, to recognize the teenager's voice as Johanna, screaming in pain, begging for mercy that didn't come. But the raspy growl of the teacher on top of her was unmistakably familiar. Adam Hill.

This was the video of Hill assaulting his prodigy student. A fourteen-year-old girl. Even if Holly couldn't see it, the sound was enough. He watched her face contort with disgust, and she waved at him to make it stop.

"That's the man we're talking about," Jason said, shutting off the playback.

"Jesus."

"He needs to be removed, Holly. *You* need to remove him. He can use whatever excuse he wants for the public and the media. He resigns, and then he tells you everything about his connections with the Chinese. Every contact. Every secret he's exposed. Every other mole and buried agent he knows about. He leaves public life, he never goes back into politics, and he never works with children again. He can slink back to Texas and work in a car wash in Dallas for all I care."

Holly pursed her lips. "And if he refuses?"

"I kill him."

He could see her working through the pros and cons, the strengths and vulnerabilities.

"You'll leave the evidence with me?"

"Most of it. Some of the DNA evidence I'll keep back."

"Because you don't trust me?"

"Because I trust no one. But you'll have enough for Hill to realize you can finish him."

Holly nodded. "All right. Hill will take the deal. I'll make sure of it."

Her slim fingernails stroked Sugar's head. The dog whimpered, and Holly sighed with resignation. She snapped her fingers, giving the dog permission to bound across the room to Bourne. They were old friends. The dog licked his face and wagged her tail furiously at the attention. Then, when Holly called her name, Sugar immediately returned and sat beside her master.

"I'm curious," Holly went on. "If I could see, if Sugar weren't here, would you have shot me?"

"We'll never know."

"I guess not."

Bourne got to his feet in the darkness and holstered his Glock. He headed for the doorway, but Holly reached out and took his arm. Her voice was calm and cool. "We both know you're lying about Adam Hill, Cain."

"What do you mean?"

"I know you. I know what it means for you to lose someone like Johanna. You're going to kill him anyway."

Jason thought about the video he'd watched in Salzburg. He hadn't wanted to see it, but he'd forced himself to endure it. To watch it over and over, to burn every detail into his memory. He pictured it in his head again, the innocence of a girl destroyed, the savage betrayal of a groomer and predator. He'd watched the other video, too, where Annie took her revenge, where he could see the abused teenager becoming the strong, troubled woman he would meet years later.

Who would she have been if none of it had ever happened?

Their paths would never have crossed. He would never have loved her and never have lost her.

"Of course I'm going to kill him," Jason said.

"Be careful. If I can figure it out, so can he."

"I want him to figure it out. I want him to go back to Dallas and live in fear every day of his life, not knowing when I'll come for him. I want him looking over his shoulder every time he drives his car, or takes out the garbage, or turns out the lights in his bedroom at night. I want him to know that someday he'll see my face and know what I'm going to do to him. I want him to die a thousand times before he finally does."

"You know what they say about revenge, Jason," Holly murmured.

"I don't care about old sayings."

"Well, maybe it's enough for him to believe you're going to kill him. Let him wonder, let him be afraid. And then don't do it."

"You don't think he deserves it?" Bourne asked.

Holly exhaled long and slow. "Oh, I know he does. I wish I could do it myself. But as soon as you pull the trigger for your own reasons, Cain, you become a killer. There's no going back from that. You've killed many times, you've become the man that David Abbott made you, but at heart, I don't think you've ever really been a killer. I know what Hill took from you, but selling your soul won't change that."

"So what do you suggest I do?"

"You grieve," Holly told him. "And then you let her go."

———

BOURNE WENT BACK TO PARIS.

He found an apartment not far from Notre Dame, and he spent days walking the city, mile after mile through the arrondissements, letting memories come back to him. It seemed as if every corner he visited in Paris triggered new flashbacks in his mind. He began to put his life back together piece by piece, but memories didn't fill the emptiness. The raw pain of Salzburg gave way to a dull ache and then to nothing at all. He didn't cry about Johanna; he had no tears left. But he spent sleepless hours at night in bed, eyes wide open, staring at the ceiling and smelling the dank city air through the open window.

He loved her. He missed her. Nothing changed that.

In the U.S., Adam Hill resigned as vice president. He claimed that he was battling pancreatic cancer, and Bourne wondered if karma had actually caught up with Hill's sins, or if this was simply the lie he was hiding behind. But he realized he didn't care. Holly was right. It wouldn't change anything to murder Hill; it wouldn't bring Johanna back. He couldn't dig down and find the anger to get on a plane and go to Dallas.

A month passed.

Then two.

He began to think that the world had forgotten about him. Wherever he went, he eyed the streets to make sure he wasn't being followed, and he checked for threats in the parks and in the Métro stations. But no one had found him. No one even seemed to be looking. If Putin still wanted him, he was lying low for now.

When he'd explored seemingly every street in Paris, he began taking trips around Europe. He went to Zurich. Hamburg. Holy Island in the UK. He rented a boat in the Mediterranean and spent a week alone on the water. He found himself retracing every step he'd taken with Johanna, as if he could go back to those places and feel her presence, or invite her ghost to whisper in his ear. But Johanna was dead, and she told no tales. Seeing where they'd been only hollowed him out further.

Three months passed.

Then four.

Summer became fall. December arrived. The Paris rains came down, hard and cold. He walked, he ran, he exercised, he trained, he went to movies, he went to bars, he went to cafés, and he began to wonder if this was it, this was the rest of his life. But a week before Christmas, as he walked along the Seine, a baseball cap on his head against the spitting rain, he spotted the abandoned houseboat he passed every day. A brand new bicycle was chained to the deck, looking out of place.

Treadstone was back.

He made his way from the river to the gardens of the Tuileries.

This time, he counted half a dozen agents establishing a security perimeter around the rendezvous. Nash Rollins was dead, but someone else was waiting for him, making contact after months of silence. As he neared the fountain and the pond, he spotted her sitting on one of the green benches, an umbrella protecting the wave of her blond hair. It was early, and wet, and they had the area mostly to themselves.

Bourne sat down on the bench next to Shadow. She still looked perfect. Beautiful. Cool. Distant.

"I wasn't sure I'd ever see you again," Jason said.

"I wasn't sure you'd want to."

"You're right. Five months ago, I hated you."

"And now?"

He shrugged. "Now you're Marlen. I can't hate Marlen."

They stayed silent for a while, as if round one in the battle between them was over. A draw. The rain dappled the pond, and some of the spray from the rain glistened on her face. Her tongue slid across her deep red lips. She reached over and put a hand on his leg, which was the last thing he expected from her.

"I need to say something, Jason. I've never said this to you before. Honestly, I'm not sure I've said it to anyone before. I'm sorry. I always believed—my father always told me—that I should live life without regrets. Never look back. But I can't do that with you. I'm sorry. I'm sorry about Johanna. I'm sorry for everything you've lost. Most of all, I'm sorry that I betrayed you, not just now but in the past, too. I could give you lots of explanations. I'm attracted to you, I'm threatened by you, I'm probably in love with you. I don't do very well with any of those things. But for what it's worth, I'm truly sorry."

"I know that wasn't easy for you to say," Jason replied.

"It was easier than I expected."

"So where do we go from here?"

She took her hand back and brushed a loose strand of hair from her eyes. "That's up to you. If you say the word, I'll go. Abbott and I talked about it. You are officially released from Treadstone, if that's what you decide you want. You've sacrificed more than we ever had a right to ask. Tell me to leave, and I'll walk away. I'll be out of your life, and you'll never see me again."

"Is that really true?"

"It is."

Bourne felt the warmth on his leg where her hand had been. "And what if I don't want you to go?"

She smiled. "Then I'm Shadow, and I own your ass."

He couldn't help but laugh. Not that she was joking. As long as they were together, they would fight for the upper hand, one trying to control the other. He knew what Johanna would say if she were here, if she were watching him right now. *Don't trust her.* And he didn't. He never would. But he also knew things about Shadow that he hadn't known in the past. He knew her weaknesses, her vulnerabilities, her complications, her desires. He knew how she liked to be touched. He knew the workings of the gears behind the machine.

He also knew how it felt, seeing her again. Suddenly, some of the barren emptiness of the past few months had been lifted.

"So why are you here?" he asked. "Why now?"

"I have a mission for you," Shadow replied.

"Treadstone?"

"Yes. I need you. If you're ready."

He turned and stared at those icy blue eyes, and she stared back at him through the chill of the Paris rain. Something was different; something had changed inside him. A switch flipped, a spark flew, and he was alive again.

"I'm ready," Bourne said.

DIVE INTO THE WORLD OF ROBERT LUDLUM'S™ JASON BOURNE

FROM BESTSELLING AUTHOR BRIAN FREEMAN

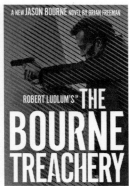

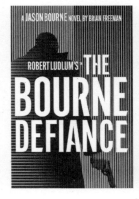
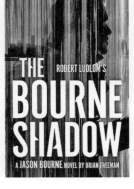
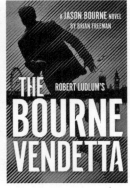